GHOSTLING

Circle of Seven
Book 1

Ash Harrier

*This book is dedicated to my backers on Kickstarter, who loyally and generously pledged to support the book.
We did it!*

Ghostling is also dedicated to Georgie, whose eye for the visual is always invaluable and who turned the Circle of Seven mandala into something truly magical. To Reef, who has a radar for a powerful story and brilliant merch energy. And to Trevor, who became my fiancé during the writing of this book, and whose belief in me and my writing is unmatched.

1
My Own Particular Unique Challenge

Most people thought it was just one bone, but in fact, it took twenty-two bones to make up the human skull.

The frontal, occipital and parietal bones of the skull's dome were fused by sutures as delicate and wriggly as a river system on a map. These were best drawn with a very fine pen, no thicker than a 0.05 nib.

"Hi!"

I looked up at the call, but the glass balcony of my parents' short-stay apartment was smeared and blurry. I got out of my chair and looked down. Three teenagers who'd been splashing and shouting at each other in the swimming pool below were gazing up at me.

A boy with water-swooshed hair waved. "What's your name?"

I hesitated, putting my sketchpad on the table. They looked friendly, but you could never be sure.

"Miette," I answered, but it came out too quiet.

"What?"

"Miette!"

"What does that mean?"

"Never mind. I get called Mimi."

"Jayden." He pointed. "This is Chloe and that's Holly."

I waved.

"Where're you from?" Holly called.

"Perry Ridge."

"Where's that?"

"In the north of Menoa County."

"We're from upstate," Chloe put in.

My peripheral vision was swarming with shadows like a tank full of eels. I ignored them steadfastly. Mom was inside, pretending to tidy the kitchen but actually listening in on my conversation. Probably hoping her daughter still remembered how to make a friend.

"Coming for a swim?" Holly asked, breast-stroking across the pool.

"Maybe."

"Do it!" Jayden grinned up at me, his hair a wild, wet thatch. "The water's perfect. And we don't bite."

Chloe giggled. "Only a little."

"I'll think about it." In my experience, most kids bit.

"You can tell us what your name means!" Jayden called after me.

I slid the balcony door shut. Mom was standing there watching me, her round face hopeful. "They seem nice. Are you going down to swim with them, Mimi?"

I sank into a chair and opened my sketchbook to my half-finished skull. At my shoulders stood three dead people my mom couldn't see: an old man, a young woman and a soldier.

"I don't feel like swimming."

Miette, as it happened, meant crumb.

It was French for *sweet little morsel*, technically—but the French used it to mean a crumb. As soon as I found out what it translated to, I switched to my nickname. Perhaps "Mimi" made me sound like a fluffy little dog, but it was better than crumb.

It was too late, anyway—my name was a self-fulfilling prophecy. By age twelve, I had crumbled. I'd stopped having friends. Stopped going to school. Stopped leaving the house unless I absolutely had to.

I'd always seen shadows—patches of darklight that accumulated when I was scared—but I thought little of it. Everyone had those, right? Everyone saw dense swirls of blackness in their peripheral vision when their distress levels spiked. *Right?* The shadows hovered constantly, but only moved, pushed forward, when I was upset. They didn't speak. They didn't have faces. They were just there, like reverse light beams.

The ghosts, on the other hand, were people. Ex-people. The first one came through when I was four. I was playing in my plastic junior kitchen, pretending to bake, when I looked up and noticed a boy in the room with me. He was about my age, wearing a long white nightgown. He said his name was Walter. He smelled like wood smoke—just a little. Enough for me to associate that smell with him ever after. His lips didn't move when he spoke and his eyes were in shadow. Blurred. It didn't alarm me. At four, you accept uncanny things more readily.

Mom and Dad thought it was cute at first: Mimi and her imaginary friends. Dad, who's a skeptic, nicknamed me Ghostling and encouraged me to tell him stories about Walter. Then Walter left and my next imaginary friend didn't seem so adorable to my parents—a fifteen-year-old boy called Mortimer who'd died from a snakebite on a sugar plantation. Nor was the next one: a fifty-eight-year-old woman named Ethel who'd drowned in a ferry accident. The older I got, the more I insisted they were real. Mom and Dad grew increasingly worried.

Word got around—I was the girl who still had imaginary friends in middle school. A handful of the other kids were nice to me, but most treated me as if my eyes might roll back in my head at any moment. I learned not to talk about the ghosts, but my reputation stuck. I was an outcast. It wasn't long before I was refusing to go to school at all.

The three imaginary friends I had with me now were my biggest spiritual crowd ever. I'd only ever had a maximum of two at a time. But earlier this year, my long-termers, Hannah and Albert, had been joined by Marvin. It was getting crowded. Car trips were especially unpleasant.

Hannah died in 1904. She was a maidservant, she said, same age as me. A particular herbal scent told me when she was nearby. Albert had died from complications of his injuries after the Second World War. He smelled like cigarette smoke and made a thumping noise with his cane when he walked. And Marvin had died on the streets. When he moved around, he occasionally left snowflakes that melted into droplets of water on the floor.

I could see why my parents were worried. Most teenagers, even the troubled ones, didn't believe they were accompanied by invisible people who'd died grisly deaths. Dad tried to get his little Ghostling some help. First it was therapy with my school counsellor, then he and Mom joined an online support group for parents of kids with unusual disorders. On the advice of the other group members, Mom tried to get me to explain what I saw. Initially, I complied, eager to talk about the ghosts. She pretended to be calm and interested while she listened, but later that day, it was obvious she'd been crying. I didn't say anything about the ghosts after that. But I still wouldn't go to school.

They'd recently taken me to see a top psychiatrist. My dad had known the guy a long time and said he really knew his stuff. I saw Dr. Mayer every week for several months, my parents adjusting the household budget to pay for the expensive sessions. I told Dr. Mayer the truth about my ghosts. Maybe it *was* a syndrome of some sort, and maybe he could help. I liked Mayer. He never once looked like he didn't believe me, and nothing I said seemed to shock him.

But he got the diagnosis wrong. He told Mom and Dad I had unresolved trauma from some childhood incident I'd repressed, and that I needed either a stay in a mental health clinic upstate, or to go to a special school where they could give me extra support. My parents talked about it for a week, then decided we should try the school. Although I was pretty sure I had no repressed trauma, I was cautiously willing to try Etherall Valley Academy. I wanted to get into college, and the curriculum was getting beyond our homeschooling capabilities. What's more, this school asked students to apply with a creative portfolio, and I loved making art.

Also, it was hours away from my old school. Surely no rumors could follow me that far. I'd be careful at this new school. Keep my mouth shut about my imaginary friends. Keep my head down and focus on getting the work done so I could go to a good college. No need to make friends. I would treat it purely as a place of learning, a pathway to higher education. We sent off the application with samples of my art—mostly line-work drawings of skulls, organs, antlers and feathers. Mom implored me to draw some flowers or something, but anatomical art was my thing. Luckily, the principal wasn't put off by my artistic style and I got offered a place.

Hell of a drive south, though. Three hours in the back seat, shivering uncontrollably. Mom and Dad had no idea how cold I was, snuggled up in the back seat with three ghosts. The icy blast of air people talk about when it comes to hauntings? That's a thing. Whenever I'm in close proximity with my ghosts, it's like being in the freezer section at the supermarket. Let's just say I've learned to always take a jacket.

I tried to stop my teeth from chattering, my gaze fixed on my dad's broadening bald patch and my mom's smooth bob. Mom chattered about their upcoming trip to Paris, adding notes on her phone every time she thought of something else she wanted to see in the City of Light. Mom was a complete Francophile—hence the French names for me and my brother Lucien—and had been planning this trip for as long as I could remember. They'd saved up and finally taken the plunge, booking it for January on the proviso that I'd be living safely at boarding school.

They were amazing, my parents. They'd hardly had any fun for the past few years, while I was in that bad space. Even now, Dad had taken time off work so they could both come and stay in Etherall Valley for two weeks while I settled into the academy. Only after we were all confident it was going to work out would they head home—and then Mom was to start at a new job so they could afford to keep me at this expensive school.

They'd both sacrificed so much for me. I had to make this work.

So when Dad glanced at me in the rearview mirror, I smiled and pretended I wasn't freezing my ass off, sitting with three dead people.

"Look," Mom had said when we were only about forty-five minutes from our destination. "There's that religious commune, Dale's Run."

I followed her gaze across the open, hilly country. A wooden gate hung wide at the top of a long driveway. The track meandered down the hill to a cluster of cottages with a church in the middle, like a mama duck with all its babies.

"I've always wanted a closer look at Dale's Run," she said, rolling down her window. Warm air, sweet with the scent of cut hay, rushed in.

Dad glanced down the hill. "You know it's a fundamentalist community?"

"Of course I do. But it's so picturesque and old-fashioned looking. It's lovely."

"There are quite a few religious sects that call Menoa County home." Dad read and listened to podcasts a lot, and loved info-dumping. "There's these guys—the Dale's Run community—who reject technology and arrange their kids' jobs and spouses. There's a druid association floating around, too. And the Wiccans, obviously."

My Aunt Aurora—Mom's sister—had taken up witchy hobbies in the past few years. She was always busy with her coven on full moons.

"I've even heard there's some group that believe they can transcend this dimension." Dad chuckled. "Maybe they're waiting for the mothership to come pick them up."

"I'm curious about the Dale's Run lifestyle." Mom was only half listening to him.

"They're extremists," Dad said.

"I think they're harmless," she replied. "They just have a simple way of living. In a way, it's quite beautiful."

Dad shook his head. "Arranged marriages? Doesn't sound harmless to me."

Mom pointed. "Look, the gate's open and there's no 'keep out' sign. Why don't we drive through the village and have a closer look?"

Hannah touched my hand, a featherlight caress. I whipped it away, cowering against my seat.

"No, miss," she whispered. "Don't let them stop."

"Beware." Albert's word smelled like smoldering tobacco.

"Tell her no!" Marvin snapped.

"Don't stop here!" I exclaimed, and Mom turned to look at me, surprised.

"Why not? What's wrong, Mimi?"

I recovered myself as best I could. "I mean, um, I think I'm carsick. Can we just keep on going?"

Dad tried to see me in the rearview. "Of course. You should have spoken up, Mimi."

"Yeah, I know," I said weakly.

I tried to get the shuddering under control. I didn't even care what the ghosts' reasoning was; I just rubbed my arm, fought the rising nausea and tucked my right hand with its missing finger into my sleeve. I wasn't scared of my ghosts, as such, but there was one rule: don't let them touch you.

Mom twisted around to assess me more fully. "She's very pale," she told Dad. "You'd better stop so I can swap places with her. We're only half an hour from the apartment now," she added to me. "You'll feel better riding up front."

No shit.

2
Not Here to Make Friends

I woke early, nervous about my first day. It was set to be warm again, and the apartment swimming pool sat as still and pale as a square-cut aquamarine. It looked icy, sitting in the shadow of the apartment building. Jayden and his friends had forgotten an inflatable lobster, and it floated on the surface of the water, smiling up at the sky.

I dug my black one-piece swimsuit out of my case and wriggled into it, threw a hoodie over the top and caught the elevator down to the pool, clutching a towel. My ghosts appeared in the pool yard as I slipped through the gate. I checked the balconies of the apartment block, but no one was around. I whipped off my hoodie and dove in.

The cold hit me like an explosion of painful ecstasy. I came up gasping and, as soon as I'd gotten some air, went immediately back under. I thrashed my arms in the water, letting it chill every part of me. My swimming style was inexpert—probably ungainly—but nobody was around. I freestyled to the ladder, pulled myself out, then dove in again. This time, the water didn't hit as cold, but its work was already done. I climbed out, wrapped up in the towel, and left the pool yard. I dripped all over the elevator floor, but I felt clearheaded and calm. Rebooted. My ghosts were waiting for me when I got back inside the apartment.

My parents and I had been asked to come to school early. I breakfasted and showered and, despite the forecast warmth of the day, opted for my usual hoodie and jeans. I had my own air conditioning in the back seat with my ghosts, anyway.

Etherall Valley Academy was a sprawling, enclosed acreage a little way out of town, sitting across the road from a woodland. At the front, a massive slab of polished granite had been planted in the turf like the first stage of a new Stonehenge. It bore the institution's name in carved letters, along with its motto: *Peace Through Learning*. A symbol bloomed in the middle: an interconnected triple spiral vaguely resembling a fidget spinner.

Mom parked and I climbed out, helping Dad heave my two roller cases out of the trunk. Clouds sprayed foam-white across the sky and the air seemed to hum. Was there a storm coming in? A crow sat on the spiked metal gate and cawed obnoxiously, like it was taunting me. I ignored it, peering through the gate. Beyond a big old oak tree, a manicured lawn rolled up to a red-brick structure that appeared to have been modeled on the Smithsonian Institution. It had conical roofs and shining spires, stucco panels, lead-light windows and arched doorways. Even a gargoyle or two.

"I wonder if I'll be in Gryffindor or Slytherin?" I said, flicking up the handle of my big case.

My parents laughed and Dad gave me a quick squeeze. "The school was once a quarantine station."

I wrinkled my nose. "Nice."

"It's beautiful," Mom enthused. "Fully restored."

"They use the infirmary as the admin block these days," Dad went on. "They had additional wards at the back, which have been modernized and converted to classrooms and dormitories."

Mom pressed the buzzer and gave them our names, then the gate rumbled open. I was chewing my lip so much I tasted blood. The crow's buddies had arrived and were having a loud argument as they wheeled above our heads, the noise ramping up my anxiety. My parents ushered me past rosebushes covered in dark red blooms, all the way up to the palatial admin block and through glass double doors.

Inside, we crossed a velvety crimson carpet, passed a mahogany staircase and stopped at a reception desk so wide you could have held a disco on it. So many of my fear-shadows were slithering around in every corner of my field of vision, I almost turned and ran back outside. I steadied myself and took a breath. The shadows receded slightly.

Out the windows on the other side of the office, the classroom blocks resembled, more than anything, cottages where old spinsters might live in between solving murder mysteries. About a dozen of those cottages dotted the school grounds, flanked by rainwater tanks and gardens. It gave me British village vibes. The only anomalies were the solar panel array on each roof and the high cyclone fencing ringing the property.

The school secretary welcomed us to the academy and immediately had me hand over my laptop and phone. A stressed-looking IT coordinator came and fetched them both. I watched forlornly as she took them away with her down a dim corridor.

"She'll install the school intranet and set up site blocking for banned websites," the secretary explained. "Your laptop will be waiting for you in your room by the end of the day, and the head of the girls' dorm will keep your phone in her office safe."

Mom and I exchanged dismayed glances. The secretary said the principal could see us immediately and showed us into his office. It was dark and elegant, with varnished rosewood shelves and rich midnight-blue drapes. My ghosts seemed to fit, in a way.

Mr. Boxe, on the other hand, did not. With his towering height and loud voice, I found him intimidating, despite a comically bushy ginger mustache. My fear-shadows reactivated, swirling and hovering around the corners of his office, pinging off my stress levels. Given the nature of the school, I'd expected something more like Dr. Mayer with his soothing voice. Boxe's manner didn't seem to match Etherall Valley Academy at all.

He told me in a jolly, blustering tone that I wasn't the only new kid starting today. I didn't know what to say to that, so I just stared at anything I could focus on: the pile of papers on his desk, the wedding ring on his finger. Thankfully my mother took over, asking about the no-phone policy. Mr. Boxe explained that taking our phones was an important part of the wellbeing focus at the school. When teens were permitted phones, he said, they engaged with life less and became unable to find their own entertainment or explore different forms of fun. The same song most teachers sing. Put that way, Mom agreed, as long as she could call the dorm supervisor to get through to me in an emergency.

My nerves were hitting a new peak, making my jaw clench. Very soon, my parents would be driving away and I'd be left here on my own. Yes, they were staying in town, but this was boarding school, so I wouldn't see them again until Friday afternoon. Mr. Boxe said Mom was allowed to go with me to check out the girls' dormitory, so I kissed Dad goodbye. He squeezed me in a big dad-hug and whispered that I knew where they were if I needed them. I attempted not to cry.

The principal led us across the grounds to the girls' dorm. Classical music floated on the breeze under the noise of the crows—were they seriously piping Beethoven through the outdoor speaker system? That must deeply annoy the student body. Vestiges of the school's former life as a quarantine station remained: a granite block with weathered carvings pointing to the cemetery and isolation ward; an old stone well, covered for safety with a rusted iron grate.

Mr. Boxe explained that the dining and common rooms were separate for boys and girls. He rattled off the schedule: school from eight thirty until three, then study time. Then it was showers and room cleaning until dinner, finishing up with more study until quiet time in our own rooms at nine. Lights out at ten. We would help with serving the meals and clearing away on a roster system.

Prison vibes.

The girls' dormitory was built from that same red brick and had its own square stucco spires and grinning twin gargoyles above the door. Mr. Boxe handed us over to Ms. Samvedi, the dorm head. She was small and wiry, with black hair cut short and a no-bullshit manner. She also had a pretty tattoo of a ring on one of her fingers. I cautiously liked her.

Other girls, the ones who boarded on the weekends, trotted back and forth between their bedrooms, the dining room and the bathrooms, staring at me with undisguised curiosity. I kept my eyes on the varnished floorboards. Ms.

Samvedi showed us to my room, then my mom immediately asked about food, so the dorm head took her off to the kitchen to talk her through the menu. I sat on the single bed and looked around my new room.

Plain white walls with the odd trace of adhesive from the previous tenant. My posters would improve the blandness. The furniture consisted of an oak desk, chair, nightstand, wardrobe and dresser. Hannah was already sitting beside me on the bed, filling my nostrils with her herbaceous scent. Albert had claimed the chair, resting his cane against his knee, and Marvin was on the floor, leaning up against the wall in the corner.

"What do we think, team?" I asked. There were no objections.

The window above the desk overlooked the playing field. I got up and peered out. Kids were jogging around for what must be their own fitness purposes. *Ick.* It may have been my paranoid imagination, but they all looked tanned and long-legged.

I checked the small wall mirror and was rewarded by my anxious face glaring out at me, frown lines between my eyebrows. My bottom lip looked raw and red from all the chewing. I sighed. At least my hair was good. My dead-straight, long, dark hair had always been my best feature.

Mom came back, looking happier than I'd seen her in a long time.

"This place is wonderful, Mim! The menu looks delicious, and Isha—Ms. Samvedi—said you and I can have a little chat on her office phone tonight." *First-name basis already?* "And guess what? They've got some really cool social activities planned for the term, including a fall dance."

I smiled inwardly. It was cute that Mom thought I'd go to a dance.

"This is a nice room, don't you think? And you can make it your own with your things. I think—I think this place is just right for you!"

For an instant I was hurt. *Is she glad to be leaving me here?* But I got it, too. She'd been worrying about me for years. This was going to be like a holiday for her, to hand me over and let the school worry instead. She deserved a break. I promised her silently that I wouldn't screw it up.

Other girls were arriving at the dorm now, which meant it was time for Mom to leave. Ms. Samvedi could see things might get emotional, so she facilitated a quick, clean departure, then plonked me in a beanbag in the common room to wait for the start of the school day.

I had a good view of the Monday morning proceedings. Some girls—the ones who lived local—only boarded during the week and went home for weekends. They were turning up now with their weekend bags, hugging their friends like they'd been away for months. There was no uniform here, and a relaxed dress code. Most girls wore casual tops, some cropped, with shorts, skirts or jeans. There were even a few light summer dresses.

I panicked for a few minutes, thinking they all looked as confident and glamorous as influencers. Then I gave myself a reality check. These were normal girls: a mix of ages, shapes, colors and demeanors. A soft, round one paused in front of me, clutching a buff spiral-bound notebook. She had frizzy hair and sharp, intelligent eyes, and wore knee-length denim cutoffs with a red tee that said, *Genius shirt: just like a normal shirt, but with me in it.*

"New girl?" she asked. "I'm Mona."

"Mimi."

She smiled. "Oh, wow."

"I know. But it could be worse."

She laughed and plopped into the beanbag next to mine, putting her notebook in her lap. "Weird time of year to start—three weeks into first term."

"Trust me, I'm aware."

"What school did you come from?"

"Homeschooling."

"Ah." Mona tipped her head. "But not anymore?"

I shook my head. My throat was getting tight with fear. It was like I'd forgotten how to talk to other kids after all these years of solitude. *Fly under the radar, Mimi.*

Mona's gaze rested on my missing finger for a moment, and I drew my hand reflexively back into the sleeve of my hoodie. "My family lives in Etherall Valley," she said. "You?"

"We live three hours north."

"Yikes, three hours. Don't worry. There are others in the same boat."

A bell rang and girls poured out of the bedrooms, all heading for the glass doors. Ms. Samvedi shouted over the top of their chatter. "If you haven't signed in, make sure you do so before you go to class! Melita Borgen! Your phone, please!"

A girl with a tight ponytail scowled and passed her phone to the dorm head.

Mona grinned at me. "Come on. Let's find out what homeroom you're in."

Mona was in a different homeroom, so she dropped me off at the door of one of the cottage classrooms.

"*Gambatte ne!*" she said as she turned to leave.

"Huh?"

"It means good luck in Japanese."

"Oh. Thanks."

I went in. The teacher introduced herself as Ms. Deering. She was small and sweet-faced, but had eyes like a raptor's: unblinking and everywhere at once.

She told the homeroom group my name. I was instant fresh meat for the twelve kids—excellent fodder for stares and whispers. They enjoyed themselves immensely and didn't make any effort to hide the fact. I tried not to look at anyone's face, but still they came at me. Only one kid had his back turned. He was bent over a book, wearing black on black, dark hair falling over his face. If only I could hide in a corner like him.

Ms. Deering attempted to rescue me, asking me questions about my previous school and generally being encouraging. But I was monosyllabic—a hermit who'd been living in a cave so long she'd forgotten how to talk. One girl was especially curious. She was in a crop top and had glorious red curls and thick makeup, possibly to cover her freckles. She ran her round blue eyes over my jeans and hoodie.

"Why did your parents send you to Etherall Valley Academy?" she demanded.

I couldn't keep a nervous stutter from my voice. "Th-they just liked the sound of it."

"Liked the sound of it?" She gave a cold laugh. "No, we've all got a backstory here. Unless they just wanted a special school for their precious princess."

"Call off the dogs, Cassie." A boy with golden-brown hair winked at her, and her mouth twisted into a smile almost unwillingly—as if she didn't want to be amused but he'd made a good joke.

He looked back at me with warm brown eyes above a slightly crooked nose, possibly previously broken. When he smiled, it lit up his face and crinkled his eyes. He wore braces on his teeth.

He stretched out his long legs under the desk. "Don't worry about Cassie. I mean, she's right—we're all suffering from something here. Cassie's got chronic snark."

"And Gabe's got shocking case of overconfidence." Cassie smirked at him.

"When people start at Etherall Valley Academy, we always ask, 'What are you in for?'" Gabe said.

A couple of the other kids agreed, volunteering their own reasons. Someone had been running with the wrong crowd at their old school. Someone else had a late diagnosis of ADHD and another girl been a school refuser, like me.

"Four years hard labor for, you know, being an outcast or failing—or getting expelled or having mental health issues." Gabe shot me that bright smile again, but I wasn't about to share my story. I flicked a look at my ghosts: Albert, inspecting the noticeboard, Hannah, standing beside Ms. Deering, and Marvin, wandering the room.

"You kids don't know how lucky you are," Ms. Deering admonished them. "Sure, EVA is for kids who need extra support, but only if they show genuine promise and commitment. Your parents pay a lot of money for you to get a superior education that recognizes individual talent. A lot of other kids get lost in the system.”

“The trouble is, with talent comes ego.” Gabe gave her a cheeky grin.

“That can be the case,” she acknowledged with a laugh.

“And what if there’s no talent—just ego?” This was a new voice.

It took me a moment, then I saw they were all looking at the boy with his back turned. Some of the kids rolled their eyes and resumed their own conversations, but Cassie bit.

“What’s that supposed to mean, Drew?” Her voice had gone a little shrill. Clearly, this guy knew how to press her buttons. He turned his head.

I had the sensation of bellyflopping into a freezing lake. He was a goth, his face painted so white it was almost blue. Raven-black hair, long on top with the ends hanging over his eyebrows. A spiked dog collar on his neck, eyebrows pierced with black barbells, and thick, dark eyeliner. One eye bore a white contact lens and the other was an unlikely agate green. But under all that, the curves of his jaw and cheek were, frankly, stunning. I had never been attracted to the goth look, but I responded to his face like I’d just spotted my favorite celebrity.

Drew addressed Cassie, but had his eyes on Ms. Deering. “I don’t see *talent* when I look around. I see spoiled brats with delusions of grandeur.”

Cassie bristled, Gabe looked amused, but Ms. Deering met his stare. “Respectful language,” was all she said.

Drew rolled his white-and-green eye medley and shot me a disinterested glance. Then he stopped, fixating on my face with something that resembled shock. The silent moment went on for way too long, my cheeks growing hot under his scrutiny until I finally ripped my eyes away. When I checked back, he was looking down at his book. Had I fantasized that exchange?

"Whoa." Gabe was glancing between me and Drew.

"What?" Cassie still sounded annoyed.

Gabe peered at me like he was trying to read something written under my skin. Then he shook his head, as if to say, *Nothing.*

"Everyone at EVA has earned admission on the basis of a *talent*," Cassie tossed at Drew. "Even you, Poetry Boy."

Gabe leaned toward me. "If you won't tell us the crime that got you a spot at EVA, Mimi, at least tell us your talent."

My throat went tight again. I didn't know how to answer him, so I stayed silent. I stared at my intertwined hands, the half-missing finger hidden by the others, and cringed inwardly while Cassie sniggered.

Ms. Deering stepped in. "Maybe we should stop bombarding the poor girl with questions on her first day. If you must know, Mimi will be in the art program."

"Nice." When I checked Gabe's face, he gave me another smile. No sarcasm detected.

Cassie, however, sniffed like she thought art was a weak entry portfolio. A couple of the other kids asked me questions about what sort of drawings I did. My awkwardness levels were at *painful*, but I told them I liked portraiture. That was probably the best way to describe my anatomical drawing without sounding weird. I was determined simply to be Mimi the solitary, arty girl. Not Mimi the freak. Not Mimi and her imaginary friends.

3
Identified as Having Exceptional Qualities

Etherall Valley Academy was a small school—less than two hundred students from ninth grade up to seniors. That meant a lot of classes in common with the kids I'd met so far.

Mona helped me find my way around. She talked nonstop, pointing out specific people, describing their personalities and supplying facts about the school—assembly being called *Lyceum*, for instance, which she explained was Ancient Greek for *gathering of learners*. Etherall Valley Academy liked to be fancy. Thanks to Mona, I quickly learned which teachers would check homework, the shortcuts to different classrooms and the people to avoid. She and Gabe sat with me during lunch, too. I couldn't work out why they were being so friendly. Perhaps the faculty had asked them to look after me.

I kept a low profile and made it through my first few days. The teachers were a diverse lot, but obviously all highly trained in mental health support. In a school for students facing "unique challenges," you had to be able to cope with constant chaos. Every teacher at EVA had one thing in common: the solid composure of that old oak tree in the front quad.

Snarky Cassie hung out with a mixed-age group who had one thing in common: they were obnoxiously loud. They interacted with an undercurrent of aggression that emerged in "playful" shoving and wrestling. Cassie seemed to have taken a dislike to me. I occasionally caught her watching me across the cafeteria at lunch or the dining hall at night.

Gabe said Cassie was in the dance program. Everyone was aligned with one of the school's special programs. Gabe's was media—filming, podcasting, web development. He wanted to go into the entertainment industry. He also loved sports of every kind. Mona was in the school's language program, studying French, Spanish *and* Chinese. They introduced me to their friend Ed, who was in the math program. Ed wasn't confident like Gabe, but he had a calming presence I liked. He was on the short side, but wiry, and had a habitual, shy half-smile. He was growing some dreads and often mentioned the beach, using words I didn't know to describe his surfing adventures.

A flaxen-haired girl called Patience caught my attention. She was Poetry Boy Drew's friend—perhaps his only friend. They were both in the literature program, Mona informed me. Patience kept her hair in two long braids and wore a crew-neck t-shirt or a plaid button-down with the worst jeans I'd ever seen. I mean, I was no fashionista—I rocked a no-brand hoodie—but these jeans were like something your grandfather would wear.

I watched Drew covertly during our shared classes, as well as in homeroom. It was perfectly plain to me that under all that hair, makeup and metal, he was breathtaking—tall and lean, with the fine, beautiful features of a movie elf. But it was as if no one else could see past the goth façade. None of the other kids spoke to him—except for Patience—and he spoke to nobody except her. Maybe that was why no one bothered with him: he simply ignored them if they tried.

He didn't make eye contact with me at all, although I occasionally felt like he was watching me. I tried to catch him out, but every time I looked up, he was writing in a leather-bound book, or reading a novel, or talking with Patience. I pictured him reading me one of his poems, then mentally slapped myself. The guy was profoundly unlikable and I wasn't interested in him, except perhaps artistically. The bone structure.

Mona didn't only attach herself to me, but also the other new kid, Axel—a tall, skinny guy with wire-rimmed glasses who seemed as overwhelmed as me. She introduced the two of us during lunch, then abandoned us to get to know each other while she went to grab a juicebox. My ghosts were hovering around the cafeteria, then Marvin came and stood right beside poor Axel, who gave a little shiver and zipped up his jacket.

The guy was watching me so expectantly, I felt obliged to converse. "It's fun starting at a new school mid-term, huh?"

Axel looked startled. "You think?"

Oh, he wasn't fluent in sarcasm.

"I'm finding it a challenge," he said. "Mona's been really nice, showing me around, but I've already gotten lost more times than I can count. And I've just found out there's a section of math they covered last year that I haven't learned yet. The teacher said I'll need to do after-school work with her to catch up."

"Was your old school not so great?"

"I was homeschooled."

That explained things a little. "Me too."

"Oh, that's a coincidence!" He gave me a big, hopeful smile.

"Did you have a problem with regular school?" I asked, then wished I hadn't. "I mean, if you don't mind me asking."

"I don't mind. No, we just didn't have a parochial school nearby, and my faith is important to me, so we opted for homeschooling." His hazel eyes brightened. "And you and I are both in the art program, too, right? Another coincidence."

"I guess we were lucky they took two of us into the art program at the same time."

"True. I heard someone left unexpectedly at the start of term. The art teacher—Mrs. Shaw—she seems really accomplished, don't you think? She knows everything there is to know about painting."

"Yeah, but this project she wants us to do—copying a portrait by a master—is intimidating."

"Do you know what you're going to reproduce?"

"Maybe *Girl with a Pearl Earring.*"

"That's a good choice! I'm thinking of doing a Leonardo da Vinci."

"I'm terrible at drawing whole people," I confessed, then realized how odd that sounded and hurried on. "And I know zero about oil painting. I'm more of a pens and pencils kinda girl."

"I like working in oils," he said.

"I might be coming to you for help, then." I said it in a casual way, but Axel's face lit up and he nodded eagerly.

"Anytime!"

Clearly I wasn't the only one coming to this school without a friend to my name. The only difference was, I was quite happy to keep it that way.

My bedroom was two doors down from Mona's and directly across the corridor from Cassie's. We had free time every day, between study hour and dinner, during which we were supposed to shower, tidy our rooms or play board games. If the showers were full, I stayed in my bedroom. I'd decorated the walls with my posters and art cards by now, and my room looked good. Homey. I didn't need to socialize.

On Thursday, during free time, I was on my bed, listening to music through my headphones. Hannah was sitting at the end of the bed, Marvin was on the floor and Albert was pacing in my small bedroom. *Step, step, step, turn. Step, step, step, turn.*

I pushed one headphone off my ear. "You've got a bit of a rhythm going there, Albert," I told him, nodding along. "You're stepping in time to my beats."

He paused, then resumed pacing—out of time.

I raised an eyebrow. "Well, that's just passive-aggressive." I swear Albert smirked.

"Hey." Mona's face appeared around my semi-closed bedroom door. "Who you talking to?"

"Just myself. I'm weird that way."

She smiled. "Got a minute?"

I pulled my headphones all the way off. "Sure."

She pushed open the door and let Cassie and Patience in before her. Patience gave me a timid smile, but Cassie's lips were a hard horizontal line. Mona shut the door behind them and they all stood in a row, looking down at me.

Oh, hell. Was this some kind of mean-girl initiation? I hitched myself upright.

Cassie scanned my walls, taking in the Victorian anatomical drawings, skeletons, vital organs and band artwork. "Who's that?" She pointed at one of the band ones.

I repressed a wince. "Hoodwynk."

Cassie's delicate nose wrinkled. "Never heard of them."

"They're an indie band from the U.K."

Her shoulders rippled like she was barely holding in a shrug. It was extremely crowded in my room now, with three dead people as well as four living. Marvin stood up, his thin shoulders hunched in his battered coat, and inspected Cassie at close range.

"Don't be afeared, miss," Hannah said unexpectedly from where she sat on the end of my bed.

Afeared? I wasn't even sure what that meant.

Mona sank onto the floor, crossing her legs, and Cassie sat on my chair. Patience stayed where she was, her hands clasped neatly in front of her. Something doll-like emanated from her, with those long braids and the smooth, round face.

"So," Mona said. "Tell us about your last school."

"I haven't been in school since seventh grade," I said. If they were just here for information, I could give them enough to keep them satisfied. *Solitary, arty Mimi,* I reminded myself. *Not Mimi and her imaginary friends.*

"Why not?" Cassie asked.

I kept my face up, although my cheeks were going hot. "Mental health stuff."

She stared at me. Hard.

"Nothing... happened at your old school?" Patience asked in her soft, low voice.

"Like what?"

Mona nudged Patience's ankle in a way that was supposed to be undetectable to me. "Like, did you have any issues there with people or, I don't know, stuff going wrong?" She said it casually, but it came across as oddly intense.

If I told them I'd been bullied, they might ask why, or what the kids had done. "Nothing specific."

"So there's nothing special about you?" Cassie asked.

I tensed and pulled my eyes away from Cassie. Mona laughed uneasily. So it *was* a mean-girl thing.

"No, nothing special." My chest and face were burning. "Not a precious princess at the special school."

"Defensive much?" she sneered. The irony.

"Sorry, Mimi," Mona said. "We didn't mean to come over all interrogatey. We're just curious about our new friend."

Did she realize how sinister that sounded?

Patience was watching me with a frown. "Do you… do things?" she asked, and Cassie sucked in a breath.

"Like what?" I asked, honestly baffled.

"Come on, Patience. Mimi obviously doesn't want to talk to us. Let's go." Cassie stood up and led an unwilling Patience out the door. She stepped right through the middle of Marvin on the way, and I saw her hesitate, shudder and rub her nose.

I bit back a smile. That wasn't anywhere near what it felt like for me to walk through my ghosts, but it was good to see she got at least a little serving of otherworldliness. Patience whispered something as they left, and I caught the word "Axel." Crap, what was going on? Had I inadvertently stumbled into some kind of crush triangle?

Mona was still sitting there. "How's the *dépaysement*?"

"The...?"

"It's French. It means the feeling of not being in your home country, you know? Feeling like a foreigner."

"Oh, right." I hunted for something to say. "My mom's learning French. She's obsessed with French things."

While I spoke, Mona's eyes had dropped to the floorboards. I shifted slightly to see what she was staring at, and the light from the window fell on some droplets of water suggestive of footprints. *Marvin*. Mona glanced at my feet. My dry, socked feet.

"Have you had your shower yet?"

"Yeah," I lied.

She transferred her attention to my desk, where my shower bag sat ready beside a change of clean clothes and my dry towel. I kept my face up, jaw clenched, ready to make up a story but also angry that she'd backed me into this corner.

She kept her gaze on me for a few moments. "Okay." She got up. "See you at dinner, Mimi."

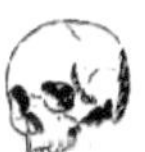

My relief to step into a weekend with my parents was palpable, especially when I heard that Cassie and Patience were weekend boarders. I would have been left with them if I'd stayed—with no Mona as a buffer, since she was one of the students who went home for the weekends.

Mom and Dad picked me up and drove me to the apartment, full of suppressed hope and excitement. They asked me what I thought of the school in that gentle, upbeat manner I had become accustomed to. I had misgivings about Etherall Valley Academy, but after everything my parents had done to make this work, I jettisoned my doubts.

"I like it. There are some nice kids and the workload isn't too bad. The food's good and the teachers are supportive."

They exchanged a look of delight that warmed my heart and simultaneously sank it. I'd done it now. I'd committed. I was staying at EVA, like it or not.

At dinner—celebratory takeout—Mom announced they'd had a call from Ms. Deering. I looked at her with apprehension. Had I done something wrong already? Attracted the attention of a concerned teacher?

But Mom was beaming at me. "They want you in the school's gifted program, Miette."

"Gifted program?" My insides underwent tectonic plate movement. "What gifted program? I thought everyone was supposed to have some kind of talent at this school?"

"Yes, the school's philosophy is to nurture special abilities—but the *gifted* program is reserved for those with extraordinary talent." My mom's eyes were shining with pride.

"But I've only had two art classes…"

"It's not about art. Ms. Deering has recognized exceptional qualities in you." Dad was grinning at me, too. "She thinks you belong in the program. It's elite, Mimi. Only six other kids in the whole school have been accepted, and Ms. Deering says it will help you get into a good college."

Was this some kind of con? Could my parents have pulled strings at this new school to get me into the program—to boost my self-esteem or something? I eyed them, but it seemed unlikely. Not really their style.

"I'm not gifted," I said. "I'm average."

"You're far from average, honey," Mom said loyally.

"It's more holistic than that," Dad added. "It's not just about grades—they consider the whole person. They'll work on building your confidence and skills. There's even a camp later in the term."

No, no, no, no, no. I didn't want to be exceptional. I wanted to blend in. "Do I *have* to join?"

They looked identically crestfallen. "No, it's not compulsory," Dad told me slowly.

I couldn't bring myself to say no immediately—not with those looks on their faces. "I'll think about it. It will probably just mean extra homework, though."

I never intended to think about it. I knew I wouldn't be joining some kind of hyper-brain society at Etherall Valley Academy to develop my leadership skills or confidence. That sounded like a no-refunds ticket to attention and expectations.

But almost immediately, my ghosts started behaving strangely. First, it was Hannah. She sat on the end of my bed throughout Friday night and watched me expectantly. I ignored it, hoping she'd stop and trying not to think about the last time she'd done that. But she was still there at four in the morning.

"Could you give it a rest, Hannah?" I pleaded at last.

Her soft, lilting voice came out of the air next to my ear. "You must go, miss."

"Where?"

"To the gifted."

"You want me to join that program? Why?"

Silence.

"I'm thinking about it," I lied. "Now, can you let me get some sleep?"

I lazed in bed in the morning. At school, the ever-present crows sat in the oak tree during the day but roosted on the roof of the girls' dorm at night. All week, they'd woken me early with their discordant chorus. The other girls were so used to them, the noise didn't seem to bother them anymore. I took advantage of the quiet morning at the apartment and slept in.

When I eventually woke up, Albert was acting odd. He was pacing the laminated floor of my bedroom, back and forth, tapping gently with his cane. Eventually he came to a halt in front of me, standing at military-style attention, as he always did when he had something to say.

"Yes, Albert?" I spoke in a low voice so my parents wouldn't hear.

"You must join," he told me. "Join the gifted."

Dammit. "Hannah already told me."

Albert nodded and waited.

I groaned. "I'm trying to work it out in my head, okay?"

"You must join."

"Why are you guys being so insistent about this?"

"You must join."

"Can you just let me have my weekend, Albert?"

He bowed slightly before departing, tapping his cane as he passed through my bedroom wall.

By Sunday evening, I felt sick with worry. Mom asked me gently if I'd finished thinking about joining the gifted program yet. Dad reminded me that we needed to confirm it with Ms. Deering. Talk about pressure.

Then it was Marvin's turn. I was brushing my teeth before bed and raised my head from spitting and he was there in the mirror, behind me.

"Marvin," I gasped, choking on minty-fresh flavor. "Don't do that to me!"

"Go to the gifted, kid." His tremulous, elderly voice was stern in my ear.

"I'm considering it," I retorted, striding from the bathroom. "Now leave me alone!"

They were active in my room that night. Every now and then, one of them spoke. *Go to the gifted. Join the gifted.* I shoved my pillow over my ears and squeezed my eyes shut. They hadn't tried to make me do something for over a year now.

Then, abruptly, it stopped. I peeped out from under the pillow. All three of them were standing beside my bed, gazing down at me with shadowed eyes. Hannah took a step forward, and I squeaked in terror, scrambling backward so I was pressed against the wall.

"Okay!" I panted. "I'll join the damn gifted program!"

Hannah stepped back. All three of them retreated, finding places to sit or lean around the room.

Either there was something significant about this program or my ghosts were even more concerned than I was about my chances for a good college.

4

The Garden Shed Society

My hair was still wet from my dawn swim when I got to school the next morning. The plunge had given me just enough of a reset to cope with Monday anxiety. When I dropped my weekend bag off in the dorm, I found a note on my door from Ms. Deering. Location and meeting times for the gifted program. They met twice a week, on Mondays and Fridays. I had to give up my cooking elective for it. Thanks to my ghosts' coercive tactics, I would never learn how to make a soufflé.

Fourth period was gifted class. I crossed the school grounds, scowling at the crows that cawed at me from the science block roof, and found the designated classroom. Did I say *classroom*? Try caretaker's hut. It resembled the forgotten outbuilding of a farm: an ageing wood cabin on stilts, choked with ivy and climbing roses. It wasn't like the other classrooms—it looked more like an afterthought. I knocked and got a "Come in, Mimi!"

Ms. Deering waved me inside. Six sets of eyes watched my entrance, and to my surprise, I knew every one of them. Gabe, Mona and Ed all wore welcoming grins, Cassie watched me coolly, practically exuding indifference; Patience nodded a greeting, her face expressionless. Beside her, Drew bent his white-and-green gaze back to his leather-bound book.

"Yeah, *Mimi*!" Mona sounded like she'd won a bet.

"Welcome to the gifted program, Mimi," Ms. Deering said. "I hope you'll enjoy our meetings. There are some spare chairs near Drew."

I tried not to react. Why had she said it that way? Some spare chairs, plural—for Mimi and her imaginary friends? Hell, I was being paranoid. I took a seat near Drew, who didn't look up or move.

I took it all in. The room was lit by a single struggling globe hanging from a cable. Bookshelves covered one wall, packed full of what looked like a collection of vintage tomes—all tattered cloth bindings and the smell of mildew. Faded and peeling posters adorned the walls: chakras and tarot symbolism, and even some anatomical stuff resembling my own poster collection. Kinda fun.

"I think we'll spend today just getting to know each other again, since we've got a new member." Ms. Deering paused to look at the other six class members, and they all nodded like she'd given them a covert instruction of some kind. "Mimi, I doubt you're keen on public speaking, but it would be great if you could tell us a little about yourself. How about *we* all go first, and then, if you feel okay with it, you can do your introduction at the end?"

Did I have a choice?

"My name is Bronwyn Deering," she said. "I'm thirty-seven and I was born and raised upstate. I spent a lot of my twenties traveling around the world, working and exploring in other countries. I studied social work and teaching, and worked with homeless kids for a few years before I started work at Etherall Valley Academy. My hobbies: I love martial arts and camping."

I tried to relax my rock-hard shoulder tension. This shouldn't be too bad. Surely I could think of a normal-sounding hobby. I didn't particularly want to admit to drawing anatomical art or my obsession with a band nobody had heard of. Maybe I could say I liked baking. Or skiing. There was no way they could check.

"I'm a sentry," Ms. Deering added. "I have a calling to guide and protect young people with preternatural abilities."

My mouth fell open. Six heads swiveled to see my reaction.

Joke. It's a joke. I checked Mona's face, hoping to catch a glimpse of something—some hint of humor that would tell me this was a weird teacher prank. But Mona was nodding at me, eyes bright. Gabe had nothing but sympathy in his steady gaze. Drew was now giving off distinct powder-keg vibes.

It was perfectly clear they'd heard it before. This was an orientation.

"Let's see." Ms. Deering looked around. "You can go next, Cassie."

Cassie shook her curls back over her shoulders and shot me a self-conscious glance. "Cassandra O'Meara. I grew up in Pinetree Glades and went to school there until I came to EVA. I have three brothers and a chocolate Labrador. I'm into dance. Ballet and jazz."

"Jazz hands," Mona murmured.

Cassie ignored her. "I can control animals."

My mouth was still hanging open. I closed it, swallowing with difficulty. I was trembling.

"A beastmaster," Ms. Deering supplied for my benefit.

"Beast*mistress.*" Mona made a whiplash dominatrix noise.

"Mona cracks jokes when she's nervous," Gabe explained, and she thumped him on the arm.

"Go ahead, Mona," Ms. Deering said. "You next."

"Mona Thomas, born and bred in Etherall Valley. I have one older sister and I like piña coladas and getting caught in the rain."

The others groaned, except for Patience, who had the blank look of someone who didn't get the gag. And Drew, who remained stormy.

"I'm a polyglot—silly name, serious talent." Mona said it like a marketing tagline. "It means I can understand and communicate in all different languages, whether I've studied them or not."

"Gabriel Cavendish," Gabe broke in, obviously busting to tell his story. "I'm from Meadowvale, about an hour away. I live with my moms, plural. Only child."

Cassie snorted. "Syndrome much?"

He paused. "What?"

"Only child syndrome. You think the world revolves around you." She gave him a bright smile.

Gabe seemed unfazed. "Ironically, Cassie couldn't be more wrong. I feel what others feel, so I'm extremely aware of other people, whatever Madame Snark says. By the way, Cassie's feeling intimidated."

"Stop it, asshole."

"He's an empath," Ms. Deering told me. "Sensitive to others' emotions."

"I like to call him the *Insensitive Sensitive*," Mona added.

"That's just because you're overexcited," Gabe told her gently, and she feigned a scowl in reply.

"Ed?" said Ms. Deering.

"Wait!" Gabe wasn't finished. "I also like basketball, movies and shy girls from the north." He grinned at me meaningfully. I looked down at my hands, taking time out of "stunned" to check in with "embarrassed."

"Ed?" Ms. Deering repeated with a sigh.

"Edwin Farrow." Ed looked almost as awkward as I felt. "I'm from Windy Cove. I have an older brother at university and a younger sister at Windy Cove Central High. I can help fix injuries and sicknesses. Make them better."

"Ed's a healer," Ms. Deering told me.

She turned to Patience. The flaxen-plaited girl seemed to have tears in her eyes, and the other kids tactfully looked around at other things. Drew had his head down, moving a pen rapidly over his notebook, pouring out words I couldn't read.

Patience took a breath. "I come from Dale's Run."

I blinked. Dale's Run was the place we'd passed on the drive to Etherall Valley—the devout commune of families that lived without technology. The place my mom thought was beautiful.

The place my ghosts didn't want me to visit.

"I have two brothers and two sisters. My father permitted me to come here, to Etherall Valley Academy, because he was worried about me. He could see me doing ungodly things and didn't know what to do about it. Mr. Boxe told him the school could help me. I..." Patience steadied her voice. "I can make things appear."

Drew stopped scribbling and reached out to put his hand on Patience's arm. She gave him a grateful smile. My shock stopped buzzing long enough for me to get a peculiar pang, right in the heart.

"Patience is a conjurer," Ms Deering told me.

"Best gift of us all, and she doesn't even want it," Mona grumbled.

"Drew?" Ms. Deering prompted.

He pulled his hand away from Patience's arm and glared at Ms. Deering, his fury back in an instant. She didn't flinch. He said nothing.

"Maybe you'd prefer to wait until the end," Ms. Deering said, although she sounded a bit hopeless. "Mimi, please tell us about you."

How did she expect me to make a coherent sentence after what I'd just heard? If there was another Mimi, a logical one that could step outside of my own body and look at the situation objectively, she would say: *Get a grip. This is bullshit. These people are playing the cruelest prank in history.* But logical Mimi had gone AWOL. I believed them. Deep in my soul, without any doubt, I knew they were telling the truth.

I launched into speech, sounding so unlike myself, even I got a shock. This was a tone I hadn't heard in years. Excited. *Happy*.

"Mimi Alston. I come from Perry Ridge. I have one brother, who's much older and lives with his girlfriend in Canada. I love drawing, especially anatomical art. I had a nickname when I was little: Ghostling. And at my old school, they called me Mimi and her imaginary friends, because—"

Hell, was I really telling them my secret? A secret I'd been so determined to keep, I would have faked my whole personality every single day at this new school?

Yes. Yes, I was telling them.

"—because I used to talk about my ghosts. I have three at the moment. Hannah, Albert and Marvin." I pointed at the chairs where my ghosts were sitting. The others' eyes were wide as they followed my gesture, and even Drew raised his head, his scowl falling away.

"Hannah was a kitchen maid." My words were practically tumbling over each other, desperate for liberation. "Early twentieth century. When she was seventeen, she got pregnant with her master's child. She tried taking a mixture of herbs to get rid of it but got the quantities wrong and died of poisoning. Albert was a soldier during the Second World War. He got sent home with a shrapnel injury to his leg and died a while later. His wounds kept getting infected and his organs eventually failed. Marvin's the most recent of them all. He was homeless due to gambling debts and died of hypothermia during a cold snap. It hasn't always been these three, but they're who I've got right now."

"Holy shit," Ed muttered.

Patience couldn't take her eyes off the empty chairs beside me, and Mona released a slow, shuddering breath. Even contemptuous Cassie looked impressed. Gabe, on the other hand, watched me curiously. It was as if he hadn't heard quite what he'd expected.

"You're a necromancer," Ms. Deering said.

Mona scribbled in her notebook. "*Necro*. That means dead."

"And *mancy* is divination," Ms. Deering affirmed. "Mimi calls the dead."

"I *call* them?" I was indignant. "I never called them! I didn't ask them to hang around!"

Ms. Deering gave me a rueful smile. "I didn't mean you actively call the dead. I meant you attract them. You can't help it."

"I'm dead," Gabe threw in.

Ms. Deering ignored him. "You communicate with them," she told me.

"Why?" I asked.

Mona gave a short laugh. "The million-dollar question. Why do any of us have these gifts?"

"You can hear them speak?" Patience's arctic-blue eyes were on me.

"Yes. They tell me what happened to them, and sometimes they give me advice—" I bit off the words *that I have to follow*, my mind drifting somewhere I didn't let it go very often. I yanked it back, putting it on a short leash.

"Drew." Ms. Deering adopted the firm tone of a parent who's had enough of your crap. "Please tell us about you."

He cast her a baleful glare, then got up and shouldered his backpack. "Enjoy Club Delusional." He directed that at me before making his way to the door and wrenching it open. He left without a backward glance, yanking the door shut and stumping down the timber steps.

"He has a shoulder surgery appointment," Mona said. "For the chip."

Ms. Deering had an air of defeat, but it didn't last long. She turned to me, a smile brightening her sweet face. When she spoke, her voice was warm with hope.

"We're so glad to have you, Mimi. You're the seventh. And that means the circle is complete."

I couldn't concentrate. My brain felt like a galaxy of scattered stars, orbiting planets and careening supernovas. Gabe, Mona and I sat together in science class and the teacher gave us a group exercise to work on. This meant we could talk and get away with it, which was lucky, because I would have exploded if I hadn't been able to talk.

"How long has this been going on?" I whispered.

Gabe leaned across Mona. "I've been at the academy since the beginning of ninth grade. It was just Patience and me for a while. Then Ed and Drew arrived partway through the year. That's when Ms. D started the gifted program."

"And Cassie and I both came to EVA last year," Mona put in.

"Doesn't anyone get suspicious about the gifted program?" I asked.

Mona grinned. "The high achievers here hate it. They say it's not fair, why don't they get to be in the gifted program, why are all the students in the program in the same grade, yada, yada. They call us the Garden Shed Society. Ms. D just sticks to her guns. I think she tells Mr. Boxe we need extra support. Trauma or whatever."

"I guess that's fair," I said. "Having a psychic power can be traumatic." Gabe chuckled like I'd made a joke. "But what does Ms. Deering teach you?"

Mona nudged Gabe out of her personal space. "It's more like a regular bonding session—a kind of *parea*."

"A what?" Gabe asked.

"Oh, that's Greek. Sorry," she added to me. "I accidentally use non-English words without noticing sometimes. *Parea* is when a group of friends come together to share life experiences, philosophies, values. Ideas. We get together and talk over what's happened with our gifts, describe anything we may have sensed or experienced throughout the week—good or bad. That sort of thing."

"Like a supernatural support group?"

Gabe and Mona seemed to find that hysterical. "Paranormals Anonymous!" Gabe snorted. The science teacher glared at us.

Mona dropped her voice again. "Not just support. We do research and stuff, too. We *theorize*."

"On what?"

"Spiritualism. Psychic phenomena. Other gifted people in history. We try to put it all together and make sense of it."

I chewed my lip. "And what's Drew's story?"

"Mr. Sunshine?" Mona grimaced. "He's having a little trouble accepting his reality."

"Poor Drew." Gabe wasn't joking.

I raised my eyebrows. "Poor *Drew*? He seems to be making everyone else suffer."

"He's seen some weird crap."

I was unimpressed. "I've seen some weird crap too."

Gabe grinned. "True."

"What's his gift?"

Mona opened her mouth, but Gabe put his hand on her arm. "Not our place, Mona. Let him tell her when he's ready." She closed it again.

"Is it the same as mine?"

They shook their heads. "We're all different," Gabe said.

"But why did you think that?" Mona wanted to know.

"He seemed shocked when I told you about my ghosts," I replied. "He actually looked up."

"He was shocked," Gabe confirmed. "And then he felt… I don't know—disappointed?"

That stung. "Why?"

Gabe shrugged. "I sense the feelings, not the reasons. There's something else," he added, "but I'd be breaking the bro code if I told you."

Mona punched his arm. "Spill," she demanded.

Gabe abandoned the bro code without further ado. "There's a pull. Like a sort of compulsion. Drew's got it, toward *her*." He indicated me with his head.

Hopefully Gabe couldn't feel what was happening inside me at that moment. "A compulsion? Why?"

"Feelings, not reasons, yeah?" he reminded me. "Could be your air of mystery. Or your pretty face."

My stomach fluttered and I tried not to blush.

Mona elbowed him. At this rate, he was going to be covered in bruises. "Stop, Gabe. Remember the rules." She leaned past him, catching my eye. "Ms. Deering likes us to stay in the friend zone in the gifted program. Hasn't been a problem for us so far—we're like siblings. Frankly, the thought of dating any of them is *ick*."

"Ms. Deering controls who we see?" I mean, I'd never dated, and it was unlikely I would be anytime soon, but still…

"Don't worry." Mona patted me on the arm. "I'm a master matchmaker. I'll have you sorted out with a nice little romance outside the gifted group in no time. All I need is your favorite band or anime character and your sexual preferences."

On a bathroom break before final period, I studied my face in the mirror. *Pretty?* I was pale by Etherall Valley standards, and my dark hair emphasized it. Gray eyes. One ear that stuck out a little more than the other. My features weren't symmetrical enough to be pretty. I had an angular nose and a wide mouth that was usually red-raw because of the lip-chewing habit—so bad today, it looked like I was wearing lipstick. I was almost grayscale, except for the lips. I guess you could say it gave me an interesting "painted vintage photo" look.

Patience's fair hair and ice-blue eyes drifted through my mind. Did Drew like demure blondes?

Why was I even wondering about that?

I shook myself and went into a mental pep talk: *You're not here to build a social circle. You're here to finish your education.* The existence of others like me was a bonus, an opportunity to reveal my gift/curse to people who didn't think I was lying. Or out of my mind. A buzz of sheer, unadulterated euphoria hit me from nowhere. *Others like me.*

The effect on my face was shocking. My eyes sparkled, the frown vanished, my mouth curved into a smile, and for a split second I *was* pretty.

My final class was English, and Drew was already there. Only one seat remained—possibly because I'd been in the restroom looking for *pretty* in the mirror—and it was next to him. I went over, a mixture of dread and excitement curdling my stomach. He glanced up as I took my seat. The white contact lens was gone now, revealing two agate-green eyes.

I found it hard to concentrate on Mr. Cambridge's explanation of character archetypes. Then he announced a partner task: we had to discuss the archetypal roles of characters in our assigned novel. Everyone broke into conversation, but Drew kept writing illegibly in his leather-bound notebook.

"Uh, are we going talk about archetypes?" I asked.

He didn't look up. "Are you serious?"

"Good. I don't want to either, but it'll look weird to Mr. Cambridge if we don't talk at all."

Drew wrote more furiously. I waited. Finally the pen went still and he turned to me. My mouth went instantly dry and my heart tried to decide whether to palpitate or arrest.

"What is *with* you?" It was low and vicious.

I shrank away, aghast. I'd never seen a look like that directed at me—a look with so much fury and loathing in it. It made my whole face prickle.

Compulsion? More like revulsion. I turned away and attempted to collect myself, flicking blindly through the set novel. How long could I pretend to do this task without our teacher wondering why we weren't speaking?

"Sorry, Mimi. Just—sorry." His voice had lost its bitterness.

A tear was trying to spill. I kept my eyes motionless, head tilted to prevent gravity from betraying me. Mission failure. *Shit.* I brushed my hair back so I could swipe past my cheek, removing the evidence, then acted like I was scratching my nose to sort out the other side.

"What's your problem?" It sounded clipped and indifferent, not weepy or nasal. I congratulated myself.

"Don't get sucked in by them. This *gift* bullshit isn't real. Bronwyn Deering is encouraging their delusions."

I got angry. So angry, my voice shook with the effort to stay quiet. "Oh. My. God. Do you realize how long I've thought there was something wrong with me? You can pretend it's not real all you like, but I won't. I just got released from solitary confinement, and maybe I'm finally going to get my life back."

I flipped through the novel again, waiting.

He bent over his notebook and resumed scribbling. "This isn't a life. You just wait."

I was done here. I raised my hand and excused myself, then went straight to the girls' dorm and claimed a migraine. Ms. Samvedi took my temperature and peered into my eyes for a moment but seemed to believe me. She sent me to lie down.

I went into my room, my ghosts trailing behind me. As I lay on top of the covers, staring at the ceiling, my mind went like a robotic assembly line, processing disconnected thoughts and spitting out ideas. The incident from last Thursday—Cassie, Patience and Mona cornering me in my room—suddenly made sense. They'd been trying to work out if I was their missing piece. And I *was*. Warmth blossomed through my chest. *The seventh.* They'd been waiting for me to complete the circle.

Well, some of them had. Obviously not Drew.

A crow cawed outside my window and the sound had a mocking tone. Drew's hostility was the reminder I needed. Friendship was never a certainty—it could turn in an instant. I'd be better off staying wary. Let them in too quickly and I'd be handing them my tender heart on a platter, inviting them to slice it up.

But that tender heart was ignoring my tough brain, having its own little party with champagne, canapés and dance beats. I could hardly wait until the next time I'd be sitting in that garden shed with the other gifted kids, discovering more about what we could do. I had a *gift*. These three dead people sitting with me—one on my swivel chair and two on my floor—were real. They weren't figments of my imagination.

Who cared what Drew thought? Maybe this wasn't quite *getting my life back*, but it was better than the living death I was used to.

5
Forbidden Liaisons

I dreamed of dark feathers that morphed into black spikes of hair on a boy who had his back to me. A rhythmic thudding arose, as if someone was beating a drum. I woke up and realized the thudding was coming from my door. I squinted at the clock. Five p.m.

"You okay, Mimi?" Mona's voice.

"Yeah," I croaked, staggering across the room to let her in.

"Sorry. Were you asleep? I thought you were having a post-reveal panic attack or something."

"I flaked out." I rubbed my eyes.

Mona plonked herself down on my swivel chair. Albert slid noiselessly out of the way to accommodate her. "Got anything to eat? I'm starving."

I dug some cookies out of the food stash Mom had sent back to school with me and handed them over before flopping back onto my bed. Mona munched contentedly, holding her ever-present notebook against her stomach.

"What's in that?" I asked.

She clutched it a little closer. "It's my most important tool. I write down *everything*. It helps me solve puzzles."

"Puzzles?"

"Mysteries." She waggled her eyebrows. "I love mysteries."

"Like what?"

"Like your gift. I've been trying to work out what it was since Ms. D told us the seventh had arrived. First, I had to work out if it was you or the other new kid."

"Axel?"

"Yeah. Gabe thought it was him. I was ninety-two per cent sure it was you, though. Then I tried to work out what your gift was."

Which was why she and Gabe had been so friendly all week. See? Friendship was a fickle bitch.

"What were your theories?" I asked, reaching for a cookie.

She consulted her notebook. "Telekinesis. So bummed none of us has that. Telepathy. Glad none of us has that. Psychometry—"

"What's that?"

"Detecting things about an object by touching it."

"That'd be interesting. What's your gift called again?"

"Not too sure. Ms. Deering could classify most of our gifts, but with mine, the best she could come up with was xenoglossic. That means knowing other languages without being taught. I prefer polyglot. Xenoglossic is too close to xenophobic."

"Do you speak every language?"

"Not *speak*, as such. But I understand every language. Every language I've experimented with, anyway."

"What about Inuit?"

"Yep. Or should I say *ii*? And the language is Inuktitut, by the way; the people are Inuit."

I thought back to the podcast Dad had us listen to on the drive south. It had been about Celtic history. "Can you speak Manx?"

She paused. "Like the cat?"

"Like from the Isle of Man."

She took a bite of cookie. "Not sure. I'll check later. Thanks for the suggestion." Mona glanced around my room. "Cool posters. Do they hang around you all the time?"

I frowned. "My posters?"

"The ghosts."

"Oh. Yeah. Most of the time. You booted one out of that chair."

She shrieked and jumped up. I couldn't help laughing, and Mona shot me a look of outrage.

"Sorry!" I said. "True, though. Albert was sitting there."

"Damn, Mimi." She grimaced, sinking back down. "I thought Drew had it tough, but you got the short straw, gift-wise."

"Tell me what Drew's gift is."

She shook her head. "Gabe was right. Not fair to tell someone else's story."

"But I'll never hear it if you don't tell me. He hates the world and hates me, and I wasn't exactly patient with all that this afternoon."

Mona's eyes gleamed. "Slay."

"Will you tell me what his gift is, if he decides he won't?"

"He will. I know this sounds weird, but we have this connection. It doesn't make a difference if we get along or not—the connection is still there. Can't explain it."

I was dubious. "Even *him*?"

She grinned. "He has flashes of compassion and even wit occasionally, in amongst all that wading through self-pity."

"What's the deal with him and Patience?" I made it sound nonchalant.

Mona shrugged. "He's got more time for Patience than the rest of us. I guess he can relate to the self-loathing. She has religious hang-ups and thinks she's possessed by the devil."

I choked a little. "Whoa."

"Yeah. She can't help it. It's just how she was raised. We're used to it. Drew looks out for her. Maybe he considers her special and pure, or whatever—or maybe he just feels sorry for her. It's frustrating, the way she thinks Satan's made a little nest in her soul, but at least she tries to deal with her gift. She knows it's real. Drew, on the other hand, thinks we're having a mass hallucination."

"For real?" My heart dropped. Could he be that deeply in denial?

"It's ludicrous," she told me flatly. "He'll be telling us about one of his experiences, then next minute he's telling us to forget it, don't pay attention, it's all a load of crap, et cetera, et cetera."

"His experiences?"

Mona eyed me. "Nice try. Now, I want to know all about your ghosts." She opened her notebook, pen poised.

Hannah looked up from where she sat on the floor, catching my attention. "Miss," she whispered urgently into my ear, her mouth pressed into a line. "Hold your tongue."

I only had time to be baffled for an instant before a knock on the door startled us both.

"Miss Alston," came a man's voice. "May I have a word?"

Mona frowned at me. "Sounds like Mr. Boxe," she told me in a low voice. "He never comes to the dorm."

I opened the door to our principal. He seemed even bigger now he was standing in my bedroom door, and that fluffy hair made him look like a giant, shaggy dog. He'd toned back the hearty manner and was smiling down at me kindly. "Ms. Samvedi said you weren't well. I thought I'd better check on you."

"I'm okay now, thanks." I tried to appear a bit weak and wan.

"Good! I know how tough it can be to change schools and thought you might be feeling the pressure." He noticed Mona over my shoulder. "Oh! Hello, Mona. What are you doing in here?"

"Same as you, sir," Mona said brightly. "Checking on Mimi."

"Well, that's kind of you, but it's probably better to let her rest."

"My head's much better," I said hastily. "Mona's been keeping me company."

Mr. Boxe chuckled. "I'm glad you've made a friend already."

He left us alone, and I side-eyed Mona to see how she'd taken being called my friend. She gave me a conspiratorial grin. With a strange twist of my gut, I smiled back.

For the rest of that week, Drew sat with other people in every class we shared. I couldn't even catch him sneaking a peek in my direction. He'd upped the goth look to *extreme*. Both white contact lenses were in every day. Every spare inch of him was covered in black, only broken up by the occasional row of chain or spikes. Yes, EVA's dress code was all about self-expression, but I was surprised he got away with it. It was as if he were covering himself up, preparing to go into battle. His look was a message: *leave me alone.*

Well, if that's how he wanted it.

On Friday, the day of our next gifted class, I was popping. I was first into the cottage, followed by Patience, then Gabe. Mona, Cassie and Ed entered as a noisy group, and Ms. Deering arrived last. No Drew. I should have been relieved, but to my annoyance, I felt a little disappointed.

Maybe the session would flow more smoothly without Drew. It was my first "normal" gifted class, and I pulled out my sketchpad. Drawing was the only thing that grounded me when I was this keyed up. I sketched shapes and random symbols, listening while the others spoke. Eyes were one of my go-tos. Those and skulls. It probably didn't look like it, but I was fully tuned in to the conversation.

The other five talked through their week's experiences with their individual talents. Mona had experimented with ancient texts, looking up papyrus scrolls on the internet and trying to translate the snippets of writing. She confirmed proudly that she could understand Manx. Ed shared a story about helping an injured seagull at the beach on the weekend. That was brilliant—but I couldn't help thinking of the good he could be doing with a gift like that.

"Why aren't you working in a hospital?" I blurted. "In the emergency room? Or the cancer ward?"

Silence descended. Ed, Patience and Gabe looked at Ms. Deering and Cassie rolled her eyes. Only Mona kept her gaze on me, doing a poor job of suppressing a grin.

"Like all of your gifts, Ed's is still developing," Ms. Deering answered for him. "He can help with small injuries at this stage."

"Oh! Of course." I flushed at my faux pas and grimaced at Ed, hoping I hadn't offended him.

"Same as how I can only pick up vague vibes of what other people are feeling," Gabe put in. "And Cassie can only encourage animals to do what she wants until they don't feel like it anymore, and then they bite her."

Cassie's stare was withering. "That was only once. And parrots are notorious biters."

"And I can only make simple objects," Patience said in her soft voice. "And they don't last very long before they disintegrate."

What did that mean for me? Was my gift in its fledgling stages too? Would more ghosts come? It was already quite a crowd.

"Not me," Mona said without a glimmer of modesty. "I can already translate pretty well anything I see or hear, no matter the language. And I get a hundred per cent in all my French, Spanish and Chinese exams."

"Tell us about your week, Mimi," Ms. Deering invited me. "How did your gift manifest?"

"Well, um, just the usual," I said. "They're always around."

"What about when you shower?" Cassie asked.

Heat flared in my cheeks. "Yeah, they're here all the time. But they don't *watch* me or anything."

She wrinkled her nose. "I should hope not! I couldn't handle a pervy ghost."

"I don't always notice them these days, to be honest. Only when I look for them, or if they do something unusual."

"Have they done anything unusual lately?" Ms. Deering asked.

I thought back over the past week. "They've been speaking to me more often than usual. Last weekend, as soon as Mom and Dad told me I'd been invited into this program, they all told me to *join the gifted*. A lot. So they obviously know about *this*." I waved my hand around the group.

That sent a ripple through them. Cassie shuddered and Ed said he thought he'd felt a cold spot as he came into class. Mona squinted at the air around me as though, if she tried hard enough, she might see my ghosts. Gabe gave me a pensive look. Wait, was he attempting to reach in and feel around for my emotions? Oh God—I could *feel* him prodding around the edges of my consciousness. I responded with a psychic stab of disapproval, and Gabe withdrew his scouting mission, looking sheepish.

"Are they angels?" Patience practically whispered at me.

I shook my head, biting my lip to stop a giggle. "I don't think so. I mean, they're a bit hazy, but otherwise they look pretty normal. Definitely no wings or halos."

"Do they look gory?" Cassie wanted to know. "Can you see how they died?"

"No, they're not bloodstained or anything." Damn, it felt good to talk about it so openly. "They look like regular people, except they're wearing the clothes from their times.

They don't speak normally, though. Their lips don't move and I hear their voices close to my ears."

Patience shook her head, apparently aghast at the idea. Maybe I was tougher than I'd realized. I was so used to being haunted, I rarely experienced so much as an uncanny shiver these days. It was only the thought of them touching me that gave me a sense of dread.

The door opened and Drew came in, slumping into a chair near Ed. My fine-liner hovering above my sketchpad, I waited for his explanation of his tardiness. He didn't offer one. He pretended he couldn't see us and kept his gaze on the dusty Turkish carpet as if the pattern was fascinating to him.

Cassie barely spared him a glance. "If we're bragging about what we can do, I made a horse jump a post during the summer break. It was grazing in a field and I told it to go over a pole jump, and it did."

Gabe raised an eyebrow. "A horse?" She nodded, smiling. "Too easy. Horses are compliant. Try something challenging next time."

"Yeah, like a cat," said Mona. "Now that would be impressive. *Nobody* can tell my cat what to do."

Cassie glared. "You two are freaking hilarious."

I was only half listening. Ms. Deering was still watching the black-haired boy staring at the carpet.

"Drew," she said firmly, like she'd had it up to here with his moody tantrums. "What's been going on for you this week?"

The silence went on for so long I nearly giggled nervously into it, but Drew suddenly answered. "There was a silver bus. A tiny dog with a diamante collar. A key in a lock set in varnished wood."

Mona was scribbling in her notebook, and I squinted to read the words. *Silver bus, small dog diamante collar, varnished wood with key.* What was so important about those three things that she'd write them down?

"Thank you, Drew," Ms. Deering said.

The conversation resumed and I went back to my doodling, practically twitching with curiosity. What the hell was Drew's gift? The others were still talking, but I couldn't stop speculating. Was he a fire starter? A water diviner? Could he levitate? I caught myself drawing an eye with a white iris and hastily shaded it darker.

Not much of the period remained; it had hardly been worth Drew turning up at all. When the bell rang and he rose to leave, I seized my gear and scrambled out of my seat to follow. I caught up to him just as he reached the corner of the cottage.

"Drew." I pretended I also happened to be walking super-fast to my next class. "I know you don't like me, and I don't particularly care, but would you at least tell me what your gift is? I mean, you know mine. And *they* all know yours. And I know about everyone else's. And Mona says it's not their place to tell."

Drew slowed to a halt and turned, dragging his white-lensed eyes upward to meet mine. Why did he have to do everything with such drama? Okay, my heart rate may have hiked a couple of notches, but I didn't falter under his gaze. He glanced around as if to check if anyone was hovering, but the other five were still inside the cottage. Only a lone crow watched us, perched on the slate roof of the science block.

"What have you got next?" Drew's voice was clipped, as if he could barely stand to speak to me.

I checked the back of my hand. I'd scrawled my day's timetable on there so I wouldn't forget where to go. "PE."

"Skip class with me. I need to get out of here for a while. I'll tell you the truth."

For someone who refused to go to school for four years, I was surprisingly hesitant to skip a class. I didn't enjoy PE—but I didn't want to break the rules and have the academy calling my parents, either.

He must have seen my hesitation. "Randall never takes attendance in PE."

"What are you talking about, 'get out of here'? The school gates are locked. There's no way out."

"I know a way out."

I hadn't asked him to spend a whole period with me; I'd only asked him to explain his gift. After Monday's hostile exchange, it made no sense. Gabe's comment about Drew being drawn to me snagged in my brain, and I made an irrational decision even I didn't understand.

"Fine. Show me."

Drew set off. He could walk really fast. I half jogged to keep pace with him, staying close to the line of trees bordering the school's lush gardens. He went to a point where a thick shrubbery grew around both sides of the cyclone fence and, after a quick scout for witnesses, dove in. I followed, immediately getting slapped in the face with a branch of spruce.

A narrow but well-worn trail cut underneath. Obviously we weren't the only Etherall Valley Academy kids who knew about this escape route. It took us to a wrenched-open part of the cyclone fence hidden by the shrubbery. Drew squeezed through the split and stepped out into the parking lot. By the time I got through, he was already across the road. I dashed after him into the quiet woodland.

"This way," Drew told me. "The trail leads to a water hole. We can talk there." His voice was tight, like he had to break bad news.

We walked without speaking until we came to the point where a trickling stream widened into a pond. A weathered wooden dock clung to the nearest bank, and on the opposite side, a big old willow was dipping its leaves in the water. The crows hadn't followed us here, and the air was warm and full of darting bugs and flickers of sunlight. Dragonflies balanced on the water's surface like a magic trick.

I dropped my bag on the bank and went to sit on the dock. Drew joined me, sitting at a safe distance, then unlaced his boots and dropped his bare feet into the water. I followed suit, pulling off my high-tops and socks and rolling up the cuffs of my jeans. He glanced at me repeatedly while we got settled, and I had the sense that he was wound up tighter than a python around a rat. I relaxed a little the instant my feet touched the cool water. After a few moments, Drew's tension seemed to ease as well.

"It's shallow," he said, as if I needed reassurance. "Even though you can't see the bottom."

"I love water," I said. "The deeper and colder, the better."

He was silent for a moment. "So, you're a swimmer?"

"I swim okay. I don't usually stay in for long. I just like the reset you get from that first plunge." Was I babbling? I closed my mouth.

The sunlight was warm on our backs, and Drew shuffled off his leather jacket to reveal a death-metal t-shirt. His arms were much browner than I'd expected, and the contrast with his white face was almost absurd.

He caught me looking. "What?"

I pulled my eyes away. "Nothing. Let's talk. What's your gift?"

"My curse?" he said.

"Curse, gift, same thing."

"Ms. Deering calls me a prophet."

I turned that over in my mind. "You predict the future?"

Drew didn't quite nod, but he didn't disagree. "I see flashes of things that have significance in future events."

"Like what?"

"Like the silver bus, the little dog—that kind of stuff. I don't know what its significance is until something bigger happens. Then I connect the two, and realize the *something* was what I'd seen in my head."

"How do you see the future flashes? In dreams? When you close your eyes?"

"Visions. Something will flicker in front of me like a single frame in a movie reel, so fast I'm not always sure I really saw it."

"What are some of the visions you've had that came true?"

He rubbed his face hard, like he was tired, and lay back on the jetty, looking up at the trees overhead. "Once, I saw a chain with a shark's tooth pendant. That week a guy in my literature class turned up wearing it. Another time I saw a coffee mug with a picture of an old building on it. I went to visit my dad at work later that week and his colleague had the mug. He knocked it while he was talking to someone and spilled cold coffee down his pants."

I laughed. Drew didn't.

"Another time, I had a vision of a paper shopping bag on a bench. The next day I was riding the bus. A bunch of people climbed on at a stop, including an old woman. I noticed the paper bag on the bus stop bench. Just before the bus moved, the woman realized she'd left her shopping on the bench and tried to rush back out the door. She fell and hurt herself—bad. They had to call an ambulance."

I chewed my lip. "So sometimes you foresee accidents? And other times there's no accident?"

"Or there is, but I don't find out about it."

"Do you only have visions of objects?" I asked.

"What do you mean?"

"It's never full scenes or events? I mean, is there any way of knowing *what* will happen in advance?"

"Not that I've been able to figure out. It's usually specific objects I see."

I pulled my feet out of the water and shuffled around to look at him. Drew watched the trees overhead steadily. I opened my mouth twice but couldn't find the right words.

"Don't hold back." Bitterness made his voice brittle.

"I just want to know why you refuse to accept your gift," I said. No answer. "Mona says you think we're all deluded."

Drew's face contorted. "How can you be okay with these powers? We shouldn't be proud of them. We're sideshow freaks! And Ms. Deering encouraging us—trying to develop the powers in us—it's not safe. I mean, you hang around with dead people and that's *okay* with you?"

"That's all I've known since I was four, so yes, I'm okay with hanging around dead people. And I'm definitely okay with finding out I'm not the only one who has a power. And I'm extremely okay that I'm not the only one with a secret most people wouldn't believe. I mean, I *could* decide what I see isn't real, but that won't make them go away." I glanced at Albert pacing the shore, Hannah seated beneath a tree and Marvin sitting against a post. "*Nothing* makes them go away."

He sat up and stared into the water, his face miserable. "I think you and I are different. Very different."

That meant *I don't get you.*

I turned around and dropped my feet into the water again. "How could our gifts hurt anyone? If anything, they can help people. Like Ed and his healing. Or Mona being able to translate anything."

Drew's jaw tightened, his black lips pressed together in a hard, straight line. "Not long ago, I saw a vision of a handful of coins in front of a faded Batman t-shirt. The next week, I saw a guy feeding coins into a parking meter in the same shirt. There were three men coming the other way. One of them bumped into the Batman guy and made him drop his coins. He swore at them. They jumped him, started throwing punches. A few people tried to break it up, but before we could do anything, they knocked him down and he hit the ground headfirst." The lines of his face were sharp with torment. "He died in the hospital that night. I foresaw a death."

I took an audible breath. "Okay, that would be upsetting." Drew opened his white-lensed eyes wide at the word. "Devastating," I corrected myself. "Terrifying. Having powers is terrifying for all of us. Does that mean we should repress them or pretend they're not happening? How does that help?"

"You don't think maybe we're playing with things we don't understand? I mean, what if Patience is right, and there *is* a malevolent spirit pulling the strings? Maybe we're being manipulated. Deering is so—so *reckless*. She doesn't think about what damage we could do, armed with our wild theories and party tricks."

"They're not party tricks. And—"

Drew interrupted me, his voice coming as a hiss. "What if I'm not just seeing these things? What if I'm *causing* them?"

"No. That's wrong. You're not causing any of it. It's all just life going on around you, and you're seeing moments in advance."

"How could you possibly know that?"

"You're not a god," I told him. "You don't call the shots. You just see stuff."

He gave me a look brimming with skepticism. "Well, if you're happy to play with these deadly toys…"

My anger fired. "You know what, Drew? You don't get to tell the rest of us to stop having gifts. Yes, I *am* happy. I haven't been happy for four years. *Four. Years.* And now I find out I'm part of something. So yes, I'm happy. I'm not deluded, I'm not alone, my curse is a gift, and I'm *happy*."

I pulled my knees up and brought both feet down hard into the water, making a splash that sprayed us both. Then I laughed in his startled, water-sprayed face.

Instead of shouting like I thought he would, he gave me a reluctant smile. "You're weird."

For an instant it stung. Then the supremely inadequate word made me laugh again. "You're weirder."

He eyed me, then checked his watch. "The final bell's going to ring in five minutes."

That meant my parents would be here to pick me up for the weekend. We got our shoes back on and headed for school. The car park was filling up with parents' cars and the bell rang just as we ducked into the shrubs and scrambled through the split fence.

"Are you a weekend boarder?" I asked, avoiding the hostile spruce branch.

"No, I live in Etherall Valley, so I go home on weekends."

"Right." I glanced at him and did a double take. My splash had messed up his makeup. Trails of black eyeliner streaked through the dissolving white on his cheek, revealing tanned skin underneath. It felt naughty—like I was seeing him partially undressed. My heart sped up at the thought.

I coughed. "The water's melted your face. You look like a sad clown." I raised a hand, then stopped myself. *You can't touch his face!*

I dug a clean tissue from my bag and offered it to him. He dabbed at the streak, and all it did was expand the window to his real face.

"Is it getting better?"

I nodded wordlessly, my eyes locked on his face. It was, if anything, worse than before, but I wanted him to keep wiping. I wanted to see all of him.

"Drew!"

We both swung around in response to the call from the direction of the school buildings. It was Patience. She was standing at the corner of the science block, watching us with horror. Drew stepped away from me like I'd insulted his mother and strode toward Patience, his head down. A crow landed on the top of the fence post behind me and gave a scornful caw.

When Drew reached Patience, she said something to him, he nodded, and they both headed for the school buildings. She glanced at me over her shoulder as they departed, and there was something accusatory in it.

Nice. I went in the direction of the girls' dorm to get my packed weekend bag, my cheeks burning. He'd smiled. Drew had actually smiled while we were sitting on the dock, after I splashed him. Then Patience appeared and magically turned him back into a rude asshole.

I was angrier at myself than her, to be honest. She didn't *make* him walk away from me without a word of farewell. He did that all by himself. Maybe he had something going on with that bone structure, or whatever, but the guy was sitting at a flat-earther level of reality denial and a day-twenty-seven-of-my-menstrual-cycle level of moody bitch.

And I had plenty more metaphors to mix for him where those came from.

6

The Excavation of Mimi Alston

Mom and Dad collected me for our last weekend together before they were to drive three hours north and leave me alone in Etherall Valley. At their apartment, I sat on the balcony with my ghosts and sketched, hoping to take my mind off the hour I'd spent with Drew. The memory of it was dancing on the edge of obsession. I tried some charcoal scenes, including one of the little, dark water hole with the dock and the willow tree. When I caught myself sketching a male figure sitting on the jetty, I forced myself to put my sketchpad away and went inside.

I chewed my lip for a minute, then came out with it. "Mom, I was wondering if we could go shopping this weekend. The weather's warm here and I think I need some new clothes. I have some birthday money and gift cards I can use. Could you take me?"

"New clothes?"

Mom looked at me like someone had replaced her daughter with a doppelganger. I hadn't been involved in my own clothes shopping in years. She'd got me by on plain gray, blue or black tees, and hoodies and jeans she occasionally picked up for me. And black sneakers. Anything else, I'd rejected. I hadn't wanted more attention than I'd already been blessed with.

"Yeah. My wardrobe doesn't really work for Etherall Valley weather. Maybe some shorts and tops. A skirt or whatever. Would that be okay?" Did she have tears in her eyes? "Mom!" I protested. "It's just shopping!"

"I'd love to take you, honey," she said with a sheepish laugh.

So we went to the local mall on Saturday. I was as surprised as Mom, but we ended up having a great day. My ghosts stayed at a distance, fading in and out of view while Mom and I browsed. I only registered them from time to time, like seeing people you recognized but weren't obliged to chat with.

I didn't buy much; I was, after all, still me. But I got a black skirt like I'd seen some of the other girls wearing, as well as some shorts and a few different colored tops. Mom talked me into a dress, saying there might be some occasion where I'd need it. It was red. I tried to tell her it was unlikely I'd wear it, but she was determined. She wanted me to get some more shoes, too. I negotiated some green high-tops— a variation on my usual black. By then, I was done. Past done. Mom would have kept going, but I pleaded being shopped out.

"I had so much fun today, Mimi," she said as we got into the car.

"Me too." And I had.

We sat in comfortable silence as Mom drove back to the apartment. I pulled out my sketchpad and fine-liner and doodled an eye, reflective and thick-lashed. Beneath it I started a skull. Most people didn't know it, but there were seven bones in an eye socket.

Mom spoke into the quiet. "I was going to try to talk your dad into staying in Etherall Valley for one more week. Just to make triply sure you've settled into your new school. But you seem to be doing so well…"

"I am, Mom. I really like it. I think I fit in here." She started crying again. Remorse snagged in my heart like a serrated tooth. "I'm sorry I've been so much trouble in the past. I promise I'll be okay. You guys go home."

"You're never too much trouble, honey. All we ever cared about was that you're okay."

But I knew it had been appalling for them—four years of having a daughter so solitary she wouldn't even sit on the porch in case she was seen by someone from her old school. "Well, now it's your time." I tried to say it lightly, but I meant it. "I'm safe. I'm happy. You and Dad can go home and plan your big trip to Paris, and enjoy not having to worry about me."

"I can't promise I won't worry. Or that I won't miss you."

"You'll be so busy slaying at your new job, you won't have time to miss me."

She chuckled. "I don't know about that. I've been out of it for so long, I'm terrified the tech's moved on without me and I'll be sitting there like a… like a…"

"Like Grandpa at a self-checkout?" She snorted and nodded. "You're smart, Mom. You'll pick it up fast."

"Hope so. I need this job."

Another twinge of guilt. My new school was the reason she needed it.

"Anyway, none of that's important," she went on. "I'm just so glad you're happy at Etherall Valley Academy, Mimi.

And if you're ever sad or anxious, just get on the phone and let me know."

I went back to shading the eye socket. "I will, Mom. Promise."

I tried out a new look on Monday. It was warm, as usual, so I wore a singlet under a loose crocheted top and teamed it with denim cut-offs and my green Converse. I checked myself out in the bathroom mirror. Did I look too dressed up? But most of the girls at EVA dressed this way. *I look just like any other Etherall Valley teenager.* Well, maybe not quite as tanned.

In strange kind of synchronicity, Axel had also tried a new look. I caught sight of him before homeroom. He'd gone demi-goth—definitely not on Drew's level, but he wore black jeans and had gotten himself some spike jewelry. Perhaps he was simply trying out a new style, but I got the feeling he was attempting to align himself with Drew. At lunchtime, I even spotted him hanging around near the oak tree, where Drew and Patience tended to sit together. I felt sorry for Axel, then wondered for a moment if I was doing the same thing as him with my new clothes. But I didn't feel like I was trying to squeeze myself into someone else's mold—it was more like I was uncovering a long-buried part of me.

I almost escaped without drawing comment, but Gabe had been at the orthodontist during homeroom and didn't see me until gifted class. So when I let myself into the cottage, he did a hammed-up double take and announced, "Mimi has dialed her cuteness up to eleven." Then everyone except Drew turned to have a good look. Cassie even snorted.

My cheeks went hot and I slid into my seat as unobtrusively as possible, annoyed at Gabe and regretting my choices. Ms. Deering, angel that she was, deflected the attention by asking us all to talk through anything relating to our gifts from the weekend.

"I listened in on conversations between tourists in a souvenir store," Mona said. "They didn't say anything interesting, but it was fun. There was a Dutch couple, a Pakistani family and a Scottish guy. Turned out he was speaking English, but I still had to use my gift to understand his accent."

Gabe, now he'd gotten his moment of humiliating me out of his system, was also anxious to share. "There's a girl in ninth grade—"

"Ew, Gabe, that's way too young for you." Cassie shot him a malicious grin.

He ignored her. "I've picked up on something from her. Something dark. I've noticed it for a while now, but it's spiked recently. She's seriously unhappy and feels out of control."

"Who is she?" Ms. Deering looked more alert than I'd ever seen her.

"I don't know her name," he admitted. "She's got short blonde hair, kind of skinny. Oh, wait—she's got a birthmark on her arm."

"Juliet," Mona and Cassie said in unison, then Mona elaborated like she had a dossier on the kid. "Juliet Banks. Weekday boarder. Quiet kid. Gets targeted by the delightful

Melita Borgen on a regular basis. Maybe it's getting too much for her?"

"I'll look into it." Ms. Deering made a note in her file.

"She's spiraling," Gabe said, and he seemed genuinely worried. "I'll try to engage her in conversation—maybe she'll open up to me, since I'm outside the situation with the other girl."

I got fidgety with excitement. *This* could be why we had these gifts: they gave us the opportunity to help people in trouble. If Drew would just pay attention to these moments, he might feel less bleak about our powers. I shot him a glance. He wore black contacts today, so his eyes looked like demonic pools.

"Drew?" Ms. Deering inquired, like she'd seen my glance.

"I saw a near miss with the silver bus from my vision," he said. "The driver pulled out and nearly hit a kid riding past on a bike."

"But he didn't actually hit him." Patience said it softly, as if trying to comfort Drew.

"No. He was lucky. My mom was giving me a driving lesson when it happened. We were stopped, waiting for the bus, and I saw what was happening so I hit the horn. The bus braked just in time."

Cassie broke in. "Oh, hey, another one of your visions came true! My aunt and cousins came over on the weekend and they have a new dog—a Chihuahua. She was wearing a diamante collar, like in your vision, Drew. She's *adorable*. I taught her to sit during a half-hour visit. Honestly, I can do *anything* with dogs." She pushed her curls behind an ear. "I've even trained my Labrador not to run away at the park—

as long as it's me walking him and not *the boys*." *The boys* was how she described her brothers whenever she mentioned them. And it was always with a disgusted inflection, as if they were a lowlife criminal gang.

"Are they okay?" Drew asked. "Your aunt—the dog?"

Cassie paused. "Yeah. Why?"

"Just checking."

Dismay spread slowly over Cassie's face. "Wait, you think something bad might happen to the puppy?"

He said nothing and turned his attention back to his page. Cassie stared at him, her eyebrows cinched together, and picked at her nail varnish.

"Mimi?" Ms. Deering prompted, possibly to gloss over Drew's pessimism.

"Nothing to report," I said.

"Patience?"

With a mixture of high excitement and deep shame, Patience confessed she had conjured over the weekend. "I needed to do my math homework, and I only had old, blotchy pens. I got in trouble with Ms. Huang last time I used a pen like that, so I thought I'd try conjuring one. Maybe because it's such a simple thing, it's lasted better than most of the other things I've made. It still works." She pulled it out of her pencil case.

I leaned in eagerly. "Can I hold it?" She handed it over, and I examined the pen. It truly looked like a normal, plastic, black ballpoint pen. If anything, it was slightly smoother and more perfect than a regular pen. I tested it, and it wrote beautifully.

"No disintegration yet?" Ms. Deering asked, and Patience shook her head. "Your skills are improving. Keep it up."

Patience's cheeks went pink and she exchanged a look with Drew. It was almost apologetic—and in return, he looked like he was saying, *Forget about it.* Their unspoken communication stirred an unpleasant feeling in my chest. They were close—so close they could have whole conversations in silence. How deep did their relationship run?

Ed was telling a story about his weekend. He'd been at the beach and come across one of the other surfers who'd been stung by a jellyfish.

"It wasn't one of the dangerous kind, but he looked like he was in a lot of pain. I wasn't sure if I should try healing a human, but my gift took over, in a way. I didn't decide to do it—it was more like an instinct. I put my hand on his shoulder where the sting was and all this energy flowed into my hand, and when I moved away, he wasn't in pain anymore. He was like, 'What did you do, man?' and I was like, 'Uh, uh, I poured vinegar into my hand to neutralize the sting.' The skin didn't even look red anymore; it just healed up like he never even got stung."

"That's brilliant, Ed!" Ms. Deering looked as proud as if he'd written an A-plus paper.

"What does it feel like?" Mona asked him. "When you heal?"

He scratched his fledgling dreads. "My hands heat up. It feels like—like my cells are buzzing with energy."

"I wonder if your energy can run out during a healing," she mused. "Like how keeping an app open on your phone runs down the battery."

Ed shrugged. "Who knows? I feel tired after healing, so if it was a really intense healing, I guess I could potentially run out of zap altogether."

"If you're comfortable to do so, keep practicing your gift whenever you can," Ms. Deering told him.

What would my homework look like, if she gave me any? She might ask me to try to make contact with my ghosts more often. I didn't relish the idea.

Mona looked up from her notebook as if she were going to ask how to spell a word. Instead, she threw a grenade posing as a question. "Why are all seven of us here at EVA at the same time, Ms. D?"

Ms. Deering leaned back in her rickety chair and gazed at a constellation chart on the wall. "I wish I knew. I know the number seven has spiritual and magical weight across the world and throughout history. Across different cultural belief systems, it's a symbol of completeness and perfection. Seven days of the week. Seven years to renew every cell in the body. It's all through the Bible... seven seals, seven thunders, seven spirits of God. Psychologically, it's the limit to the number of short-term memories we can hold at any moment."

"It's a prime number, too," Ed put in.

"Yes." The faint lines between her eyebrows deepened. "But my intuition tells me that this point in time, now all seven of you are together, is powerful. It's a convergence, as much as a coming of age. An upward shift in the power of your gifts."

It was an impressive response. Most of us sat and thought about that in silence, but Mona sniffed and shook her head. "There must be more to it than that. There's got to be some kind of role or task for us. Why would we be gathered here together like this, by you or the universe or whatever, just to improve our gifts? What's the use of these powers if there's no *quaesitus*?" We looked at her blankly and she realized what she'd said. "It's Latin for quest."

Gabe and Cassie laughed at her, but Patience looked hopeful. "Maybe we have some good to do in the world? A duty we must fulfil?"

"Yes!" Mona was nodding eagerly. "Like a rescue effort in a plane crash!"

Ed looked alarmed—probably because it would be the healer who would really have his work cut out in a plane-crash scenario, whereas Mona would only need to translate for injured tourists. What would I do? Corral the perished souls?

Drew shifted in his chair. "Maybe it's our duty to keep ourselves under control and make sure we don't accidentally hurt someone with these *gifts*."

He didn't sound as sarcastic as usual, and glanced at me after he spoke. The glance expanded into a long, hard look at my face. He pored over it with those demonic pools as if looking for something he'd missed. It simultaneously infuriated me and sent my breathing out of whack. Gabe was swiveling his head between us like he was watching a tennis match.

"That's a good point, Drew," Ms. Deering said unexpectedly. "The potential is there for us to get carried away and do some unintentional damage. We must tread with caution."

The bell rang.

"It's good that we're asking these questions," Ms. Deering said as we packed up our gear. "I'd like to continue this discussion next time."

We dispersed, and I snuck a look at Drew as he wandered off with Patience. The chat in the woods had taken place only three days earlier, but it already seemed like weeks ago. He'd been infuriating. Single-minded and immovable. Even in gifted class, he was still full of gloom and throwing out warnings. So why did I kind of want talk to him again? Did I honestly think I could change his mind?

Maybe I could sit with him in English and have a conversation. But when I arrived at our English class after science, he'd joined a table full of other people. I went to sit with Axel and a girl called Olivia.

Axel brightened when I joined them. "Mimi! How's it all going?"

"Good. You?"

"Great. There are some nice kids at EVA."

"I heard you got into the gifted program," Olivia said from his other side. "Congratulations."

A sideward look told me they were both watching me. "Thanks."

"What's it all about?" Olivia wanted to know.

"Yes," Axel said. "I'm curious, too, I must admit. You're already doing extension work for art, so what does *gifted* actually mean—in the context of a gifted program? Are you all high-IQ geniuses?"

Uh-oh. Mona had warned me about this, but I was unsure what our official line was on the gifted program. I should have asked Ms. Deering.

I gave a semblance of an explanation. "I think they consider us to have, um, potential for, uh, leadership? The teacher does collaborative project work with us." There. Not the worst lie I could've come up with.

"Cross-disciplinary stuff?" Olivia asked.

I wasn't even sure what that meant. I nodded anyway. "Yeah. And, um, personal development. Leadership skills."

"I wish I was in it." Axel gave a small sigh.

"Me too," Olivia said.

"I'd love to do that sort of extension work," Axel continued. "I'd really benefit from the teamwork skills after being homeschooled forever. Plus, I *like* everyone in the gifted program. I feel like I'd fit in."

"Hmm." It was all I had.

Olivia was watching me expectantly. "How did you get in, Mimi?"

"Was there an aptitude test?" Axel asked.

I couldn't hold in a snort of laughter and tried to turn it into a cough when they both looked startled.

"Careful, miss," Albert warned, close to my ear.

"Mimi?" Olivia prompted. "Was there a test?"

"Ms. Deering invited me in," I said. "You should talk to her if you think you belong in the program."

Axel nodded. "Oh, okay. Yeah, okay, I will."

I felt bad for him and Olivia, but I doubted either of them would want anything to do with the gifted program if they knew what it really took to get in.

7

Mixed Messages and Other Half-Truths

I had a mountain of science homework. After school, I headed straight for my room to get started, but Mona caught up to me in the dorm corridor.

"Samvedi's looking for you."

"Oh! Thanks."

Hoping Mom was on the phone, wanting to speak to me, I went back up the corridor against the student traffic to Ms. Samvedi's office. She was on her computer, but when she saw me, she waved at a seat beside her desk and swiveled on her chair to face me.

"Mimi, I've had it reported to me that you skipped a class on Friday."

Heat crawled up my neck and my stomach suddenly hurt. Black patches of nothing swirled in the air behind Ms. Samvedi. I didn't speak.

"Mimi, that's not how we do things at EVA. If you're going to skip classes or refuse school, you'll need to leave."

I found my voice. "No! I'm sorry. I don't want to leave. I won't do it again."

She considered me, her head tipped slightly to one side. "Why did you do it?"

"I—I don't like PE."

"And where did you go?"

"Um, I hid in the girls' bathroom. Did Mr. Randall notice I was missing?"

"Someone noticed you were missing and let me know. They were merely worried about you."

"Oh." I racked my brains to work out who would have done that. If it wasn't Randall, it must have been someone in my PE class. But I barely knew the other kids in my PE class. They had us in a mixed group, all ages. Olivia was the one girl from my grade who shared my PE timetable, and she didn't seem like the type to rat me out. The only other person who knew I'd skipped was Drew—and that was because he'd been skipping too.

"I need to give you an official warning, Mimi."

My panic accelerated, making the shades loom and slither. "Please, please don't, Ms. Samvedi! My parents will be so disappointed, and they've been through so much—it was a bad decision, but I know that now and I promise on my *life* I won't do it again. Please just make it a verbal warning this time. I'll—I'll clean toilets as punishment. Anything!"

Her eyes twinkled a little. "We've got paid staff for that, but thanks for the offer." She pushed some pieces of paper around her desk, then looked back at me. "All right, I'm going to take your word for it that this was a one-time slip-up. But if it happens again, Mimi, it will mean an official warning *and* I'll be speaking to your parents."

"Thank you," I said breathlessly. "Thanks, Ms. Samvedi!"

She nodded at me to leave her office. All the way back to my room, I sent up fervent thanks to the god of penitent truants. I should never have let Drew convince me to skip.

What was wrong with me? I needed to stop thinking about him—stop being fascinated by him—or I'd end up in trouble. In trouble or badly hurt.

I sat down and ate one of Mom's cookies to reset my system. The shadows receded and dissipated, and a crow hopped along the grass outside my window. I opened my laptop to start my science homework and discovered a little blue icon blinking in the bottom corner: C8.

What now? Was this malware or something? The technician had added the school portal on my first day—but I'd only really looked at the email inbox. I clicked the C8 icon, hoping I wouldn't regret it. A window popped up.

Welcome to Collabor8, Etherall Valley Academy's proprietary chat program. If you can't find your group project in the menu, ask your teacher to set it up. Please observe the EVA anti-bullying guidelines while using this program and note a profanity filter is in place.

Mona Thomas has opened a Collabor8 under GIFTED PROGRAM PROJECT.

I clicked *Accept.*

Mona: *Hi, Mimi. What did Samvedi want?*
Miette: *Hi. What is this project?*
Mona: *It's not a real project. Ms. D set it up for us so we can chat outside school hours. C8 is supposed to be used for group projects, but she figured we might need to communicate sometimes.*
Miette: *So everyone in the gifted group is in this chat?*

Mona: *No, I've opened a private chat. It's just you and me.*
Miette: *Can the teachers read our messages?*
Mona: *It's an end-to-end encrypted system, so outside perverts can't hack in to talk to kids. But the teacher in charge of each specific channel can access our chats—that's Ms. D for the gifted program—and she told us she won't invade our privacy. So what did Samvedi want?*
Miette: *To bust me for skipping a class last week.*
Mona: *Mimi! Bad girl! When and why?*
Miette: *To tell you the truth, I went to the woods over the road with Drew. He agreed to reveal his gift to me.*
Mona: *I'm assuming that's not a euphemism.*
Miette: *Mona!*
Mona: *Skipping was a bad idea. They won't let you have day passes on the weekends if you don't have good standing.*
Miette: *It's like you're speaking English but I can't understand.*
Mona: *Didn't anyone explain it all to you when you started?*
Miette: *Possibly, but I was so anxious I may have forgotten to listen.*
Mona: *If you don't get any official warnings, then you keep your "good standing." But if you lose good standing, you can't go on outings or to social events, or even apply for a day pass until the following term. A day pass allows you to get out of the dorm on the weekend so you can live some semblance of a normal life and come to sleepovers at my place.*
Miette: *Ah. Well, I got lucky. Samvedi decided not to give me an official warning this time.*
Mona: *How did you get caught? Did Drew get a warning too?*

Miette: *Someone noticed I wasn't in PE and reported me. I can't work out who it was. Do you think Olivia would do something like that?*

Mona: *She's not a snitch. Did Mel Borgen see you? That's just the sort of stunt she'd pull.*

Miette: *Don't think she's in my PE class. Only Drew knew about it, I thought. Oh, wait—Patience was waiting for Drew when we came back in.*

Mona: *She wouldn't have done it. I mean, she's a good girl, but she wouldn't deliberately get you into trouble.*

Miette: *Even if she was "worried" about me?*

Mona: *I don't think so. Probably not.*

Miette: *Could she be jealous, maybe? She might have a thing for him.*

Mona: *For Drew? Ha ha! Not a chance.*

Miette: *It wouldn't be that far-fetched.*

Mona: *He's not her type. He's not anyone's type.*

Miette: *You don't think he's attractive? I mean, objectively speaking.*

Mona: *I can see he's pretty. But he's such an asshole, the pretty's all worn away for me. He's got a Backpfeifengesicht.*

Miette: *A what?*

Mona: *It's German. It means a face that should be slapped. I tell you what, let's ask Patience if she knows anything once study hour is done.*

Miette: *No, it's fine. Anyway, I've learned my lesson. I won't be doing it again.*

Mona: *I should think not. The woods is where EVA kids sneak off to, well, get a little privacy, if you know what I mean.*

Miette: *We were just talking!*

Mona: *He stares at you constantly.*
Miette: *He does not. He avoids looking at me.*
Mona: *No, Mimi. He avoids looking at everyone. He TRIES to avoid looking at you but fails. We all see it. Poetry Boy's got a little obsession with the new girl. Gabe's mentioned it a few times and Cassie denies it vehemently, which means it's definitely true and she's pissed off he's not staring at her.*
Miette: *So Cassie likes Drew?*
Mona: *Hah! No, she's got her sights set on Tyler Van Wyk. But she thinks all boys should be slaves to her beauty.*

This conversation had my mind whirling. None of the straight girls were into Drew? I mean, didn't they have *eyes*?

A tone sounded out in the corridor.

Mona: *There's the end of study hour. Meet me in Patience's room.*
Miette: *No, Mona! I said I don't want you to ask her*

Mona Thomas has ended the session.

Crap! I dashed for the corridor and caught sight of Mona disappearing into Patience's bedroom. I wove around the girls spilling into the hallway and knocked on Patience's door.

"Come in," came her soft call.

I stepped inside and shut the door. Her room was so neat it made me feel like a messy object myself, and I didn't know where to sit without disturbing the perfection. Mona had parked herself on the floor, so I sank down beside her and tried to tell her with my eyes not to ask about my class-skipping snitch.

Mona nodded acknowledgement at me, then did exactly as she pleased. "Okay, Patience, we have a question. Mimi got sprung skipping class with Drew on Friday and you're the only other person who knew. Did you report her?"

"Mona, no!" I turned to Patience apologetically. "I don't think it was you."

She'd gone bright pink—right to the tips of her ears.

"Did you?" Mona persisted.

I opened my mouth to apologize again, but Patience got in first. "Yes. I'm sorry, Mimi."

My mouth remained open.

"That was a crappy thing to do, Patience." Mona sounded almost as surprised as I was. "She nearly got an official warning. Why would you do that?"

"I didn't want her to get caught breaking the rules." Patience's eyes were cast down now, and she was standing in front of us with her hands clasped together like an ashamed little girl.

Mona did her most suspicious squint. "Did you report Drew as well?"

"No."

"That's not very fair, is it?"

Patience formed the word *no* with her mouth but didn't make any sound.

Mona's squint was relentless. "Look me in the eyes, Patience." Pale blue eyes lifted unwillingly. "Tell me the truth. Why did you report Mimi?"

For a moment I thought she'd say nothing, then she sighed a long, wobbly sigh. "Because Drew asked me to."

Miette Alston has opened a Collabor8 under GIFTED PROGRAM PROJECT.
Drew Ellery has accepted.

Miette: *Would you like to explain why you got Patience to report me for skipping school after YOU talked me into doing it? Was that some kind of ridiculous prank?*
Drew: *What?*
Miette: *Don't play dumb. She told us.*
Drew: *I honestly have no idea what you're talking about.*
Miette: *So you're saying she's lying?*
Drew: *No. Patience doesn't lie. Oh, wait.*
Miette: *Wait?*
Drew: *Oh, hell. I think she might have gotten mixed messages from me.*
Miette: *She wouldn't be the only one.*
Drew: *What does that mean?*
Miette: *What mixed message did Patience get?*
Drew: *It's private.*
Miette: *Well, your private mixed message almost got me an official warning.*
Drew: *Sh*t.*
Miette: *I deserve an explanation.*
Drew: *Yeah.*
Miette: *Go ahead.*
Miette: *Hello?*
Drew: *I don't know how to explain it.*

Miette: *Try.*

Drew: *Okay! I asked Patience to stop me doing things like that.*

Miette: *Like what?*

Drew: *Like skipping class with you.*

Miette: *So this is her solution? To get ME caught?*

Drew: *She must have thought you'd get a verbal warning and maybe it would put you off doing it again.*

Miette: *What's that got to do with YOU not doing it again?*

Miette: *Hello?*

Drew: *I'm trying to put it into words. Give me a minute.*

Miette: *I've given you a minute.*

Drew: *There's no easy way to say this. I've asked Patience to help me not to associate with you.*

Miette: *Huh? Why?*

Drew: *I'm not a good friend.*

Miette: *Why me, specifically? You can be friends with everyone else in the gifted group but not me?*

Drew: *They're not friends. They're acquaintances.*

Miette: *Except Patience.*

Drew: *Yeah, I guess she's a friend.*

Miette: *Did you ask her to help you not to associate with ALL of us?*

Miette: *Drew??*

Drew: *No. Just you.*

Miette: *Nice.*

Drew: *Sorry.*

Miette: *What did I do to deserve this?*

Drew: *Nothing.*

Miette: *Then why don't you want to associate with me?*

Drew: *I just don't.*

Miette: *Unbelievable.*
Drew: *Sorry.*
Miette: *No, you're not. Anyway, whatever. I'm not going to ask again. I couldn't care less if you don't want to associate with me.*
Drew: *It's got nothing to do with what I want.*
Miette: *What?*

Session end. Thank you for using Collabor8! Chat hours are 3pm to 6pm.

The dinner bell was ringing. I swore at my screen and tried to reopen the chat window but it was gone. The app was locked for the day.

During dinner, I told Mona what had gone down in the chat with Drew—all except the last thing he'd said. I was almost sure I'd misread that. Anyway, I certainly didn't want Mona speculating on what it meant, even if I obsessed over it in private.

"Told you he was an asshole," she said, and this time I had to agree.

He turned up each day of that week in his body armor, wearing leather and spikes so outlandish, younger kids veered around him in the schoolyard. Only Patience trotted along at his side in her pink t-shirt and awful jeans, blonde braids swinging. They were like a grotesque street performance duo. He didn't speak to me. He didn't even look at me anymore.

Like I'd told him, I couldn't care less. I tried to focus on people who knew how to interact like ordinary humans: Mona, Gabe and Ed. They looked out for me, saved me a seat, made me laugh. They even laughed at my jokes. And Olivia, another senior weekend boarder. The only problem was, she often asked me questions about the gifted program. She wanted to know what projects we were working on, what syllabus we were following. She openly wished Ms. Deering would invite her to join.

"It ramps up whenever a new kid joins," Mona told me privately. "Everyone wants to be special. Ms. Deering should have called it the Good Deeds Club or something. That would've put other aspirationals off."

Mona wanted me to visit her place for a sleepover, which sounded fun, but she hadn't been able to work out a date yet. Her dad took her to her grandparents' farm almost every weekend. I was starting to go a little stir-crazy staying in school all week and contemplated applying for one of the day passes she'd told me about. Maybe Olivia would come out with me. I asked Mona how to get a day pass in science on Friday, and Gabe overheard.

"You want to get out of school, Mimi?" he asked. "I know Etherall Valley pretty well. We could get day passes and do something. I've got hockey practice on Sunday, but I'm free tomorrow."

I had to admit it would be preferable to hang out with the gifted kids. "Okay. Let's invite the group."

"I can't come," Mona said. "But Cassie, Ed and Patience are all weekend boarders."

"Should we ask them?" I said to Gabe.

He hesitated. "Yeah. Yeah, okay, I'll speak to them and I'll message you later."

I waved them goodbye at the end of the period, feeling lighter at the prospect of getting out on the weekend. Maybe a movie. Or we could go swimming, if there was a pool somewhere in Etherall Valley. It would be good to get into the water again.

Then Drew was standing right in front of me, forcing me to a stop. "Can we talk?"

I was speechless.

"Can you skip class?"

I blinked at him. "You're kidding, right?"

"Patience won't report you, I promise. That was a misunderstanding."

"No. I'm not doing that again. The school will call my parents, and they've been through enough without me messing this up too."

"When, then?" Urgency had crept into his voice, making me pause and reconsider.

"Monday," I offered. "In homeroom, or at lunch."

He shook his head. "That's too long. Could I chat with you through Collabor8 this afternoon, after school?"

"I thought you went home on the weekends?"

"I'll use a computer in the library before I leave." He must have seen the suspicion in my face, because he slumped a little and stepped away. "Don't worry about it."

"You can open a chat with me," I told him stiffly. "I'll be around after school."

I headed for my next class.

8

The Donkey in the Room

Not going to lie, the rest of the day dragged. I was burning to know what Drew needed to talk to me about. I kept coming back to Mona's words: *Poetry Boy has a little obsession with the new girl.* And Drew's final message from the day before.

Then again, he and Patience had deliberately gotten me in trouble. I speculated more and more wildly, chewing my lip red raw and only listening to my teachers with half an ear. By the time the final bell rang, I was alternately imagining Drew inviting me out on a date and threatening to take out a restraining order against me.

During study hour, I paced my bedroom, glancing anxiously at my laptop every few seconds. Within minutes, I got a ping.

Drew Ellery has opened a Collabor8 under GIFTED PROGRAM PROJECT.
Accept?

Drew: *I apologize for nearly getting you an official warning.*
Miette: *Okay...*
Drew: *It was unintentional.*

Miette: *All right. Just please don't do it again. And I'd appreciate it if you could unmix your messages to Patience so SHE doesn't do it again, either.*
Drew: *Already done.*
Miette: *Good. Apology accepted.*

I waited. There was a long silence in which neither of us seemed to have anything else to say. I folded first.

Miette: *Is there something else?*
Drew: *Yes. Look, about my visions. Maybe I'm not exactly making these things happen, but there's never a happy ending, and it gets depressing after a while.*
Miette: *I understand. But could you try to, I don't know, be patient? Maybe your gift is still developing, like Ed's. He could only heal birds and animals at first, but last weekend he healed a human. And my gift—it seems pointless, too. Why have ghosts around? But they tell me things sometimes, and I'm starting to get a feeling that's significant. Like the way they told me to join the gifted, and then I found out I was one of the seven.*
Drew: *I've seen too much pointless tragedy.*
Miette: *But could you try to simply BE with it? Accept it? Stop fighting and see where it takes you.*
Drew: *When I was seven, I had a friend called Chelsea who lived next door. I had a vision of a broken rope. Three days later, she went on a rope swing at a park. The rope was weathered and it snapped while she was swinging. She fell and broke her spine, ended up paralyzed.*
Miette: *Hell, I'm sorry.*

Drew: *Don't be sorry. Just understand why I can't accept this "gift." I don't want it. I'd do anything to get rid of it.*

Ping.

Gabriel Cavendish has opened a Collabor8 under GIFTED PROGRAM PROJECT.
Accept?

I hesitated over the *Accept* button. No, Gabe would have to wait. I couldn't do another conversation while this one was going on. I closed down the blinking window.

Miette: *I get that you're in pain, that it feels like unwelcome knowledge you're getting, but there's another way to look at it.*
Drew: *And what's that?*
Miette: *As an opportunity.*
Drew: *An opportunity to foresee death and misery. Lucky me.*
Miette: *An opportunity to find out more about these people or the circumstances of their tragedies.*
Drew: *Don't you get it? Fate. It's real. These people—their numbers are up. They don't get second chances.*
Miette: *I don't believe in fate.*
Drew: *I'm a prophet. I don't have a choice.*
Miette: *Why did you start this conversation if you're just going to try to make me think like you? I never will, Drew. If someone tried to tell me my fate was to, say, flunk out of college and become a chauffeur for reality TV stars, then I would defy anything that pulled me that way. I'd fight. I'd*

study every spare minute until I got my degree. I'd never learn to drive. I'd get around in a hot air balloon or on a donkey.

There was a long moment of stillness. Even the animated ellipses that showed when someone was typing a reply were motionless.

Miette: *Are you still there?*
Drew: *Picturing you on a donkey. For some reason, you're wearing a sombrero.*

I giggled, shocked. Drew had a sense of humor? Then Collabor8 pinged again and another request popped up from Gabe. I sighed and accepted the session this time. I'd make it a quick chat so I could get back to the conversation with Drew, which seemed to be on an unexpectedly upward trajectory.

Gabriel: *Miette Alston.*
Miette: *Yes, Gabriel Cavendish?*
Gabriel: *So I thought we could go to the old granary market tomorrow. I checked with the others to see if they wanted to come. Cassie's got dance rehearsals, Ed's surfing all weekend and Patience already has plans with Drew.*

Wait. Drew was going out with Patience on the weekend? So in one moment, he's picturing me riding a donkey in a sombrero, and the next, he's flitting around town with his *Handmaid's Tale* girlfriend? Something bleak and angry hit me like a concrete tsunami, and I went back to the chat with Drew without pausing to think about how weird I was being.

Miette: *Got to go. Making plans for the weekend.*
Drew: *What are you doing?*
Miette: *Not sure. Gabe's taking me out somewhere.*

I waited. The chat window sat open and motionless, while the one with Gabe pinged in the background.

Miette: *Well, bye.*
Drew: *Are you going swimming?*
Miette: *Um, I don't think so...*
Drew: *Let me know if you are. I'll see you next week.*

Drew Ellery has left the session.

I took an exasperated breath and went back to the chat with Gabe.

Gabriel: *They have some good stalls at that market, and food trucks.*
Gabriel: *Do you like pizza?*
Gabriel: *I'll buy you lunch.*
Gabriel: *Hello?*
Miette: *I can buy my own lunch.*
Gabriel: *I want to buy you lunch! You'll need to apply for your day pass tonight, though. They don't give out same-day passes.*
Miette: *I haven't applied for a pass before.*

Gabriel: *It's easy. Just go to the school portal and click on Dorm Support. Day Pass is in the menu. Five hours is the maximum they'll give you on a day pass, so I was thinking, 10 till 3?*
Miette: *That's a long time just to go to a market!*
Gabriel: *No, that will give us plenty of time to catch a bus there, chill, have lunch, and start looking for a bus home at about 2pm.*
Miette: *Oh, okay. I'll go apply now.*
Gabriel: *Yay! Can't wait. I'll be at your dorm door at ten.*

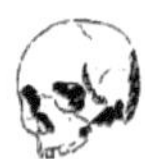

Gabe was outside the glass door of the dorm at ten sharp, his sunny face full of smiles. He waved at me energetically while every weekend boarder in the girls' dorm commenced whispering about us and I died a thousand deaths inside. Ms. Samvedi had given me my phone for the outing—it was considered a security measure.

"Have fun, Mimi!" Olivia called, just in case anyone hadn't been alerted to my outing with Gabe. I should have invited her to come with us, since all the other gifted kids had bailed on me and Gabe. I'd remember to ask her next time.

Patience's day pass was also for ten o'clock, so she stepped outside with me.

"Catching the bus?" Gabe asked her.

"Yes."

"Same," he said. "Sit with us."

Two crows cawed at us as we crossed the lawn. Gabe clapped at them, which caused them to flap away. He told us a story about a food fight that had erupted in the boys' dining room the night before and I laughed, but Patience listened in silence. She'd been quiet around me since she'd ratted me out to Ms. Samvedi. She didn't seem malicious, but I couldn't quite forgive her. She hadn't even apologized to me—Drew had done that for her. Then again, perhaps there really had been some misunderstanding—some instruction from him that she'd screwed up. I couldn't respect her, knowing she was taking her orders from Drew, but she probably wasn't intentionally evil.

Once we were on the bus, my ghosts chilling the back of my neck in the seat behind, I caught her eye. "What are you and Drew getting up to today?" I asked as nonchalantly as possible.

"I think we're going to the market," she said.

"Snap," Gabe said, but he didn't look thrilled about it. "Maybe we'll bump into you guys there."

I took advantage of having access to my phone to exchange some messages with my parents and brother, catching them up on how school was going. Mom wanted to call me, but I didn't want to have a conversation on the bus. I said I'd call her later. Gabe was doing the same thing—messaging with family and friends, scrolling his feeds. Patience obviously didn't have a phone—probably something to do with her upbringing at Dale's Run. Poor girl. How did she function? She sat there in silence, gazing out the window.

Knowing Drew was waiting for Patience at the other end of the bus trip did nothing to prepare me for the actual sight of him. I didn't recognize him at first. Then it hit me that the shaggy-headed young man leaning against a brick wall in a plain gray t-shirt, jeans and Converse was Drew.

"Drew's gone goth-lite today," Gabe observed. "I haven't seen him look like that for over a year."

Drew glanced up as the bus pulled in. Just a light layer of white makeup and a vague effort at eyeliner. Rings in the eyebrows instead of barbells. His black hair hung in a clean, product-free tangle. No black lipstick. No contacts.

Oh, my holy mother of God. He was gorgeous.

I twitched my clothes so they sat right. I'd tried the black skirt with a yellow knit top and my black Converse, and now I looked at myself, all I could see was "punk librarian." *I have no idea what I am doing and shouldn't be allowed out in public unsupervised.*

We spilled out of the bus and stopped in front of Drew. He was plainly shocked to see us and stood staring. We both stood staring.

Green eyes, as green as the ocean on a cloudy day.

"They happened to be on the bus, too," Patience told him apologetically, but he didn't take his eyes from my face. I was hot and tingling all over my body, but I couldn't look away either.

Gabe cleared his throat. "Shall we head to the market, Mimi?"

"Do you guys want to hang with us?" I blurted, barely aware of what I was saying.

"No, thank you," Patience said at the same time as Drew said, "Yeah, sure."

Drew turned to Patience. They had one of their silent conversations, then Drew's eyes strayed back to me.

"Maybe just for a while?" he said to her.

She gave an extremely reluctant shrug, and I must have smiled, because suddenly Drew was smiling back at me. It took all the oxygen from my lungs. Patience started walking in a resigned manner and Gabe, frowning, fell into step with her, leaving me and Drew to follow along behind.

9

The Healing Power of a Good Gozleme

Drew and I walked along the street behind Gabe and Patience. It was as if my brain had been emptied of all knowledge of social interaction.

"You look…"

Drew waited.

"Very different," I managed.

"I couldn't be bothered today."

"I suppose it's quite a commitment every morning, maintaining your style." That sounded critical. Or sarcastic. I hadn't meant it that way. Why couldn't I converse normally? I checked his face, and he was wearing a wry half-smile.

"You're not wrong."

"You're more like Axel-level goth today."

He glanced at me. "The new kid? I noticed he's changing his look. What's that about?"

"Not sure. Maybe he wants to be your friend. Mona thinks he's interested in Patience."

Drew's expression shifted a little and he glanced at Patience, who was replying to something Gabe had said. "Patience has very specific standards."

"Like?"

"Devout. Old-fashioned."

We arrived at the market, and the buzz of the place was a welcome relief. We could lose ourselves here without having to worry about getting our words right.

"Have you seen the book exchange?" Drew asked us. "They have the most amazing books. I found a 1910 edition of Dickens last month." His enthusiasm was wildly out of character and adorable. It was as if he hadn't had a chance to put on his psychological mask, let alone the physical one.

While I was in the book exchange, my ghosts wandered at a short distance, as if they were giving me my space. I appreciated it. I stood beside Drew to look at the books, just inches from touching. Drew exclaimed when I spotted an early edition of *One Flew over the Cuckoo's Nest.* He bought it, his excitement intoxicating. Pity I hadn't been there to see his face when he found that old Dickens book.

Patience cast us occasional worried glances but didn't interfere. She went to look at the memoir section. Gabe flicked through old DVDs for a while, then complained about being bored and asked me to go look at other stalls. If he thought Drew would stay behind in the bookshop, he was wrong. Drew and Patience both came with us.

We wandered the rows, the air heavy with a rough-knit blend of soap, roasted coffee beans and donuts. We perused anime stickers, handmade candles, vintage clothing, succulents in pots and artisan chocolate. I noticed some little gemstone skulls and bought a green agate one for my shelf.

"You like occult stuff?" Drew asked.

"I like anatomical art," I said without thinking. "Bones, organs, that sort of thing." *Oh, shit.* Why did I tell him that about myself?

But Drew only nodded, the ghost of a smile on his lips. Gabe wanted to watch a juggling performance, then he asked if I was hungry. I wasn't really, not with this turmoil inside me, but knew I should probably eat. Patience tried to talk Drew into going to a café across the road for lunch, but he wanted to come with me and Gabe to the food trucks parked behind the old granary that housed the market.

"I don't know what to have," I said after I'd been around all the trucks. "Japanese, Indian or pizza?"

"I'm having pizza," Gabe announced. "Should I get you some, Mimi?"

I chewed my lip indecisively.

"Have you tried gozleme?" Drew asked me. He nodded at a Turkish food truck. "They do a really good one."

"I've never had it. What is it?"

He took me over and showed me the fried, filled flatbreads. It looked good, so I ordered one stuffed with fetta. He got the chicken one. Gabe got pizza and Patience chose a sandwich, and we all sat down at the table to eat. I squeezed some lemon over my gozleme, and—*oh my God*—it was amazing. Crispy, pastry-like bread, salty cheese, all hot and melted, and the tang of lemon juice. On the first bite, I opened my eyes wide and Drew chuckled, nodding his agreement. His laugh was quick and low, and I treasured the sound. I wanted to take it home with me.

I stuffed my face because it was simply too delicious, and suddenly I was starving. Drew stuffed his face too. We stuffed together. The others may have stuffed their faces as well, but I didn't notice.

"Should we go for a walk at the park now, Drew?" Patience asked when we'd finished lunch.

"Do you want to try the arcade, Mimi?" Gabe asked me, but there was a kind of hopelessness to it that was totally warranted, because Drew and I locked eyes again.

"We could go to the arcade," Drew said.

"I'm happy to walk at the park," I said.

Seriously, we could have been trawling through a garbage dump. I didn't care. If I could just keep looking at those green eyes, I'd be happy.

We went to the park. It was shaded with trees turning golden, leaves just starting to fall, despite the lingering summer heat. Gabe found a forgotten soccer ball and challenged us to a two-on-two soccer game. I explained that I was terminally uncoordinated and Drew said he'd referee, so Gabe played Patience. She seemed to like games, and I was quietly relieved to see the two of them enjoying themselves. Drew and I sat on the edge of a stone fountain to watch.

"Can I ask you something?" I said.

"If I can ask you something."

"Okay." I turned his way slightly. "Why do you dress like you do? You don't seem to be into the scene at all—the music or the culture. Just the look."

Drew's eyes stayed on the game. "It makes people uncomfortable."

"You want to make people uncomfortable?"

"It keeps them away."

"You don't like people?"

"I don't want to like people."

He looked like he didn't enjoy talking about this, but I couldn't stop picking at the edges of Drew to find out what was underneath. "Are you worried people might guess about your gift?"

At first he didn't reply. He examined a leaf he'd found on the edge of the fountain and, after a long silence, finally spoke. "I'm worried they might fall victim to my curse."

"It's not a curse."

Drew sighed. "I don't know if things happen to these people because they're around me, or if I just get hints about their shitty destinies beforehand. Either way, I don't think it's a particularly good idea to get close to anyone."

I was tempted to ask, *What about Patience?* "I think that's sad," I said instead. "You're too scared to let anyone get close to you in case you lose them? What kind of a life is that for you? You're going to hide behind makeup and contacts and spikes forever, just to protect yourself from getting hurt?" The irony that *I* was giving someone else this advice was not lost on me, but he didn't need to know that.

"It's not that I'm scared of getting hurt. I'm scared of *them* getting hurt."

"Maybe you've been left scarred by what happened to your friend Chelsea. You might be frightened that you'll see something related to someone you care about in one of your visions, and that would be terrible." I let my fingers trail in the clean water of the fountain. "So you've found a way to stop yourself from caring about anyone, because then you don't have to deal with the pain."

He opened his mouth like he was going to argue, then closed it again.

"Sorry," I said. "I don't have the right to say things like that."

"Someone's got to cut through my bullshit, I guess." He gave me a lopsided smile that made my heart hammer.

"Goal!" Gabe lifted his arms in appeal to us. Drew gave the thumbs-up and I applauded dutifully, although neither of us had seen it.

"You could have come as yourself today," I said when the game resumed. "Just Drew, no mask. I mean, the others have all seen what you really look like, but I haven't. I've only ever seen you in your armor."

His brow furrowed. "You want to see what I look like?"

I nodded, trying not to look too eager.

For a few moments, it was as if Gabe and Patience and everyone else at the park—the geese wandering around and the dog barking across the lawn—all faded into background noise. Then Drew shrugged, turned around and crouched over the fountain edge. He scooped water in his hands, splashing it over his face. He did that a few times, rubbing at his skin, and the makeup came off, white and black blending into gray, dripping into the water and dispersing in tiny swirls.

Eventually he shook his head like a dog would, swung around and sat back down beside me on the stone edge. There he was. Drew Ellery, no mask. Sitting beside me with a gray t-shirt and jeans; hair flopping damply over his forehead; green eyes regarding me apprehensively while his skin glistened and dripped. For the first time, I could discern the natural fall of shade and light on his cheekbones and jawline, the water running down the hard lines of his neck, into the opening of his shirt. Presumably down his chest.

"You look much better." I tried to say it in a neutral manner but choked halfway through.

Time to look away, Mimi. He's going to notice you're staring. Turn away now. He'll think you're a maniac. MIMI, LOOK AWAY NOW!

"Just normal and boring underneath," he said.

That wasn't what I was thinking. I wasn't thinking anything, really, except *kiss me, kiss me, kiss me.* My God, was there something wrong with me? I didn't care that I'd never kissed anyone and wouldn't know what I was doing. I didn't even care that Gabe and Patience were right there. *Kiss me, kiss me, kissmekissmekissme—*

"I suppose this must be like meeting me for the first time." He grimaced self-consciously. "Hi, I'm Drew." He stuck out his hand for me to shake.

"Nice to meet you." I shook his hand, and my body zinged to life at his touch. This was awful. But wonderful.

Instead of letting go, he turned my hand over, holding it so he could see the half-missing finger. "So here's my question."

My stomach tightened. "Let me guess."

He released my hand. "You don't have to tell me."

For some reason I didn't mind telling him. "It was my first ghost. He held on too long."

It took him a moment, then Drew caught up. "What—so it caused damage to your hand?"

"Frostbite. Ghosts are cold."

"They can touch you? I always thought people could pass right through ghosts. Well, to be honest, I didn't think that because I didn't even believe in ghosts until a couple of weeks ago."

I straightened. "What happened a couple of weeks ago?"

"You turned up."

"Oh!" I flushed and laughed sheepishly. "Yes, most people pass through them. Not me."

"What happens when you try?"

In answer, I held up my left hand, all fingers folded except the middle stump.

"Are you flipping me the bird, Mimi?"

"No. I'm flipping you the *ird*. It's like the bird but the top part's missing." This was my dad's bad joke, and Drew broke into laughter. I thanked Dad silently for his service.

Then he stopped laughing and studied my face. My pulse hitched right along with my breathing.

"Drew, it's two o'clock." It was Patience, standing near us with Gabe at her side, both of them puffing and sweating. "We'd better get to the bus stop so we can be back at school in time."

We walked to the stop and, when the bus arrived, said goodbye to Drew. He was already walking away by the time our bus pulled out from the stop.

"Well, that was weird." Gabe watched him out the window. "Drew was like a different person today. Maybe he's only annoying at school and on the weekend he's a normal guy. Like a reverse superhero. Other than him monopolizing your attention, I could get used to this Drew."

I could *definitely* get used to this Drew.

"He's a good person." Patience's cheeks had gone pink again, and she sounded faintly annoyed. "He cares a lot."

Gabe chuckled. "I know he does. His emotions are loud as hell. I'm just not sure what he cares about."

She frowned. "He wants to protect people."

"From what?" I asked.

She looked away, staring out of the window. "From himself."

10
What It's like Going in Reverse

You know how it feels when you finally break through into a new level of connection with someone and you just know everything has changed? It's like a wall has crumbled. You understand why they've been acting a certain way. You've clicked, and you just know things are going to be different—forever.

That was how I knew it would be with Drew after our day together at the market.

Except it wasn't.

He turned up to homeroom in full goth gear again, complete with white contacts and a new piercing: an iron spike through his beautiful lip. He didn't even spare me a glance. He sat as far away as possible, his back to the room, and scribbled in his leather-bound book. Gabe looked my way and raised an eyebrow. I felt sick.

The mood was heavy in gifted class, too. Aside from the fact that we had Edward Scissorhands sitting in the corner, probably composing a eulogy for my hopes and dreams, Ms. Deering had some news.

"You're probably wondering where Cassie is. One of her close relations is in hospital and it's serious."

"Is it the aunt?" Mona jumped straight to conclusions. "The one with the little dog?" She glanced at Drew.

He remained motionless in the corner, his white-lensed gaze tethered to his open page. He already knew.

"Yes," Ms. Deering said. "It's that aunt. She took a fall and was injured. Cassie's keeping vigil at the hospital with her mother."

"Wow, Drew's visions are getting really accurate." Mona sounded impressed.

Drew's jaw tightened.

"But it could just be a coincidence," I blurted. "It's not like he saw her fall downstairs or whatever. All he saw was the dog they adopted."

"Do you have any details, Ms. D?" Mona asked.

Ms. Deering cleared her throat. "Cassie's aunt tripped over their new puppy and hit her head on the bottom step."

"Holy shit," Ed breathed. "Okay, no coincidence there. But she's alive?"

Ms. Deering flicked a glance at Drew. "Yes."

"In a stable condition?"

Ms. Deering hesitated this time.

Drew spoke into the silence. "She's in a coma. She might die."

My heart felt like a cold stone lodged in my ribcage. Gabe, seated beside me, had his gaze locked on Drew. Was he was doing his empathy thing? Reading Drew?

"She's in an induced coma while they try to get her brain swelling down," Ms. Deering clarified. "Yes, Drew's vision was accurate. It's an unfortunate accident. Cassie and her aunt are close, and I imagine the whole family's suffering. All we can do is hope she recovers."

Mona had been making notes, but now she looked up. "If we can connect Drew's visions with a specific individual again in future, then maybe we have the chance to do something about it. We should have taken it more seriously—we knew Cassie's aunt might be in danger when Drew told us about the vision and Cassie connected it with the diamante collar on the Chihuahua."

Ms. Deering was shaking her head. "How could any of us possibly have known what was going to happen? It was such a random accident. There must be thousands of possible accidents we could try to predict from that vision, from a bee sting while walking the dog, to a child choking on one of the diamantes."

Exactly! I wanted to shout. But Ms. Deering's words were Drew's breaking point. He stood up so fast, his chair crashed to the floor behind him. He was gone in moments, the cottage door left hanging open.

Patience looked imploringly at Ms. Deering, who nodded. She gathered her gear, then Drew's, and hurried out to follow him, closing the door quietly after herself.

Pressure was building behind my eyes. Gabe nudged my arm and grimaced sympathetically. My God, was he constantly listening? I turned away slightly.

The scent of old-fashioned cigarettes filled my nostrils, and Albert's voice came close to my ear. "Some injuries can be healed, miss."

I snapped my head around and stared at him, with his shadowed eyes and clipped mustache.

Healing… bee sting… jellyfish sting…

I gasped. "Ed! Ed could try to heal her!"

Ms. Deering gave me the kind of look teachers give when they've already warned you once.

Ed put his hands up in defense. "Mimi, I wish I could, but I'm not good enough yet. The most serious injury I've ever healed was on a pigeon that flew into our kitchen window. I wouldn't be any use to Cassie's aunt—I mean, she's got top doctors looking after her, and my energy wouldn't…" He trailed off. "My energy probably wouldn't…" Ed stopped again. His eyes were bright and he was scratching his short dreads, like he wanted to try but was almost sure he'd fail.

"My ghost literally just said some injuries can be healed," I told him. "I think you should try."

Ed processed my words, then turned to our teacher. "Can I?"

She shook her head. "There's no way to make it happen, Ed. You know students aren't allowed out midweek."

"What about if you smuggled him out?" I asked.

"If I got caught, I'd lose my job. Then who's going to run the gifted program and look after you seven?"

That stumped us all. I sat and chewed my lip, trying to think of a way around the rules.

Ms. Deering stood up. "Speaking of duty of care, I need to go and track down Drew and Patience. I'll be back shortly."

As soon as she was gone, Mona yanked her chair around and faced Ed. "We need to get you out to help Cassie's aunt."

He opened his eyes wide. "How, though?"

She turned to Gabe. "It's up to you. You need to cover for Ed while he sneaks out tonight."

"I could take a bus," Ed mused. "If I can only get out without Mr. Lemmon noticing I'm gone."

"Cassie's house is in Pinetree Glades," Mona said, hopping onto Ms. Deering's open laptop and running a hasty search. "The emergency hospital for the district is St Jude's. At lunch, I'll go to the library and email Cassie on her personal email address and confirm the details."

"But how do I get out of the dorm?" Ed asked.

Mona made an impatient movement. "Say you need to do some library research and get an after-hours pass."

Ed brightened. "Actually, I have to do a major math investigation this week. I could say I need time in the library and Ms. Huang should give me an after-hours pass."

"Perfect. You can sneak out, take the bus to St Jude's, do your thing and be back by five. Gabe, you keep watch for Ed, and make sure the dorm door is unlocked when he gets back."

Gabe looked unenthusiastic but shrugged his assent.

"Can I help?" I asked.

"You could get a library pass, too," Ed told me. "Then if any of the teachers are looking for me, you could say I'm in the bathroom or whatever."

I nodded. "Done."

"I was going to do that." Mona seemed slightly aggrieved, but then she tugged a pigtail and made a note in her book. "It might be better if I'm the comms base, though. I'll monitor Collabor8 with you two and email with Cassie." She made a frustrated noise. "I wish there was a way you could have your phone, Ed."

Gabe ran his hand through his hair. "Guys, I feel like we should tell Ms. Deering about this. She can smooth things over if there's any hassle with the staff."

"Under no circumstances will you tell her," Mona commanded. "She'll veto it. Like she said, she could lose her job. We can't put her in that position. Trust me."

Gabe obviously hated the plan, but it was hard to say no to Mona. I understood Gabe's hesitation—I was nervous, too—but I loved that we were doing something real.

"What about Drew and Patience?" I asked. "Do we tell them?"

Mona considered the question, then consulted Gabe. "What was Drew's vibe? I saw you reading him."

"Yeah. He was loud today. He's in free fall."

"What do you mean?" I asked.

"Distressed. Disturbed. Discombobulated. All the disses."

"Let's keep them out of it," Mona decided. "Drew might freak out, and Patience will do whatever he says."

"It's so stupid!" The words burst from me, startling them all. "He goes around acting like he's at the center of these incidents, but how could he be? He's just seeing pieces of the future!"

Mona resumed her seat. "You're preaching to the choir, Mimi. But Drew's got an overactive sense of responsibility. A guilty complex."

"He thinks he's failing them," Gabe corrected her. "Thinks he should know how to stop it all from happening."

I chewed my lip. "Do you think Patience found him when he ran off?"

"Probably," Mona said. "She can usually talk him off the ledge."

The knife of worry in my gut gave another twist, but at that moment, Ms. Deering came back. "Sorry about that," she said, puffing slightly. "They're in the library. Be gentle with Drew, won't you?" she added. "He's struggling today."

None of us spoke, and Ms. Deering paused, eyeing us one by one. Ed coughed awkwardly, and I went instantly hot in the cheeks.

Mona rushed into speech to create a diversion. "We were talking about how we can help. Could we send Cassie's aunt some flowers, Ms. D?"

Ms. Deering softened. "That's sweet, Mona, but let's give the family some space. The most useful thing we can do is to offer sympathetic ear when Cassie gets back."

Things were going smoothly so far, Mona reported in a whisper as we walked to the girls' dorm at the end of school. Ed had gotten a study pass from Ms. Huang and Gabe was in place, ready to cover for Ed at the dorm. Cassie had emailed instructions about how to get to St Jude's Hospital and promised to meet Ed at the door.

I had my own pass from the history teacher, so I dropped off my bag, signed out of the dorm and headed back to the library, my ghosts trailing behind. The crows were out in force today, cawing and croaking from trees and classroom rooftops. Ed was already in the library, putting in an appearance. We exchanged a look, then I distracted Mr. Winton in the history section, pretending to be unable to find a book while Ed crept out. From the corner of my eye I saw the top of the library door slide closed and breathed a silent sigh of relief. Hopefully he could get across the school grounds and through the split fence without being spotted.

I took a seat and opened my laptop to the Collabor8 app to report the mission was going as planned. The scent of tobacco drifted into my nostrils and Albert tapped his cane on the floor.

"They'd better not go into the sickroom after sixteen hundred hours, miss." Beneath his darkened eyes, his lips were pressed together in an earnest line.

"Why?" I whispered.

Albert's cane tapped as he wandered away.

Shit, shit, shit!

I opened a chat with the gifted group, not pausing to think.

Miette: *Mona, tell Ed not to go into the hospital room after 4pm!*
Mona: *What? Why not?*
Miette: *I don't know! Albert said he shouldn't.*
Patience: *Who's Albert? What's going on?*
Mona: *One of her ghosts. The soldier. Why 4pm, Mimi?*
Miette: *He didn't say, sorry.*
Mona: *Are they reliable, your ghosts?*

I had no idea how to answer that. I wasn't used to sharing what my ghosts told me to do, and it made me feel oddly exposed. I glanced at my half-finger.

Miette: *Yes.*
Mona: *Okay, I'll contact Cassie to warn her.*
Drew: *WTF is happening here?*

Mona had gone silent. I held my fingers over the keyboard, unsure what to tell Drew and Patience.

Gabriel: *Ed's sneaking out to see Cassie's aunt. He's going to try to heal her.*

There was a long moment with no reply.

Drew Ellery has left the session.

Gabe broke down the mission for Patience, who surprised me by being on board with it. Mona confirmed that Cassie had read her email about the four o'clock deadline. The chat went quiet for a while. I sat in the library and pretended to study. Poor Ed. If I felt this twitchy just sitting waiting, imagine how tense he was.

The wait dragged on. I distracted myself by raking over how Drew had receded into his goth armor. *Dammit.* I still couldn't shake the sensory joy of Saturday: hot gozleme, the smell of old books, laughing at my dad's borrowed joke and those moments of eye contact. That physical jolt of energy when he took my hand. The way his agate-green eyes seemed to see something deeply important in me.

The chat window with the gifted crew was still open, if inactive. I opened another Collabor8 window and searched for Drew's name, then hovered the cursor over the *Request* button. What could I even say to him? No amount of logic seemed to cut through the noise of his guilt and self-loathing.

Mr. Winton wandered up to me and I snapped my laptop shut so fast I wouldn't have been surprised to find the screen broken.

"Have you seen Edwin?" he asked, gazing across the library. "I've looked everywhere for him."

"He went to the bathroom," I gabbled. "And he was heading back to dorm after that. He said he was finished."

He sighed. "He could have let me know."

Mr. Winton went back to his desk, and I opened my laptop—screen thankfully intact. Hannah shifted behind my chair, and I slid the cursor back onto the *Request* button and willed my finger to click.

The other screen started blinking.

Gabriel: *Ed's back! I spotted him sneaking along the fence line. He's signing in right now.*

I didn't wait a minute longer. I scooped up my laptop and dashed for the door. "Thanks, Mr. Winton! Bye!" He waved.

Back at the dorm, I practically ran to Mona's room, checking the common room clock on my way past. Quarter to five. I knocked and went in without waiting. Patience was sitting cross-legged on the floor, her pale blue eyes wide with anxiety. Mona beckoned me in, and I shut the door behind me.

"Ed says he got there with fifteen minutes to spare before four o'clock," Mona reported. "He's exhausted from the healing effort. Wait, Cassie's just emailed." She scanned the screen, then read it aloud to us. "*Ed did what he could, but there's no change in my aunt's condition. My grandparents visited at four, so it was lucky Mimi told us to get Ed out by then. They would have wanted to know who he was. I should be back at school tomorrow unless things go bad here. I appreciate the effort.*"

We all deflated. "No change," Patience murmured.

Mona seemed angry. "Well, so much for your ghosts being reliable."

It felt like a personal insult. "Are you serious? Albert said not to go after four, and that's exactly when Cassie's grandparents turned up!"

"But why did he say Ed could heal him if he couldn't?"

I glanced at Albert, who was standing silently in the corner, as if he'd powered down for the day. "I don't know. Maybe that wasn't what he meant after all. It's not always clear what they mean, and if I ask, they don't always answer."

"What happens if you don't do what they tell you?"

An involuntary shudder went through me—deep and cold. They both saw it.

"Next question," I said.

Mona's hand crept toward her notebook. "Come on, spill. I'm the knowledge keeper for this club, and I pride myself on maintaining incredibly thorough records on everyone's gifts and gift-related problems."

"I don't talk about this, Mona. I hate even thinking about it."

Patience apologized immediately, even though she hadn't been the one pushing. Mona just gave me her best interrogative squint.

"It's bad, then?"

"It's bad," I confirmed.

"Does it hurt?"

Cold, cold like a planet unreached by the rays of the sun. I shook off the feeling.

"They get insistent." She opened her mouth to ask another question, and I put my hand up. "Enough."

Mona's gaze flew to my missing finger. "Does *that* have anything to do with it?"

I pulled my hand down and clenched my fist.

"Leave it, please, Mona," Patience said in her soft voice.

"Fine." Mona opened a drawer, rummaged inside, then closed it again. "Ugh, I need sugar to deal with this stress. Can't you conjure us something, Patience?" She said it as a joke, but Patience hesitated and Mona's face lit up. "You *could?*"

"I've done jellybeans before."

Mona's jaw dropped. "You have? Could you conjure some now?"

Patience held her hand out like she was waiting to accept a gift and closed her eyes. A colorful fizzing began in the air above her hand, like multicolored glitter in a snow globe. It gathered, forming into irregular shapes, leaving a slightly deformed set of pink, green and white beans sitting in her palm. She cautiously opened her eyes.

"You're amazing!" Mona squealed. "I mean, they're a bit weird. More like miscellaneous jelly shapes than jellybeans. A jelly vegetable medley. But you did it, and I bet they taste just like the real thing!"

Before she'd even finished talking, each jelly lump popped out of existence in a pink, green or white puff of powdered sugar, making us all jump and gasp. Suddenly, like a pressure valve had been released, the whole thing was hysterically funny. Mona, Patience and I ended up lying on the floor, breathless and aching from laughing. Just one glance would set us off again, and the only thing that broke the cycle was the chime of the dinner bell.

Damn, I hadn't laughed like this in over four years. I'd forgotten how high it made me feel.

11
In the Name of Science

Drew wasn't in school the next day, but Cassie was. I first saw her at the homeroom door, looking completely different than usual. Her eyes were shadowed and red-rimmed, her face thin and pale, the freckles standing out on her makeup-free skin.

But when she locked eyes with Gabe and me at our table, she broke into a grin and practically danced across the room to join us.

"It worked!" she whispered, slipping into a chair.

Gabe was already grinning back at her, immersed in her happiness, but I didn't dare believe it until I had details.

"We got the call at midnight. Aunt Gail woke up! The doctors are calling it a minor miracle."

My hands started shaking, eyes watering, and I couldn't work out if it was relief or awe. Cassie's words poured out, tumbling over each other in her excitement.

"I took Ed straight up to the ICU when he got there. I knew we didn't have much time. Every second that the nurses left us alone with her, Ed had his hand on Aunt Gail's head and just, like, went into the zone. He was super gentle, didn't say anything, just kept that hand right there. I thought it hadn't worked. I was just about crying when he left. But then the phone call. I can't believe it. Dad wanted me to stay home today, but I had to come—I wanted to tell you guys in person. Ed's a goddamn superhero!"

The Garden Shed Society held a special meeting under the oak tree during lunch, the crows cawing triumphantly from the branches above our heads. Drew still wasn't around, and Ms. Deering obviously had no idea what was going on, but the rest of us were there. We heaped praise on Ed, who was beaming and bashful. Cassie had regained some of her composure during the morning and was back to the snarky Cassie we knew, but she couldn't hide her gratitude.

"We're going to have to up our games, people," she said. "Ed's saving lives, and what have the rest of us got to show for ourselves? He's the magical equivalent of a Michelin-starred chef and we're over here like college students making ramen."

"That's a good point." Mona glanced around at all of us. "We should practice working together as a group. I mean, did it occur to any of you that what happened with Cassie's aunt was the first time we've combined our efforts? It was Ed who healed her, but Drew, Ed and Mimi were *all* involved in how it went down."

Patience nodded. "I was thinking about that last night."

Mona's fingers shredded a dry oak leaf feverishly. "What if Drew's visions are foreshadowing events we can act on *together* to prevent? Or at least help, somehow. Drew's vision, Mimi's ghost, Ed's healing. This has never happened before. We've never had our gifts synergize like this."

"But the clues are so sparse," I said. "How are we supposed to reverse-engineer a scenario from one of Drew's split-second visions?"

"And Drew having a vision of the puppy didn't stop the accident from happening to Aunt Gail," Cassie put in.

"No, but the visions *alerted* us to the incidents," Mona answered. She warmed to her subject, talking fast. "I wonder if we could somehow induce Drew's visions? Or get him to focus more on the context when he sees something like a silver bus or whatever. We might be able to work out where things are set to happen beforehand. Then we could *really* help."

Patience shook her head. "That's too much pressure on Drew, Mona."

Gabe agreed. "And even if he could work out where the things in his vision are located, what do we do with the information? Stake out a bus stop and do twenty-four-hour surveillance until something happens?"

"Of course not, but we could at least keep an eye out for incidents that happen in a place," Mona replied. "Then we could send Ed in to heal, or whatever is needed."

I saw Ed's face fall. "That's too much pressure on *Ed*," I said.

She pretty well ignored me. "But if we start to triangulate the gifts around Drew's visions—"

"Are your gifts getting stronger?" Gabe interrupted, looking around at us all. "I feel like mine is, ever since Mimi arrived."

"That's not your *gift* getting stronger, Gabe." Cassie smirked, and for once he was flustered into silence.

"Ew," Mona said. "And yes, your gifts are definitely getting stronger. I've been taking notes." She flicked back a few pages. "Ed's healing humans. Patience's conjuring has less disintegration. Gabe's getting more accurate with the emotions he picks up. Mimi's ghosts are giving us advice."

"And I got a squirrel to run in a perfect circle three times around our yard," Cassie put in.

Mona paused. "Oh. Is that difficult?"

Cassie's eyes opened wide. "Have you ever considered how a squirrel thinks? They're like toddlers on yellow M&M's. *Yes*, it's difficult."

"What about you, Mona?" Ed asked. "Is your gift getting stronger?"

Mona shrugged. "Mine's already as strong as it can be."

No one said anything, but I could practically feel everyone thinking a little humility would be a nice thing. Gabe shot me a private smile.

"I've got an idea," Mona went on. "Let's try an experiment. Let's *test* our gifts."

"And report back?" Ed asked.

"No, I mean now—together. Demonstrate them." She turned to Patience. "Could you conjure some candy again?"

Patience was pink-faced, but she nodded. We checked around for witnesses, but the only students anywhere near us were playing a ball game across the lawn, and the ancient oak tree hid us from the admin building. Patience went into her mini-trance state, hand cupped, and called some cosmic dust.

I got shivers of excitement all down my spine, watching the dust spark and fizz until a patch of color appeared, thickening and solidifying into a long raspberry twist. She opened her eyes and presented it to Cassie, glowing with delight as the rest of us clamored for a share.

"It's good." Cassie's blue eyes were wide as she chewed. "And it's my favorite!"

"I know." Patience was smiling.

By the time she'd made three more, she'd run out of magical steam. She was even sweating. "Sorry, I don't think I can do any more."

"It's not dematerializing." Mona was scribbling so hard in her notebook, she almost missed out on her share.

"Me next," Gabe said through a mouthful of raspberry twist. Then he hesitated and gave a defeated laugh. "I just realized it's impossible to demonstrate my gift."

"How am I feeling right now?" Mona asked.

"Curious. Determined."

She had to admit he was right. "But you knew that anyway from the things I've been saying. Can you read Patience?"

He focused on Patience. "Excited. Proud. Happy."

She went pink again but nodded.

"What about me?" Cassie broke in.

Gabe paused, then shrugged. "You asked. Fascinated and attracted to something… or someone."

She didn't need to confirm he was right—her glare was enough. I glanced surreptitiously at Ed and Gabe, wondering which of them she was into, and whether Ms. Deering's friend-zone rule had ever been broken. That led me to thoughts of Drew.

"What about Mimi?" Mona asked.

Gabe shot me a smile. "Mimi keeps her walls up, but she's got excitement mixed up with a bit of anxiety spilling around the edges."

My cheeks heated up. He was good.

"And me?" Ed asked.

Gabe studied him. "On a high. You feel like you won a prize."

Ed shrugged acquiescence. "It's nice to know you can break someone out of a coma."

"I'll go next." Cassie put her hand flat on the dirt and tapped her finger rhythmically a few times, concentrating hard. Then Patience gasped as a white butterfly alighted on her hair. Everyone exclaimed and laughed, but Cassie wasn't done. Four ladybirds flew into the circle and landed near Ed. They crawled onto his shoe and steadily up his ankle before taking simultaneous flight. Then she glanced up at the three crows making a racket above our heads.

'Shoo,' she said softly, and they all took flight.

We all broke into spontaneous applause. Cassie gave a seated curtsey, grinning.

"Tough act to follow," Ed remarked. "But I think I demonstrated my gift last night, unless one of you wants to volunteer to sprain a wrist for me to heal right now."

Gabe thrust out a long, hairy leg, revealing a graze on his knee. "I did this at hockey practice on the weekend. Feel free to fix my boo-boo."

Ed didn't hesitate. He covered the half-healed wound with his palm and, just moments later, moved his hand away, exposing unbroken pink skin. We all exclaimed in shock and delight.

"So fast!" Patience breathed.

"Mimi." Mona turned to me. "What have you got?"

"Three ghosts I have absolutely no authority over."

"Tell us something about them, then," she urged. "Ask them some questions."

"They probably won't answer. What do you want to know?"

"How did they know to come to *you*?" Patience asked immediately, as if she'd been holding the question in for a while.

"What do you mean?"

"I mean, did they *know* you'd be able to see and speak to them? Is that why they chose you?"

It was a valid question and something I'd obviously wondered about from time to time, but it had never occurred to me to ask them. Hannah was standing nearby, Albert was wandering along the line rosebushes and Marvin was perched on a tree root behind Ed.

"Why did you come to me?" I asked them softly, feeling only a little silly.

Hannah glanced over but said nothing. Albert didn't even appear to register my question.

Marvin, to my shock, answered. "The boundary's thin around you, kid."

I reported that back to the other six, and Mona scratched her pen in her notebook. "I need to do some research on this boundary thing."

The other four watched in silence, perhaps a little paler than they'd been a moment before.

"What is the boundary?" I asked. No answer. "*Where* is the boundary?" I tried.

This time, Hannah answered. "Between the before and the gray place."

Her words gave me a chill, and I hesitated to pass on the message. Was I supposed to be sharing this information about the dead? This felt oddly like a secret—like sacred knowledge.

"Where are they right now?" Ed saved me by asking.

I pointed at them in turn. "Hannah's right there and Albert's over there. Marvin's here, sitting behind you."

Ed turned and felt around in the space I'd indicated, but Marvin moved away. After a few moments, Ed shrugged.

"I don't feel anything."

"What's so funny, Mimi?" Gabe asked, although I didn't think I'd smiled.

"It's just that they tend to get out of the way if people move into their space."

"He moved?" Ed asked. "Would he let me sit beside him, then?"

"Maybe." I pointed to where Marvin was now standing on the other side of the oak. "Go stand there. A little to the left—no, your left. That's it. You're right next to him."

A slow change came over Ed's face. He blanched, his smile dropping away, and an involuntary shiver ran through him. An instant later, he'd scrambled away from Marvin and was back on the ground beside Cassie.

"What was it?" Mona asked. "Did you feel something?"

"I don't know." Ed's eyebrows knitted as he looked at me. "Are they cold?" I nodded. "It felt like… like an energy suck."

Patience clutched the little silver cross she wore around her neck. "I don't think we should be playing around with Mimi's ghosts," she said softly.

"You do realize my ghosts are no weirder than your ability to conjure raspberry twists?" I retorted. *Things you never think you're going to say to your schoolfriends, number 243.*

"Hey, guys. What're you doing?" It was Olivia. She'd appeared with Axel, and we'd been so caught up with our experiments that none of us had noticed. They both had weird looks on their faces. How long had they been standing there?

"Hi," Mona said curtly. "What's up?"

"Nothing." Olivia looked around at us all. "Is this a gifted group thing?" she asked, waving a hand to indicate our sharing circle.

"Yes, we're planning for a group project," Gabe said quickly, smiling at her. "Not very exciting."

"Where's Drew?" Axel was wearing black jeans, a metal band shirt and a fake eyebrow ring. It was such a poor version of Drew's extreme goth, I had to restrain an eye-roll.

"Sick, I think," Ed answered. "He stayed in bed this morning."

Olivia edged forward. "Could we join you? Axel and I have both decided to apply for the gifted program. It'd be nice to get an idea of what you're working on."

"We were just finishing up, actually," Mona told her.

I couldn't help but think that was a little rude. "Want to go for a walk?" I asked Olivia and Axel. "I need to stretch my legs."

"I'll come too," Gabe said, jumping up.

"Hey, your knee's much better!" Axel said, staring at Gabe's leg. "I heard you saying last night that you were worried it wouldn't heal in time for your next game."

Gabe was speechless for a second, then he grinned. "I know, right? I slept with an advanced healing bandage on it, and it's practically gone today. Amazing shit." He threw a grin at Ed and leapt upward, smacking a tree branch over our heads. It sent down a shower of tawny oak leaves.

Olivia laughed and caught one. "I get a wish!" she said. "Catch one, Mimi."

I tried and failed.

"Terminally uncoordinated," Gabe said, snatching a leaf and passing it to me. "There you go, make a wish." He leaned close and whispered, "And stop worrying about Drew. He's always been like this."

Wow. He was *really* good.

For the rest of the day, Mona talked about experimenting with Drew's visions. I started to get tired of it. I was pretty sure she was going to corner me and keep talking about it after study hour, so I went to the common room. She could go chew Patience or Cassie's ears instead. But Mona came and found me, plonking into the beanbag beside mine and whispering at me.

"Can you stop?" I said at last, maybe a little more firmly than I meant to.

She hesitated. "Stop what?"

"Stop trying to force Drew into doing something he's not capable of. He's drowning, Mona, and we need to throw out a lifeline, not hold his head under."

She regarded me in silence for a minute. "Do you like him, Mimi?"

I fought my blush like a rock fights gravity. "I think he's a complicated, toxic pain in the ass. But I feel sorry for him.

And we're never going to function properly as a group—use this synergy you keep talking about—if he doesn't get past his psychological block, right?"

She twisted her hair around her pen. "That's true. But maybe if we made a group decision to act, to pull our powers together and conduct another rescue mission, then he would have something to focus on. A distraction from the *litost*, you know?"

"From the what?"

"It's Czech. It means the torment of your own misery."

"But not all of us have fun gifts like you," I said. "It's okay for *you* to want to increase your power, but think about what that will mean for Drew, or me. Or even Gabe."

An odd look crossed her face, as if she didn't like hearing that. Then she opened her mouth to speak again, but I'd had enough. I struggled out of my beanbag.

"Olivia," I called across the room. "Want to work on the jigsaw puzzle with me?"

Olivia closed the dragon coloring book she was working on. "Sure."

I left Mona alone in her beanbag and crossed to the table where Ms. Samvedi's current puzzle was set up. It was the biggest one I'd ever seen—five thousand pieces, sitting on a massive wooden board on top of the table. The picture was a map of the County of Menoa, so kind of boring, but educational, I suppose.

Mona stayed where she was for a few minutes, and I could feel her watching me. My shadows roiled quietly in my peripheral vision. At last she headed down the corridor, probably to seek out Patience or Cassie. I felt a little bad, but also frustrated with her. Just because she was ready for anything and eager to move on to some sort of "next phase" didn't mean everyone else wanted the same thing.

"How's your gifted program project going?" Olivia asked.

I repressed another sigh. *Is there* anything *else we could talk about?* "Fine."

"What's the project about?"

My imagination failed me. "It's a bit involved," I said flatly.

She grinned. "Sounds like you're really into it. I'll take your spot in the program if you don't want it."

I smiled apologetically. "Honestly, it's not that much fun."

"Yes, but it'll look so good on your transcript when you're applying for college."

Dear Admissions Board,

Mimi was in a handpicked dysfunctional group of teenagers with freakish powers. She demonstrated a particular talent for wrangling the dead.

"I doubt any college would be impressed by a non-accredited program like this. They'll be more interested in our grades and, I don't know, extracurricular activities. Attitude and behavior, that sort of thing."

We worked on the puzzle together in silence for a few minutes. I tried to find a piece of Perry Ridge.

Olivia brushed her hair behind her ear. "You've probably heard the rumors about my dad," she said out of nowhere. "But they're not true."

"What about your dad?"

"About why he's in prison."

I blinked.

Olivia chuckled weakly. "Okay, maybe not. I assumed someone would have gossiped about it."

"I'm really sorry. I didn't know."

"It was felony burglary," she said. "But he *didn't* assault anyone, no matter what Mel Borgen says."

I groaned. "I've been here for literally four weeks and I already know not to believe a word that comes out of her mouth."

Olivia told me the full story. Her father had a gambling addiction. He'd tried to rob a closed store one night and got sprung by a security guard, who pepper-sprayed him, then called the cops. He was halfway through a three-year sentence in the county prison.

"He's trying hard in there," she said, trying piece after piece in the bottom corner of the puzzle. "He's doing counseling for his addiction, trying to finish his high school diploma. I'm trying, too. I used to mess around in my old school, but I want to make Dad proud when he gets out. I'm getting good grades now, and I'm going to try for a scholarship to an Ivy. That would be the most amazing present I could give him."

"You'll do it," I said. "You've got the determination and the brains." She shot me a smile.

Did I really deserve to be at this school? So many of the kids here had trauma, family problems and mental health issues to contend with, and here I was, perfectly fine other than having some ghostly companions. If I were a better person, I'd give up my spot for a kid who needed it more than me—but I wasn't a better person and I wanted my place. More every day.

I thought about my mom working at her new job so I could stay at the academy. I should do something nice for her and Dad. Make them a card or send them a sketch or something—anything to show them how grateful I was.

At dinner, Mona seemed a little reserved. Maybe I'd hurt her with my comments. Damn, I was *not* good at this crap. She hadn't done anything unkind to me, so maybe I should apologize. In my room, I emailed Mom a quick, loving message, then stared at the wall for a few minutes.

"What do I do?" I asked Hannah.

She had no wisdom for me. As for the other two, Marvin was sitting against the wall and Albert was pacing on the lawn outside my window. *Ugh.* Friendship was like a complex code I needed to learn.

The thought of a code sparked an idea. I did a little online searching, then headed down to Mona's room with my headphones and sketchpad. I knocked, and she called, "Come in!"

I shut the door behind me. "I'm sorry for being a grumpy bitch earlier. I didn't sleep that well last night. All that worry about Ed and his hospital visit. I'm not great on broken sleep."

She gave me a big, relieved smile. "That's okay."

"Can we hang out?"

"Yeah, grab a seat." She turned back to her computer.

I settled on her bed with my sketchpad, flipping through to find the raven feather I'd been penciling earlier.

"You were right, anyway," Mona blurted.

"Huh?"

She turned back to me. "About our gifts being different. Yours is more—more magical than mine."

I frowned. "That's not what I said."

"It's true, though. Think about it. Anyone could learn my gift if they studied long and hard enough. But no one can teach themselves to call the dead, or conjure things, or see the future."

Her need to make herself useful to the gifted group abruptly made sense. I put aside my sketchpad and reached out my hands. "Pass me your laptop."

"Why?"

I nodded at the laptop until she gave in and handed it over. I thought for a few moments, then searched for *Anglo Saxon poetry*, angling the screen away from her. "Okay. Excuse my pronunciation. *Oft him anhaga are gebideð.*"

I knew I'd butchered it, but Mona only had to think for a few seconds. "Often the solitary one," she said slowly, "finds grace for himself."

I turned the screen to show her how she'd translated it perfectly. "Have you ever learned Anglo Saxon?"

"No, but—"

"Mona, stop. Not only can you translate a mispronounced line in a language you've never studied, you can do it with a *dead* language no one even uses anymore. And it was word perfect. Don't tell me that's not magical."

She was fighting a smile now, her color deepening. "Whatever."

"Now, I have a challenge for you. Have you come across the Dorabella Cipher? My dad heard about it on a podcast and told me the story last year. It's over a hundred years old and still hasn't been decoded. I figure if anyone can do it, it's you."

She hesitated. I'd hooked her, I could see it. She retrieved her laptop and ran a search on Dorabella. Within moments, she was fully absorbed. I concealed a smile, put on my headphones, set my mom's old iPod to play Hoodwynk and settled in to draw.

12
Unsuccessful Ways to Avoid Dating

Yet again, no Drew in homeroom.

"Has anyone told Drew your aunt is okay?" I whispered to Cassie.

She rolled her eyes, but I'd learned not to take that personally by now. "Of course. I emailed him yesterday. He didn't bother to reply."

Then Ms. Deering slipped us a note. She wanted us to meet in the garden shed in the second half of lunchtime. A panicky knot formed in my gut. Was it bad news? Was Drew leaving school or something? Was he sick?

Or was he in a crisis, spiraling?

None of the others knew anything. We ate our lunch fast and assembled in the gifted program cottage to wait for our teacher. She turned up a few minutes later, a crease between her eyebrows. She didn't sit down, but leaned against a desk, looking worn out.

"First up, I'm so pleased to hear about your aunt's recovery, Cassie." Ms. Deering smiled at Cassie, and the rest of us avoided looking at one another. "Now," she went on. "Drew's family had some personal bad news yesterday, so he's taking a little time at home with them."

"Is everyone okay?" I asked, my chest tightening again.

"Yes, everyone in his family is fine. His sister lost someone she knew at her school. But the students are being supported, and Drew should be back tomorrow."

"Wait." Mona sat up straight. "Was that the accidental shooting—the Etherall Valley Junior High kid?"

"Yes." Ms. Deering tried to forge on. "So, I want to—"

"Oh my God," Cassie broke in. "I heard about that! Some boy got hold of his father's gun and it went off. He died, right?"

"I heard that too!" Ed shook his head. "Poor kid. He was only fourteen."

"That's the same age as Drew's sister," Patience put in.

"How did it happen?" Gabe wanted to know.

"Olivia used to go to EV Junior High," Mona said. "One of her old friends emailed her with the story. The gun was loaded and the kid didn't realize. His dad had locked it in a drawer but left the key in the lock."

A thought flashed into my mind and I pointed at Mona's notebook, my throat locked against speaking. She frowned at me, but Ed gasped. "Wait—didn't Drew have a vision about a key last week?"

Mona's eyes grew big and round. She scrambled to open her notebook, then sucked in a breath. "*Varnished wood with key.* Drew's vision was about this kid!"

"Oh no." Patience's voice was so soft that most of them missed it. "Poor Drew."

"You see?" Mona demanded, looking around at us all. "If we'd been able to get more information from Drew, we might have saved the boy!"

Even without the context of yesterday's discussion under the oak tree, Ms. Deering looked angry. It was the first time

I'd seen that sort of reaction in her. "Mona, no amount of speculating would have helped us work out what was going to happen, let alone when, where or to whom."

Mona had to concede the argument, but in that moment, I was glad Drew was away. What she'd said was the last thing he needed to hear right now.

I thought about him for the rest of the day, sitting at home suffering under his storm cloud of helpless guilt. I couldn't resist: during study hour I emailed him, hoping he'd log in to his school account and pick it up.

Hi, Drew,
Ms. D. told us you've had bad news and Mona guessed it was in relation to the local high school boy who died. Patience thought he might have been a friend of your sister's. I just wanted you to know I'm really sorry. It's a horribly unlucky thing to have happened. I hope your sister is doing okay.
See you at school.
Mimi

I used the word *unlucky* as a sort of code word, trying to remind him that it wasn't his fault. By the time I went to bed, there was still no reply—nor had he sent anything when I checked in the morning.

I walked from the dorm to school with Mona and caught sight of Drew getting off the bus. He was in deep goth, his armor completely reinforced. The very way he carried himself told me he was weighed down with self-blame. He came into school from the bus bay, passing right by us, and his white-lensed eyes stayed firmly on the ground. He'd seen us; I knew he had. But he ignored us.

"Damn," Mona said softly.

In homeroom, he sat across the room by himself. When I took a step as if to join him, he spread his gear across his table and put his bag on the chair next to his.

After school, I argued with myself for an hour before sending him a message request on Collabor8. He declined. I tried again. Okay, I tried again three times. The third time, he picked up.

Miette: *Hi, thanks for accepting. I know what's probably going on in your head and I'm hoping you'll let me be a voice of reason.*

There was a pause, animated ellipses showing me he was writing a long reply. But when he finally sent it, there were just six words.

Drew: *STAY THE HELL AWAY FROM ME.*

Drew Ellery has left the session.

There's nothing quite like being told to stay the hell away from someone for making you stay the hell away from someone. I didn't want to (a) make things worse, (b) lose my self-respect or (c) experience the hurt of hearing that again.

In homeroom the next day, Drew sat alone and read a novel. He didn't even look in my direction. At lunch, he sat with Patience and they talked in quiet mumbles. I interacted with him twice: once, I took the empty seat beside him in English. He said nothing in reply to my tentative greeting, and I sat there for the rest of the session, my cheeks warm from the humiliation.

The other time, I was alone in the library doing research on the art of Vermeer when Drew stepped through the door. He saw me. I sat up straight, using every nonverbal social cue I knew to practically plead with him to come and sit by me. This would be the perfect spot to have a conversation—in his safe space, uninterrupted by other students and with Mr. Winton sitting in his office, engrossed in something librarian-ish.

Drew hovered on the doorstep. I could see he was considering it. I smiled hopefully. But it was as if a piranha had smiled at him. He looked, if anything, totally triggered. His face clouded and he turned away, exiting the library.

And *there* was the pain I'd been attempting to avoid.

At the end of the day, I lay on my bed, playing with the little agate skull I'd bought at the market. I'd come to a decision: I could not help Drew. Every time I reached out, he slashed like a cornered cat and I ended up wounded. And I wasn't just hurt anymore; I was *angry*. Drew was messing with my head and I didn't appreciate it. I'd struggled for years before coming to Etherall Valley Academy, and it had just begun to get better. Now here he was, undermining my new confidence. I couldn't afford to play with my mental health.

Hell, how had I been so monumentally deluded to think I could help him relinquish his self-loathing and denial? I was just one seventeen-year-old girl. He needed a team of therapists. I'd leave Ms. Deering to manage Drew's moods and fancies from now on.

His rejection was a good lesson. A timely reminder not to let people get too close.

Ping.
Gabriel Cavendish would like to start a Collabor8 session for GIFTED PROGRAM PROJECT.
Accept?

Gabriel: *Miette Alston.*
Miette: *Gabriel Cavendish. What's up?*
Gabriel: *I just wanted to chat. Are you busy?*
Miette: *Not really. I've got most of my homework done.*
Gabriel: *I have a question.*
Miette: *Go on.*
Gabriel: *You and Drew—you got a formal arrangement in the pipeline?*
Miette: *No way. Why?*
Gabriel: *I had a vibe.*
Miette: *An empath vibe? Or just a vibe?*
Gabriel: *Both. To be honest, I thought something was going on that day at the market, but over the past week or so, you guys haven't spoken at all. Did you have a fight?*
Miette: *No. He just stopped talking. He's complicated and it's exhausting.*
Gabriel: *You're over it?*
Miette: *Emphatically yes.*

Gabriel: *It was a surprise, I'll admit, seeing him being so friendly to you that day. Drew doesn't normally mix with new kids. Or any kids, for that matter.*

Miette: *Except Patience.*

Gabriel: *Yeah. That weird thing with Patience.*

Miette: *What is the thing with Patience?*

Gabriel: *He looks after her.*

Miette: *What does that mean?*

Gabriel: *Hah, that sounded bad! I don't think they have THAT kind of relationship. He helps her feel better about her gift. She looks after him too. You've seen how when Drew storms out of class, she sometimes goes after him. Calms him down. They've got a connection.*

Miette: *Despite their differences.*

Gabriel: *Yep. I feel sorry for them both. They've got waves of secrets and self-hate coming off them. If I didn't know better, I'd think they'd committed a murder together.*

Miette: *Sounds like a fun way to live.*

Gabriel: *You know Patience's family thought her gift was a religious thing? Boxe had to tell them she had a "psychological problem," not possession. He said he could manage her problem here at EVA, and once they got her here, Ms. Deering put her into the gifted program.*

Miette: *That's wild.*

Gabriel: *Her mom and dad were glad he took the problem away, I think. They believe Boxe is giving her therapy, but Ms. D tries to train her to hide her gift from her family. It doesn't stop her feeling guilty and believing she's Satan spawn.*

Miette: *Mr. Boxe doesn't know anything about our gifts, does he?*

Gabriel: *No, he doesn't know anything, but he still lets Ms. D run the program. Sometimes I wonder why. He must know we're not geniuses. She's protective of us. Doesn't let any of the other staff know what's really going on.*
Miette: *No one would believe her anyway.*
Gabriel: *Good point.*
Miette: *Well, I guess I should think about finishing this last bit of English.*
Gabriel: *Want to come to the school dance with me?*
Gabriel: *Helllooooo? Mimi?*
Miette: *I'm here. What dance?*
Gabriel: *On the 20th. Friday night, two weeks from now.*
Miette: *Oh. I haven't heard about it.*
Gabriel: *It's all over the notice boards. Cassie's on the organizing committee.*
Miette: *Right.*
Gabriel: *You're quiet. Dodging a reply? Or is this awkward for you?*
Miette: *Kind of.*
Gabriel: *Is it unwelcome?*
Miette: *Haven't been asked to a dance before.*
Gabriel: *Bullsh*t. Oh, that's right! You were homeschooled. I forgot. So. Will you come with me?*
Miette: *Thanks, but no. I don't do dancing.*

"Accept his invitation, miss," Hannah said in my ear.

I swung around. She was sitting on my bed. "Hannah, I can't go to a dance. I never go to dances."

She watched me steadily.

Gabriel: *Aw, come on! I won't make you dance if you don't want to. Just come and hang out with me.*
Miette: *It's really not my scene.*

"You need to go, kid." It was Marvin this time. He was standing beside me.

"Come on. This is ridiculous. You can't make me go to a stupid school dance!"

Marvin tilted his head slightly as if to say, *Can't we?*

A prickling started at the base of my skull and developed into a full-body shiver.

Gabriel: *You're going to be on school grounds on dance night anyway. Might as well be in the gym, hanging with the coolest people.*
Miette: *Is Mona going?*
Gabriel: *Yes, she is. She's partnered up with Ed, going as buddies. And Cassie's going with Tyler.*
Miette: *Are Patience and Drew going?*
Gabriel: *No way. Patience never does dances and Drew's banned because he lost good standing again—but he wouldn't go even if he could. So, what do you say?*
Miette: *I really don't think*

The smell of tobacco hit my nostrils and I didn't even get to press send before Albert's hand was on my shoulder. Where he touched me, the blood went still in my veins, the leaden chill of death spreading through my muscle and tendons. I wrenched myself out of his hold so fast I smacked into the bedroom wall and landed on the floor. I scrunched myself up as far away from Albert as possible and peered up at him through my tangle of hair.

"Please, no, Albert! Okay, you win!"

Albert hovered there, his hand extended toward me while I cowered away from his touch, my shoulder aching like I'd been stabbed, the other arm stinging where I'd hit the wall. He didn't move, and although I couldn't see his eyes, I had the distinct sense Albert was remorseful for what he'd done. That he wasn't so much pursuing me to pour more cadaver vibes into my flesh as wishing he could help me up. He moved back.

I clambered to my feet, not taking my eyes off him. Albert retreated to the corner of the room and passed silently through the wall. I slid into my chair, deleted the last line and retyped it with shaking fingers.

Miette: *Okay, I'll come.*
Gabriel: *Yeah? Yay!*
Miette: *We can go as a friend group. You, Mona, Ed and me.*
Gabriel: *I wanted to go with you as my date.*
Miette: *But Ms. Deering doesn't want the gifted kids to date.*
Gabriel: *That's more of a guideline. Not a rule.*
Miette: *Let's go as friends. Or if you want to take a date, maybe ask someone else.*
Gabriel: *I want to go with you. I'll go as friends if you like, but I'm still going to think you're pretty.*
Miette: *Be serious, Gabe.*
Gabriel: *I am. You really are pretty.*
Miette: *Stop.*
Gabriel: *Okay, stopping. Except to say your modesty about your prettiness makes you even prettier.*

Miette: *STOP.*

Gabriel: *Don't panic, Mimi. This is all very natural and normal. Handsome guy meets pretty girl, asks her out. It happens in schools all over the world, promise.*

Miette: *Gabe.*

Gabriel: *Stopping now, for real. I don't want you to change your mind.*

Miette: *Friends.*

Gabriel: *Friends who think friends are pretty.*

Miette: *Goodbye, Gabe.*

Gabriel: *Wait! You're still going to the dance with me, yes?*

Miette: *Yes.*

Gabriel: *Yes! Okay, bye.*

Gabriel Cavendish has ended the session.

What the hell just happened? Hannah was still seated placidly on my bed and Marvin was back in position, slumped against the wall. The only sign he'd moved was the melted snow tracking across the floorboards toward me. Albert was probably wandering the garden, but frankly, I didn't care where he was at that moment.

I maneuvered my hand through the collar of my shirt and rubbed my shoulder. It felt like it had been directly under an air-conditioning vent running full blast. Like a piece of meat pulled from the freezer. I twisted my head around to inspect it. A couple of tiny broken blood vessels were the only sign of physical damage. I checked my other arm where I'd hit the wall. A big red mark promised a bruise.

It appeared I was going to the school dance.

I realized the next day that this dance was a big deal at EVA. Now I knew about it, I saw posters for it everywhere. Cassie talked about it constantly. She was going with one of the rowdy guys she loved mixing with, and she was hyped for it.

Mona confirmed that she and Ed were going as friends, but raised her eyebrow at me when I told her Gabe and I were doing the same.

"I'm not sure that's what *he* thinks. It was the first thing he told me this morning. You'd think he won the lottery. Have you got a dress yet?" she added. "I've ordered mine online. It's long, white with blue flowers. I just hope it gets here on time. It was supposed to arrive last week. If it doesn't come, I'll be stuck with one of my old things, unless I beg something off my sister. Hey, do you want to get ready at my place? We can play music and have snacks. You know, *voorpret*."

"What?"

"Oh, it's Dutch. It's like pre-fun. The fun before the fun."

Voorpret sounded good to me. Mom had wanted me to go to a dance for years. Every time the homeschool network hosted one, she'd pleaded with me to go, often resorting to bribery. She almost got me once with the promise of a full set of Copic markers. So when I got an email from her reminding me to message Aunt Aurora for her birthday, I casually mentioned the dance in my reply. A few minutes later, Ms. Samvedi came to fetch me, saying I had a phone call from home about an "important family matter." She put me in her office for privacy, shutting the door behind her.

"Mom? Is everything okay?"

"What are you going to wear, Mimi? You need a dress!"

"Oh my God, Mom, I thought it was something important!"

"This *is* important."

"It's not formal. It's just a casual thing."

"You still need something to wear. Not jeans, that's for sure."

"I think other kids are wearing jeans."

"Oh, no, Mimi. You'll find most of the girls will wear dresses. Have you got a color preference? I'm looking at some beautiful dresses online right now. Oh, this one is gorgeous! Do you still hate pink?"

I had a moment of genius. "I'll wear that red dress you made me buy last month. It's not too formal, but it's still pretty."

I practically heard her brain working. "It *is* a lovely dress. Have you worn it yet? Or even tried it on?"

"I've tried it on," I lied. "It fits perfectly. And if I wear that, you won't need to spend more money on me."

She sighed in disappointment when she realized she wouldn't be buying me a pink dress. "You're right, Mimi. That red dress is just right for a casual dance. But what will you do for shoes?" She sounded like a deranged fairy godmother.

"I'll wear my—"

"Stop right there, young lady. You will *not* wear sneakers to a dance."

"High-tops. Not sneakers."

"No."

I could be as stubborn as her. "It's what I feel comfortable in."

"I'll order you some shoes and get them delivered to school."

"That's nuts. It's a waste of money. Save the money for your Paris trip." She was quiet for a moment. "Mom?"

"Mimi, please don't wear sneakers to a dance."

The only way to stop her nagging was by agreeing to go shoe shopping on the weekend.

"By the way," I threw in. "Mona's invited me to get ready for the dance at her place. Could you email Ms. Samvedi to say I have permission?"

"Who's Mona? Wait—you've got a best friend?" Mom choked up, and I wanted to die. "Is she wearing sneakers, too?" she asked through her tears.

"Oh my God. No. Mona will make sure I look nice, okay? You don't need to worry."

All week, in homeroom and our other shared classes, I barely looked at Drew. It was a deeply committed and mutual not-looking-at. Thursday was the only time we had a brush with acknowledging each other's existence. There was an incident in the cafeteria at lunchtime. A ruckus arose from another part of the room, and although Mona stood up and craned her neck, she couldn't make out what was going on. Cassie was over there in the thick of it—I caught a flash of her red hair.

"Is it a fight?" Gabe asked. "I think Tyler's involved."

Tyler was the guy Cassie was taking to the dance. If it was a fight, I wasn't surprised he was part of it.

Then a black shape materialized, climbing over a table and leaping to the floor, running for our table at full speed. It was Drew, chains clanking, boots thudding across the timber boards. He skidded to a halt by my side, smashing into me so I spilled my juice into my salad.

"Ed!" he snapped.

Ed was on his feet in a split second, scrambling after Drew toward the source of excitement. Before we could get over there and find out what was going on, staff members appeared and took control, clearing the outliers like us from the cafeteria so they could deal with the incident.

We got the full story in Friday's gifted class. Most of us already knew the details—it had gone around the school faster than a stomach virus—but Cassie had witnessed it at close range.

"It happened in total silence," she said, her eyes so wide we could see the white space around her irises. "None of us even realized Ada was choking on a chicken tender until she banged on the table with her hand. She was purple! Tyler pulled her up and did the Heimlich maneuver on her and it worked—it got the food out of her throat, but he accidentally hurt her while he was doing it."

"He cracked a rib," Mona put in. "People *heard* it crack."

"He was trying to save her life!" Cassie shot back. "Anyway, as soon as she could talk again, she started complaining about her ribs, then Ed got her to lie down in the recovery position, and while he was helping her, he just put his hand on her rib and did his thing—and the next moment, Ada was fine!"

Gabe clapped Ed on the shoulder. "Nice work, man. Now you're laying hands upon people, you can build your own cult following. You'll make millions—hallelujah!"

Mona shoved Gabe, indicating Patience with her head and calling him the Insensitive Sensitive again. I glanced at Patience to see how she would react, but she was focused on something Drew was murmuring to her.

Ms. Deering got everyone settled down. "Tell me how your week has been, everyone. Any issues or achievements? Gabe, do you want to go first?"

"Achievements?" He flashed her a grin. "Well, maybe I didn't heal a broken rib, but I did get a date for the school dance with the cutest new girl at EVA."

Mona and Ed groaned. I went hot in the face and glared at Gabe. But he was eyeing Ms. Deering, waiting for her reply. Wait—had he done it purely to check what the reaction would be?

Ms. Deering raised an eyebrow. "I understood we didn't date within the gifted group?"

Gabe deflated. "Well, I guess Mimi and I are going as friends, then."

Cassie made a snorting noise. Ms. Deering nodded. "Let's stay focused. Anything to report on your gift, Gabe?"

"I've started talking to that freshman, Juliet. I'm sure there's something wrong there. She's got this huge shadow of fear and sadness sitting over her. I can almost see it. It's always at its worst on Mondays."

My ears pricked up. A *shadow* of fear? Could Gabe know something about my shadows? *Mental note: sound him out.*

Ms. Deering didn't like hearing it. "I checked into Juliet's records. This doesn't leave this room, got it?" She stared around at us, and we all nodded in answer. "Juliet has a similar wellbeing profile to a lot of the other kids here—depression, anxiety. She was in a bit of trouble at her old school. Do you think there's old trauma resurfacing, Gabe? Is she not coping?"

He shook his head. "It's not like the anxiety I pick up from the other kids. It's like she has a sense of being under threat, but if anything, it reduces when she's around other kids. It's hard to explain."

"Like she's got something after her, and she's only safe in company with other people?" Mona suggested.

"Yes!" Gabe looked grateful. "That's it."

"So, she feels unsafe," Ms. Deering murmured.

Gabe nodded. "I was going to keep talking to her, gain her trust. See if she lets anything slip."

Ms. Deering approved. "I'll let Mr. Boxe know there may be something amiss with Juliet and he can rally the staff to support her. Cassie?" she asked, moving on.

Cassie shook her head. "I've been kinda distracted," she confessed. "My aunt's recovery and organizing the dance."

"That's all right. Patience, have you conjured anything new?"

"I've refrained this week, miss."

Patience sounded like a naughty monk who'd managed not to commit any sins since his last confession. I caught the flicker of dismay in Ms. Deering's expression, but she didn't comment. She turned to me.

"Mimi, any changes?"

I was about to shake my head, then the thought of Tuesday night slid into my mind. My shoulder twinged in response. "My ghosts are talking to me more. Since I came to EVA, they've spoken to me at least once a week."

"Interesting." Ms. Deering studied my face. "Can you share what they've said?"

I glanced at Albert, striding up and down the lawn outside, scattering the crows. Did I really have to admit what had happened? That the three of them had gone all psychotic matchmaker on me and forced me into going to the dance with Gabe?

I was *not* telling them that. Nor could I tell Ms. Deering how they helped us sneak Ed out of the school against her wishes. I snatched at the only alternative I could think of. "When my parents were driving me to Etherall Valley a few weeks ago, we passed Dale's Run. My mom wanted to drive in and get a better look, but my ghosts told me we shouldn't go in there."

Spots of color appeared in Patience's cheeks. "Dale's Run is my home. It's not scary or freaky; it's just a bit old-fashioned compared with what you're used to. We may not have TV or computers, but we do use electricity and read books. We're not backward."

"I didn't mean to offend you," I said, feeling terrible. "Personally, I don't have a problem with the place. It was just that my ghosts wouldn't let me go there."

Mona was scribbling earnestly. "And it wasn't just one of them?" she asked me. "All three of them said it?"

I nodded, remembering their touch. One of those deep, uncontrollable shudders came out of me—a body memory. If only there was some way to convert those shudders into a shrug or a stretch, but they were like an overflow of creepiness. They had to go somewhere. Gabe clearly felt it too, and gave me a commiserative grimace.

"Thank you for sharing that, Mimi," Ms. Deering said. "Nothing else? What about you, Mona?"

Mona talked brightly about all the unsolvable codes she'd decoded since I introduced her to the Dorabella Cipher. She presented us with messages people had been trying to read for centuries. They were surprisingly dull. Ms. Deering agreed with Mona that she should keep this "just among us" and allow the rest of the world to decode them in due course, using non-supernatural means.

"Drew," our teacher said at last, "anything to report?"

Drew obviously didn't want to speak, but he made the effort. "A pink rose. The number thirty-four in dark green paint. A red ribbon tied around a post. An old car, kind of dirty blue and rusty."

Mona wrote more notes, and Drew looked down at his leather-bound book. Even from across the room, I could see heavy black ink on the open page, spiked letters forming a single word: *Drowning.*

He stared at it as if he couldn't remember writing it, then reached out to flick the book shut.

13
Too Little, Too Late

After school, I went to the art room to work on my painting. Albert wandered around the herb garden outside the door, Hannah sat neatly at one of the art tables and Marvin did his usual slouch against a wall. After about an hour, when I was deep into the Pearl Girl's headscarf, Axel turned up.

"Hello!" He stopped to look at my canvas. "How's it going?"

I gave my work a critical examination. It wasn't looking good, objectively speaking. The girl's eyes seemed to stare right through me, and the bone structure was too pronounced, as if her skull was trying to emerge from her skin. "I know it's not quite right, but I'm running out of time, so it's just going to have to stay that way."

"I know what you mean. My Mona Lisa's smile's not right."

Could confirm. His Mona Lisa looked unhinged.

Axel set up his artwork in another part of the room. He hadn't attempted a goth look today, and I was glad. Frankly, I didn't need to be reminded of Drew. It was a pity Axel felt the need to be a social chameleon. He needed to understand that he was enough, without trying to shoehorn himself into a subculture. Or maybe he needed to hear that he wasn't alone, even if he hadn't made any close friends yet. I couldn't think of a way to reassure him that wouldn't make me sound like a Christian youth group leader.

"Are you going to the school dance on the twentieth, Mimi?"

"Uh, yes. You?"

"Definitely. Do you have a date?"

"No, I don't date. I'm going with Gabe. As friends."

"Oh, right. Do you know if Mona is going?"

Was he going through a mental register of girls he could ask? And why were my shadows swirling in the corners of the room like that? "Yes, Mona's going with Ed."

"Oh. And Patience?"

"I don't know about Patience."

"Do you think she—"

The door swung open and Mr. Boxe stuck his head in, his hair sticking up like a fluffy halo. "Hello, hello!" he said in his usual jolly tone. "I'm doing the rounds of all the hard little workers toiling away after school hours! I've just come from the dance studio and the media room." He let himself in and went over to Axel's easel. "Excellent, excellent. That's a Leonardo DiCaprio, if I'm not mistaken?"

I smothered a smile, and Axel politely explained his project.

"Fascinating, fascinating. Portraits in oils. Gaining skills by reproducing a masterpiece. Well, well." Mr. Boxe made his way over to me, and I unwillingly stepped back to let him see my work. How did he manage to take up so much space?

He tipped his head to one side like an expert art critic. "Very interesting. Nice use of color."

"Thank you, sir."

"Who was the original artist?"

I told him about Vermeer. While I spoke, his gaze strayed to my open sketchpad with its many attempts at working out Pearl Girl's eyes, and a few of my usual skulls, hands and hearts thrown in for good measure.

"Veneer, eh? Fascinating." He clapped, making me jump. "All right, I'd better move on. I still need to visit the kids in the literature program." He leaned his head toward me and dropped his voice. "No more migraines, Mimi?"

I froze and blanked. I felt called out in a lie, or like my privacy was being invaded. I mumbled an answer in the negative, and he studied my face for a moment before nodding, turning away and striding from the room.

Maybe he'd rattled me more than I'd thought. Around the edges of the room, serpentine pockets of darkness loomed and slithered more than ever. I turned around slowly to take them all in, trying to work out if they were moving closer. I glanced at Hannah, and her voice came soft in my ear.

"Perhaps you'd be better off back in your room, miss."

"Are you all right, Mimi?" Axel was watching me over his easel with a puzzled frown.

"Yeah. I think I'm done for the day, though. Mr. Boxe broke my flow state."

I spent a good chunk of the weekend in the art room with Axel, working on our master reproductions. Mrs. Shaw wanted us to finish them off so we could move on to creating our own original portraits this week. Clearly she didn't understand how many years of work it would take before the Pearl Girl looked anything like a living human.

While Mona and I walked from the dorm toward school on Monday, the crows providing their usual chorus of jeers, she pointed out Gabe talking to a girl with short, fair hair just inside the gates.

"That's Juliet," Mona told me. "The freshman he's worried about."

The girl was picking at the skin on her arm, staring at the ground while Gabe spoke to her.

"Why do you think he's so concerned about her?" I asked. "He barely knows her."

"Gabe feels everyone's feels, remember? So, if something's really bothering someone, it kind of becomes his problem."

A pang of sympathy hit me. Imagine having to wear everyone else's feelings as well as your own. Especially in a school like this, where everyone had a "unique challenge."

I watched Gabe. He was practically oozing big-brotherly kindness as he listened to Juliet speak. It softened me toward him to see him being so sweet to her.

"Let's go say hello," Mona said.

"Don't do it, miss," Hannah said in my ear. "She's nearly ready to speak."

I grabbed Mona's arm to stop her from striding toward Gabe and Juliet. "My ghosts say no. Let's leave Gabe to it."

But in homeroom I waited for Gabe, doodling in my sketchpad. As soon as he arrived, I waved him over to where I was sitting. He joined me, looking pensive.

"Any news on Juliet?"

"She wants to talk, I can see it. I can *feel* it. Something's going on. I can't just come out and ask her, though—that'd spook her."

"She'll have to trust you first." I crosshatched an anatomical heart on my page, trying to work out what would have made a fourteen-year-old me trust a seventeen-year-old boy. The answer was: pretty much nothing. "She needs to know you won't gossip. Maybe it would help if she thinks, I don't know… that you're hoping to become a student leader, or something like that."

His face lit up. "That's genius, Mimi. How about I tell her I'm trying to start a peer mentoring system here at school?"

"Yes! For younger kids to have a trusted older friend to talk to about any problems they're having!"

We fist-bumped, then Hannah's herbal scent filled my nostrils. She was across the room, right near where Drew liked to sit in his Dark Corner of Solitude. I found his eyes on me. He'd reduced the armor down so it looked like more of an afterthought today: a faint dust of white across his face, no eyeliner. A band t-shirt and jeans.

He gave me a tentative smile, and my heart tried to exit my chest via my ribcage. To say it was an effort not to smile back would be an understatement. It took all my physical strength to fight the response my body had to that smile, but I couldn't let him keep messing with me.

Drew's face clouded and the smile fell away.

"Mimi," Gabe was saying. "Did you hear me? Ed's older brother is lending him his car for Friday night. He can pick us all up for the dance. I'm going home to get ready, so he'll swing by mine, then we'll come get you and Mona from her place."

"Nice!" I was determined to act normal. "That'll be fun."

But as we headed for our respective classes, Drew was waiting for me. I tried to follow Gabe without making eye contact, but Drew spoke.

"Mimi, can I talk to you?"

Gabe hovered a moment, then walked on. I'd stopped, but I folded my arms and stared at the ground, deliberately resisting looking into Drew's eyes. "What about?"

He paused, maybe to assess my body language. He was probably accustomed to Keen Mimi. How eager I must always have seemed before now! My cheeks warmed up.

"The usual," he said.

"Sorry, I need to get to class."

I congratulated myself as I walked away. Not one moment of eye contact, and I'd stayed polite but clear. Yes, I felt torn, but I'd stuck to my resolution.

I maintained my distance during our shared English class, too. Drew looked like he might come and speak to me again after the school day ended, but Gabe and Mona appeared and we all headed toward the dormitories together, leaving Drew behind. Gabe glanced back as we walked away.

"Something go down with Drew?" he asked.

"No," I said.

Mona looked back too. "Why do you ask, Gabe?"

Gabe shrugged. "He's giving off a truckload of emotion. Another angsty day in Drewtopia."

Mona snorted, but I couldn't quite bring myself to laugh.

I spent an unhealthy amount of time over the next couple of days wondering why Drew had wanted to speak to me and low-key hoping he'd send me a message. He didn't.

Friday rolled around, then it was all about the dance. Mom had emailed her consent for me to get ready at a friend's place, so Mona's older sister picked us up from school and we started the *voorpret* with churros.

Mona convinced me to let her do my hair and makeup. I called Mom and put her on speaker phone while Mona gave me smoky eyes.

"What sort of shoes did you end up getting?" Mom asked.

I pulled away from Mona, gesturing at her to stay quiet. "Oh, some red slip-ons."

"Do they match the dress color?" Mom clearly didn't trust my taste—probably for good reasons. "You don't want two different shades of red."

I glanced at my black Converse and grimaced. "They match perfectly."

"Mona, you'll put some jewelry on her, won't you?" she begged.

"Hell yes, Mrs. A."

When Mom had gone, Mona released me from her eyeshadow brush. "Your mom is adorable. Where are these red shoes?"

I confessed about the Converse, and Mona shook her head.

"I refuse to let it happen. What size are you?" I told her my shoe size. "Same as Keisha. Come on."

Mona grabbed my dress and me, then banged on her sister's door. "Keish! Mimi needs to borrow some shoes to wear with this hot little red number."

Keisha was instantly invested. She examined my dress while I protested weakly, then pulled open her wardrobe to reveal an impressive shoe collection. She selected a pair of strappy black heels.

"Try these with some black accessories."

Mona made me get dressed, shoes and all, then added black rose-shaped earrings and a velvet choker with a matching rose pendant. She held a big blue zirconia pendant against her chest and looked at it critically.

"Statement piece, I think." Against the odds, Mona's dress had arrived on time and fitting perfectly. It looked gorgeous on her—long, satiny and just casual enough to suit a school dance.

"What do you think?" she asked when we were done.

We stood side by side in front of the full-length mirror. Mona had badgered Keisha to cornrow her shoulder-length hair, and her curves looked incredible encased in the clinging dress. The zirconia hung on a long silver chain around her neck and she'd added big silver bangles. On her feet she wore jute wedges. She looked summery and full of fun.

My red dress had a flaring skirt and V-neck that gave the impression of curves where I had much less than Mona. Although I was wobbly in the heels, they made my legs look long and toned. The black rose pendant sat nestled in the hollow of my neck. Mona had barely touched my hair, declaring it to be "naturally awesome." All she'd done was clip it up at a couple of invisible points to give it a trendier style. She'd made me up with red lips and eyes smokier than a forest fire. I couldn't hold in my delight to see us both looking so good.

"You're amazing, Mona."

"You're an easy subject to work with."

I sent Mom photos and then we heard the doorbell, so I wobbled down the stairs on my heels after Mona. Her mom had let Gabe and Ed inside, and they both looked great. Gabe was in jeans and a fitted button-down shirt that showed off his physique—which, I suddenly noticed, was pretty fine. Ed was cute and scruffy with his dreads, a surf tee and yellow high-tops.

Gabe didn't make a secret of his admiration. "Damn!" he exclaimed, opening his eyes wide. "You just... *Damn!*"

"What he said." Ed gave us both hugs. "You two look *hot*!"

That was kind of a weird note on which to introduce the boys to Mona's mom. We got out of there in a hurry, bundling into Ed's brother's car: a red eighties number with gleaming silver spoilers. Mona's mom gave Ed a stern look before we drove away, but I liked his driving. He was focused and careful.

Was this what it felt like to be normal? Here I was, Mimi Alston, styled and heading to the school dance with two great guys and an amazing girlfriend. Only a couple of months before, I'd lived in neutral hide-me clothes, trying to be invisible. Even my ghosts had decided not to come in the car with me tonight. They were around somewhere—I could still sense them—but not sitting in our laps, for which I was enormously grateful.

"I feel for the kids who lost good standing," Mona was saying. "Imagine being in the dorms and having to watch everyone get dressed up and put on makeup."

"Or sitting at home while everyone sends you fit-check selfies," Gabe added.

Unbidden, Drew jumped into my head. What would he think if he saw me looking so good? *In your face, Drew.* But he would never see me looking so good because he was at home, probably writing a poem about how excruciatingly scorn-worthy people who went to school dances were.

Gabe reached for my hand, and I shot him a look. He stopped. "Thought I felt you having a black moment," he said apologetically.

He was too sweet. I gave his hand a squeeze, then released it.

The dance committee had set up disco lights in the gym and a tenth-grade girl was acting as DJ. Cassie came over to greet us like she was the host of this party. She was on her best behavior, squealing that we looked *beeeea-u-ti-fullll*, then waiting patiently for us to compliment her in return. Actually, she looked fabulous in a short, tight baby-pink dress and the highest heels I'd ever seen. How on earth could she walk? I'd already stumbled twice on my mid-heels. Gabe even had to catch me once, preventing me from face-planting into the snack table.

"Tyler bought me a corsage," Cassie whispered. She seemed happier than I'd seen her since we met. "Isn't that sweet? It's not even prom!" She showed us a blush rose with baby's breath in her hair, casting an adoring glance over at Tyler, who was laughing with his friends. "I'll see you later." She tottered off to join them.

This dance wasn't at all like I remembered my elementary school dances being, but sort of what I'd expected: loud music, some occasional dance floor drama and regular warnings from teachers when couples got too close.

Axel appeared, dressed in a surf shirt, jeans and trainers. He had his hair gelled into messy spikes that were more like thick stalagmites—a unique look.

"This is sick, eh?" he said, his eyes bright behind his glasses. I'd never heard him say "sick" before, and it jarred. "Do you want to dance, Mona?"

Mona consented, a little bemused. She only gave him one dance, though, then danced with several different guys and in a group. Axel came to ask me next. We danced holding hands, with his arm around my waist like he'd been having lessons. I didn't particularly enjoy it.

"Patience not here tonight?" he asked.

"She's not a fan of dances, I think."

"Bummer." He paused and glanced over at Ed, who was loading up a plate with sushi. "These lights are sick."

Oh my God. He was mimicking Ed. Not that Ed spoke like that—did anyone say "sick" anymore? But Axel was obviously attempting a surfer style: the t-shirt, the trainers, the attempts at something like dreadlocks. Slang. He'd transitioned from trying Drew's style on for size and now he was trying Ed's. Pity gnawed at me. He was so lost. Even I was doing better than Axel at our new school, socially speaking.

"Yeah," I said brightly. "Sick. The music's not bad, either."

He grinned. "You like it?"

"I hate it," I confessed.

He did a double take, then laughed. It might have been the first glimpse of the real Axel anyone'd had all night.

I danced a few times, but only when the floor was crowded and I could blend in. Definitely not to any of the slow dances. I made sure Axel was included in the circle when we danced as a group, although I could see others found him uninteresting, maybe even annoying.

But I claimed sore feet from Keisha's heels when Gabe tried to pull me up to the floor for the final song of the night. It was a couples' dance. He scolded me for breaking his heart and sat down beside me to watch. Cassie and Tyler attempted to steal a passionate kiss and got broken up by Mr. Lemmon. Mona stared at them from where she was dancing with Axel. She was frowning through the speckling disco lights.

"Mona's worried about Cassie," Gabe said as if he'd read my thoughts. "She's been anxious all night. I asked her why, and she said, 'The pink rose.'"

"Huh?"

"That's what I said."

Then a memory strobed into my mind. "Oh! Drew's vision!"

Gabe had to be reminded that a pink rose was one of the things Drew had seen in a vision. "Oh, yeah. Doesn't mean it's *that* rose he saw, though. He didn't say he'd seen the rose in Cassie's hair—just the rose, right?"

"But that's how his visions work."

I chewed my lip until all the lipstick was gone. Cassie wasn't exactly a friend, but she was one of us. I didn't like the thought of her being in danger—or even at risk of a minor incident. I pictured someone spilling a cola down her baby-pink dress. Snarky as she could be, this was a special night in her life, and I didn't want anything to ruin it for her.

I got up and crossed to Cassie where she was standing by the dance floor with Tyler, looking sour.

"Can I talk to you?"

Her mood spilled out onto me. "What do you want?"

I moved to her other side so Tyler couldn't hear. "Drew had a vision of a pink rose, remember?" I nodded toward the one in her hair.

"What?"

"Drew had a vision—"

"I heard you. So what?"

Seriously? After what had happened to her aunt? "I just thought you might want to be careful. I don't want you to get hurt."

"The only person who's going to get hurt tonight is Mr. Lemmon if he doesn't stop interfering in my love life." She glowered at the teacher, who was patrolling the dance floor, looking for more public displays of affection to stifle.

I crossed back to Gabe. He was smiling wryly. "She took that well, then?"

"She wouldn't listen."

"There's no point, Mimi. Cassie's so mad at Lemmon right now, I'm frankly amazed she hasn't tried to summon a bear."

A few minutes later, the dance was all over. Mr. Lemmon switched on the overhead lights, then Mr. Boxe thanked the organizing committee and directed everyone to pack up the chairs and tables. Not a particularly atmospheric end to the evening.

Gabe and I walked Mona and Ed to the gate. Mona's sister was already waiting for her, and Ed waved out the window as he edged his brother's car onto the road. Tyler was driving Cassie home to her place and spun his wheels as he turned out of the car park. His car looked like a heap of junk to me, and there was a blend of appreciative hoots and derisive laughs from the weekend boarders still hovering. I chewed my lip so hard it bled.

Mr. Boxe locked the gates and everyone trailed to the dorms. Gabe walked slowly, falling behind the crowds, despite my attempts to hurry him along. I couldn't wait to get these shoes off. At the point where the path forked in one direction to the boys' dorm and the other way to the girls', I turned and said goodnight, but Gabe didn't leave. He stood there and eyed me.

I eyed him back and put up my mental walls. "You're not feeling for feelings, are you, Gabriel?"

He grinned. "Only a little."

"Stop."

"I'm kidding. But some feedback would be helpful."

"Feedback? Dance moves, five out of five."

"Style?" He spread out his arms to show off his outfit.

"Four, just to keep you humble."

"Ouch! Chivalry? How'd you like that moment when you stumbled on your heels and I caught you?"

"Five for effort."

"Effort! Oof. What about how it felt? Does *that* get a decent score?"

I hesitated, unsure what to say. Did he have to look so sweetly eager? I didn't want to hurt him.

"Gabe, we're waiting for you!" Mr. Lemmon called from the lit-up entry to the boys' dorm.

He groaned but jogged away, calling, "I want an answer to that, Mimi!" as he went.

I walked back to the girls' dorm, puzzling over it. How did I feel? I was flattered that Gabe was interested in me—

but there was no electric zing. The excitement level, if I had to put a temperature on it, would probably be sitting at warm. My treacherous mind drifted back to the vision of Drew seated on the fountain's edge, his skin dripping with water. Reaching for my hand. Excitement level: scorching.

He was never any good for you.

Anyway, Ms. Deering had banned all romance and I wasn't at Etherall Valley Academy for relationships. Except for getting ready at Mona's place and sharing cookie stashes. And giggling with Patience over spontaneously combusting jellybeans. And worrying about Cassie. And trying not to hurt Gabe. Unease wavered through me. I wasn't doing isolation as well as I normally did.

Back in the dorm, bare feet had never felt so good. The dance-goers collected around the big table in the common room and drank late-night hot chocolates. Mel Borgen glowered at us from her circle of loyal acolytes, loudly criticizing our outfits, trying to self-soothe her disappointment at having missed out on the dance.

Soon enough, Ms. Samvedi pointed us to the bedrooms and told us we had fifteen minutes to take off our makeup or finish chatting. I switched on the light in my bedroom, and had to bite back a squeal of shock. My ghosts were all standing there as if they'd been waiting impatiently for my return.

"At the gate, miss," Hannah said, bobbing her head.

Albert stood tall and straight. "Go out to the gate."

"Gate, kid," Marvin mumbled.

"I can't go out there," I protested. "The dorm doors are locked. Anyway, it's against the rules to leave without permission—especially at ten thirty at night."

"The door's open," Albert said.

"Go to the gate," Hannah insisted.

Hell, how could I do this? I hesitated a moment too long, and they surged toward me. This time I couldn't hold in my exclamation of fear.

"You okay?" Olivia asked, pausing at my open door.

I nodded. "Thought I saw a spider," I lied breathlessly. "Just my imagination."

She laughed and continued on.

The three of them were just inches away. "Okay!" I whispered. "I'll try, but this is going to get me an official warning, you realize that?"

They weren't interested in my argument. They just hovered like they would move into my personal space in a heartbeat if I didn't move right now. I dropped Keisha's heels by the door and checked the corridor. A freshman was walking toward the bathroom, but it was otherwise empty. I dashed down to the common room and crossed the darkened space to the glass doors.

Somehow, they were unlocked.

I opened one as quietly as possible and stepped into the cool night air. My ghosts were already out there, waiting for me.

"The gate," Marvin growled.

"Yeah, I get it!" I snapped.

I shut the door and crept around the side of the dorm, checked the grounds for stray staff members, then ran across the damp lawns to the school gate. I didn't stop until I reached the spiked structure, puffing slightly.

"What now?" I asked Hannah, who was right there.

A rustle in the shrubbery to the side of the gate made my heart do a brief break dance. Raccoon? Opossum? Psychopath?

Drew?

14
On a Beautiful Night

He'd come through the secret fence split. It was the real Drew, too. No makeup. No black clothes. In fact, he was wearing a white t-shirt with jeans. He didn't see me; his gaze was on the lit-up gym where some of the teachers must still be socializing.

"Um, hello?"

"Mimi!"

He was in front of me in three strides, then he stopped as if he'd hit an invisible wall. A harsh parking lot lamp was still on, and it had him in a spotlight, his face pale and strained, his eyes glittering. Even the cords in his neck and his collarbones stood out. He looked utterly uncertain, like he might turn and run at any moment. Then—*oh, God*—he did that thing again, the thing where he ran his eyes all over my face like he couldn't take enough of me in.

I folded my arms defensively. "What are you doing here?"

He didn't answer for a long moment. "It's a beautiful night. I wanted to see the stars."

I turned away. "I'm over your shit."

"Wait," Albert told me.

"Wait!" All the carefully cultivated hostility had been stripped from Drew's voice. "How did you know I was here?"

"My ghosts told me. And you didn't answer my question. *Why* are you here?"

"I needed to speak to you."

I turned back. My skepticism must have been palpable, because Drew raised his hands, palms up, as if to show me he was unarmed.

"I want the truth," I said.

"This is the truth. I've been here for hours, watching from across the road. I wanted to see everyone going to the dance—having fun. I wanted to see you."

I stayed outwardly motionless, pulse hammering.

"A-all of you," he stammered on. "I wanted to see what I was missing out on, because I deserved to miss out. I've been such a…"

"A dick?"

He blinked, then nodded. "Yeah. I've been a dick."

That was satisfying.

"You've been ignoring me at school," he added. It wasn't an accusation—just a statement of fact—but it infuriated me anyway.

"*You've* been avoiding *me* for weeks."

"You're right."

"And screwing with my head. Friendly one minute, pretending I don't exist the next. I can handle people's mental health issues or poor social skills, but your behavior—it's been *mean*, Drew. Childish."

He winced. "Can you forgive me?"

I stared up at the bugs circling the parking lot light, trying to formulate a reply. "I forgive you, but I can't do it anymore." My heart argued loudly with me, trying to stop my words, but my resolution held. "I never know where I stand with you, and that's messed up."

"I know I've been all over the place. I need to explain why. I want to tell you everything."

I couldn't unsee the vulnerability in his face. My iron will corroded rapidly, my breathing growing audible to my own ears. "Go on, then. Tell me everything."

He swung around and paced a few steps, gripping the back of his neck with one hand. "You said I've been wearing armor to stop people from getting close to me because I'm scared I might get hurt. That stung because it was true. I thought I was scared of hurting *them*, but I was more scared of how it would hurt me. What you said—it was like you shot an arrow into a bull's-eye. You forced me to face it, and now all I can see is how spineless I've been. You're right about my visions, too. I'm not causing this stuff to happen; I'm just getting previews. I need to grow up and deal with it. See if I can create some good from it."

I waited. It wasn't enough.

He stopped pacing. "When I met you, it blew my mind. To find out what you'd been living with—your gift. I was disgusted by how weak I'd been. Even though I wanted to get to know you, I thought it was safer for both of us if I stayed away. But I couldn't. I kept getting pulled back to you.

"I must have looked unhinged, sometimes seeking you out and other times avoiding you. Patience knew about it. I asked her to help me stay away from you—to protect you.

She did what she could to prevent us from—" He stopped himself, and I held my breath. "From becoming friends. Even when I didn't want her help, she would remind me of what I was trying to do. I'd hold strong until I needed to see or speak to you again, then I'd buckle."

He stepped closer, voice shaking. "Please, can we start again? I swear I won't be an asshole this time."

My resolve was now dead, upside down at my feet with its little legs curled. Warmth was filling my chest, spreading outward to every extremity like molten honey in my veins.

I tried to keep my voice hard. "You've got one more chance."

His face lit up.

"Ask him about the danger, kid," Marvin rasped in my ear.

The danger? I had to think furiously—then I remembered. "Hang on, what are you talking about, 'safer for both of us' and 'to protect me'? What makes you think I'm in danger?"

Drew scratched his arm, his mouth becoming a tight line. The night seemed to grow colder.

"Drew, you said you'd tell me everything."

He came close and caught my hands, making me jerk backward in shock. "I've seen you in a vision."

I froze, then wrenched my hands away. "When?"

"A while ago."

"How many times?"

"Just once."

"Are you sure it was me?" My throat had gone so tight my voice sounded weird. "You didn't know me until a few weeks ago. Maybe I just look a bit like the person you saw."

He shook his head. "It was just over a year ago, and it—it made an impression."

It was my turn to pace. "But you've had visions that have turned out to be nothing sinister, right? The spilled coffee and the shark's tooth necklace. Or even near misses, like the silver bus. There've only been a couple of instances where your vision ended up in injury or…" I couldn't say the word.

Drew looked how I felt: like he was barely holding it together.

"What exactly did you see?" I demanded.

"Your face. Underwater."

"*Underwater?*" My demand wavered. "Drowned?"

He nodded wordlessly. I turned away, trying to process it. My lungs were abruptly unable to capture any oxygen, and when I tried to suck in more, it ended up as a sob. Drew was there in an instant, folding himself around me, capturing me in a hug so I tight I could hear his heartbeat and smell his skin.

"I don't know what it means," he whispered against my hair. "Maybe it isn't what it seemed." He released his hold so he could see me. "It could be something else, right?"

My tears were still leaking. "I don't want to die." The confession fought its way out, against all my efforts to choke it.

Drew pulled me close again, his words coming as a fierce whisper. "I won't let you."

I held on tight, not about to let go unless I absolutely had to. Which happened an instant later when a voice came from the direction of the gate.

"Drew! Mimi! Let me in!"

It was Cassie, standing barefoot and disheveled on the other side of the gate. She still wore her baby-pink dress, but the stilettos were missing and the rose hung tangled in her hair beside her ear, most of the petals gone.

Drew and I dashed over to her. "What happened?" I asked, wiping my eyes. "I thought you were going home?"

"I was. We were going to drive to a lookout so we could make out before Tyler took me home. But he didn't go to the lookout. He kept driving and wouldn't stop, even when I screamed at him."

My stomach flipped sickeningly. Cassie's face, now we were near enough to see it properly, was a veneer of fury over deep-set horror.

"I tried to get out of the car and he grabbed my arm, wouldn't let go. It was so weird. I don't know what he thought he was going to do." A shudder ran through her.

"Come through," I urged her. "There's a split in the fence."

Drew ran for the shrubbery and dived in, emerging on Cassie's side of the fence. He guided her back into school grounds the same way.

"Come here." I put my arm around Cassie's cold shoulders. She tensed for a moment, but permitted my arm to stay. "How did you get away?"

"He had to slow down to go around a bend. I was scared—shouting at him, trying to pull my arm away—then suddenly I imagined myself a wolf, snarling and biting. I've never felt anything like it before. A couple of moments later, three dogs were right there, in front of the car. Tyler hit the brakes, then they had their heads through his window, growling and barking like wolves, snapping at his face. I got the door open and sort of fell out while Tyler was trying to fend them off. He drove away—with my phone still in his damn passenger seat." Her eyes were enormous with shock and fear. "Turned out the dogs were just a couple of black retrievers and an Alsatian. They were licking my hands and whimpering like they were upset, too. I was terrified Tyler would come back, so I asked them to stay with me while I got some help. He didn't come back, though. I sent the dogs home as soon as I came into view of the school."

She held on to me for balance and lifted one foot, then the other, examining them in the parking lot light. I gasped. They were torn up and bloody.

"That asshole still has my beautiful shoes. I've walked three miles barefoot on the road. Oh my God, I want to kill him. My mom and dad are probably in a frenzy by now—I was supposed to be home ages ago."

"Let's go inside," I said. "Ms. Samvedi will know what to do."

We started toward the dorm, then I stopped short and looked at Drew.

He read my meaning. "Yeah, I'm not supposed to be here. And you're not supposed to be outside."

"Leave," I told him. "Go home. I'll tell Ms. Samvedi I spotted Cassie from the dorm window."

He nodded and jogged back toward the split in the fence.

I supported Cassie to walk on her sore feet back to the girls' dorm. The ruckus when we arrived back was pretty extreme, but Ms. Samvedi was the personification of efficiency. She pulled Cassie and me into her office, called for backup—luckily, some of the other staff were still in the gym—then got us to tell her the full story. We left out the bits about Drew being there and Cassie mystically channeling wolves.

Ms. Samvedi summoned Cassie's parents, then phoned the police to let them know they'd be coming in to make a report. Last of all, she washed and bandaged Cassie's feet and inspected the big, hand-shaped bruise blooming on her left arm. If only Ed were here. He could have her injuries sorted out in a second. Cassie's dad turned up after about forty-five minutes, looking strained and pale. He took her away, clutching her close to his side.

"I think you'd better call your parents too, Mimi," Ms. Samvedi said after she'd chased all the other girls back into their rooms. "Mr. Boxe and I will be emailing all parents to advise that an incident has occurred, and everyone is safe, but I think you ought to let yours know about your involvement."

I chewed my lip for a few moments. "I'd rather call them tomorrow, if that's okay. It's almost midnight and my mom will freak out if I call now. She won't sleep. I'll tell them in the morning."

Ms. Samvedi assented, then peered at me. "I don't quite understand how you spotted Cassie from the dorm. None of the windows face the school gate."

The ever-present shadows moved a little closer from the corners of the room. I sat in silence, hoping she'd let it go.

No such luck. "Mimi? Were you already outside?"

I weighed up my options while panicking, which was about as easy as it sounds. "Yes," I blurted at last. "I saw the door was unlocked so I stepped out. Just for a minute."

"Why?" The shadows swooped and slithered.

I gave the first excuse that landed in my head. "It's a beautiful night. I wanted to see the stars."

"Need I remind you about seeking permission to leave the dorm at night?"

"No. I know the rules."

"So…?"

"I'm sorry." I kept my eyes down. "I was buzzing after the dance. I needed some air. I wasn't going to do anything wrong. I wasn't sneaking out to meet anyone. I just needed to breathe."

She evaluated my story as only a woman who works with teenage girls every day can. "I think you ought to visit Mr. Lemmon this coming week."

Mr. Lemmon. School therapist by day, boys' dorm head by night. I sagged. "Really?"

"Just for a bit of extra support."

Gossip around the dorm was off the charts. There were dozens of emails and Collabor8 chats between the gifted kids, too. For us weekend boarders, the lack of access to our phones was a source of major inconvenience.

Mom was so freaked out about what had happened with Cassie that she wanted to come down and see me immediately. It took a massive effort to talk her out of it. Honestly, it would have been better *not* to tell Mom I was the one standing there when Cassie got back. It only made her fret.

Somehow, Mona found out about everything that followed. Cassie had made a police report. Tyler had been called in for questioning. Of course, he denied any of it happened. He said they were parked, chatting in the car, when the dogs came and attacked him through the window. That he panicked and drove off, leaving Cassie there. I mean, that would have been poor form too, but not quite on the level of unlawful restraint. Cassie was determined to see him pay for what he did. We all sent her messages of support.

As if that wasn't enough to churn me up, Drew's vision kept dropping into my head at odd times, stinging like a graze exposed to cold air. The next minute, I was high on the memory of seeing him so bare and honest. I kept replaying the vulnerability in his face, the burst of electricity when he touched me. The yearning to feel his arms around me again was as wild as roaring whitewater, and I didn't know what to do with it. I fidgeted and paced around the dorm all weekend, unable to focus on anything except drawing.

I couldn't wait to see him again and at the same time dreaded it. All I wanted was to hold his gaze like it was just us in the entirety of the world. But what would we say to each other next time we met? I contemplated messaging him, but my courage failed me. I checked my laptop a thousand times, but Drew didn't reach out. Maybe his courage was failing him, too.

When Monday came, it felt like Christmas. Unfortunately, Ms. Samvedi hadn't forgotten her ruling, and I was required to visit Mr. Lemmon before school. He was a tall, skinny guy with thick black hair and a colorful shirt. He had a chunky garnet ring on one hand, like a championship souvenir. Former basketballer? I'd met more than my fair share of school counselors, chaplains and youth workers over the years. There was definitely a type.

"Ms. Samvedi tells me you're experiencing a few bumps in the settling-in process," he said.

I'd made up my mind to get through this as quickly as possible. "No, honestly, it's been good. People are being really nice to me."

"But you've got a penchant for wandering?"

"A what?"

"A habit. You like wandering." He cocked his head, smiling. The shadows swooped a little.

"Um, no. That's not really fair. I messed up by trying to skip PE, but I won't do it again. On Friday night, I just wanted some fresh air. I didn't realize it was breaking the rules just to step outside. I thought I would only be doing something wrong if I actually went somewhere."

"And you didn't go anywhere? To talk to Gabriel Cavendish, perhaps?"

"No!" I said it so vehemently, he held up a hand.

"All right. Just checking."

"Seriously, I really like EVA. I'm not going to mess this up if I can help it. I don't always pay attention when people are explaining things to me, though—maybe I missed a couple of the rules when I first enrolled."

"There's no issues with the other students, then?"

"Definitely not."

"What about your anxiety? Is it manageable?"

I gave him a half-smile. "It's at about a six. Manageable."

Mr. Lemmon smiled back. "Well, is there anything in the rules you'd like to go over now, if you didn't take it in when you first enrolled?"

It was the perfect way to get out of this session without having to spill my inner feelings. I asked him to go over the EVA code of conduct with me, and the rest of the session was relatively painless. Mr. Boxe went past the office door at one point and caught sight of me through the glass. He did a one-eighty, knocking on the door and coming straight in before Mr. Lemmon even answered.

"How's our newest student?" he asked.

Even I knew the rudimentaries of client confidentiality in a therapy situation. Mr. Lemmon was frowning, and the shadows swooshed so busily in the corners of his office that I couldn't help flicking them a nervous look.

"I'm fine, thanks." I gave Mr. Boxe a tight smile. "And don't forget about Axel—he's just as new as me."

"Oh, of course!" He slapped his cheek lightly, as if punishing himself. "So everything's tickety-boo with you, Mimi?"

Apparently we were talking like Victorian orphans now. "Yes, it's just that Ms. Samvedi thought I should go over things with Mr. Lemmon after what went down on the weekend, that's all."

The principal's face fell like I'd given his school a bad online review. "Yes. That's fair. It was an awful thing to have happened. I'm truly sorry you had to be involved."

"I wasn't really involved. Anyway, Cassie's okay—that's the main thing. And she's safe from that di—I mean, that guy."

Mr. Boxe looked even gloomier. "Yes."

I took the opportunity to escape. "Do you mind if I go now, Mr. Lemmon?" I asked, getting to my feet. "I don't want to be late for homeroom."

Mr. Lemmon said I could go, and I left them murmuring together in the counselor's office. As soon as I exited the room, relief washed through me and the shadows backed off. Maybe if Ms. Samvedi had known how going for a session with Mr. Lemmon would ratchet up my stress levels, she would've let me get on with my life without the extra "support."

In homeroom, I was confronted by a sight that would thrill any red-blooded straight girl: two handsome guys who sat straighter when I walked in, and both smiled like I was the best thing they'd seen all morning. Gabe touched the chair beside him and Drew nodded at me with an invitation in his eyes. I froze, not wanting to send the wrong message to either of them. I spotted Cassie and sat with her instead.

"You okay?" I murmured.

"I sure am," she said, her jaw set. "I've been telling the rumor spreaders some home truths all morning and working out who my real friends are. There's nothing like a social cull."

I gave her a fist bump, and we sat in silence for a minute. I was thinking about the moment she'd turned up at the gate, then about the moment before that when Drew had his arms around me. Across the room, he caught and held my gaze. I somehow went hot and shivery at the same time.

"Sorry I didn't listen to you." Cassie's words came out stilted, and she looked like she would rather eat glass than be saying this. "At the dance."

"It's fine."

We left it at that.

During gifted class, Cassie told everyone exactly what had happened with Tyler. She had a spectacular bruise on her upper arm and was still in pain with her feet, so Ed got her to take off her shoes, then he sat on the floor beside her chair and held her feet while she talked. By the time she'd recounted the events, the skin of her soles was perfect. Not a scratch or a blister.

Patience, who'd been listening with her eyes wide and horrified, reached over and put her hand on Cassie's. "I'll pray to God that the scars on your heart and virtue heal."

Cassie burst into laughter. "Um, okay. My virtue's my business, not God's, but thanks for the thought. I'm going to be okay, as long as that asshole gets what's coming to him. Mel Borgen is already trying to tell anyone who'll listen that I made the whole thing up." She pulled a face. "I just wish I'd gotten the dogs to remove the parts of him that can do other girls harm."

"It's incredible, how you called them," Ms. Deering said. "So you didn't consciously compel them, like you've been doing when you practice?

"No, it was totally different. I imagined myself as one of them, and then they came to my rescue."

"I wonder if the adrenaline of the situation enhanced your ability," Mona mused. "Or allowed you to connect directly with the animals, instead of talking to them as a human."

Cassie shook out her curls and grinned wickedly. "I love being able to defend myself."

"I was worried all night." Mona put down her pen. "As soon as I saw Cassie wearing the pink rose from Drew's vision. I wish I'd said something."

Cassie grimaced and shot me a look. "Not sure I would have listened. I was kinda focused on Tyler."

"I screwed up worse," Gabe said unexpectedly. "I've always had a strange vibe from Tyler. The guy hides his feelings, and the ones that slip out from time to time are ugly. I should have warned Cassie ages ago—when I first saw her hanging around with that crew."

Cassie groaned. "Could you stop blaming yourselves? Mimi mentioned the rose to me, if you must know, and I ignored her. And yet I know better than anyone what Drew's visions mean, since my aunt's accident."

My throat seemed to dry up as she said the words, and I bent my head, drawing a little set of pawprints running up the side of my sketchpad to distract myself. I didn't look at Drew.

Mona was still caught up on what Gabe had said. "What do you mean, Tyler hides his feelings?" she asked.

"It's hard to describe. Some people keep their emotional volume down low. Others are up high. The majority are in the middle."

"So you can easily tell what the loud people are feeling, but not others?" Mona was intrigued. Her pen nib hovered over her page.

"Loud doesn't mean clear," Gabe told her. "I feel it when people are having strong emotions, but I can't always distinguish what they are."

"Do you have to be near the person to pick up the signal?" Ed wanted to know.

"Yeah. Same room, preferably. With the loud feelers, I can pick up on their emotion through walls—it spills out into the space around them. Quieter feelers, I need to fish around a bit."

I looked up, remembering the times he'd poked around in my feelings. "But people can feel you fishing, can't they?"

"Some can. Not many." He grinned at me. "The clever ones can mentally slap me for it."

"Mimi can feel your brain-vasions?" Mona squinted at him suspiciously. "Have you ever tried fishing for my feelings?"

Gabe waggled his eyebrows. "That would be telling."

Her squint became a glare. "If I ever catch you in there, I'm gonna kick your ass into next week."

The others chimed in their agreement, even Drew.

Gabe chortled. "Don't have to go fishing with you, Drew. You're an open book. Your emotions are screaming every time I'm anywhere near you." Drew looked dismayed. "I have to shut you out a bit sometimes."

Drew stared at his desk, coloring deeply—and because he had no makeup on, we could all see it.

"What's going on with the look, Drew?" As always, Mona was the first to come straight out with it.

He didn't meet anyone's eye. "I've been covering up. I'm not going to do it anymore. Mimi made me see that I was running away."

Mona looked aggrieved. "I could have told you that the first day you put on your costume."

"You look much better like this." Cassie examined him head to toe, somewhat clinically, without the least attempt to hide it. "You're actually quite hot, Drew. And now the freshmen won't be terrified whenever they see you in the schoolyard, so that's something."

"I'd almost forgotten what he looked like under all that goth," Ed remarked.

"It's so clean and simple," Mona said. "Like when you reset your phone and all the pointless apps are gone."

Drew kept his eyes fixed on his desk, his cheeks still flaming.

Gabe, however, was frowning at him. "What do you mean, 'Mimi made you see' you were running away?"

Drew shrugged. "No matter what gets thrown at her, she just handles it."

Now it was my turn to blush.

"Oh my God," Cassie said. "I might vomit. When did we get all warm and fuzzy?"

Gabe was looking back and forth between me and Drew, his expression perturbed. I felt a little nudge at my consciousness and shot him a warning glare. *Don't you dare*.

Mona took the heat off us. "It's amazing. Since Mimi came to Etherall Valley, we've all come so much further than we've ever gone before. It used to be so *individual*, you know? All of us experiencing little bits and pieces of our gifts from time to time. But now, it's like we're getting closer to working as a team every time!"

Watching Mona's bright eyes dance brought a smile to my lips. Pride bubbled unexpectedly inside me at the thought of being essential. Look at them: Ed sitting there healing Cassie's feet while she admitted she should have listened to us. Drew confessing how he'd been hiding behind his armor and promising he wouldn't anymore. A decision solidified deep inside me: I was *not* going to be consumed by the vision Drew had told me about.

Hopefully he wouldn't tell the others. I didn't want anything to change in our group dynamic, especially if it meant they might treat me differently. Maybe my life was in danger. But I was Mimi Alston, girl with the ghosts, and I'd been afraid and in isolation for *years* before I arrived here in the circle of seven. The prospect of dying wasn't going to scare me back into misery now.

15
Garage Sale Negotiations

Ping.
Gabriel Cavendish has opened a Collabor8 under GIFTED
PROGRAM PROJECT.
Accept?

Gabriel: *Miette Alston.*
Miette: *Gabriel Cavendish. What's going on?*
Gabriel: *Just wanted to talk. You busy?*
Miette: *Doing homework.*
Gabriel: *Can you take a break? I want to ask you something.*
Miette: *I guess so. You can explain to Mr. Bin Osman why my geography assignment is late tomorrow.*
Gabriel: *Consider it done.*
Miette: *What can I help you with?*
Gabriel: *Since you're so good at blocking my attempts to catch your emotional vibe, I thought I'd better come out and ask.*
Miette: *That is the conventional human method, yes.*
Gabriel: *So, can we have an open conversation?*
Miette: *Of course.*
Gabriel: *I want to know how you feel about you and me.*
Gabriel: *You there?*
Miette: *I'm here.*

Gabriel: *Mimi, I'm going to tell you the truth. I like you. I REALLY like you. I hope you like me too, but I'm not sure.*

Miette: *Of course I like you.*

Gabriel: *And?*

Miette: *You're a really great guy.*

Gabriel: *And?*

Miette: *And a good friend.*

Gabriel: *Oof. There's the smackdown.*

Miette: *I'm a bit of a noob at friendship, but I think we have a pretty good one. Why risk that by changing it?*

Gabriel: *I've changed it already and I like it even better.*

Miette*: Gabe, I'm sorry, but I don't think I'm ready for anything else. I've just started at EVA. I'm trying to get my head around having friends, being in the gifted group, my studies. Everything.*

Gabriel: *And then there's Drew.*

Miette: *Please.*

Gabriel: *He's into you.*

Miette: *What?*

Gabriel: *He said he wasn't when I asked him after that day at the market, but he spills his feelings everywhere.*

Miette: *Don't tell me his feelings.*

Gabriel: *You don't want to know?*

Miette: *It's not fair. You don't even know what his feelings are. You said yourself you don't always recognize what they mean.*

Gabriel: *Yeah, but when you come into the room, he gets on a rollercoaster. One minute, he's in a silent scream. Next minute, there's a great big tornado of happy that lifts him up out of his usual misery. Sunshine, lollipops, rainbows, etc. I recognize it. It's a lot like the feeling I get when I see you.*

Miette: *Stop, Gabe.*

Gabriel: *You've got a thing for him, haven't you?*

Miette: *I'm trying to discuss this maturely here.*

Gabriel: *You're private, hard to read, but you drift away from other people when he's around.*

Miette: *Stop.*

Gabriel: *I was hoping it was just your curiosity about him. Last couple of weeks, you even seemed to dislike him. Hence asking you to the dance.*

Miette: *Stop it, Gabe! I don't want to talk about this.*

Gabriel: *Why won't you be honest with me?*

Miette: *It's not your business.*

Gabriel: *Come on, Mimi. You're good at hiding how you feel, but not that good. If it's him, just come out and say so.*

Miette: *You're being really unfair. Stay out of my head.*

You have left the session.

Great, now I was angry-crying. *Thanks for putting that tension between us, Gabe.* Hell, he'd taken me to one dance—supposedly as friends—and he thought we had a thing? I liked being Gabe's friend and didn't want to lose that. What was wrong with not wanting to take things further?

And if *Drew* were asking me…?

I pushed the thought away.

The trouble with Gabe was that he'd begun to rely on his gift instead of using normal methods of understanding people. Then when their emotions were mixed, or changed rapidly, he felt ripped off. Tricked.

Well, that wasn't my fault. And I shouldn't be obliged to confess everything to him just because he had his own exclusive advance screening of my feelings, either. I was entitled to my privacy, no matter what glimmers of the truth he saw. Then I thought about Gabe's sweetness to that freshman Juliet, and how good he'd been to me since I started at EVA, and felt bad. I didn't want to be his enemy. Perhaps I could pour this out to Mona—maybe even get her to talk to Gabe.

After study hour, I visited Mona in her room. I longed to unburden, but by the time she'd let me in and settled me on her bed with a contraband brownie slice, I'd lost courage. I watched her scribbling in her ubiquitous notebook.

"What are you writing?" I asked.

"Stuff about Cassie's wild dog experience."

"Why?"

She paused. "I don't know. I feel compelled to. I write about all the things that get talked about in class, or whenever I hear or read something I think might be relevant. And the things that happen from day to day—Ms. Deering's intuitions. Your ghosts talking to you. Gabe's strange vibe about Juliet. Drew's visions."

Drew's visions... "How far back do your notes go?"

"Since I started in the gifted program. I've got three notebooks full of stuff. You can see them if you like. I don't mind the gifted crew seeing them."

Three! My heart sank, but I nodded. "Yes, please."

Mona told me to turn around. I heard her digging among papers, maybe even moving furniture, behind my back.

"Okay," she said after a few moments. "No offense, but I have a super-secret hiding spot I don't tell anyone about.

That's where I keep the notebooks." She held out three identical spiral-bound notebooks.

"Thanks." I lay back on her bed to start reading.

I flipped through the books as Mona switched over to her German homework. There was a lot in each book, but she'd organized it all by date and name.

Drew: laptop on bed with words "astronomical events" typed into the search bar. Blue beach towel with picture of unicorn.

There were entries about me in the most recent one.

Mimi: "Albert" told her not to let Ed and Cassie visit aunt after 4pm.

I went back to around the time when Drew started at EVA and read all the entries about him I could find. There were a lot.

"You catching up on the history of the gifted program?" Mona asked me after I'd been lying there flipping pages for half an hour. "Crash course?"

I smiled. "Guess so."

I kept reading. Mona finished her German and went on to geography, sighing frequently because it was climate studies, and apparently the one thing she hated deciphering was a pressure system.

Finally I found what I was looking for. The word *drowned* leapt out at me from an entry written a year ago, stuck between an account of Patience conjuring a doll for her sister and Mona's translation of an overheard conversation about achieving a higher state through meditation.

Drew: dead girl's face underwater, eyes closed. He doesn't know her, but thinks she's someone important.

A shudder racked my body. Somehow, seeing it written in ballpoint pen on ordinary lined paper, dated a year earlier, made it real. Hannah sat beside me and laid a single ice-cold finger on my hand, as light as a snowflake.

I jumped up, freeing myself of her touch, and snapped the book shut. "Fascinating," I declared. "Thanks, Mona. I'll leave you to the joys of barometric pressures."

"Thanks," Mona said wryly. "See you at dinner."

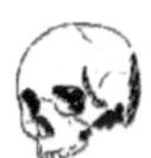

Thanks to Gabe, homeroom was officially relocated to Awkward City. When I arrived the morning after our Collabor8 conversation, he was talking with Cassie. He only paused to give me a cool glance, then went back to his conversation.

I went to sit with Drew, who'd noticed the exchange. "What's with Gabe?" he asked.

I bent over my sketchpad and let my hair fall so he wouldn't see my face. "Who knows?"

But at lunchtime, sitting with Drew, Mona, Patience and Ed, the topic was a hit. "Gabe's super pissed at you," Mona announced, squeezing ketchup over her mashed potato.

"I haven't done anything," I said, aggrieved.

Mona looked up. "I was actually talking to Drew, not you."

The blush was deep and painful. Drew raised his eyebrows at her. "Me? What did I do?"

"He called you a lying, two-faced *something* I can't repeat in front of Patience." Mona peered at us both. "Ah. This is about Mimi." She chuckled. "I should have known."

I glared down at my food tray, dying inside. "If he must be annoyed, he could just be annoyed with me. It's got nothing to do with anyone else."

"Does Gabe think Drew stole you away from him?" Patience sounded shocked.

Mona had the full story and didn't hesitate to enlighten Patience. "A couple of weeks ago, Gabe cornered Drew and asked if he was interested in Mimi. Gabe was planning to ask her to the dance but first wanted to check if there was something already going on with Mimi and Drew. Drew told him to go for it, and now Gabe says Drew's broken the deal because he and Mimi are"—she peered at me—"whatever they are."

Drew and I studiously avoided eye contact.

"If he was so serious about it, he should have said so," he muttered.

A vestige of pride reared up in me. "Maybe there shouldn't be *negotiations* behind my back, like I'm something you both spotted at a garage sale and Gabe thought he'd better check if you wanted it first."

Mona laughed so hard she almost spat out her mashed potato.

Ed was grinning too. "It's not 'negotiations,' Mimi. Gabe was just trying to make sure he wasn't muscling in on another dude's hot prospect."

"It'd be nice if the *prospect* was asked for her opinion."

"Okay." Ed gestured at me. "What does the prospect want?"

"Respect, for a start."

"Um, this is high school dating," Mona reminded me. "But I admire your idealism."

By Friday, Gabe was still ignoring me and still glaring at Drew. I braced myself for the hour in gifted class with him. Homeroom was bad enough, but at least there were twelve or so kids in there to dilute the effect of his anger. But with just the seven of us, Drew and I would be direct targets.

But Gabe wasn't there. Ms. Deering said he had an appointment and handed out notices she'd emailed to our parents. We all read them curiously.

Dear Parent/Guardian,
Gifted program students are to attend a team-building weekend at Blackmere Pool Forest Cabins from the 10th to 12th of this month.
The weekend will include trust and confidence games and other recreational activities. Attending staff include Ms. Bronwyn Deering and Mr. Theodore Boxe.
Weekday boarders will not go home on the Friday, but stay at school so all students can go straight to camp by bus after

school. They will return to school on Sunday afternoon and may go home for the night or remain at school, depending on your preference.

Please return the attached medical form and permission slip as soon as possible.

"Mr. Boxe is coming?" Cassie's nose wrinkled. "Why?"

Ms. Deering looked apologetic. "I've been feeling like you seven need time together to really connect, which is why I organized the camp. Because it's such a small group, I thought we'd be exempt from the school policy of a minimum of two staff for an overnight activity, but apparently even the gifted program can't get away with flouting that rule. Mr. Boxe put his hand up to come along. He used to work at a recreational park in Davenport and absolutely loves that sort of thing."

"He's going to cramp our style," Mona said.

"Mr. Boxe is a good man," Patience said in her soft voice.

"Yeah, but he doesn't know about our gifts," Cassie drawled. "Which means we'll need to hide them."

Ed moaned a bit about missing out on surfing for the weekend, and Patience wondered out loud if her parents would let her attend. Cassie said the cabins had better not be too basic, and Mona claimed she was an expert at camping after her years in the Girl Scouts. I just sat there feeling pumped. A whole weekend with all of them. With Drew.

He didn't look quite as happy. In fact, he was reading the note again in the seat beside me, his jaw clenched.

Blackmere Pool.

"Will there be swimming?" I asked Ms. Deering. "Or canoeing?"

"No," she said. "Unfortunately, the school's insurance won't cover swimming without lifeguards present. The weather's getting too cool for watersports, anyway."

I nudged Drew, and the corner of his mouth quirked into a half-smile. My heart did its own little flashmob. This camp was going to be amazing.

Ping.
Gabriel Cavendish has opened a Collabor8 under GIFTED PROGRAM PROJECT.
Accept?

Not now, Gabe.
It was Friday afternoon, study hour was almost up and I was contemplating emailing Drew to ask if he wanted to do something over the weekend. Frankly, I couldn't handle a grim conversation with Gabe while I was mustering the courage to ask Drew out.

Ping.
Gabriel Cavendish has opened a Collabor8 under GIFTED PROGRAM PROJECT.
Accept?

There was a movement beside me. Hannah was looking at me from where she sat on the end of my bed.

"Let him speak, miss," she advised in a whisper near my ear.

I sighed and accepted the session.

You are in a Collabor8 with CASSANDRA O'MEARA, PATIENCE ROSE and GABRIEL CAVENDISH.

Gabriel: *Hi all.*
Cassandra: *Hi. Where were you today?*
Gabriel: *Got my braces removed, so I took the rest of the afternoon off school to chew gum and eat toffee.*
Patience: *Did it hurt, getting them taken off?*
Gabriel: *I'm fine. I wanted to tell you guys what's happening. I got an email from Juliet and she wants to meet me tomorrow. She's finally ready to talk. I've applied for a day pass.*
Patience: *Have you told Ms. Deering?*
Gabriel: *Kid made me promise not to tell any teachers.*
Cassandra: *What do you think is wrong with her?*
Gabriel: *Something's going on at home, I think. She said she'll wait for me at a park near her place in the afternoon.*
Cassandra: *Gabe, are you sure she doesn't just have a crush on a hot older student?*
Gabriel: *100% sure. Yes, I'm hot, especially with these perfect teeth, but this is serious.*

My attention was caught by Marvin, shifting restlessly on the floor where he'd been sitting slumped against the wall. He and Hannah exchanged a look, then she turned to me.

"You'll need to go with him, miss," she told me.

"I can't," I said. "This is Gabe's thing."

"You must, miss," Albert said.

"Guys, honestly, I can't. Gabe doesn't like me at the moment. Please don't make me do this."

Marvin heaved himself to his feet. He came shuffling toward me with intent. I panicked.

"Okay! Okay."

He stopped and returned to his corner. I reluctantly tapped out the words.

Miette: *My ghosts just said I have to go with you.*
Gabriel: *Not going to happen. I've been working on Juliet for weeks now, trying to gain her trust. She won't talk if there's someone else with me.*
Miette: *Gabe, please. I can't defy them. I have to go with you.*
Gabriel: *Why can't you defy them?*
Miette: *They get upset.*

I could almost feel the irritation in his silence.

Miette: *Please?*
Gabriel: *Fine, but you've got to stay out of sight.*
Miette: *Of course.*
Gabriel: *Get a day pass sorted. I'll see you at the bus stop at 1pm tomorrow.*

16
The Dysfunctional Rescue Squad

I was antsy as hell in the morning, watching my ghosts with half my brain, worrying about being alone with a resentful Gabe with the other half. It wasn't cold, but the sky matched my mood—deep gray clouds, heavy with unwept rain, like it was only waiting for me to step outside before it could hurl itself at me. The smell of it crept in through the window and doorframes.

Axel had emailed to ask if I'd go to the art room with him. It seemed like a good way to ease the chatter in my head. He was already there when I arrived and seemed happy to see me.

"Have you chosen a subject for your personal portrait yet?" he asked when I'd set up an easel and donned my apron.

"Yes. My grandmother. I've emailed my dad for a photo, but he keeps forgetting to send it. Also, Grandma is super fussy about pictures of her and she'll probably hate anything I do." I doubted she'd like a portrait that made her look like a skeleton, either, but I'd deal with that problem later.

Axel was chuckling. "I'm sticking with a safe option: my mom. But I'm cheating. I'm going to do her face in profile, partly turned away. I struggle with getting mouths symmetrical. It's my downfall."

"Mouths are hardly ever symmetrical in real life."

"True, but people expect it in a portrait."

I chatted with him a while longer, delaying starting work. Axel had joined the school's annual production as crew and told me enthusiastically about how good the show was going to be. They were putting on a musical. Cassie had mentioned it already—she had a starring role. Axel was on set design. He spent a good ten minutes trying to talk me into joining the crew. The guy had more school spirit than anyone I'd ever met. It was a shame EVA didn't have student leaders, because Axel really needed something to put his energy into.

Listening to him was becoming more painful than working on my portrait, so I finally set up a canvas and starting blocking in a background. I was tempted to start painting Grandma from memory, but all I could picture was the bones of her temples and that receding jaw. What the hell was wrong with me? It was like I couldn't see people as anything other than a collection of body parts. I'd have to jog Dad's memory about the damn photo.

"Want to take a break?" Axel called across the room midmorning. "I brought tea." He showed me a thermos.

"Tea! That's quaint. What type?"

"Earl Grey, of course."

The dual ideas of Earl Grey tea and taking a break from my unsatisfactory project drew me across the room. Then I realized the shadows had thickened, heaving and roiling in the corners. *What the hell?*

At that moment, Mr. Boxe came into the room. "Hello, hello! You two again? What are you working on now?"

It was hard to concentrate on explaining my project while the corners of the room pulsed with patches of black. My eyes kept sliding upward to check on the shadows.

"Is everything all right, Mimi?" Mr. Boxe was staring at me in perplexity.

"Go back to your sleeping quarters, miss," Albert said in my ear. "Now." He was watching me intently, hovering like he would rush at me any moment.

I backed away, glancing between the shadows and Albert, not sure which I should be most afraid of. "I've had enough," I gabbled, whipping off my apron and practically throwing my brush into the jar of paint thinner. "I'm gonna leave this here to dry. I'll pack it up tomorrow."

I got out of there, leaving Axel and Mr. Boxe staring at me with astonishment on their faces. I half ran back to the dorm, not stopping until I was in my bedroom. Only then did I sink onto my bed and shoot a look at Albert.

"Okay?"

He nodded, his eyes deep behind their dark blur. "All's well now, miss."

"They feed on fear, you know," Hannah said.

"What?"

But she didn't say anything more. Albert sank into my chair, gazing out of the window. Hannah sat on my bed, facing away from me, and Marvin stared at nothing from the corner.

After lunch, I pulled on some shoes, collected my wallet and donned a hoodie. I went and claimed my phone from Ms. Samvedi for the outing. Mel Borgen, perennially without good standing, watched me leave. Her face couldn't have been sourer.

The first thing I did when I got out of the dorm was call my mom.

"Mimi! I didn't expect to hear from you today. How's everything? How's your poor friend?"

I walked toward the gate slowly so I could chat for longer, holding a hand over my ear to shut out the noisy cawing of the crows. "Cassie's good. She's bounced back really strong."

"And have they tossed that boy behind bars and thrown away the key? I've emailed the school to ask a couple of times, but they haven't gotten back to me yet."

"Well, he's still suspended. I'm not sure what's happening. Hopefully they won't let him back in."

"Well, as long as everyone's supporting poor Cassie, that's the important thing."

"How's your new job going?" I asked.

There was a brief pause. "Not too bad."

"Mom?"

"It's fine, honey. It's just a bit of a learning curve."

"You'll be running the place in no time. Did you tell them you've booked your Paris vacation for January? Were they okay with it?"

Another tiny pause. "Yes, that's all fine."

"You sure?"

"Oh, and your brother called. They've set a date! Next November."

"Oh, wow. Are they coming home for the wedding?"

"They're considering having two weddings—one here and one in Québec."

I'd reached the school gate by now and felt much better. Mom's power to comfort never failed. While I waited for a staff member to buzz me out of the gate, I caught sight of Gabe waiting at the bus stop.

"I'd better go, Mom. I'm meeting a friend."

"Is it the boy who took you to the dance?" she wanted to know. "Gabriel?"

I admitted it was, and she wished me a good time, unable to keep the delight out of her voice. But Gabe's expression as he noticed my approach became carefully blank. I sighed inwardly.

He was reading the bus schedule when I stopped beside him. "There's one due now—hopefully it hasn't already gone past. The one after that is due in fifteen minutes, but we'd need to walk a bit further at the other end. It doesn't go by the stop we want."

"There it is," I said, seeing the silver flash of a bus turning into our street in the distance.

We dug out our bus passes. Then Marvin shuffled up and stood right in front of me.

"Not this bus, kid," he wheezed.

"Huh?" I said.

Gabe glanced at me questioningly.

"Get out of sight," Marvin told me.

I grabbed Gabe's arm. "One of my ghosts just told me not to take this bus. And to hide."

His impatience was plain on his face. If Gabe didn't listen to me, I'd have to let him get on the bus alone. No way was I going to refuse Marvin. I tugged at Gabe's arm, and he must have picked up on the fear engulfing me because he muttered a curse and let me lead him around the back of the bus shelter.

The bus pulled in and the doors opened. Some kids got out, chattering. We couldn't see them from where we were hiding behind the timber shelter, but I recognized the voices of EVA girls—sophomores, I thought.

"Well, Mel says Cassie wanted Tyler to be exclusive, but he only wanted to hook up," one said.

"I know. And I wouldn't put it past Tyler, if I'm honest. But trying to, like, practically *kidnap* her? Really?"

"Don't you think it's a little extreme to make up a story like that? Cassie's a bitch, but I didn't think she was this bad. This could ruin his life."

"Mel's got inside info. Tyler's her cousin, or second cousin, or something."

"He is?"

"Yeah, but they're not supposed to discuss it."

"Why not? There's nothing wrong with having your cousin at the same school."

"I know, but there was some reason, something to do with how Tyler got into the school. I don't know the details."

"I think he *did* do it. Mel's deluded. I mean, Tyler is hot, but he's a creep. Always looking at your boobs, you know?"

"Ugh, agreed."

The conversation faded as they crossed the road and pressed the gate buzzer. Gabe and I exchanged a look.

"Do you think that's important?"

I shrugged. "Maybe. Mel and Tyler being secret cousins—who'd have thought? I'll get Mona to put it in her notebook."

"That was impressive." Gabe was thawing a little. "Thanks, ghost."

"Marvin." I waited for the younger girls to meander across the school grounds and out of sight.

"Thanks, Marvin." Gabe checked the bus schedule again, then we both sat on the shelter bench to wait.

"That's the second time I've been spoken to today," I said. "Albert got me to go back to the dorm from the art room this morning."

"Why?"

"I don't know." I chewed my lip, then forced out the words. "Gabe, I've got these shadows that hang around me."

He frowned. "You mean your ghosts?"

"No. My ghosts look like people. These things are just shapes. Blobs of darkness. They literally look like shadows—translucent dark patches. They hover around the perimeter of my vision and get active when I'm nervous."

He was staring now. "Only when you're nervous?"

"Yeah. Or upset. You're the expert on feelings—do you think they might be something like *manifestations* of negative emotion?"

"Could be…"

"Is that what you've been seeing around Juliet?"

"No, I don't see anything. I just feel her fear." I deflated, and Gabe studied my face. "Do you see anything for happy feelings? Like, rainbow ones?"

I laughed. "No such luck."

"What does Mona think about these shadows?"

"I haven't told anyone before."

"Why not?"

"I don't know. It felt unnecessary. I have three perfectly formed ghosts wandering around with me all the time. Why would I question swirly shadows?"

He shook his head. "You must have nerves of steel, Mimi. I think you should tell Ms. Deering about this."

"Maybe."

It started raining, and Gabe checked his phone for the time again, but it wasn't long before the next bus appeared. We boarded this one without incident.

"We should still get there close to the time I promised Juliet," he said.

"What do you want me to do when we get there?"

"She'll probably freak out if she sees I've brought someone with me. Especially someone she knows from school. We should split up before we get to the park. Wear your hood and keep your distance so she doesn't recognize you."

"Okay."

I texted Mona to tell her what was happening. She didn't reply. She was probably at her grandparents' farm again—she'd complained about their poor phone signal before. We got off the bus somewhere unfamiliar and trudged through the steady rain for a few blocks before Gabe slowed down and pointed out a park up ahead of us.

"That's the meeting place. I'll go on ahead. Make sure you stay well away from us, got it?"

I got it. Gabe jogged away, and I slowed my pace, trailing behind him. He went through a line of trees and veered left. A moment later, I'd lost sight of him.

When I got to the corner of the park, I put my hood up and hung back, scanning for Gabe. There he was: sitting with Juliet in the distance. They were perched on the picnic table under a shelter beside an empty playground. I went to a table on my side of the park and sat down with my back to them. My ghosts all sat opposite.

"Why did you want me to come with Gabe today?" I asked quietly.

Hannah said nothing and sat watching Gabe and Juliet. Albert was straight-backed, observing me, and Marvin gazed at his holey shoes. I opened my phone and started scrolling, catching up on a bit of light entertainment from the worlds of art and funny pets.

It was a long wait. I got my sketchpad out and penciled some oak leaves. Then tree trunks. Then tree trunks with eyes. My mind drifted to the place it went whenever I had spare time: Drew. Letting me know he was out there at the school gate on the night of the dance was probably the best tip-off my ghosts had ever given me.

I hugged the memory of him, stripped of his armor. The smell of him. He had a clean, sharp fragrance with something like pine needles in it. But beneath that, when he was very near, Drew's scent was warm and male, and it made me want to breathe him in. Sitting there, I could almost feel the sensation of him pulling me close against him after the dance, as though he couldn't stand it if anything happened to me.

Surely that couldn't be faked.

Where would this take us? I felt a lot more than friendship toward him, and he'd been looking eager to see and speak to me ever since that night—no more reluctance, feigned or otherwise. I rewrote the school dance with him in it, imagined myself on a date with Drew. *His* face when he saw me all dressed up; *him* stopping me from falling into the snack table. Dancing up close with him on the dance floor, my arms around his neck.

I glanced guiltily over my shoulder, checking on Gabe. It wasn't that I didn't have a good night with him. It was just that it could've been so much better.

Gabe and Juliet were on their feet. My phone told me an hour had passed while I'd been sitting there daydreaming about Drew. I got up and packed away my sketchpad, watching the two of them surreptitiously.

They set off, heading for the street on the other side of the park. Gabe glanced over at me as they walked away—did he want me to follow or wait here? I hovered for a few moments, then made the decision to follow. Mona finally replied to my messages.

What? A covert operation I'm not involved in? I'm fuming! Keep me posted!

Will do, I replied.

I stepped off the curb and onto the road where Gabe and Juliet had gone. They were out of sight. *Great.* They must have turned up a side street. There were three to choose from.

I stood there indecisively for a minute. Should I go on, or just wait for Gabe to—hopefully—return for me? My ghosts stood with me but offered no advice.

I unlocked my phone. *Help, Mona! I've lost Gabe. I'm guessing Juliet has invited him to her place. Do you know where she lives?*

No, but I can try to find out, came back immediately.

I waited. After a few minutes, Mona messaged me again. *She lives at 12 Lloyd Turn, EV.*

I opened the map app and brought up directions to Juliet's house. I walked partway there, but stopped on the corner so

I could keep watch for Gabe. Hopefully their conversation wouldn't go on too much longer. I couldn't help but think of Cassie's comment from yesterday. Was it possible Juliet *had* swindled an older crush into spending time with her on the weekend?

Albert touched his icy hand to my back, and I pulled myself away from him so violently that I almost fell over. "Go after him, miss. They need to be quick."

Shit! I started jogging down the road, turned into the driveway of number twelve, then stood frozen with uncertainty for a second.

"Hurry," Albert urged me. "Knock at the door."

I ran up the porch steps and knocked. After a minute, Juliet answered, Gabe hovering behind her. His eyes opened wide and he shook his head, gesturing at me to go away.

Juliet was oblivious to his silent performance, peering at me. "Aren't you from school?" she asked in surprise. "What are you doing here?"

Gabe touched her shoulder. "Go finish packing, Juliet. I'll take care of Mimi."

Suspicion flooded her face, but when he urged her again, she did as he said.

"What the hell are you doing?" he snapped as soon as she was gone. "You're messing everything up! Her father's been violent toward Juliet and her mom—I'm trying to get them out of here."

"My ghosts told me to get you to hurry!"

That shut him up. "Why?" He glanced over his shoulder. "Her mom's out cold—she's taken tranquilizers. And her dad's out of the county for work today."

"I don't know why!" I was practically hopping on the spot with anxiety by now. "Albert told me to hurry you along; that's all I know."

"I don't want to rush her—she'll panic."

"They need to hurry up!" Albert exclaimed, bringing his cane down on the porch so it made a bang.

Gabe shoved past me and peered around the door. He scanned the area where Albert stood. "What was *that*?"

I went rigid with shock and swung around to face him. "You heard that?"

"Yeah, of course! Someone spoke and there was a thump." Gabe stood staring at the porch, but when I checked, Albert had vanished.

I felt around in the empty space with my hand. Unsurprisingly, it didn't change anything.

Gabe watched me. "Mimi? What is it?"

"That was Albert you heard—my ghost," I managed. *Where'd he go?*

My phone buzzed in my hand, and I checked it reflexively. *Drew just emailed everyone,* Mona had messaged. *He had a vision of a fist coming at him.*

Too many things were happening at once. I clung to the one thing I needed to make sense of. "Where's Albert?" I asked Hannah, but she just stood there looking at me sorrowfully. "Marvin? Where's Albert?"

No answer. They just lifted an arm each and pointed to the driveway. I turned around just as a blue car with rust stains pulled in.

"Oh, God," I whispered. "Juliet's father. He's home." I'd never seen the man at the wheel before in my life, but I knew.

Gabe dove back into the house, calling for Juliet. The big man got out and heaved himself up the porch steps. His face was sallow and mean, his eyes bloodshot.

"Who are you?" he demanded.

"Juliet's friend," I said, my voice shaking.

His face darkened. "She's grounded. You'd better go."

I went down the porch steps in a show of obedience. He opened the screen door and let himself in, then locked it behind him, hollering for his daughter. But I didn't leave. I ran to the side gate and clambered over, messaging Mona at the same time. The message was supposed to say, *Call cops,* but, thanks to typing while running, it didn't come out looking anything like that. I shoved my phone in my pocket and hoped Mona would work it out.

Shouting and wailing arose from inside the house as I dashed for the back door. A bark drew my attention to the corner of the yard—it was a gigantic Rottweiler and it was coming for me. I ran harder, praying the back door was unlocked. The patron saint of trespassers was listening, and I swung myself inside, slamming the door in the dog's face right as it made up its mind that I deserved to die a grisly death.

Juliet's father was screaming incoherently at Gabe, who was backed up against the kitchen wall, holding up his hands to defend himself. Juliet was crying and yelling at her dad to stop, but he only paused to throw terrible names at her. From nowhere, he swung at Gabe, catching him on the side of his face and making him stagger. Juliet shrieked.

I grabbed the nearest thing—a can of bug spray—and threw it at the man with all my might. It bounced off his back, making him grunt, and he turned on me, advancing with his fist held high. Gabe recovered and charged, shoving Juliet's dad so he stumbled backward and fell against a door. It flew open; he crashed down a flight of steps and landed on the mid-stair landing. He went still. Juliet screamed again.

Gabe went down the basement steps and prodded the man with his shoe. "He's breathing," he called.

Juliet's father began to stir, lifting himself up on one elbow.

"Gabe, get away from him!" I cried.

Gabe scrambled back up the stairs. I yanked the door shut, but there was no lock, and Hannah was pointing us to the front of the house.

"Come on!" I ran for the front door.

Gabe seized Juliet's hand and dragged her through the house. "Wait!" She was gasping in panic. "My mom! She's still in her bed!"

"Juliet?" called a weak female voice.

Gabe and I exchanged a look. He shoved Juliet at me. "Take her out of here!" He raced for the bedroom.

Gripping Juliet's hand, I got us out the front door and off the porch, then kept running. A siren whooped so close we both stumbled and squawked. Two police cars pulled up, and within moments, an officer had put himself in front of us, demanding our names.

"Get in there!" I cried, pointing at the house. "There's a man in the basement. He attacked us. My friend's trying to help a woman get out."

The officer went nowhere, but his buddies stormed the house, weapons raised. I ignored the officer's repeated questions, listening and watching, pleading silently with the universe to get Gabe out safe.

Then he appeared. He came barreling out through the front door and stumbled across the lawn, straight into the solid frame of another police officer. She held on to him.

"He didn't do anything!" I called, running back to the yard. "He was trying to help her." I pointed at Juliet, hoping she'd back me up, but she was far too freaked out to speak.

Gabe was also trying to explain, but had the sense to obey when an officer told him to get on the ground. Another was radioing for paramedics, reporting a woman affected by tranquilizers. A minute later, a cop came out of the house with Juliet's father in cuffs. My legs went weak with relief.

The man stopped struggling and staggered to a halt, catching sight of his daughter. "Jules, honey," he called, his tone wheedling and thick. "Tell 'em the truth—that I was defending us from this scum!" He aimed a kick at Gabe and missed.

Beside me, Juliet was so pale I thought she might faint. My heart turned leaden. This would be the moment Gabe and I got charged with breaking and entering because Juliet was too terrified to speak out against her father.

But the girl shook her head. "No, Dad. I'm done."

17

The Consequences of Our Actions

We got a ride back to school in a police car. Gabe's mother had already been to the station with him while he made his statement. My parents were to drive down in the morning and take me in for my turn.

The squad car turned into the EVA parking lot and Gabe glanced at me. "Holy hell." It was the first thing we'd said to each other since we got out of Juliet's house.

A bruise was darkening on his chin and he had a small cut on his lip. He saw my gaze and touched his jaw gingerly.

"You should get Ed to look at that," I whispered.

He nodded. "Where did the cops come from?" he asked under the conversation of the officers in the front.

"I messaged Mona."

"What... *happened*?"

I knew what he was referring to. *Albert.* Every time I thought about losing him, I got a pain in my chest like someone was cracking my heart open with a hammer and chisel. Albert was a ghost, for God's sake. Why did it feel so bad to know he was gone?

"You're devastated," Gabe said.

"Thanks, I'm aware of that."

He took my hand. "I'm here for you, Miette Alston."

I held it together, but only with a supreme effort.

The cops walked us to our dorms, then went to have a meeting with Mr. Boxe. Ms. Samvedi took me into her office and made me explain what had happened. Having no idea what Gabe had told the police, I kept my story as vague as possible, but it was as if Ms. Samvedi was looking for holes. She wanted to know where Gabe and I had met Juliet, and why we decided to help her run away instead of reporting what she'd told us. She even asked where we thought we were going to take the girl. Did any of this matter, considering Juliet's life had been in danger?

I pled ignorance. "Gabe was arranging things. Juliet doesn't know me very well, so she wanted his help, not mine. She trusts him. He got me to hang back while she told him what was going on."

At last, I claimed a headache and exhaustion and Ms. Samvedi allowed me to go to my room. Mona had switched from messaging to email, knowing I would have handed my phone in by now. I found a long message in my inbox, but I was genuinely too tired to attempt a proper reply, so I responded to say I'd talk to her tomorrow.

Collabor8, which only worked within the school intranet, was running hot between Gabe, Patience and Cassie. I didn't scroll back to read the full chat; I just jumped in.

Miette Alston has joined the session.

Gabriel: *There she is! Mimi the Magnificent and her ghost squad.*

I glanced at Hannah and Marvin. My room felt too empty, and it made my eyes sting. I tried to focus on the chat. I needed Gabe to help me get my story straight without being too obvious. You never knew when the police were going to subpoena your chat records and, even though these Collabor8 chats vanished when we ended each session, everyone knew that nothing online ever really disappeared.

Miette: *Ms. Samvedi was curious about how everything went down. Asking lots of questions. I couldn't remember some of the details.*
Gabriel: *Hard questions?*
Miette: *Some of them were.*

Thankfully, he got it.

Gabriel: *Well, you must remember that we were going to get waffles at Granny Goopy.*
Miette: *Um, okay. Where is that?*
Gabriel: *Oh my God, you haven't tried Granny Goopy's waffles in central Etherall Valley? Next weekend, kid, we're going for waffles.*
Cassandra: *They are good waffles, Mimi.*
Gabriel: *So, we were going for waffles, but we spotted Juliet at the park and went to say hello. She spilled her story and said she wanted to get out of home. She needed our support. Her dad was away for the weekend (or so she thought) and she was waiting for her mom to wake up so they could go stay with friends, start the separation. We encouraged her to make the move and offered to help her pack. Her mom was dead to the world on sleeping tablets and her father got home unexpectedly. The rest, you saw up close.*
Miette: *Got it. Thanks.*

Cassandra: *Gabe said he HEARD one of your, you know, friends. What happened?*
Cassandra: *Mimi? Are you still there?*
Miette: *I've got to go. Tell you about it later.*

The burst of tears shocked me. I dropped onto my bed and wept hard, face in my pillow to muffle the sobs. It was short but intense. Afterward, I flipped onto my back and stared at the ceiling, picturing Albert with his olive-colored uniform and chestnut hair.

This was deranged. Why was I grieving for a ghost? A ghost that could turn my flesh into frozen meat—that had once stepped into my physical space and left me debilitated for days?

"Oh, Albert." It came out as a shaky sigh.

My mind ran back over the other times my ghosts had left me. Walter, the first one, had vanished on a family picnic day for my father's work at Easter time. A man who worked with Dad bent down to chat with me, asking if I'd ever done an egg hunt before. I was going to say, "Yes, but Walter might not have," when Walter picked up a full wine bottle that was lying on the picnic blanket and whacked the poor guy on the leg. By the time the hullabaloo settled down, Walter was gone. The man sat with an ice pack on his knee, bewildered about how he'd managed to stumble on a wine bottle.

Lying there, I tensed with shock. Walter had *picked up a wine bottle.* How had I never thought about that properly before? He'd interacted with an actual physical object! A second incident popped into my mind: Mortimer, another of my ghosts, throwing a glass at a basement wall before he vanished. And Albert, thumping his cane on the porch timbers today. All of them, making themselves known to other living humans—and then vanishing.

I sat up. Wait, did they have to leave once they'd revealed their presence to people other than me?

I cast my mind feverishly back to the other ghosts who'd left. Ethel, when I was eight. I was crossing the road and a man on a bike had come unexpectedly around a bend. Ethel shoved him and made him fall off his bicycle. I got blamed—although, to be honest, if she hadn't done it, I would have been the one who got hurt, because the cyclist was coming right at me. Maybe Ethel had done it to protect me.

Mortimer throwing the glass. A bunch of kids in middle school had devised an innovative way to make me feel awful, involving a Halloween party, a Ouija board and a boy dressed in a sheet with a pair of lips drawn on. Then Mortimer scared the hell out of them all by smashing that glass against the wall.

Had he been trying to protect me too?

And Albert, trying to warn me and Gabe about Juliet's father today—had he also sacrificed his existence to protect me?

My heart was racing. I looked up at Marvin in the corner and Hannah, seated on my bed. "Is that it? Your warnings, showing yourself to others—is that all to keep me safe?"

Neither answered. I drew my knees up to my chest and wrapped my arms around them. This was a revelation. They weren't trying to hurt me. They were trying to protect me. The information they gave me—the way they forced me to do things or stopped me from doing other things—wasn't random. It wasn't designed to keep me scared. The ghosts knew things I didn't know and were actively working to keep me safe. I mean, Walter smashing that guy's knee still made no sense, but maybe the man had been a danger to me in some way.

A crow cawed excitedly from the lawn outside my window, as if it had also had a brilliant idea. I addressed Hannah and Marvin again. "Thank you." They both nodded, and triumph surged through me. "Are either of you planning to go anywhere?" I added.

"We all go eventually, miss," Hannah replied. "But others will take our place."

"A bit of advance notice would be nice, so I can say goodbye. You guys have grown on me over the years. It's hard to share every meal, shopping trip, car ride and visit to the bathroom with another soul without getting a little bit attached."

Hannah said nothing, but I felt like she might be smiling if she knew how, and old Marvin made a very quiet harrumphing sound.

I had a lot of explaining to do when Mom and Dad came to take me to the police station the next day, but making a statement wasn't as bad as I'd feared. In fact, with Juliet's accusations against her father and her mom backing her up, not to mention Gabe's statement, my account seemed like a bit of an afterthought.

Afterward, Mom and Dad took me out to get something to eat. A military truck passed us going the other way, and the memory of Albert made my throat ache and eyes prickle.

Every time I thought of him, it landed all over again that he was gone. Beneath my parents' argument about the relative merits of burgers and Mexican, Dad's eyes caught mine in the rearview mirror and he frowned. I gave him a quick smile, moving out of sight to wipe my eyes.

Right then, cruising along the main strip in Etherall Valley, I spotted a big pink sign: *Granny Goopy*.

"Let's go there!" I cried.

Gabe and Cassie were right. Granny Goopy waffles were crunchy and squishy, with just the right syrup-to-whipped-cream ratio. I sat there with a mouth full of deliciousness, reflecting on how good my life had become. I'd even managed to get some time with my parents, despite the circumstances.

Then my mom dropped a bomb. "Honey, Dad and I are looking around for another school for you."

I commenced choking on my food.

"What? No!" I exclaimed as soon as I could talk again. "Why? I love it at EVA!"

Dad patted my arm. "We know you're settling in well, but we can't help but worry, Mim."

A shadow wobbled in the corner of the restaurant's ceiling. They were gathering. "No," I said again. "I know it's a long way from home, but I'm fine, honestly."

"It's not the distance—"

"Is it the cost?"

"It's not just the cost. It's the people you're mixing with." My mom's round face was lined with worry. "First, your friend Cassie being detained by that boy. Now this. Another friend—a victim of family violence. And you were at her house! With the perpetrator! In *direct* danger."

Dad was nodding. "She's right, Gho—Mimi. We feel sorry for these kids, and they deserve extra help through the school, but we don't feel right about you mixing with people whose lives are impacted by this much dysfunction."

"How can you say that? No one should have anything but sympathy for Juliet and Cassie! Neither of them had control over what happened to them. Cassie was simply on a date with a boy from school when he showed his true colors. Who could've predicted that? And Juliet—she's been trying to tell the truth about her father for years. We should be grateful she's at EVA, in a place where she felt safe enough to tell someone what was going on."

"But you were right there," Dad reminded me. "Both times—first when Cassie escaped from the boy's car, and then trying to effect a *rescue operation*."

"No, I wasn't trying to rescue anyone. I just happened to go along with Gabe to Juliet's place to help her get packed. We were sure her dad was out of the county, or we would never have gone to her house."

My voice had gone high-pitched with passion. Dad raised his hand. "Look, there's no need to panic. We wouldn't put you back in a mainstream school. But we are looking around. Your mother and I both feel we could find you a school that's just as good as this one—without the drama."

I tried to control my tone. Snapping at them never worked, and this was important. "There'll be drama at any school. Honestly, it's just a fluke that there have been a couple of instances here. It's the best school, Mom, Dad—it really is. I love it. I'm getting my work done, I love the art focus and the gifted program, and I've got friends here. *Real friends*."

They exchanged a long look. Mom sighed. "Nothing's going to change for now. But Mimi, please stick with the quiet kids—the good ones. The ones who don't attract trouble, if you know what I mean. *They're* the ones who will be the best friends for you."

Relief washed through me and I didn't try to correct them again. They couldn't possibly know how wrong they were.

In gifted class, Ms. Deering made it known how furious she was about being informed of our escapade *after* it had occurred. I'd never seen her look like this before. Her delicate features were creased, her blue eyes hard.

"I knew, as soon as I was told Juliet, Gabe and Mimi were involved, it had something to do with your gifts. What I want to know is this: why did none of you think to let me know what was going on?"

Gabe hung his head. "Sorry, Ms. D. Juliet made me promise not to tell any teachers."

"No one else had promised any such thing, though—had they?" She cast her gaze around the room and landed on me. "What about you, Mimi? Couldn't *you* have reached out?"

"Uh…" It was all I had.

"To be fair, even *I* didn't know what was happening until they'd already boarded the bus," Mona said as if she were our command central.

This only inflamed matters. Ms. Deering looked one move away from *I'm not angry, I'm just disappointed.* I could only imagine what she'd say if she knew we'd sneaked Ed out to help Cassie's aunt.

"You're right, Ms. Deering," I hurried to say. "I should have messaged, or emailed, or whatever. I didn't think."

"It's not her fault," Gabe put in. "Mimi was only with me because her ghosts made her go along for the ride. It was for the best, too. They had lots of good intel."

Ms. Deering double-checked that we all had her contact details and extracted a promise from each of us that we'd contact her if anything was going down. Then she let Mona get on with her mental acrobatics. She'd already identified the old blue car belonging to Juliet's dad from one of Drew's visions. There was also the fist vision and Albert's intervention to hash out. Mona wrote pages of notes while we discussed the events.

"One last thing," Ms. Deering called when it was almost time to finish. She gave us a pleading look. "Things are moving faster all the time. I don't know where your gifts are taking us. All I know is this: we shouldn't go making reckless decisions or diving into dangerous situations. Work with me, people—please." She sighed, looking tired. "The weekend after next, I'm supposed to be taking you all on a camp. I'm starting to think it's a mistake. Having Mr. Boxe—an outsider—along with us could make things too complicated. I wonder if I should cancel it."

There was a general outcry. "Come on, Ms. D," Mona said. "We'll be good! I've been looking forward to a weekend camping with my paranormal pals."

"We'll be careful," Gabe said. "We can pretend to be academically gifted, no problem."

"Especially around Mr. Boxe," Ed added. "When he's in earshot, we'll act like total nerds."

"I had a letter from my father," Patience said in her soft voice. "The campsite isn't far from Dale's Run, and we've been invited to visit for afternoon tea on our way back from camp."

Ms. Deering's eyebrows shot up. "All of us?"

Patience nodded. "Father said he wanted to meet my classmates and teacher. He said he was writing to Mr. Boxe to ask him."

Marvin shuffled across the room toward me under the ensuing outbreak of chatter. "You're not to go there," he told me.

"You mean…?" I murmured.

"To Dale's Run, kid."

I checked with Hannah, and she nodded. Marvin shuffled away.

"Um," I said to Ms. Deering, hoping not to attract the others' attention. "Apparently I'm still not allowed to visit Dale's Run." Inopportunely, a random silence fell just as I spoke.

"Your ghosts have warned you again?" she asked me.

I nodded, going warm in the cheeks. Patience pressed her lips together and said nothing, but she looked angry. Hurt.

"Look." Mona got out of her seat and crouched down to get a better look at the floor. "Water, again!" She glanced up at me. "Is this from your ghost?"

I shrugged. "Marvin died in the snow. He leaves snowflakes sometimes."

There was an odd stillness in the room while everyone studied the melted droplets that led from an empty corner right up to me.

Cassie shuddered. "At least we know she's not making it up."

My mouth fell open.

"We never thought you were making it up, Mimi," Ms. Deering assured me. "Now get to your next classes, everyone. I'll let you know what's happening with the camp when I've had more time to think about it."

In English, Drew had saved me a seat. I slid in next to him, attempting not to reveal how damn happy it made me feel.

"Are you all right?" he asked in a low voice.

Were my eyes still swollen from yesterday's cry-fest? "I'm fine."

He studied me. "You're not hurt?"

"Gabe was the one who got smacked in the face. The worst thing that happened to me was almost getting eaten by a Rottweiler."

"You lost a ghost."

My annoying eyes threatened to leak again. "Yeah. Feels like someone died—isn't that weird?"

"I'm sorry."

"Thanks." I attempted a lighter tone. "Hey, do you ever wish we just had the usual teen problems?"

"What, like restrictive parents, disastrous dating, online bullies, that kind of thing?"

"Yeah. Although, laid out like that, it sounds terrible. Not sure I'd be able to cope with being normal."

He dipped his chin in agreement. "We wouldn't know where to begin. Like sloths at a samba class."

I laughed, and Mr. Cambridge called the class to attention. He made us sit through a slideshow about rhetorical devices in fiction, then set us on a partner task identifying them in the set novel.

"Got a pen?" Drew asked. I held one ready over my page. "Analogy, metaphor, allusion, foreshadowing. Oh, and juxtaposition. There. Now let's go back to the previous conversation."

"Ooh, I like being teamed with a lit geek. I think we were talking about sloths in a samba class."

"Alliteration."

"Smartass." I started sketching an eye in the corner of the page. "Know what? Since I started at EVA, I feel more normal than I have for years."

He raised an eyebrow. "Even with us weirdos?"

"Especially with you weirdos. I'm doing normal stuff. Taking the bus, going out on weekends, sneaking food into the dorm…"

"Dating?"

I caught my breath and turned it into a dismissive laugh. "I haven't dated."

"You dated Gabe."

"No, we went to the dance as friends."

"I wish I'd had my epiphany earlier. I would have kept good standing and gone to that dance."

"You would've hated it. They weren't playing your kind of music. Screamo, right?"

His mouth twitched. "Smartass. I don't even know who half the bands on my t-shirts are. I'm a bad goth."

"It's pretty disrespectful, the way you were appropriating the subculture before your epiphany."

"I know." He paused again. "You know what caused my epiphany?" I waited. "A chicken tender."

I stared. "What the hell?"

"True story. That day when Ada choked on a chicken tender in the cafeteria? I racked my brains trying to match up my visions with what happened to her and came up empty. It was like something clicked. I realized that bad things happen to people all the time and it's got nothing to do with me."

"That was all it took? Years of guilty agonizing and all you needed was for Ada to choke on some breaded chicken?" My outrage made him laugh.

Mr. Cambridge called on us to share our findings at that moment. He'd probably detected we were having a real conversation. Drew took over, describing how the dog in the set novel was a metaphor for civic responsibility and participation, and the wolf was a metaphor for resistance and isolation. Mr. Cambridge reluctantly agreed that Drew was right, then talked us through cumulative sentences and asked us to write an example.

"Smooth," I murmured when everyone was working again.

"Watch this, then."

He bent over my paper and wrote: *She went to the school dance, feeling normal, looking amazing, and ready to shake it until her shoes disintegrated.*

"Cumulative sentence," he said. "Not even fictional."

"A-plus," I said, but my heart was hammering now. I took my turn. *He went to the school dance, although he never made it onto the dance floor, preferring to hide in the shrubbery like an axe-wielding serial killer.*

Drew's mouth twisted and his eyes glittered with amusement. "Gives a whole new meaning to 'cutting in.' Did you dance much?"

"No. No one goes to dances to dance, do they?"

"Where did your shoes go, then?"

I groaned with the memory. "My mom and Mona conspired to put me in heels. Little did they know I would seriously endanger a table full of chips and dips. And they hurt like hell. I took them off as soon as the dance was over, which is why I was barefoot when you saw me, not because I danced my shoes into dust."

"Why wouldn't you dance at a school dance?"

"They weren't playing my sort of music."

"Screamo?"

I shot him a smirk. "Yeah, screamo."

He contemplated me with his incredible green eyes, which made me a little sweaty. "What sort of music do you actually like?"

I shrugged. "Lots of different kinds."

"Like what, though?"

"Have you got a cumulative sentence to share, Mimi?" Mr. Cambridge asked, making me go into an instant panic.

I looked at the sentences we'd written on my page. *Shit.*

"Um…" I thought fast. "She likes listening to music, across lots of different genres, from indie pop to folk."

"Not bad," Mr. Cambridge said. "I wouldn't call it grammatically perfect, but you've got the idea."

"Smooth," Drew murmured.

After class, we headed for the dorms. I'd been flirting hard for fifty minutes straight and was kind of stunned at how easily it had come to me. I was also lightheaded from the euphoria and needed a cold shower.

Drew paused at the fork in the path. "Are you rescuing more freshmen next weekend or did you want to get a day pass and do something? Maybe."

I played it cool. "Maybe."

"Saturday?"

I'd promised Axel I'd do a painting session with him on Saturday. That could be rearranged. "Saturday works."

"Anywhere you want to go?"

"I don't know the area very well. What's fun?"

He thought about it. "I don't do fun very often. But I know a few places we can just hang out and talk."

"That's my kind of fun."

We parted ways, and I went back to my room for study hour. Very little studying was done during that hour, or the ones that followed. *I'm going on a date with Drew this weekend!* My brain and heart held hands and skipped off together into daydream land, picturing intimate conversation, flirtatious whispers, intense eye contact and my first kiss. There may have even been a gondola on a Venetian canal.

Hannah stirred on the end of my bed. "Patience, miss."

It sounded peculiarly like a warning.

When the dinner bell chimed, I joined Mona at a dining room table where she sat scribbling in her notebook.

"What's with you?" she asked.

"Huh?"

"You look all bright-eyed and sparkly."

I tried to temper my internal buzz. "It's lasagna night. Isn't everyone excited?"

Mona went back to her note taking. Two incomprehensible words were written on the facing page:

Vakk xoopd

"What language is that?" I asked, pointing.

She hesitated. "What do you mean?"

"*Vakk xoopd*?" I attempted to make the sounds work.

"No, it says, *Call cops*." Mona frowned at the page. "Oh, wow. I see what you mean. That was the message you sent me when Juliet's dad turned up."

"*That* was what I sent when I was trying to get you to call the police?" I held my breath in awe. "But to you, it's *call cops*?"

Mona was studying the words as if she'd only just seen them for the first time. "Yes. I mean no. Both. I can see the words you sent, but in my head it's *call cops*. That's weird, huh?"

"*Weird*? That's telepathic-level communication skills."

Mona grinned like I'd handed her the moon.

"What are you doing?" Olivia was peering across the table at Mona's open page. "Is that your gifted program project?"

Mona slammed her book shut.

"Mona loves codebreaking," I blurted. "Especially the hard ones."

"You like *really* hard codes?" Olivia asked her.

"Love them," Mona said. "The harder the better."

Our table was summoned to the serving counter. "Have you heard of the Lydenburg code?" Olivia asked as we headed over with our plates. She paused at the still-incomplete giant jigsaw puzzle of Menoa and pointed to a forested area. "Here's Lydenburg, in the south. Years ago, some papers were found in an old ruin. They were in code. It was a big deal when I was in elementary school—they used to take us on excursions to the museum and try to get us cracking it." She grinned. "Maybe they thought one of us would actually hit on the real key. No one's ever been able to break it, though. I think the Menoa County officials eventually issued a statement that it was just made-up gibberish, probably done by kids. But who knows? Maybe it's just an impossible code."

Mona's eyes gleamed as we followed Olivia to the counter. She leaned over to whisper in my ear. "Challenge accepted."

18
Acts of Service Are My Love Language

The weather was a little cooler on Saturday morning. Jeans weather. I spent way too long trying on an array of tops before I settled on a Hoodwynk t-shirt I treasured beyond all else. Drew had no idea how privileged he was to see this shirt.

I took my sketchpad, knowing I'd need something to do with my hands if I didn't want to melt into an anxious puddle of sweat. I waited for him outside the school gate. Hannah and Marvin hovered nearby. It would have been nice to have some alone time with Drew, but I had a new appreciation for my ghosts since I'd worked out why they got a little heavy-handed with me at times.

I was early and had five minutes of wondering if Drew had back-pedaled on his epiphany and I was about to be stood up. He was dropped off at the corner by a woman who must have been his mom, just as my phone told me it was ten. He was in a t-shirt and jeans, too, Converse on his feet. Cosmetic-free, hair natural, and light on jewelry—just the eyebrow rings and a stud in his lip. My heart was doing jumping jacks, and when he smiled at me, it improvised its own modern dance routine.

He said we were going to the Etherall Valley Botanical Gardens. We caught the bus, my ghosts sitting a few rows behind us. It was like Drew and I had to cram our entire life histories into one bus ride. He told me about his younger sister Piper, calling her a bossy pain in the ass, but I could tell he adored her. His mom was an ambitious go-getter in sales, while his father was a wannabe writer who'd emigrated from India as a kid and ended up working in a warehouse. His dad was so excited when Drew got headhunted for an EVA scholarship after winning a local poetry prize, he spent weeks talking Drew's mom into letting him take it up. She eventually gave in, saying she supposed Drew should pursue his interests.

I told him about my mom and dad's trip of a lifetime to Paris that was happening in January. Then I told him about my older brother Lucien, and how he went to Québec in his gap year to work in a ski resort and ended up getting engaged to a Canadian girl. I asked if Drew had any pets, and he said he had a cat but for a few minutes wouldn't tell me its name. At last he looked away and admitted it was a fluffy ragdoll called Mimi. It was only awkward for a moment, then I laughed my ass off.

At the botanical gardens, Drew led me to a kiosk where we could buy a picnic pack. The best thing about that concept was that we could find a spot to be alone—well, alone-ish. Marvin and Hannah wandered the gardens nearby.

We picked out a shaded patch of grass and set up our picnic. He asked about my shirt and I told him about Hoodwynk, then he opened the music app on his phone and played one of their songs. It felt so personal, I might as well have been playing and singing for him myself. He listened with his head tipped to the side and his eyes fixed on the flowerbed opposite.

"They're good," he said at the end of the song. "Powerful lyrics. Mostly about isolation, don't you think?" He set his phone softly playing a Hoodwynk album while we ate and talked, and I wondered if I could get any happier.

"Why do you think your ghosts don't want you to go to Dale's Run?" he asked over lunch.

"I wish I knew. Ms. Deering said I'll probably have to go home in Mr. Boxe's car while the rest of you visit Dale's Run in the minibus." I made a face. "Have you ever been there?"

"No. Patience has told me about it, though."

"What's it like?"

"They live off-grid. Woodfires, gas lamps and generators. No phones—not even a landline. Patience has to wear long dresses when she's at home—no jeans. The teenagers get their marriages arranged by the pastor in charge."

"That's what I'd heard. No offense intended to Patience, but that sounds like hell to me."

"Before she came to EVA, the pastor kept trying to exorcise her demons."

"*What*?"

"They kept her locked in the church, had her 'fasting' to starve out the devil. It was practically a rescue situation by the time Ms. Deering and Mr. Boxe intervened."

I swore softly. "Poor Patience."

Drew loaded a cracker with cheese and an olive. "Maybe your ghosts are worried about something happening there."

"Maybe. They generally seem to act in my interests."

"Except for…" He nodded at my missing finger.

"Actually, when Walter did that, he was trying to protect me."

Drew paused with the cracker partway to his mouth. "What do you mean?"

"I was trying to cross a bridge over a creek, and it was unstable. He held on to me to stop me running across. The next kid who went over the bridge crashed through the middle of it. The poor girl got stuck under the timbers and nearly died."

Drew didn't move or speak for so long that I got a little worried. At last he released his breath in a long exhalation. "It's reassuring to think you've got an ethereal security detail following you around."

"Everyone needs a dead squad."

"Can they hear us talking?" he asked.

"I don't think so. It's hard to tell. I'm not sure how much they can see in the living realm, although Albert liked to walk around gardens." I glanced around at the flowerbeds. "He would've liked it here."

"Do you know much about his life?"

I hesitated. "A little bit. Do you want to hear it?"

He nodded. Was this going to weird him out? Talking about my ghosts had always been a surefire way to lose friends. But Drew was waiting. I'd had enough to eat, so I rolled over to lie on my stomach, propped up on my elbows and flicked my sketchpad open. If I was drawing, I could avoid his gaze while I spoke.

"Albert looked around thirty-five to me, maybe a little older. He had dark red hair and carried a cane topped with a brass duck's head." I was sketching an acorn. "I first saw him about four years ago at the grand opening of the Perry Ridge Memorial Garden—something my father worked on. Dad's a planner at the municipal offices in Perry Ridge, if you're wondering." I sketched a cluster of stars.

"At the start, Albert was just a human-shaped blob pacing back and forth. That's how they all come through. It's as if I'm seeing them behind a frosted glass barrier that comes closer and closer over days, sometimes weeks." I started on a skull.

"So they don't just suddenly appear?" Drew sounded fascinated.

"No, there's a buildup. Then I wake up one morning and they're through, solid and clear."

"That must be the 'veil' people talk about."

"Maybe." I outlined an eye. "When Albert came through, it was obvious he was from another time. His uniform was different from what soldiers wear today. He made a little bow as he introduced himself, and told me his full name and rank, but I've forgotten them over the years. I remember how he died. He got injured in an air raid in Italy, left with chunks of metal hanging out of his leg. Back home, they operated a few times, but the injuries didn't heal well and I guess antibiotics weren't a thing at that stage. He died from infection."

I stopped drawing and stared at the soft, young blades of grass sprouting out of the dirt beside my sketchpad. "I miss him so much. Isn't that weird?"

"Weird's our thing," was all Drew said.

I smiled and resumed sketching.

"Did Albert ever hurt you like Walter did?"

My pencil stopped.

"You don't have to tell me."

I glanced up, and the honesty in Drew's face untied a knot I hadn't even known was inside me. "I tried to ignore his advice once. I'd sprained my ankle slipping on the stairs, and the doctor gave me strong painkillers I'd never tried before. After dinner, I grabbed the new pill bottle, but while I wrestled with the childproof cap, Albert stepped in front of me and said, 'Miss, you mustn't take that medicine.' I didn't realize how serious he was. I laughed and said, 'Sorry, doctor's orders.' I tipped the pills into my hand and opened my mouth."

Drew looked down at my hand again—the one with four and a half fingers. "What did he do?"

Albert's physical pain and grief filling me up, my body growing deathly cold, tight with agony from his infected wounds, my organs failing, my life force dwindling. His voice coming like a death knell: "You mustn't take those pills."

I pushed my sketchpad out of the way, rolled onto my back and stared at the sky. "He stepped into me, and I sort of became dead for a moment."

"Dead? How?"

Albert, watching me drop to the floor, gasping for oxygen and holding my hand to my heart to make sure it was still beating. "I'm sorry, miss, very sorry, but you mustn't take that medicine."

"I'm not good at explaining it."

Drew lay down beside me, and I sensed him looking at me but kept my gaze on the blue sky.

"I used to see a psychiatrist," he said. "He wanted me to talk through something difficult once. He said talking about frightening things in a safe space neutralizes the fear. He got me to lie down and close my eyes so I wouldn't have to make eye contact."

"Did it help?"

"A little."

"I can try."

I closed my eyes, pretty sure that if it were anyone but Drew, I would have bailed on the situation by now. I snuck a peek at him. He was lying beside me with his eyes closed in solidarity.

"Where do I start?" I asked, staring at his profile.

His eyelids quivered at my voice but stayed shut. "Wherever you want."

I took a breath and closed my eyes again. "They don't say much, but sometimes they respond to things happening in my life. Like once, Hannah said to me, 'Miss, you oughtn't go today.' I had a homeschooler meetup scheduled—a social skills day at a recreation center. My parents had paid a lot for me to attend. I ignored her at first, and then I tried to get her to back off. She stood in my doorway and wouldn't let me pass. In the end I got so annoyed, I barged straight through her. That was a mistake."

My pulse was beating like a hammer in my throat, sweat forming along my hairline. "I got locked into her space with her. I looked down and saw my arms were hers, I was wearing her dress and her blonde hair was hanging over my shoulders. I was ice cold and the world looked strange— smudged and darkened, like my eyes didn't work properly. I—Mimi—started to sink away. Hannah's thoughts and memories took over. It was like my warmth, my heartbeat, they were disappearing. I became Hannah, dead Hannah, who died alone in a woodshed." It was as if my words were coming from a long-forgotten spring that had suddenly cracked the surface.

"I tried to call out for my mom, but my mouth was locked shut. Hannah's voice was right inside my head, and she wasn't just talking now, she was growling in this guttural voice, saying, 'Miss, you oughtn't go today.' I couldn't answer her. There wasn't enough Mimi left to reply. All I wanted to do was say, 'Okay, I won't go!' But I was like a speck of myself, getting smaller every moment.

"I don't know how it ended. I guess she let me out. I woke up on the bedroom floor with Hannah watching me from the corner of my room. I couldn't go on the outing, obviously— I could hardly get off the floor. I spent two days in bed, recovering."

I'd told someone. First time ever.

I opened my eyes to find Drew had moved. He was up on his elbow, leaning over me, his expression tight with worry. My breath caught. He was doing that thing where he explored my face, then his eyes seemed to go to my mouth for an instant before he pulled himself away from me.

He sat up. "Christ, Mimi."

I sat up too, trying to slow my breathing. "They don't do it very often."

"But having dead people around you all the time, never knowing if they'll turn on you. How have you coped with that?"

"I haven't." I managed a laugh. "I refused school for four years. I barely went outside. Sometimes I asked to sleep on the floor in my parents' room. I had regular appointments with a therapist or Dr. Mayer. I ate a lot of my mom's baking."

"Dr. Mayer?" A crease appeared in his forehead. "That was the name of my psychiatrist."

"Dr. Mayer in Perry Ridge?"

"Ah, must be a different doctor. Mine's here in Etherall Valley. My parents took me to see him for a few months and it didn't make any difference so we quit. It was costing a ton."

I sipped some water and surreptitiously flapped the damp back of my t-shirt. Drew took up a fallen leaf and picked small, precise pieces off its edges with his thumbnail, seemingly lost in thought. "Did you find out why Hannah didn't want you to go on that outing?"

"I honestly never did."

"What about the tablets Albert wanted you to avoid?"

"I didn't take them. I told the doctor they made me vomit and she put me back on the regular stuff."

He stared at a bunch of trees. "Deering says our gifts are increasing in power. What's that going to mean for you?"

I shrugged. "A whole cemetery worth of imaginary friends?"

He shook his head with a soft laugh. "Damn."

"What's it going to mean for you?" I tossed back.

"God knows. A career in weather forecasting? Or fortune telling?"

I laughed and tore the doodle-covered page from my sketchpad. I folded quickly it into a paper fortune teller and dropped it into his lap. "There. Something to kick-start your career."

He played with it, wearing a half-smile, then folded it up and put it in his pocket. "Come on, let's go for a walk."

I spent the afternoon picking back over my day like a kid counting candy after trick or treating. It was impossible to settle into anything constructive. I put the most heartfelt of Hoodwynk songs on repeat, rolled my little agate skull in my hands and thought about his smile, his soft laugh, those green eyes.

When I got back to my room after dinner and glanced at my open laptop, there was an email from Drew. My heart rate spiked and my head went light. This was getting ridiculous. I was like Pavlov's dog, drooling whenever it heard a bell rung, except my trigger was Drew Ellery.

From: Drew Ellery
To: Mimi Alston
Subject: Albert
Hi, Mimi,
I was thinking about Albert and how you can't remember his full name and rank.
You said you first met him at the Perry Ridge Memorial Garden. I checked, and there are a few hundred WW2 veterans who came from the county honored on the cenotaph there. I went on the website and found seven Alberts listed who died between 1941 and 1950.
You thought he was about thirty-five, right? Two of those Alberts were too young and one was too old. But there are four Alberts with memorials in that garden who died after their return home.
I used the government website showing soldiers lost in war and came up with the attached photos of three of them. There's only one I haven't been able to track down yet. Did you want to check these Alberts and see if any of them look familiar?
Drew

I clicked on the first attachment. Not him. The second one. Not him.

The third…

There was my Albert! He was gazing back at me from the screen, looking serious in full uniform. He was younger than I knew him, and his chestnut-colored hair looked dark in the black-and-white photo. His eyes were pale—probably blue. I'd only ever seen them in shadow.

Corporal Albert Goundrey, born 1906. 3rd Battalion, 15th Infantry Regiment. Succumbed to his injuries November 16th, 1946. Beloved son of Patrick and Maisie, dear brother to Catherine.

For a second, my emotions went into battle: a smile wrestled with a sob and my throat burned. Damn, I was on a rollercoaster these past few days. These moments with Drew. The escapade with Gabe. The loss of Albert and that moment when my parents suggested I change schools. It wasn't a regular rollercoaster, either. It was a triple-corkscrew, highest-vertical-drop-in-the-hemisphere, loose-seatbelt ride, and I kind of loved it.

I seized my sketchpad and started drawing. Within a few minutes I'd created a likeness of Albert. I sat back, flexing my aching hand and reviewing the sketch. It was one of the best things I'd ever done. For the first time, I'd successfully drawn a person that didn't look like a Frankenstein's monster collection of body parts. Perhaps it was because I knew him so well, seeing him day in, day out, everywhere I went. I felt lighter as I looked at the sketch, as if I'd found a way to mourn him correctly.

Hell yes. I was going to paint Albert.

19

New and Original Ways to Fail at Friendship

On Sunday, I stripped back the paint from my creepy, skeletal portrait of Grandma and started blocking in the outline of Albert. Several senior art students were in the art room today, immersed in oil paint fumes. Axel turned up after around an hour and came straight over to my easel.

"Mimi, are you okay?"

"Yes…?" I remembered in a dismayed instant that I'd had plans to paint with him on Saturday—and had forgotten to cancel. "Oh, hell, Axel—I'm so sorry about yesterday! I screwed up, big time."

The look on his face told me he was hurt, even though he pretended it was no big deal.

"I won't let it happen again," I promised. "That was not my best friend behavior."

It came out wrong. I'd meant not my best behavior as a friend, but it sounded like I was calling him my best friend. But the way he brightened made it impossible to clarify it without hurting him even more.

"It's totally fine," he assured me. "Everyone has their lapses. Last week I forgot to brush my teeth one morning. I barely dared talk to anyone all day in case I had bad breath."

"Well, you're more scrupulous than a lot of other teenage boys, that's all I can say."

Axel set up an easel next to me. He'd stopped cosplaying as his prospective friends and was back to his original checked shirts and brushed hair—not a trace of goth or surfer. I wanted to cheer for him.

"How are you liking EVA now?" I asked, squeezing a dob of paint onto my palette.

"I'm getting into the swing of it. Being a boarder's taking some getting used to. I was left hungry after dinner last night because the only vegetarian options were side dishes of boiled vegetables." He rolled his eyes.

"You're the only vegetarian in the boys' dorm?"

He nodded. "There was another one, but he left."

"Huh. That's not the case for the girls' dorms." Cassie was one of several vegetarians.

"Maybe it's considered girly, but my whole family is against meat eating."

I laughed. "Vegetarianism is not girly."

We fell into silence while we worked on our portraits. Mrs. Shaw stepped in and out, moving between her office and the supply room. Sometimes I wondered if she had a home to go to. Marvin and Hannah were around, drifting in and out of my field of view. The other kids chatted softly, but mostly the atmosphere was one of quiet hard work. I glanced at Axel's canvas. His painting of his mother was coming along, but she seemed almost ridiculously beautiful to me. Like that old-time actress who married the prince— Grace Kelly, I think it was.

My portrait was coming together, too. For whatever reason, Albert looked human. Ironic that my living subjects looked dead but I could make a dead person look alive.

I painted for two hours, but I had a load of homework waiting for me, so I eventually dropped my scraper into a jar of thinner and stretched. Axel leaned across to look at my painting.

"That's really powerful, Mimi. It looks like a period piece. Nineteen fifties?"

"Forties."

"What's going on with his eyes?"

I'd started painting Albert's light-colored eyes then smudged over them with a shadow. It was how I knew him.

I shrugged. "Eyes are hard."

"Who was he?"

For a second I thought I smelled tobacco smoke, but it was probably just the paint chemicals. "He was family."

At school on Monday, I got my lunch and made my way toward the table where Mona, Drew and Patience were sitting. Patience saw me coming, got up and left. I tried not to be triggered, flashing back to the ridicule and rejection of middle school.

I sat beside Mona and picked up my fork. "Patience not hungry?" I asked, keeping my tone light.

For better or worse, Mona never tackled anything except head-on. "She's upset that you hate her family."

"Hate her family!" It was so unfair that I couldn't even verbalize my protest.

"Because you don't want to go to Dale's Run."

"It's Mimi's *ghosts* that don't want her to go to Dale's Run," Drew said.

"Obviously." Mona pushed a pea out of her fried rice and off the side of her plate. "But Patience is sensitive; we all know that. She's jumped to the conclusion that Mimi's got the ick over her cult."

Ed and Gabe joined us. Gabe caught my vibe almost instantly. "Something wrong? Or someone wronged you?"

"Oh, you're improving!" Mona told him, reaching for her notebook. "You've identified resentment." She made a note. "A teen boy with emotional literacy—quite a phenomenon."

"I just wish I knew why my ghosts don't want me going to Dale's Run," I said. "Maybe it's not safe there."

"Maybe we should all avoid it," Mona mused.

"I wish we could," Ed said. "I sure don't want to go."

"Don't tell Patience," I said glumly. "She'll think you're judging her."

"She's been judged all her life," Drew said. "She just wants to be a good person, that's all, and her father's got her believing she has pure evil running in her veins."

"She's afraid of her gift," Gabe added. "Which makes sense, I guess, if her family hates her for it."

"I haven't helped." Drew kept his eyes on his lunch as he spoke. "She and I were like a two-person support group for recovering psychics for a while. Both of us trying to go as long as possible without using our gifts, encouraging each other. I've been an unmitigated…" He couldn't seem to find a word to do himself justice.

"Idiot? Dumbass?" Gabe offered innocently.

Drew said nothing, and I felt for him. He *had* been an unmitigated whatever, and so had Patience. I was impressed with him for acknowledging it, though.

"Patience is like an animal that's been kicked around," Gabe said. "Always in fight-or-flight. She'll need a hell of a lot of support to get over it."

"And here's Mimi saying she won't go to Dale's Run," Mona said. "No wonder Patience is feeling it."

I kept my eyes on my tray. "It's not my fault. I'd love to see the place where her cult lives."

Ed choked on a laugh. "That's the spirit."

Heat rushed up my neck. "I mean, her family. I'd go if the ghosts would let me. I'm not scared of them or anything, and I *like* Patience. I can't say I'll like her parents, knowing about the exorcisms, but I'd be respectful."

Gabe, Ed and Mona all looked up. "Exorcisms?" Ed repeated.

Drew grimaced at me. "I probably should have told you not to mention it. It's supposed to be a secret."

"Gabe knows," I said. "He already told me her family tried to exorcise her."

Gabe put his hands up. "I knew they thought she was possessed, but I had no idea they'd tried exorcism."

Mona bent her head over her book, scribbling frantically.

"Holy shit," Ed breathed. "How did they do it? Priests and crucifixes?"

I chewed my lip, panicking. "I'm sorry," I said to Drew. "I assumed they knew."

"It's fine," he said.

"Ms. Deering needs to know about this." Mona slapped her notebook shut.

"Deering already knows," Drew told her. "It was why she and Boxe had to go get Patience out of there."

The five of us sat in silence.

Ed released a long breath. "Imagine having some guy waving a cross over you, spraying you with holy water and shouting at Lucifer to leave your body."

Drew glanced at me. We both knew it had been worse than that. He looked at his tray like the thought of eating was suddenly disgusting.

In the afternoon, Mona burst through my door during study time, clutching her laptop. She shut the door behind her before Ms. Samvedi could catch wind of the transgression.

"You could get an official warning, Mona," I reminded her.

She was glowing with excitement. "Screw that. I need to show you something." She sank onto my bed, obliviously forcing Hannah out of the way, and wrenched open her laptop. "Remember what Olivia told us about the Lydenburg code? The papers that were found? I've just been on this site."

The website open on her laptop was called mysticalmenoa.org, and it was appalling. Black background, colored fonts, blue hyperlinks: the full Web 1.0 experience. It even had a button to sign a guestbook. The page was titled THE LYDENBURG PAPERS, all caps, in a gothic font. An image filled the screen: a scanned, dirty-looking piece of paper covered in inked strokes and dots.

"I was searching for stuff about the Lydenburg code—oh, and this is an amazing website, if you ever get a chance to look at it. I know it looks bad, but it's got incredible stories about ghost-lights and local disappearances and stuff—and all in Menoa County. So anyway, these papers were found years ago on a property in the back country of Lydenburg. There was an old farmhouse crumbling in a field. The family had built a new house closer to the road. One day, the farmer was pulling some of the floorboards out of the old homestead to use as firewood and found this metal chest underneath. It had the papers inside. He thought they might be from the Civil War and handed them over to the local museum, but they couldn't decipher them."

"And you can?"

"Yes, I can!"

"Anything juicy?"

"Yes! There's only the one page of the original papers available online, so I'm trying to figure out how to get hold of the rest. I might have to visit the museum. But Mimi, it's *bizarre*. It's about some ancient mystical city that becomes visible to people who are enlightened enough to reach another dimension. The city is supposed to be here in Menoa County somewhere."

"Oh, wait, my dad mentioned that when we were driving down from Perry Ridge." I tried to remember what he'd said. "I think it was something to do with pagans—or maybe it was Wiccans."

"Wiccans!" Mona reached for her notebook. "Interesting."

"I think he even mentioned aliens."

Mona's eyebrows were mid-forehead by now. I waited while she scribbled. A moment later, she slammed her book shut and fixed her eyes on mine. "Here's the weirdest bit. Whoever wrote it talks about *the seven.*"

Hannah and Marvin stirred and an icy shiver ran through me, but I tried to stay rational. "The seven?"

"Yes! Us!"

"Hang on, how do you know it's us?"

"The code is tricky—I'm still translating—but it talks about the coming of the seven evolved ones, and a new dawn for the world. I mean, don't you think it's a bit too much of a coincidence? That there are seven of us, with heightened enlightenment, and that this is all taking place in Menoa County…"

I wasn't quite sure how to break it to her that I didn't see that much connection, only the number seven. We certainly didn't have more enlightenment than the average seventeen-year-old. "Does it say *what* the abilities of the seven are?"

She shook her head, only deflating slightly at my lack of enthusiasm. "No, but *seven evolved ones*, Mimi. Don't you think that must mean us? The idea of being evolved—I mean, it would explain a lot, you have to admit, if our gifts aren't just an anomaly, but a new evolution in humankind."

"You mean we're prototypes? Or genetic mutations?"

Her eyebrows pinched together. "Sort of. Maybe we're new iterations of what humans are going to become. Our gifts are sort of like heightened sensory abilities, don't you think? Like I don't just read, but read across different languages. Gabe is a super feeler. Patience can craft things out of cosmic dust, and Cassie's like an animal whisperer. Drew sees beyond what's right in front of him at any given moment. Ed can harness his energy or, I don't know, share his immune responses to heal people. And you can see through the veil between the worlds of the living and the dead. It's like we have all the usual senses and modes of perception, but they're enhanced. So wouldn't you call that an evolution? An upgrade to the normal abilities of a human?"

"We're not Pokémon, Mona. That's not how evolution works. It's slow and subtle, happening over generations."

"But there's always a sudden mutation that kicks off the change," she argued. "You know, like the first African elephant born with bigger ears, which helped it flap the flies away and hear at a greater distance. Or whatever big elephant ears are for."

I didn't know what to say.

She inspected my face. "You don't believe me."

"Of course I *believe* you. I believe that you can translate the Lydenburg paper accurately. I just don't know if the mention of the 'seven evolved ones' is enough to be sure it's about us."

This time she did look crestfallen. She closed her laptop and got up. "Okay." She headed for the door.

"Wait, Mona!" She looked back. "I don't mean I doubt you. I want to hear more when you've translated the rest."

She gave something that combined a nod and a shrug and left my room. I'd definitely upset her.

As a kind of oblique apology, I opened my own computer and emailed Dad to ask him if he knew about the alien city in the mountains and whether it was Wiccans or pagans who were involved.

<h1 style="text-align:center">20</h1>

<h1 style="text-align:center">That Feeling Like You're Being Watched</h1>

Mona was late to breakfast in the morning and came in yawning and bleary-eyed. To my relief, she headed over to my table.

"Late night?" I asked.

"Three a.m.!" she whispered, plonking herself beside me. "I feel like I just went to sleep five minutes ago."

"And?"

"I did it. Decoded the whole page. I went into this kind of weird trance state with exhaustion and started to feel like I might be making it all up. Anyway, I finished it."

"You're amazing." I was completely sincere.

"I sent Ms. Deering the translation. We'll see what she says today."

I told her about emailing my dad, and Mona came with me to my room after we'd snarfed breakfast. I opened my laptop, and good old Dad had already replied.

"That's the thing about my father," I said. "Ask him about something he's interested in and he gets back to you immediately. Ask him for a photo of his own mother and it takes him weeks to get his shit together."

From: Kevin Alston
To: Mimi Alston

Subject: Re: Menoa magic mountain?

Hi, Mim, yes, I remember the story you're talking about, but it wasn't Wiccans or pagans. The first time I heard about this group was in a letter to the editor in the Perry Ridge Gazette. Some guy was complaining about the number of "minority religions" proliferating in this part of the county. He ridiculed the ideas of one particular group, who believed those with a special level of transcendence would move into another dimension and become able to see an ancient lost city. They would even be able to lead people to it. If it helps, I think the holy city was called Asteria or Astrea or something similar. You might be able to find something on the web if you're interested. What makes you ask, by the way?

Have fun at camp on the weekend!

Love, Dad.

"Search for Asteria," Mona urged me.

I tried it, then Astrea. We found nothing related to an invisible city. The only thing remotely like it in Menoa County was an energy company named Astera.

"Let's go back to MysticalMenoa.org," Mona said, reaching across me to type in the URL.

This website is blocked under the Etherall Valley Academy online safety policy.

Mona's mouth dropped open. "What? I was literally on that site last night! How could it be blocked?"

I tried again, and up popped the same message. Mona dashed back to her room to get her own laptop, opened it and attempted to pull up the website. Blocked.

"What the hell?" I'd never seen her so outraged. "How dare they? Why would EVA block that site, anyway? It's totally harmless." She stopped, and I could practically see the cogs and wheels turning in her head. She sucked in a breath and seemed to tense all over, her eyes popping. "We've stumbled across something important, Mimi. That's why they've shut it down."

"What?" I wasn't keeping pace at all. "Who?"

"I don't know. *They*. Maybe even someone working in the school."

"Wait, maybe the site just got flagged because it's insecure or infected with malware or whatever. Or maybe there's sketchy ads running on it. There's bound to be a simpler explanation."

She was shaking her head. "No. I know there's something wrong here. It's just a basic website run by some old guy living in Lydenburg who's fascinated by mysteries, and *bam*!" She clapped loudly, making me jump. "Locked out."

"It is weird." I didn't want to disagree too firmly and risk hurting her again. And she *did* have a planet-sized brain.

She stood up. "Let's get to school. I want to talk to Ms. Deering."

Mona was wide-eyed and fidgety with anticipation until it was finally time for gifted class. Ms. Deering was way more interested in Mona's story than I expected. She listened intently while Mona accused every staff member at EVA of sabotaging her research. Gabe sat up straight while Mona ranted, clearly picking up on how seriously she was taking it.

"Who at EVA decides which sites are okay and which get blocked?" he asked Ms. Deering.

She hesitated. "I assumed it was the IT staff, acting on the policy, but this scenario is well outside the usual protocols. As far as I know, EVA only blocks social media and gaming sites, anything eighteen-plus or R-rated. Not the kind of website Mona's describing."

I didn't need to venture my theory about it being a phishing site because Ed had the same idea and suggested it to the group.

Ms. Deering considered it. "I would agree, but this is just so unusual—for a student to be using a website and have it blocked overnight. Normally the online safety strategy is more preventative than reactive." She sank into a seat, gazing at the floor absently. Then suddenly her eyes were up on Mona again. "You emailed me through the school system last night, telling me about the site and the Lydenburg papers."

Mona clutched the edge of her desk. "You think someone read our emails?"

Ms. Deering had gone so pale she was almost faintly green. "Did you save a copy of the Lydenburg paper you translated?"

Mona opened her file. "Save it? I printed it." She waved a piece of paper covered in spidery code at us. "Try blocking *paper*, you fascist assholes."

"Language," Ms. Deering murmured, but her heart wasn't in it.

"I'm confused," Patience said. "Are you saying someone is reading your emails, Ms. Deering? Or Mona's?"

"*All* of our emails!" Mona said. "What about our messages on Collabor8?"

"We can't be sure Collabor8 isn't compromised, too," Ms. Deering said.

My heart wobbled like an old elevator arriving on the ground floor. We'd had so many chats about our gifts. There was all the stuff from before and after the Juliet incident. And Drew had emailed me the things he'd found out about Albert. We'd all been so careless.

Ms. Deering ran her hands over her face. "I'm sure I don't need to say this, but from now on, let's only speak about the gifts in person—or using our phones, I suppose, if we're outside school. If it's an emergency, you can use the school intranet; otherwise avoid it. I'll try to find out who in the school might be watching us."

She asked Mona to read her translation aloud.

"Some bits are missing," Mona told us. "Well, not missing, but I haven't been able to decipher them yet. It's one of the hardest codes I've ever seen. I can't work out the first line on this page, but the second line says: *The records from... something... describe it thus. The* something *were walking through an untouched region in the hills surrounding Lydenburg when we came to a precipice. From that point we could see great rocky outcrops and majestic trees with a river coursing through it all, very mountainous—and all but impassable.*

"*Three of our party immediately exclaimed at the sight, and it became apparent they saw a scene we could not perceive. They described a great city of stone towers,* *surrounded by a vast moat of water like a sea, reaching up to the walls of a—*I can't decode that word—*protecting the beautiful place.*

*"Each of the three who saw this vision, all advanced in the spiritual knowledge of the community, gave a different account of the city's place in time. One declared it ancient ... another said it was yet to be constructed and the last concluded it—*can't read that bit. *They all agreed this city, which they called—*can't get that word—*would be a place of refuge when a great flood rose. Then the prophesied seven evolved ones would ascend to power, bringing the world into the dawn of a new phase."*

Mona looked up.

"What does it all mean?" Ed asked.

She put the paper back into her file. "*Seven.*"

"You think that means us?" Gabe asked.

"Who else?"

Drew's forehead creased. "You can't just assume it means us whenever you see the number seven in some esoteric document."

Mona sniffed and scribbled the word *esoteric* in her notebook. "I'm hardly jumping to conclusions here. But seven *evolved* ones? It can't just be a coincidence that we're all here together being mentored by Ms. Deering in Menoa County—and there's a city that can only be perceived through extra-sensory perception *also* linked to the county."

Cassie had been observing the conversation in silence, but now she spoke. "I think you've got it out of proportion. It's most likely just some freak spouting off, probably coming off a recreational bender. Don't they say there are 'shrooms growing in the Lydenburg hills?"

Wrong thing to say. "Oh, really, Cassie?" Mona's voice was icy. "It doesn't fit into the Cassie O'Meara frame of reference, so you've made up your mind it's bullshit?"

Cassie scowled. "You always think there's some reason behind all our gifts, behind us all being here at EVA. But some things just *are*."

Mona opened her mouth to retort, but Ms. Deering raised her hand like a crossing guard. "This isn't useful. Now, Mimi, did you say your father knew something of these 'transcendents'?"

"Oh, yes." I got my laptop out of my bag and opened my email while Cassie and Mona continued their argument in snarky mutters. For a few seconds, I just stared at my inbox in astonishment, then I looked up at Ms. Deering. "It's gone."

"What's gone?"

"The email from my dad. It was there this morning. Now it's gone."

Mona practically sat on my lap to get a proper look at my screen. "Check your deleted items." I knew I hadn't deleted it, but I obeyed. "No? Your spam folder, then."

I shook my head. "It's gone."

Ms. Deering's lips were pressed tightly together. "Well, that confirms things." She cast a steely gaze across us all. "Someone with access to the school's intranet is trying to stop us from finding out about these Lydenburg papers and the events they describe. Which means we're onto something important."

Mona flashed a look of triumph at Cassie.

I wasn't at all happy to know Mona was right. It felt icky to know someone had been fishing around in my emails.

When school ended, I did what I always did when I was uncomfortable and needed to get out of my own skin. I worked on some art.

The art room was quiet; it was just me working on the painting of Albert, with Mrs. Shaw sorting out the supply closet. Axel turned up around four with a stack of library books. He read a bit about painting skin tones, then got to work on the portrait of his mother.

"Ed was saying you're all going on a camp this weekend." He smiled a little wistfully. "I didn't get into the program. Nor did Olivia."

"I'm sorry." He looked so disappointed that I really did feel sorry for him. "You're not missing out on much," I lied.

He gave me a lopsided smile. "I'm a bit of an overachiever, I guess, so it hits hard when I don't get what I'm aiming for. I'm going to ask if I can try again in a month or so."

"Maybe you should just enjoy the normal schoolwork load. There's plenty of time for overachieving in college."

He shrugged, but it was obvious a normal workload wasn't enough for him. We painted in silence for a few minutes. It was when I was deeply immersed in dabbing color on Albert's hat that Axel spoke again, dragging me out of the moment. "Can I ask you something?"

"Mm-hm." I reloaded my brush with olive green.

"Do you think Patience likes boys?"

I looked over at him. "As opposed to non-boys?"

He thought about it. "I hadn't thought of that, but yes. What I meant was, do you think she…?"

"Dates?" I offered.

"Yes!" He shot me a grateful look.

So Axel liked Patience! That might work. Drew had said Patience had "specific standards": devout and old-fashioned. And Axel had said once that his faith was important to him. He had an old-fashioned formality I'd noticed in some other homeschooled kids—he used the sort of language that came from spending most of your time with adults.

"I'm not sure. She's from Dale's Run, so she obviously has some parental rules to navigate. But she might be open to dating the right person."

Axel nodded thoughtfully. "She doesn't have a lot of friends, does she?"

"I suppose not." A pang of regret hit me. With me saying I couldn't go to Dale's Run, Patience probably thought she had even fewer friends than she'd realized.

When it was time to finish, we packed up and headed back toward the dorms. Axel's art books looked heavy, so I helped him carry a couple. Bruise-colored clouds hung in the sky and, although it wasn't cold, there was a feeling of rain.

"Your shoelace is undone," Axel said, slowing.

"I'll fix it later."

"No, you might trip." He put his pile of books on the edge of the old well, took the rest out of my arms and watched me expectantly.

Wow, he was quite the rule follower. I put my foot up on the low wall to tie my shoelace, then Axel exclaimed in alarm. His library books had slid off the uneven stones and crashed onto the rusted cover of the well. It cracked and split under their weight. I lunged for them and managed to save all but one book, which fell through the split in the iron cover and landed in the ancient wooden bucket chained to a crank.

"Oh no!" Axel took the books from me as if they were live kittens I'd somehow endangered. "It's a library book! I'm going to get in so much trouble!"

"No, they'll understand. You didn't do anything wrong." The look on Axel's face stopped me. He looked so panicked that a dark suspicion flitted across my mind: did he get in trouble a lot at home? Were his parents overly critical and repressive? Shadows swirled and gathered in the corners of my vision.

I checked the position of the book. It wasn't too far down—definitely within arm's reach. I leaned across the wall and stretched downward, my hips balanced on the flat stone, then navigated my hand through the iron grille, avoiding the sharp edges. The book was just inches from my fingertips. I leaned a little further.

Suddenly my center of gravity was on the wrong side of the wall and I was tipping, about to go headfirst through the grille. For the first time I saw the water at the bottom, black and reflective. I gasped and flailed, then something caught me and I just hung there like a human seesaw, wobbling over the lip of the well.

Axel had hold of my legs. "I've got you! Can you inch your way back?"

I squirmed backward, grabbing the book by one corner as I did so. Finally I hitched myself out of the well, landing on my butt and falling back on the grass. I gazed up at the sky, panting.

Axel dropped to his knees beside me. "Are you all right?"

"Yes! Thanks for saving me."

"Thanks for saving my book." He got to his feet, extending a hand to help me up. "I'll report that broken grille to admin. You probably shouldn't have tried to get my book, Mimi. If you'd fallen in, you might have broken a limb, or even drowned!"

We walked back to the dorms, Axel chattering about old wells and water sources, and I didn't hear anything he said.

Dead girl's face underwater. The vision scurried and tumbled around the inside of my head like a rat in a wheel.

21
Living in Close Quarters

By the next morning the old well was cordoned off with a caution sign, and by midday there were workmen there installing a new steel cover. I told no one what had happened. It wasn't anyone's business, and Drew would only blow it out of proportion. I mean, that rusted grille had been an accident waiting to happen.

Camp day arrived. Mr. Boxe was driving his own car while Ms. Deering ferried us in the school's fourteen-seater. It had the EVA triple-spiral crest on the side, which Mona told me was called a triskelion. Mr. Boxe wore a polo shirt with the same logo on the breast pocket.

Hannah and Marvin were already waiting in a seat on the minibus and Mona had saved one for me, which put a dent in my hopes of sitting with Drew. I kept an eye on him as he climbed the steps and ducked through the door. He paused in the aisle to check where everyone was seated, then got Patience to move from the spot she'd chosen up the front. They came to sit at the back near me and Mona.

Cassie made Ms. Deering play an atrocious pop radio station up loud. She and Gabe were in high spirits to be getting away from the dorms, and even Patience looked excited. Ed still seemed a little flat about missing out on his weekend surfing. Mona was utterly obsessed with her

Lydenburg papers mystery, and if we dared distract her from writing in her Notebook of Momentous Discoveries, we paid for it with a lengthy monologue on the seven evolved ones.

Cassie broke the news that the police had decided not to press charges against Tyler. "It's partly because of his age, but also because 'all he did' was hold on to my arm. Hello? The guy literally restrained me while I screamed for my freedom, but apparently that's not a crime."

We agreed with her that it was bullshit, but Patience wondered aloud if Tyler felt guilty. "God may be making him pay for his crime by suffering in his conscience."

Cassie openly rolled her eyes. "You're way off," she informed Patience. "When someone exhibits that level of toxic masculinity, the likelihood that they feel any guilt is miniscule. Don't you think it'd be better to have him off the streets, or at least slapped with a police record? I mean, imagine if you were invited on a date and you found out too late that the guy was an abductor or a sex pest."

Patience chewed a nail. "My father and the pastor will choose a man to court me when the time comes. No one at Dale's Run does anything like what Tyler did."

"Sure," Cassie said, eyebrow hitched.

Drew was studying Patience's face. "When will your dad let you start courting?" I smothered a jealous pang.

"When I'm eighteen." She was turning pink. "I'm not in a hurry."

"Do you know who's lined up for you?" Cassie asked.

Patience shrugged. "I have a suspicion."

Cassie could barely conceal her horror. "Do you like him?"

Patience shrugged again. "He seems like a hardworking fellow. I don't feel ready for dating boys, though."

"I could *not* deal with my parents choosing my boyfriend," Cassie said. "How could I like the guy, even if I did like him, know what I mean? It's the principle."

"If your parents had chosen your suitor, it might have been a nicer boy than Tyler," Patience said, then went bright red as she realized how it sounded.

Cassie glared. "So what happened was all down to my bad taste? Way to victim-blame."

Patience practically whispered an apology, Cassie gave her signature dismissive sniff, and everyone else pretended not to notice how flustered they both were.

We arrived at Blackmere Pool after about an hour on the road. Ms. Deering turned the minibus off the highway onto a gravel track and we bounced over the uneven surface into the forest. The trees towered on either side of the road, creating a cool, dim atmosphere, faintly indigo in hue. We passed a couple of cars full of tourists leaving the national park after a day visit.

Eventually Ms. Deering brought us into a clearing where a perfectly still, deep-green lake gleamed like a polished gemstone. I was glad I'd thought to throw in my bathing suit, even if there was no swimming planned for the camp. Maybe we'd get the chance anyway.

The thought of Drew's vision whispered across the back of my mind like a bad memory. I dismissed it. It wasn't like I was an inexperienced swimmer.

Massive granite boulders were perched on the banks. They had the precarious appearance of marbles, like if you pushed against one, it would roll into the water. Some teenagers were hanging around a platform where swing ropes had been looped on a wooden post. They appeared to be psyching themselves up to jump in.

Ms. Deering drove us around to the other side of the pool and past a sign pointing to *Cabins 4 Hire.* We piled out of the minibus and checked out our accommodation: three tiny wooden cabins nestled deep in the trees. One cabin had three bunk beds for us girls and Ms. Deering, and another was for the boys and Mr. Boxe. The third contained showers and toilets. There was also an open-sided kitchen shelter and a campfire circle surrounded by benches.

Mr. Boxe was already there. He blustered around, calling out for help. He was saying things like "Many hands make light work" and "Let's make hay while the sun shines," obviously in his element.

"Wait, we have to share the bathroom hut with the boys?" Cassie screwed up her nose.

"You'll take turns showering," Ms. Deering told her. "Girls then boys."

Cassie didn't lose the face. "It's all a bit crappy, don't you think? Did you see the cabin floors?"

"It's rustic." Mona was grinning. "Welcome to camping, Cass."

Cassie had more complaints: having to carry the food boxes to the kitchen shelter, lack of privacy, the state of the toilets. I got on with the tasks we were asked to do, but every time Drew and I locked eyes, it felt like we exchanged secrets. At one point, while I was lifting a carton of water bottles out of Mr. Boxe's car, he leaned in to help and we became a tangle of crossed arms, skin on skin, so close I felt his body heat and smelled his slightly piney scent. By the time we'd extricated ourselves and the carton was securely in my arms, I was lightheaded from the sheer sensory input.

We chose our bunks and Ms. Deering got us doing jobs. I was rostered onto dinner prep with Cassie, which meant cutting up the toppings for pizzas. Being vegetarian, she refused to touch the bacon or pepperoni, but also seemed to take exception to olives and mushrooms, so I ended up doing most of the work. Mr. Boxe had Patience and Gabe helping him construct a dubious "oven" out of foil and a cardboard box. The other three were told to collect firewood, but we could hear them goofing around through the trees.

To my surprise, the cardboard box oven worked and the pizzas were good. The sun dropped below the horizon as we ate, leaving only traces of blue dusk. Stars began to glitter, promising a spectacular astronomical show. Ms. Deering handed out bandanas in different colors, telling us to keep them close because we'd be switching them around depending on who we were paired with over the weekend. Mona wrapped hers around her wrist like she was a *Survivor* contestant. The rest of us pocketed them.

After dinner, we sat around the fire, chatting comfortably. My ghosts hovered among the trees, keeping their distance—a pleasant break for me. We were laughing and telling camping stories. Drew and I kept meeting each other's gaze, and I sure didn't need that fire to keep me warm.

"Righty-ho," Mr. Boxe declared suddenly, flicking on his headlamp and half blinding us all. "First activity!"

"Aw, but we're enjoying the *sobramesa*!" Mona protested, and although I didn't know the word, I guessed it meant something like the atmosphere of us chilling together after the meal.

Even Ms. Deering seemed a bit startled by Mr. Boxe's suggestion. "Er—weren't we going to wait until the morning, Theo?"

"Not enough time in tomorrow's schedule, with all we've got planned for them. And this game must be played at night. All right, so we'll start with Stalk the Lantern. One group will be the lantern keeper." He passed Mona a battery-operated lamp. "The other two groups take a radio each."

I was trying to work out how to get myself next to Drew when Mr. Boxe told us the pairs were the same as our job roster partners, so I was stuck with Cassie. We found matching green bandanas and put them on our wrists. Cassie took the two-way from Mr. Boxe and sat beside me, fiddling with it.

Mr. Boxe's voice boomed into the quiet night. "Mimi and Cassie, you're Team Lion. You'll start at the lake." Across the circle, Drew froze. "Patience and Gabe, you're Team Tiger. You'll start here at the cabins. Mona, Drew and Ed, you are Team Antelope. You'll take this lantern into the trees and evade capture, guarding it with your lives."

Patience was giggling. I'd never really seen her laugh before. Nervous giggle, maybe?

"There's no moon," Ms. Deering put in. "I'm not sure if…"

"The darkness is the whole point!" Mr. Boxe's enthusiasm was hard to counter. "They're perfectly safe. The two pursuing groups have radios to communicate with each other; the lantern keepers have the lamp, so they can navigate using that. And whistles!" He patted his pockets then drew out a tangle of whistles on lanyards and passed them to us. "Everyone takes a whistle in case of getting disoriented."

"What do we do when we find the lantern?" Patience's voice was eager and her eyes shone in the firelight. Oh, wait—she wasn't nervous. This was Patience *excited*.

"Creep up on them and touch the lantern. Once the lantern gets touched, the game is over."

"And we can take the lantern anywhere?" Ed asked. "Or are there boundaries?"

"You'll play in the trees between the cabins and the lake. If you reach the trails on either side of that patch of woods, stop. That's your boundary."

"That's a wide area." Ms. Deering sounded even less happy.

"It's about right for this game," he told her.

Mona switched on the lantern, which beamed a soft white light across the benches. Mr. Boxe showed us how to use the two-ways and then Cassie and I were sent off first.

"I can't see a damn thing," she grumbled.

I stumbled over a fallen branch. "A flashlight would have been handy."

We made it to the lakeside relatively unscathed. The sound of voices floated across the water and a yellow light glowed on the far shore.

"There's someone there," Cassie whispered.

"Must be those other kids from earlier," I replied. "Camping out, maybe."

We sat out the five minutes we'd been told to wait, then Cassie tested the radio, holding it like it might catch alight. "Hello? Gabe? Patience, are you there?"

There was a silence. "Hey, was that a flash of light?" I asked, stretching up on my toes to peer into the trees.

The radio crackled into life, making us both jump. "Breaker, breaker, Team Lion, this is Team Tango-India-Golf-Echo-Romeo, receiving you loud and clear. What can we do you for? Over!"

"Stop being ridiculous, Gabe," Cassie said into the radio.

Crackle. "That's a negative, Team Lion, no can do." Patience's giggles were audible in the background. "I've got a bogey at three o'clock—no, false alarm, that's just Mr. Boxe's portable camp toilet. Over."

I snort-laughed, but Cassie remained as sour as ever. "Can you guys see any light from there?"

Crackle. Patience's tentative voice came over the radio. "That's a negative, Team Lion, do you copy? What's your twenty? Over." This time Gabe was laughing in the background.

"What's a twenty?" Cassie demanded.

Crackle. "It means your location. Over."

"Why didn't you just say location? Where are we, Mimi?"

I took the radio. "We're by the lake, just between the two biggest boulders."

"That's a negative, Corporal Alston," Gabe answered immediately. "Only proper two-way communications will be accepted, do you copy? Over."

"Oh, copy that. I meant we're at two clicks south-southeast of the big Radio-Oscar-Charlie..." I hesitated. "What's K?" I asked Cassie in a whisper.

"How the hell am I supposed to know?"

"Sloppy," Gabe returned. "K is Kilo, which any self-respecting soldier should know. Drop and give me ten. Over."

"That's a negative, sir," I retorted. "And you can kiss my Alpha-Sierra-Sier—"

Cassie snatched the radio out of my hand. "Would you stop screwing around, Gabe?" she hissed into it. "I want to find this lantern and get back to the campfire!"

White light flashed—for real this time. I squeaked, grabbed Cassie's hand and dashed toward it. Cassie swore as she tripped over something.

"Shh!" I said, but it was too late—there was a scuffle, a burst of laughter and some crashing through the trees as our targets made a run for it. "Come on!" I ran after the bobbing white light.

"Gabe, they're coming back toward you guys!" Cassie said into the radio, doing her best to keep up as we stumbled through the undergrowth.

"Roger that!"

Cassie tugged me to a halt. "Just stop—we need to listen for a minute."

We stood still, listening, but the only noise was the sound of our panting. Then another flash of light—we both saw it simultaneously and, clutching hands, set off running as silently as possible. The lantern came into view and Cassie and I ducked down, watching from behind a bush. There was Mona, standing still, the lamp hanging from her hand.

Drew's voice arose. "I think we lost them."

"Keep the lantern low, Mona." That was Ed.

"I'm trying."

Crackle. "Team Lion, do you copy? No sign of the quarry. Over."

Mona, Drew and Ed were off and running by the time Cassie had dug the radio out of her pocket.

"You scared them off, you jackass!" she growled at Gabe. "*Over and out.*" She switched off the radio and stuffed it in her back pocket.

"Uh, I think we're supposed to keep the radio on," I said.

"We'll never catch them if Gabe keeps messing around. They headed toward the cabins. I think we should go around the perimeter of the woods, rather than straight after them. They'll be expecting us to pursue them, but we can intercept them near the campsite instead."

Whoa, okay, Cassie was taking this pretty seriously now. I mumbled assent, and she held my hand in a semi-painful grip, pulling me along after her. But before we went too much further, the light bobbed into view again. It was duller, yellower, like they were covering it with cloth. Cassie and I both went still. We recalibrated, then headed for the lantern like a couple of silent avenging angels. When we were just a couple of yards away, we stopped behind a tree. The light hung from a hand, illuminating a set of knees and shoes.

"Ready?" Cassie's voice was barely audible.

Adrenaline tingled through me. "One," I whispered back, "two… three!"

We lunged. "Gotcha!" we cried together, seizing the lantern keeper.

The figure stood motionless. Silent. He was big… too big. I let go, but Cassie held on. "Ed?" she asked uncertainly. "Drew?"

A moment later, there was an "*oof!*" followed by a squawk, and Cassie was sprawled on the ground. Then someone shoved me, sending me stumbling sideways. Footsteps thudded away across the dry pine needles, along with the light. It was a flashlight, I now realized.

"Was that—?" I stopped. *No. No way.*

Cassie grunted as I helped her to her feet. "Do we know him? Ow. I fell on my ass and the radio was in my pocket. I can already feel a bruise forming."

I touched the whistle hanging around my neck. Give a blast? Or head back to camp? That guy—whoever it was—might have been a stranger inadvertently caught up in our game. And he was gone now, not threatening us at all. But what was he even doing prowling around on his own in the dark?

"Let's go back to the cabins," I said.

Cassie had fished the radio out and turned the knob, but it didn't switch on. "Great. Maybe the batteries came loose."

We headed for where we thought the cabins were, crunching through the undergrowth. Cassie swore softly.

"Are you okay?" I asked.

"Yeah. That was just weird. Who was that? Did he… did he seem familiar?"

I blurted out what I'd been thinking. "Could it have been Mr. Boxe?"

She scoffed, then seemed to reconsider. "He was the right size, actually. But why would Boxe act like that?"

At that moment, a scream cut through the night from the direction of the lake. Cassie and I practically squeezed each other's hands bloodless.

"Come on!" came a cry from nearby—Mona's voice—and the lantern appeared.

Whistles sounded from the direction of the cabins, but I followed Mona and Ed toward the source of the screaming. My thoughts flew to that big male figure we'd encountered. Where was Patience? Then it became clear that the commotion was coming from those teenagers across the lake. We ran after Mona, who held her lantern high. Ed was outstripping us all through the nighttime gloom.

The lake came back into view, flat and still, full of the starry sky and tree shadows. Ed raced on ahead, around its perimeter. Shouts and screams came from the other side, lights jerking back and forth. I was flagging by now and had a cramp in my side. Cassie was fitter than me and dropped my hand so she could run after Ed. I caught up to Mona, and we puffed along together like the sport avoiders we were.

Someone was on the ground and the kids were arguing around him in panicky voices, their phone flashlights switched on.

"Don't move him!" Ed called. "I know first aid—what happened?"

"He dived off the bank!" The girl who answered was moving around with her phone held high in the air, trying to get a signal. "It was too shallow—he knocked himself out, came up floating."

The unconscious boy lay on his front, head turned to one side, mouth open. His body heaved occasionally. Ed crouched over him and put a hand on the center of his back, concentrating hard. Another boy standing nearby in wet shorts was hyperventilating, repeating, "Oh my God—Mason—oh my

God," over and over until the girl with the phone finally snapped at him to shut up.

The injured boy suddenly puked up some water, then gasped, but he didn't open his eyes. That was still good, I decided, sagging with relief. He was breathing. Ed kept his hand in place between the kid's shoulder blades, gazing down at him.

"Shouldn't we get him onto his back?" someone asked.

"No, his side," said someone else.

"Just leave him," I said loudly. "Ed knows what he's doing."

They backed off and Ed did his thing. Cassie was refitting the radio batteries, trying to bring it back to life, and we could hear more of our group running around the lake's edge, calling out to us, getting closer. I was seized from behind so suddenly that I let out an exclamation of shock. A pair of arms were around me. I struggled against them.

"It's not you!" The voice came in my ear.

Drew. I wrestled around to face him, ready to yell at him for scaring me—but someone pointed a flashlight at us and his expression was illuminated in full and dazzling brilliance for a couple of seconds. I stopped short. If he'd scared me, I'd *terrified* him. The chaos around us seemed momentarily to blur.

"I'm through!" the girl with the phone shouted. "Paramedic! We need a paramedic! Blackmere Pool!"

Gabe arrived next, then Ms. Deering with Patience. Our teacher joined Ed at the injured boy's side, checking his pulse. Ignoring everything and everyone, Ed steadfastly poured healing power into the boy's body. I willed the kid to wake up.

"Where's Mr. Boxe?" Cassie asked Gabe, her voice sharp.

He shrugged in bewilderment. "Back at the campsite, I guess."

But Mr. Boxe's car crunched to a halt beside us a minute later. He jumped out, leaving the headlights blazing on the scene and lugging a large medical supplies case. He had a flashlight in his other hand—a big one that shone with a yellow light. Cassie made a strange noise beside me.

"Make some room, make some room," he ordered us, getting down on his knees beside Ed and Ms. Deering. "What are you doing there, Ed? Get out of the way, son, we need to get him into the recovery position."

"Leave him," Ms. Deering pleaded. "He might have a spinal cord injury—he needs to be kept still."

Someone found a dry towel and put it over the shivering boy. He was still out of it, but there were signs of life. Ed and Ms. Deering looked after him while Mr. Boxe went into principal mode with these kids he'd never met before.

"What are you lot doing here at this time of night?"

"We were just camping," said one tearful girl. "Our parents know we're here."

"How did you get here, though? I don't see a vehicle."

"Bus," said a boy. "We've got tents to sleep in. We're catching the bus back home tomorrow."

"Well, you'd better get hold of your parents," Mr. Boxe said. "They'll have to pick you up tonight. This boy needs to go to the hospital."

"I *want* to go home," said another girl. "This place is creepy. There's some weirdo wandering around in the woods."

Mr. Boxe went still. "What weirdo?"

"A big guy," a boy piped up. "With a flashlight."

Mr. Boxe turned to us. "You kids ought to get back to the cabins. There are too many people here getting in the way. I'll sort these kids out, make sure they all get home safe. Ms. Deering can look after the boy."

"Ed's helping me," Ms. Deering called, her voice firm.

Mr. Boxe hesitated, then gave a grunt of agreement. He handed Drew his flashlight. "Go back to camp as a group, stoke the fire and get a kettle of hot chocolate on. Go on, now."

Drew released my arm, which I hadn't even realized he was still holding, and the six of us headed back around the lake.

22
The Tender Truth

"You can't do that." I kept pace with Drew, the others trailing behind us.

"Do what?"

"Freak out whenever I'm near water. I'm not going to drown, especially when I'm standing on dry land."

"People can drown in a puddle," he muttered after a moment's silence.

"Yeah, but I'm conscious, and I can swim. And even if I couldn't, other people are around and presumably they can swim, too." I tried to see his face in the darkness. "If you're so worried about me drowning, why did you take me to the water hole in the woods that day?"

"There's nowhere else to go outside of school except those woods."

"So you ignored the fact that there was a water hole there?"

"I wanted to see what would happen when you were close to water."

For a second, I was speechless. "You were experimenting? To see if I'd fall in and drown?"

"I wasn't going to let that happen. I thought that at least if I was there when it happened, I'd be able to stop it. It was a controlled exposure to the danger. It's the only way for you to be around water now."

"There's not going to be a *controlled exposure,* Drew. I love water and I'm not going to stop going in it because of your vision."

"Then you should tell me when you're going to do it so I can be around."

"No. That's weird."

Drew said nothing, but he emanated helpless tension. It reminded me of the way Dad used to look sometimes when I refused to leave the house.

Maybe that was why it annoyed me. "Could you not treat me like a glass ornament you might accidentally drop? *I'm* not scared, so why should you be? I don't believe I'm going to die. If there's some incident the future has planned for me, it's avoidable. Anyway, I refuse to be frightened. I was running scared for years, and I'm not doing that anymore."

"I know *you're* not afraid."

"If I'm not afraid, why should you be?"

"You know why. Because my visions always come true."

"How can you say that? You can't prove it. You see things you don't always understand—things out of context. Like, you saw things about Juliet, right? The old blue car, the fist. But that ended well—Juliet and her mom are safe. Gabe and I are fine."

"It's different."

Little warning lights were going off at the edges of my consciousness. *Are you honestly trying to screw this thing up, Mimi?* my heart inquired. My head ignored it. "Different how?" I demanded.

"Because I never saw Juliet *dead.*"

The finality of the word shocked me into silence for a moment, then I got even madder. We'd reached the cabins by now. Drew stoked the dying fire while Mona found a pot she filled with milk and cocoa powder and set up over the flames. She put a packet of cookies on the table, and I sat in front of them, fuming. Drew sat beside me, somehow not dissuaded by my glare, and Gabe sat opposite, observing us curiously.

Cassie tossed her green bandana onto the picnic table. "Boxe," she said flatly.

Gabe turned his attention to her. "What did he do?"

"Maybe nothing. But *some* big guy appeared in the woods while we were looking for the lantern, and let's just say he didn't act like a normal person. Shoved me over, pushed Mimi out the way, ran off without saying a word."

Gabe stared. "*What?* When did this happen?"

She shook her hair, trying to get leaves out of it. "A few minutes before the ruckus started across the lake."

"That couldn't have been Mr. Boxe," Patience said. "He was here at the campsite."

"Are you sure?" Cassie asked. "The whole time?"

"Yes."

"No, we can't be sure," Gabe told Patience. "We didn't have Mr. Boxe in sight during the game. We went down to the tree line."

Patience had to admit it was true.

"The guy was the same build as Mr. Boxe," I put in.

Mona opened her notebook, a pensive look on her face, and made a few lines of notes. Between us, under the bench, the back of Drew's hand nudged mine. He held his open, his gaze on the fire, steady and determined. My anger dissipated as if he'd raised a white flag, and I took his cool, strong hand. I couldn't resist running my thumb along his soft skin.

Drew's expression didn't change an iota, but there was a slight movement around his throat.

Gabe snapped his head around to look at us. I slammed shut the doors to my feelings and offered him the cookie packet to distract him. Drew and I kept our clasped hands concealed between us.

"How did the boy get injured?" Patience asked.

"He dived into the lakebed," Mona told her.

Patience looked distressed, and Gabe slung an arm around her shoulders. The flashing lights of an ambulance soon appeared through the trees, but we couldn't hear or see anything else. Mona made Gabe help her pour the hot chocolate into mugs, then fretted because they grew cold and the others still hadn't returned. She poured it all back into the pot.

Drew and I said nothing. We just held each other's hands under the bench while my body turned into an insanely hot and fluttery thing and my heart did the Lindy Hop.

Mr. Boxe's car finally crunched into the clearing and he climbed out, followed by Ms. Deering and Ed. They all looked grim.

"What happened?" Mona asked Ms. Deering.

"The boy's been taken to the hospital. He's not in a good way."

Ed didn't even join us at the table. He went straight to the boys' cabin and shut the door behind him. Mr. Boxe was fussing with his medical kit in the back of his car, so Ms. Deering leaned down and spoke to us softly.

"Ed's terribly upset. I imagine he hoped the boy would at least regain consciousness, but he was still unresponsive when they took him away. The paramedics kept him immobilized—they suspect a spinal cord injury."

"Ed's got guilt pouring off him," Gabe said, glancing at the cabin.

"Shit," Mona said with a sigh. "Poor Ed."

"What can we do for him?" Patience asked.

"Just be there." Ms. Deering rubbed her forehead wearily.

Mona passed around the mugs of hot cocoa and we sipped them, discussing the evening's incidents. While Mr. Boxe was in the bathroom, Cassie whispered the story of the man in the woods to Ms. Deering.

"Was Mr. Boxe here the whole time we were playing the game?" Mona asked our teacher.

She grimaced. "I took advantage of the fact that you lot were busy, and went for my shower. But I'm pretty sure he was here. He was still in his camp chair when I stepped out of the bathroom."

I looked at Mr. Boxe's camp chair. It was one of those fancy ones with loads of pockets and a mini-table you could fold across your lap.

Mona was writing in her notebook. "It's all speculation." She sighed. "Give me one good fact. We're drowning in hearsay."

With the word "drowning," Drew's hand tightened around mine for an instant, then he let go and got to his feet. "I'll check on Ed."

I watched him go, my heart sinking. I *got* that he was worried about me, but this couldn't go on. Even if this vision he'd had never came to anything, he'd always be thinking about it, expecting it. How could we have any kind of normal relationship under those conditions?

But this connection between us was so damn supercharged—it meant something. I couldn't ignore that.

Ms. Deering said we should get to bed, so I went for a quick shower. On my way back to the girls' cabin, my ghosts trailing along behind me, I met Drew heading to the bathroom with his toothbrush. We stopped in the darkness.

"There's this Spanish proverb," he said without preamble. "*Vivir con miedo es vivir a media.* A life lived in fear is a life half lived. Reminds me of you."

I wasn't sure how to take it for a few seconds. "I like it," I said at last. "Maybe I'll get it tattooed across my forehead so you can read it when you need a reminder."

"Don't be mad at me. I can't help looking out for warning signs."

"Yes, you can. I want you to be my friend, not my savior."

"I'm not trying to be your savior—but you've got to understand, you've changed everything."

"What?" My voice sounded squeezed tight.

Drew raked his hand through his hair. "My whole world was guilt and fear. It was like a cage that went everywhere with me. Then you turned up and Deering identified you as our seventh. That meant I'd have to get to know you, get close to you. I was furious, knowing I'd have to go through…" He abandoned that sentence. "But the better I got to know you, the more it felt like the bars of the cage were bending back, letting the sunlight in. When animals first get rescued, they don't always know what to do. Their feet hit the grass and they just sink to their knees as if they've forgotten how to walk. I'm like that. No idea what to do. Just lying in the sunshine, trying to understand the freedom."

I processed his words, my blood somehow churning hotter in my veins. "You said it was a chicken tender that gave you your epiphany."

He dropped his voice. "It was never a fucking chicken tender, Mimi."

In the faint glow from the cabins, his eyes were locked on mine. We were standing closer than I'd realized and both leaned in at the same moment, me tilting my face up and Drew bending his down, as if we had a secret to share. Except, when we got to the point where we should have started whispering, there were no words. His chocolate-scented mouth was almost touching me, his warmth making my skin tingle, my breaths coming fast and shallow.

Footsteps on pine needles approached and a flashlight landed on us. Drew pulled back.

"Coming to brush your teeth, you two?" Ms. Deering asked.

He nodded and turned for the bathroom.

"I've done mine," I said.

"Head back to the cabin, then," she said pleasantly.

I did as she said, trying not to loathe her for the interruption. Once inside, I climbed onto a top bunk and unrolled my sleeping bag, heart still going like a hummingbird's. Cassie sat on the bottom bunk opposite in silk pajamas, attempting to clean her fingernails with the point of a floss pick.

"What's the deal with you and Drew?" she asked out of nowhere.

The muscles down my back tightened. "What do you mean?"

"He was there at school, after the dance, and you guys looked pretty cozy. You act sketchy—both of you. Are you seeing each other in secret?"

I lay back on my sleeping bag. "No."

"I'm not going to tell Ms. Deering. But she'll split you up, you realize. She doesn't want any of us getting involved with each other."

"It's nothing," I said. "We're not seeing each other."

"Mm-hmm. Why's he changed so much, then?"

"You'd have to ask him."

She snorted lightly. "Like he'd tell *me* anything. Anyway, I'm just saying. If there's something other than a crush going on, you should probably say something to Ms. D. We're supposed to be open about stuff. That's the whole point of the gifted program and all the teamwork activities at this camp."

I rolled onto my side, preparing to give Cassie some home truths about her teamwork skills—then froze. "Uh..."

She glanced up. "What?"

"There's something in your hair."

Her hands went still. "Where?"

"At the side, partway up. No, the other side. I think it's a moth. A big one."

For someone who could commune with animals, Cassie panicked more than I expected. She jumped up and ruffled her hair with her fingers, trying to shake the thing free. Then it stretched out little wings and I gave an involuntary scream.

"It's a bat!"

Cassie shrieked, flicking at her hair, then flipped her whole head upside down and gave her hair a thorough shake. A squeak sounded and the brown bat flew free of her curls.

It came to a clumsy halt on a ceiling beam and got itself into a hanging position, chattering and stretching its wings.

"Great." Cassie was panting. "A bat lives in our cabin."

"It's probably harmless." I didn't take my eyes off it.

Ms. Deering stepped inside with Mona and Patience. We warned them about the bat, and Mona immediately climbed into her sleeping bag and covered her head.

"Bats carry diseases," came her muffled voice. "That's how pandemics start."

Patience was staring at the bat from her top bunk. "Do you think it will leave?"

"It's probably about to go hunting." Cassie eyed it. "They're nocturnal. We must have disturbed it when it was waking up."

I shot her a dubious look. "I'm pretty sure it hitched a ride in your hair from outside. It's probably been in there since we were running through the woods."

Cassie took a breath. "Hey," she said to the tiny bat in a soft voice. "Go outside now, little friend."

It stretched its wings again, and for an instant we thought it would obey, then it just wrapped itself up and hung there, one beady eye trained on Cassie. It couldn't have been more than two inches long, from its long ears to its round rump.

"I guess not," she said sourly, and rolled over to settle into bed.

Patience eyed the creature warily for a minute, then she rolled over as well. Ms. Deering yawned and lay down, and when I checked on Mona in the bunk beneath me, she was still under her covers. I turned to face the wall.

I thought about Drew, running hard to rescue me when he thought I was in danger, and that tormented expression when the light hit his face. About his words: *bending back the bars to let in the sunlight.*

But most of all, about that moment in the darkness, with his body close and warm breath against my cheek.

I woke and rolled over. Sunlight streaked through a gap in the cabin's curtains. Everyone was still asleep and my ghosts were sitting on the end of Ms. Deering's bunk, watching me.

The tiny bat now hung from the underside of Cassie's bunk, right above her head. I opened my mouth to call out.

"Never mind it, miss," Hannah said into my ear. "It's harmless."

I bit back my cry with difficulty but kept my gaze on the bat. It was just hanging there. Hannah was right: Cassie didn't seem to be in danger of attack. When she woke up a few minutes later, she didn't panic. She just stared at her little companion with a puzzled look on her face.

"What's your deal?" she whispered.

It ruffled and gave a faint squeak. Cassie raised her eyebrows and sighed as she swung herself into an upright position.

"Fine," she said softly. "Just don't be weird."

By breakfast time, Cassie's bat was in her hair again and it wasn't going anywhere. She tried to get it to fly away and go nest for the day, but it was stubborn. It was a good thing Mr. Boxe didn't notice stuff like hair accessories.

"It's a companion," Gabe said. "What do they call it when an animal hangs around with a witch?"

"A familiar," Mona supplied.

Cassie glared. "Are you calling me a witch?"

Gabe shrugged. "If the bat fits."

Ed seemed to be back to his usual self—maybe a little quiet, but not distressed like the night before. Mr. Boxe was definitely back to *his* usual self and cooked eggs over the fire, calling out to us to check the morning's job roster. I was teamed with Ed after breakfast. We had to crush any trash we'd made and walk it over to the picnic area dumpsters to prevent animal scavenging. We skirted the lake, carrying a bag of trash each. Ed stared across at the spot where the teenagers had been camped.

"Hope that kid's okay," I said.

"Mason," he said.

"Mason."

We ditched the trash bags in a dumpster and headed back, but Ed stared so hard at the diving platform, I changed route. "Come on. Let's go take a look, make sure they didn't leave anything behind."

He seemed a little relieved. We walked over to the swimming site, and I spotted a sign nailed to a tree: *Warning! Shallow water. No Diving.*

Ed read it a couple of times, a muscle working in his jaw.

"Sometimes things just happen," I ventured. "Nobody's fault. It was probably too dark for him to see the sign. Or he might have seen it but forgotten about it."

"I couldn't help him." Ed's eyes had filled with tears, and he scrubbed them impatiently away. "Nothing I did would wake him up or mend his spine."

"It's a serious injury." I longed to give him a hug but didn't want to invade his personal space. "There's no way such severe damage could instantly heal."

"I could heal Cassie's aunt," he reminded me, swiping tears again. His chest was heaving; he was only just holding it together.

"Yeah, but it took a day or so to take effect," I said. "And she'd already been treated in hospital, too. Ed, you're not expected to cure a spinal cord injury. That's way too advanced. That's like neurosurgeon-standard healing ability. Give yourself a chance to level up. You know, you only just healed your first human a few weeks ago, and that was a jellyfish sting. Think about how far you've come. I think Mason might have died if you hadn't been here."

He gave me a watery smile. "Ms. D said all this last night. Then Gabe said it all again while Mr. Boxe was out of the cabin."

"Maybe that's because it's true."

He gulped twice and stared across the lake, his fledgling dreads wobbling in the breeze. My heart squeezed for the poor guy. *Screw it.* I gave him a hug, and, far from pushing me away, Ed wept onto my shoulder.

"This is not your fault," I told him in my firmest tone. "I'm sure Mason's doing better right now than he otherwise would be—and it's all down to the healing energy you poured into him last night. I'd bet my left testicle on it."

Ed was laughing when he pulled away. "Thanks, Mimi." He used his t-shirt to wipe his face. "You're always so grounded about our gifts. Only Mona tops your confidence."

"I'm not confident! I just know that when my ghosts want me to do something, I do it, and if I don't, they take charge anyway. I let my gift do the driving. Maybe you should, too."

We walked back to camp slowly to give Ed's eyes a chance to dry. Mr. Boxe was impatient to get the first activity for the day underway, and Ed and I remained partners. I tied his blue bandana around his dreads, and he tied mine around my messy bun.

It was a decoding game. Mona's eyes lit up, then Ms. Deering practically broke her by saying, "Mona, you sit this one out. I need your help setting up my next activity." She drowned out Mona's protests with a firm command to sit and drill holes in some buckets.

Mr. Boxe handed out clear plastic tessellation puzzles. Once solved, they gave us a series of shapes that corresponded to binary coding. The code gave us a riddle we then had to solve: *I am a spirit you would not like to drink. Between this world and next, I am the link. If you were to see me, you would get a fright. If you think I'm not real, you're probably right!*

Math puzzles and a riddle about ghosts? Obviously, Ed and I won.

After lunch, Ms. Deering split us into two groups: me, Patience, Gabe and Mona in pink and red bandanas versus Drew, Ed and Cassie in blue and green. We headed down to the lakeside to start the activity, which involved figuring out how to fill a container with water using holey buckets. We all took off our shoes and rolled up our cuffs, Mona and

Cassie exchanging competitive slurs and Patience giggling in anticipation.

Gabe sat out because we needed even numbers for this game. We were slaying the other team, partly because Mona had played it in Girl Scouts and knew all the tricks, and partly because Drew was distracted by watching me like a parent would watch their toddler near a kiddie pool. I even took time out of the race to roll my eyes at him.

The joke was on me, though. While we were filling the bucket for what should have been our last run, my foot slipped on a smooth stone and I staggered a couple of steps before overbalancing and landing face-first in the cold, shallow water. I came up laughing, but Drew stood frozen on the shore, his bucket leaking water everywhere, oblivious to the shouts of his teammates. Gabe was practically busting a rib laughing at me, and only Mona's competitive streak kept the game going. She screamed at me to move my ass. I staggered upright, and we got the final bucket of water into the container before Mr. Boxe declared us the winners, grinning at my dripping form. Even Ms. Deering was chuckling.

Drew turned on her. "I thought you said we weren't doing any water games on this camp." He sounded so angry that we all fell quiet.

To cover the moment, I declared that I was going back to my cabin to get changed. As I headed off, Ms. Deering told the others to take a fifteen-minute break, and a moment later, jogging footsteps sounded behind me.

"Mimi!"

I kept walking, wringing out my t-shirt. "Drew, I'm fine. Please stop this."

"I can't take it anymore!"

He seized my wrist so I had to stop and pulled me so close I could see the droplets of lake water on his eyelashes. I forgot my frustration in an instant. His eyes were glittering with desperation, his lips parted, his face taut. It turned my insides to lava. *Kiss me, kiss me, kissmekissmekissme—*

He moved a strand of wet hair off my cheek with excruciatingly tender fingers. "We have to tell them about my vision—Ms. Deering and the others. I can't handle this constant fear. I need the rest of them looking out for you, too."

It was like I'd been stung by a hornet, right through the sternum. I stood there, dripping. Speechless. Cheated.

"No." I shook my arm free and started walking again.

"*No*?" He pursued me. "Mimi, this is killing me! You won't let me tell you to be careful and you won't let me tell anyone else to make sure you're careful."

"I *am* careful. I fell over in a few inches of water, surrounded by people who would help me if I got into trouble. I was *not* going to drown!"

"My vision—"

"Was wrong!" I interrupted him. "Your vision was *wrong*. Forget about it."

"*Forget*?" The outrage in his voice made me wince. I reached for the door handle of the girls' cabin, only stopping when he said, "Mimi, wait!" I turned back to face him with a loud sigh.

Drew took my arms, bent down and put his lips on mine. I squeaked with shock and my brain jettisoned all coherent thought. *He's kissing me! I'm kissing him! We're kissing!*

Of their own accord, my hands found his hips and I hung on, rapidly becoming unaware of anything in the world except his lips, his smell and the feel of his hands slipping around to my lower back. His kiss grew feverish, answering my urgency, and despite having no idea what I was doing, I found myself pushing my tongue into his mouth to taste him more deeply. The cold ring in his lower lip bit into mine, and in response I pressed myself hard against him, wanting to bite him back, to devour him. A soft groan rose from his throat and he broke the kiss but stayed breath-minglingly near, gripping me close. Our chests were heaving and I was at risk of bursting into flames.

"I don't want to lose you," he whispered, and my heartbeat thrummed faster than insect wings.

You won't, I wanted to say, moving in to kiss him again.

But he held me back, eyes locked on mine. "You have to let me tell them."

My chest tightened like it had silently imploded. I swore, yanked myself out of his hold and shut the cabin door in his face.

<h1 style="text-align:center">23</h1>

<h1 style="text-align:center">Battle Tactics for Beginners</h1>

"You're not eating lunch?" Mona balanced her plate of nachos on a rock and settled herself beside me, oblivious to the fact that she'd forced Hannah off her seat.

I shook my head, concentrating on my sketch. "Not hungry."

Hannah sat beside Marvin on the rock opposite. Mona crunched corn chips. "So, is it official?"

"Huh?"

"You and Drew." She smirked.

"What are you talking about?"

"We all saw the kiss. I thought Mr. Boxe was going to jog over and grab you both by the scruff of the neck."

The blush was hot and painful. "You all *saw*?"

"Well, those of us who were walking back to camp. And anyone who didn't see would have heard about it by now."

I sighed.

"What's wrong? Is he a bad kisser? Too wet? Too much tongue?"

"No," I said. "He's a good kisser—not that I'd know if he wasn't, to be honest."

Her expression softened. "Aw, that was your first kiss? That's so sweet! Sorry you had an audience."

"Me too. Especially Ms. Deering and Mr. Boxe."

"They've probably already given Drew the 'this is not an appropriate setting for that sort of behavior' talk by now. What are you going to do about Ms. Deering's rule?"

"There's nothing between us. Ms. Deering doesn't need to worry."

Mona practically choked on her mouthful. "Um, I beg to differ. I mean, I've noticed all the *mamihlapinatapai*, but—"

"The what?"

"The meaningful looks with intent. It's a Yaghan word. Anyway, it's obviously gone further than anyone realized, if you're making out on school camp."

"No, I mean it." I shaded the rock in my sketch, trying to stop my hand from shaking. "I don't think it would work. Drew's got hangups."

Her eyebrows shot up. "Like, kinks?"

"No! I mean he's overprotective. It's not healthy."

"Oh, right." She munched thoughtfully. "Huh, I wouldn't have picked that. I'm glad you've got boundaries, though. Did you break the news to him already? I noticed him looking thunderous but figured he was just annoyed you two aren't getting any *alone time* to enjoy the moment. That, or the teachers have already told him off."

"We had a disagreement," I said.

"Details?"

"I'd rather not talk about it."

Mona looked disappointed, but I truly couldn't discuss it. There was pressure behind my eyes that was threatening to burst out as tears at any moment. Was it true, what I was saying? Was this vision of Drew's going to ruin everything for us?

Typically, I had little time to dwell on it. Ms. Deering had another activity for us in the afternoon. This time it was orienteering. Most of us had no idea how to use a compass, so Ms. Deering taught us the basics. Mr. Boxe had settled into his camp chair, looking weary. I was on the red/pink bandana team again, with Cassie, Gabe and Patience. For once, I was grateful Drew wasn't in my group.

"You're looking for ribbons," Ms. Deering told us. "Red for Gabe's team, yellow for Mona's. Follow the instructions on your papers and collect each ribbon as you find it. Your goal is to be back here inside one hour with fifteen ribbons."

I could feel Drew trying to catch my eye but refused to look at him. He was probably just going to tell me to be careful near the water again.

"Mimi," Ms. Deering said, startling me. "A word, please."

Crap.

She took me to the kitchen cabin and handed me a granola bar. "You need to eat."

"Oh. Okay."

"And I've never really explained this to you before, but it's obviously way past time to do so. I have a strong feeling you seven should have equal connections."

I frowned. "What do you mean?"

"The connections you have with everyone in the group— I know you don't always get along, but you care about them. There's a sense of the greater good. You'd fight for them, right?" I nodded. "But the minute that connection crosses the line into something different between two of you, it shifts the balance. It feels wrong to me. I know it's a big thing to ask of you, but could you please try not to get romantically involved with anyone in the group, Mimi?"

Death would have been preferable to this conversation. "I'm sorry. I didn't mean to do anything wrong."

"No, *I'm* sorry, because this must feel restrictive and unfair. But it's important. I can't even explain why, I just know it matters to your safety—to the safety of the whole group."

I nodded, my cheeks burning, unable to meet her gaze. "It's okay. I don't think I'm... I don't think he's... We're not very good for each other like that, anyway."

When I risked a glance, she looked so grateful, it made me feel better. She thanked me and sent me back to the game. I joined Cassie, Gabe and Patience. Ms. Deering was right: Drew and I were disturbing the balance. *But hell, that kiss.* The confusion made me feel even more like crying.

The four of us headed for our designated starting point, Patience carrying our team's clipboard and Cassie the compass. Gabe was trying to show Cassie how to use it properly. I trailed behind with Hannah and Marvin.

"We need to decide on battle tactics," Cassie said over Gabe. "I propose we speed-run the course between targets. Mona's team will be slower because she's unfit."

Patience had the excited giggles again. Who'd have thought she'd turn out to be so competitive? "The first one is north, fifty-five degrees west. Sixty paces."

"Ow! You're pulling," Cassie told her bat. "If you must hang in my hair, at least make sure you don't wriggle."

"Aren't you worried it has fleas?" Gabe asked.

"Of course I am!" she snapped. "But it says it needs to be with me."

"It *is* a familiar." Gabe wasn't joking this time. "That's amazing! Does this mean our gifts are related to witchcraft? We need to tell Mona so she can look into it."

"I'm *not* a witch," Cassie snapped.

Gabe grimaced at me behind her back as she stalked ahead to catch up to Patience. "Witchcraft," he said. "Wouldn't that be something?"

"Sure would."

"Everything okay?" he asked.

"Yeah, of course."

"Can I ask you something?"

"Sure," I said warily.

He paused, then rushed out the words. "What happened earlier, with Drew—was that what you wanted?"

For convenience, I might as well have rouged my cheeks a permanent shade of crimson. "Isn't that kind of a private question?"

"You're upset about something."

"Stay out of my head!"

"I can't help it." Gabe sounded genuinely sorry. "I didn't go looking this time. But it's like trying not to smell or see— I just notice feelings."

I backed down. "I'm fine."

"So it was… consensual?"

"Excuse me?"

"The kiss." He was looking away now, staring into the trees. "Something made you feel bad. Angry."

"Let me have a black moment in privacy, Gabe."

"I'm just worried about you—worried he did something you didn't want."

"It was categorically consensual, I promise." Damn, was this the most awkward conversation of my life? A new personal best, for sure.

Gabe said nothing. We caught up to Cassie and Patience, who were standing beneath a pine tree, peering into the branches.

"It's supposed to be here," Patience murmured.

"There!" Cassie pointed. The red ribbon was tied to a low branch on the other side of the trunk.

"Yes!" Patience dashed over and untied it. "What's next?"

The three worked out the next bearing and jogged off, pacing out ninety steps toward the lake. I followed at a distance, wishing I could throw myself into the game like they had.

Gabe wheeled around and jogged back to me, grabbing my hand. "I don't like seeing you like this! Come on, Mimi, forget your troubles. You need some *direction* in your life. Something to stop you heading *south*. A *degree* of fun."

He tugged at my hand until I couldn't hold in a laugh and ran with him. When we caught up to the other two by the lake, Patience was searching the jetty posts for the red ribbon, but Cassie had frozen. She was staring at a tall figure further along the shore.

Gabe frowned. "Cass?"

"Is that... Tyler?"

It sure looked like him. He was coming toward us.

"Cassie!" he called.

"Are you serious?" She tucked her bat further into her hair. Patience glanced anxiously at the campsite, but we were out of sight of the cabins. She joined us where we stood in a cluster, clutching her whistle.

Tyler stood in front of us, his face shining like he'd been exercising. "Hi, guys."

Gabe moved closer to Cassie. "What are you doing at Blackmere Pool, man?"

Tyler's eyes were locked on Cassie. He shrugged. "Just hiking. Pure coincidence."

"You shouldn't be here." Her voice was ice cold. "You shouldn't be anywhere near me."

"Hey, how was I supposed to know you'd be here too?"

"Don't give me that bullshit—and leave me alone, you psycho."

His lip curled. "You're sticking to your messed-up story, then, are you?"

"Oh my God." Cassie clearly had no further words to express how angry he'd made her.

Gabe stepped forward and Tyler postured, puffing his chest like a territorial silverback.

"How about you get away from us, asshole?" Gabe suggested pleasantly.

Tyler was practically baring his teeth. "You believe her, do you? Innocent until proven guilty—ever heard of that?"

"He's dangerous." Hannah's voice came beside my ear. "Don't let your friend fight him."

Gabe's fist was clenching by his side. I stepped in front of him. "Tyler, get away from here."

He barely gave me a glance. "It's a free country."

"Then we'll get Mr. Boxe to have you removed by the police."

Hearing the principal's name got his attention. He glanced around.

"They're right over there by the cabins," I told him. "Want us to call them over?" Patience lifted her whistle to her mouth.

Tyler held up two hands and stepped back. "Damn, you nerds are weird. Enjoy your little campout." He swung around and headed for the trail that led out of the park.

Patience lowered her whistle and Gabe put an arm around Cassie. "You good?"

She shook him off, as prickly as always. "I'm fine. That creep doesn't scare me." She strode across to the water's edge and plucked a red ribbon from a metal signpost. "What's the next bearing?"

We arrived at camp just outside our time limit, but with fifteen red ribbons in Patience's pockets. The other team was already back. It was Gabe who told everyone about Tyler. Ms. Deering went pale, and Mr. Boxe, who'd looked half-asleep, sat up straight and spoke to Cassie.

"Are you all right, Cassandra?"

She tossed her hair, bat and all. "I'm fine. He left the park. I don't buy his story, though—him being here was no accident. He must have known I'd be here this weekend. My dad'll be livid when he hears."

Mr. Boxe's frown grew darker, and he stared absently at the leaf litter. "I don't like this at all," he said to Ms. Deering at last. "I think I'd better make a call to Tyler's family and ensure they keep him away from Cassie."

"I agree," she said.

"Do you think he'll try to come to the cabins?" Patience asked in a small voice. "We don't know for sure that he left the park."

"I don't expect he'd try his luck against the group," Ms. Deering said. "But just in case, we'll stick together. Anywhere you want to go, let's make it a minimum of two people, please. Even the bathroom."

Mr. Boxe had already stood up and was fishing in his pockets for his keys. "I'll go and make the call from the other side of the lake, where the signal's better," he told Ms. Deering, and headed for his car.

"Is Tyler from around here?" Mona asked Cassie.

"Lydenburg." Cassie was still making a concerted effort to appear bored by the whole thing.

"Lydenburg." Mona's cogs and wheels activated. "Interesting."

An idea hit me. "Could it have been *Tyler* we ran into during Stalk the Lantern?" I asked.

Cassie's eyes widened. "Of course! He's tall, like Mr. Boxe, and that's why he didn't say anything—he didn't want to get caught!"

"Sketchy." Ed looked repulsed. "Hanging around our campsite at night."

"I'm scared," Patience admitted.

"You're safe in our group," Ms. Deering assured her. "But let's scrap the next activity and go straight into free time. Stay where I can see you all, but take some time out to relax, yes?"

We made our way to a nearby circle of boulders and found ourselves spots perched on rocks or resting against them.

Patience looked at Drew. "Didn't you have a vision about a red ribbon tied to a post not long ago? That's what we were looking for when Tyler turned up."

Mona checked back through her notebook and seemed vexed when she found the entry. "I should have picked that up," she mumbled to herself. "Have you had any visions since we've been here at camp, Drew?"

"I had one this morning."

She looked annoyed. "This morning! Why didn't you tell me?"

He gestured toward the cabins. "Because Boxe has been around, mostly. I saw an ink drawing on old paper, all faded." Mona had begun scribbling. "A circle, with symbols all around it, and strange writing I didn't understand. The symbols were things like a feather, an eye, a skull." Drew's forehead creased with the effort of remembering. "A hand? And a star, I think. And one or two others. It was so fast, I didn't get a chance to see them all."

"Can you draw it?" Mona passed him her notebook.

Drew made a rough sketch: a wheel of fine scribble with symbols dotted around it at regular intervals. Mona asked more questions, but he couldn't give her any more than he already had. I gazed absently at the drawing. It reminded me of my own sketches of organs, bones and natural objects. Drew was watching me, I realized. My eyes surprised me by filling with tears and I turned away, pretending to fix my shoe, so he wouldn't see. I didn't even know why I was crying—whether it was because of what he'd said or Ms. Deering's rule.

Drew steered clear of me that evening, sitting with Patience while she chattered about all the games we'd played. Our disagreement was obviously as fresh in his mind as it was in mine.

I woke early and peered down through the bars of my bunk. Patience was already dressed to her sneakers. She was packing her clothes into her bag, then taking them out and repacking more neatly. Ms. Deering's bed was empty. Mona was asleep, notebook peeking out from under her pillow, and Cassie was too, her bat clinging to the underside of the top bunk again. It was pretty cute, the way it had chosen her. I wouldn't mind having a bat select me as its human— assuming it was parasite-free.

The memory of my argument with Drew hit me again. Then I thought of the still, cold lake waiting out there in the brightening dawn. I had my bag up on the bunk with me, at the foot of my mattress, so I dug out my bathing suit and did contortions inside my sleeping bag until it was on. Then I climbed down, grabbed my towel and mouthed, *Back soon* at Patience.

I stepped into the chilly morning air. The campsite was silent and empty, the boys' cabin still. Steam drifted from a window in the bathroom hut, indicating Ms. Deering was showering.

Behind me, the cabin door opened and Patience slipped out. "We're not supposed to go anywhere alone."

I deflated. "I forgot. I was going to take a dip."

"I'll come with you, if you want."

"Really? Thanks!"

We headed for the lake, the first rays of daylight streaming through the branches of the tallest trees.

"It's a beautiful morning," Patience said.

"Incredible."

"Do you swim a lot?"

"No, but if I'm somewhere like this, I do." I shot her a smile. "It's a cold water thing."

"I love being in cold water."

I did a double take. "You're the only other person I've ever met who does!"

"It makes you feel alive."

"Exactly! It's like… like…" I hunted for the words.

"Being flipped inside out and back the other way again."

I laughed. "Nailed it."

We reached the shore. A low mist hung over the water, and it was stiller than a green glass dish.

"I wish I'd brought a swimsuit now," Patience said.

"Go get it!"

"I didn't pack one."

I checked the cabins. "Go in your underwear. There's no one around, and I won't tell."

She looked so scandalized that I couldn't help laughing. I tossed her my towel and ran through the shallows, collapsing into the water as soon as it was deep enough. It closed over my head and all was icy, muffled darkness. A moment later, I burst out and sucked in a breath that was more of a squeal. It was freezing! Horrible and wonderful. Patience stood on the bank with my towel over her shoulder, laughing at me.

Movement caught my eye: someone was running through the trees, coming straight for us. Drew. He burst out of the woods and skidded to a halt beside Patience. He was in boxers, his torso bare, a hint of lean muscle curving down into the waistband of his shorts. Patience went pink and averted her eyes. I stared, my mouth hanging open.

"Mimi! What are you doing? Get out!"

My senses reconnected to my brain and I twisted away, breast-stroking toward the middle of the lake. "Go away, Drew."

The sound of splashing rose behind me. I spun around and Drew was coming for me, determination on his face. Then he tripped and plummeted forward, hitting the surface with a smack. That had to hurt. Patience was laughing her grandpa jeans off.

I waited for him to emerge. "Karma," I said as soon as his ears were out of the water.

His gaze darkened and he got to his feet, dripping. "This isn't a game."

"I'm not playing," I snapped, trying not to be distracted by his bare, wet chest and clinging boxers. "Leave me alone."

For an instant, I thought he'd keep storming through the water and try to drag me out. Instead, he swung around and headed back to shore. Then he sat down on the muddy bank and watched me. Shivering.

Of course, I then had to prove a point, so I stayed in longer than I'd intended. Only when my fingers had turned blue did I make my way back to shore at a leisurely pace, trying to conceal the chattering of my teeth. Her eyes enormous, Patience handed me my towel. I turned away and pretended to gaze across the lake while I rubbed my shoulders and hair dry, hoping he couldn't see my knees knocking from the cold. Then I turned back.

"Coming, Patience?"

"Yes."

I spared him a fleeting glance. His eyes were locked on me and I was suddenly aware that a piece of black Lycra was the only thing between his eyes and my naked body.

Karma.

I wrapped up in my towel and headed back toward the cabins with Patience. Drew trailed behind us at a distance and none of us spoke a word.

The final activity before we'd be leaving camp was a quiet reflection. We had to find a partner and a space to discuss some questions about the weekend. Before I could react, Drew and Gabe simultaneously stepped my way.

Ms. Deering nodded. "We'll need one group of three, since we've got odd numbers. You three can go together."

Drew and Gabe exchanged a look. I shrank inside.

We found a spot beneath a pine tree and sat down, leaving big spaces between the three of us. Gabe read from the piece of paper.

"What did you learn about one another this weekend?"

"That people sometimes make choices that aren't in their best interests," Drew said.

The embers of my anger had been glowing ever since our argument, and now they flared to life. "That people don't always know what's in others' best interests," I retorted.

Gabe's mouth was hanging open. "Whoa. Okay. I guess I learned that sometimes people keep secrets."

Drew and I had the decency to look awkward.

Gabe read the next question. "What was the most challenging thing you tried this weekend and why?" He flicked the piece of paper. "Well, for me, it was trying to interpret the simmering emotive drama."

I attempted to answer seriously. "Stalk the Lantern was the most challenging thing for me, especially running around in the woods without a flashlight."

Gabe looked expectantly at Drew.

"For me, it was the water games."

"Why?" Gabe asked.

Drew just kept his eyes on me.

"Next question," I told Gabe.

He was plainly curious, but complied. "Was there anything you'd do differently to succeed with the activities?"

"Probably," I said. "But I had to make the mistakes in order to learn along the way."

Gabe nodded at me. "The mistakes were the fun bits. But if I had my time again, I'd try to get paired with you for more of the games." Drew shot him a startled glance, and Gabe lifted his eyebrows. "What? I hereby declare all former gentlemen's agreements null and void."

"Agreements?" I echoed coldly.

"There were never any agreements, gentlemen's or otherwise," Drew said.

Gabe made a skeptical noise. "In light of the lady's reconsideration, may the best man win." He stuck out his hand for Drew to shake. Drew ignored it, glowering.

"Would you stop?" I said. "This isn't funny."

"I know," Gabe said, and for once, he did seem serious. "Last question: what was the standout moment of the weekend? For me it was seeing the games transform Patience into a ruthless competitor. You?"

The kiss. Drew's eyes met mine and darkened with the same thought.

Gabe sighed. "Well, I guess I know the answer to that."

24
I'm Just Trying to Mind My Own Demons

We'd packed the minibus and were all waiting around while Ms. Deering and Mr. Boxe discussed the route she should take to Dale's Run. I watched my friends joke and argue, feeling seriously shortchanged about having to do the drive back to Etherall Valley with Mr. Boxe. Patience and Drew were talking, seated together on a boulder. Patience seemed edgy—perhaps nervous about introducing her friends to her family.

Ms. Deering told everyone to get on board.

"Ready to go, Mimi?" Mr. Boxe called to me. "I promise I'll take the turns nice and steady, and have you back at school in no time. We only need to stop once, just to drop off some of this borrowed equipment at my old workplace in Davenport."

I managed to smile. The cover story for me not going on the bus was that I'd had dreadful motion sickness on the way to camp.

Hannah moved closer to me. "No, miss. You're not to go with him."

"What?" I whispered.

"Don't go with him, kid," Marvin said in my other ear. "Get on the bus."

My spirits rose. "You know what, I think I'm going to be okay, sir. My stomach feels fine today. Maybe I was just hungry on Friday afternoon."

Ms. Deering regarded me in bafflement. "I thought you felt quite strongly that you shouldn't ride on the bus, Mimi?"

"I did, but something tells me I'm going to be fine after all." I shot her a grin.

She smiled back, comprehending my code. "That's great!"

Mr. Boxe had his head tipped to the side. "Are you sure, Mimi? I wouldn't want you getting sick on a bus full of people."

"I'm sure." I bounded up the steps of the minibus. Patience sat up straight when she saw me, and the other five stared.

Mona beckoned me over. "What are you doing? I thought your ghosts said no Dale's Run for you."

"They did, but they've changed their minds! They both said I shouldn't go with Mr. Boxe."

Mona's head swiveled so she could examine our principal, who was loading one final crate of equipment into the trunk of his car. "Is that so?" She made a note.

Mr. Boxe drove away and Ms. Deering seemed to breathe a sigh of relief. She turned the key in the ignition and swiveled in her seat to face us all. "I think we made it through the camp without Mr. Boxe noticing anything unusual about us. Did you feel any signs of suspicion, Gabe?" she asked.

Gabe thought about it. "Boxe is hard to read. The most I felt from him all weekend was when we told you both about Tyler turning up. That rattled him."

She nodded. "Cassie, you probably need to say goodbye to the bat now."

"I've tried, Ms. D, truly! He won't leave. Look." Cassie stood up and shook her hair violently, and the bat held on with grim determination, squeaking in protest. "He says he needs to be with me."

"He's imprinted on you." Ed smirked. "You're soul mates."

"Shut *up*, Edwin."

Ms. Deering seemed torn. "I think it's illegal to keep a bat without a license."

"I don't have a choice in this!" Cassie huffed.

"You need to give him a name," Gabe told her. "How about Batty McBatface?"

"Batricia," I suggested. "Sebatstian?"

"Bruce Wayne," Mona called.

"He's got a name already," Cassie said. "It's Sir Percival. And none of you are funny."

She refused to explain why she'd chosen Sir Percival.

Ms. Deering got us on the road to Dale's Run, and Drew told Mona about a vision he'd had during the night. He'd seen two hands clasped together—girls' hands, he thought, but from two different people. Mona got him to describe them: one had looked rough and worn, as though with physical work; the other was smooth and soft.

As we came closer to Dale's Run, Patience's agitation reached the point where she was in tears. Drew spoke to her in a low voice, trying to calm her down. He dug in his pocket for a tissue, but when he pulled one out, a bit of paper dropped onto the floor of the bus. He grabbed it and quickly shoved it back out of sight—but not quickly enough. I recognized it as the paper fortune teller I'd made for him on our date at the botanical gardens.

He still had it?

He *carried it around with him?*

Drew gave Patience the tissue, not meeting my eye. Gabe made his way across the bus to sit in front of me and Mona, blocking my view and forcing Marvin out of his spot.

"What do you think your ghosts are playing at?" he asked.

I shrugged, wishing fervently he'd move out of the way.

"They flipped on their warning. You don't think that's odd?"

"It's *very* odd," Mona confirmed.

I stiffened. "They really did tell me I should come to Dale's Run, you know. I didn't make it up to get out of going in Mr. Boxe's car."

"I know." Gabe jerked his head toward Patience. "She's freaking out."

"Well, obviously," Mona said.

"Some of us can pick up on emotions the normal way, Gabe," I told him. "You know, facial expressions, tone of voice, asking questions."

Gabe chose to ignore that. "Do we really need to do this?"

Mona checked over her shoulder, then dropped her voice. "I heard Ms. D talking about it to Mr. Boxe. The Roses would only allow Patience to attend the camp if Boxe promised we'd visit on the way back."

We were arriving, driving past farmland I recognized from the drive with my parents a few weeks earlier. Ms. Deering turned onto an unpaved road, and there was Dale's Run with its wooden houses and large chapel. At the bottom of the road, Patience's family was waiting out the front of their house to greet us.

They'd lined up in order of height, the girls in pastel dresses and the boys in white shirts, long pants, suspenders and hats. Even Patience's mom wore one of those heinous pastel numbers. Ms. Deering pulled up and switched off the engine. Shadows swooped and wavered in my peripheral vision, reflecting my apprehension.

"Here goes," Gabe murmured, swinging himself out of his seat and following Ms. Deering out of the minibus.

Patience presented us to her father first, a big blond man with deep lines on his tanned face, then Mrs. Rose, who was small and dark-haired. Next came two teenage boys called Samuel and Matthias, then Charity, who looked about thirteen, and Faith, who couldn't have been more than ten. They all kept their eyes on their father, except for Faith, who stared at us openly. Patience went to stand with her family, looking out of place in a t-shirt and jeans.

A man emerged from a nearby house, and Mr. Rose introduced him as Pastor George Carruthers. Patience's eyes widened when she saw him, but her father spoke to her in a low voice and she slipped into their house. By now, my shadows were having a party at the edges of my field of vision.

"Welcome, one and all, to our home," Mr. Rose said. "In her letters, Patience speaks highly of her schoolfriends— and, of course, you too, Miss Deering."

Ms. Deering didn't correct the "Miss" but nodded her acknowledgement.

"Where's Mr. Boxe?" Mr. Rose asked, glancing at the bus.

"I'm afraid work has called him back to the school," Ms. Deering explained. "He asked me to give you his best wishes and make his apologies."

"Ah." Mr. Rose seemed displeased. "Well, do come into the house and join us for tea."

We followed him inside, my ghosts sticking close enough to make me shiver. The room was cramped and dim, with one small window above the sink. A farm cat sat crouched on the ledge outside. The wooden table and chairs dominated the center of the room, and more chairs were lined up around the walls. Cakes and slices had been spread across the table, as well as a teapot and homemade lemonade in a glass jug.

Patience reappeared in a long, pale-blue dress just like her sisters wore. In fact, they were made of the same fabric. They must have hand-sewn their clothing—either that or they were buying in bulk from a supplier of nineteenth-century costumes.

"Is this for real?" Cassie whispered to me.

Mrs. Rose, Patience and Charity served afternoon tea. We were directed to sit around the table, while the Rose kids were relegated to the chairs along the walls. I felt bad for them, perched like outsiders in their own home. Faith's longing gaze was fixed on the cakes. I wanted to offer her a piece but wasn't sure of the correct etiquette. Hannah and Marvin flanked one of Patience's brothers. He rubbed his arms and seemed to suppress a shiver.

Pastor Carruthers said grace, then made genial chitchat as if that might reassure us that everything was normal. *Good luck, dude.*

"Our way of life must seem rather old-fashioned to you young people," he said with a smile. "We're regular people, like yourselves, but we believe we can best do the Lord's work without the distraction of the clamor and violence so prevalent in today's world. Pastor Dale, who founded our village community in 1943, preached that if we keep ourselves innocent of the sins in the outside world, we might better focus on lives of goodness and purity. So you won't find any e-phones or i-mail in our little village," he finished.

We managed to hold it together, and Patience looked mortified at his gaffe. The pastor returned to his tea and cake.

Cassie caught my eye and winked at the cat on the ledge. In reply, it pawed at the window and yowled. This was obviously unusual behavior, because the whole Rose family looked over at it, startled. Patience glanced at Cassie and gave her head a tiny shake, and Pastor Carruthers searched our faces. My shadows loomed.

When we'd eaten, Mr. Rose suggested a walk around the village. Mrs. Rose, Charity and Faith hovered, ready to clear the table. Just as I stepped out of the room, Faith snuck a chunk of cake off the table and stuffed it into her mouth.

Outside, the pastor acted as tour guide, pointing out the barns, homes, a schoolhouse and finally the chapel, with its enormous wooden cross on the roof. Other people who lived at Dale's Run observed us wordlessly as we toured their village.

"Come inside for a look," the pastor urged, standing at the chapel door.

Patience's expression told us this wasn't what she'd expected or wanted. However, Ms. Deering paused for only a moment before stepping through the door with an air of resignation. I could understand why. The church was a big part of the Dale's Run community, and we could at least take a quick look. We filed in after her, none of us wanting to get Patience into trouble.

Once we were seated in an uncomfortable pew near the front, Pastor Carruthers offered us a blessing. This "blessing" turned out to be the dabbing of holy water upon our reluctant foreheads, followed by forty-seven minutes of concentrated prayer, urging us to relinquish sin and Satan, to reject all ungodly acts and behaviors, to obey our parents and those with spiritual wisdom, and to embrace the light of God in all its glory. We didn't dare check one another's faces. I wasn't sure if I wanted to laugh or walk out. Ms. Deering tried to put us at ease, whispering occasionally, "It shouldn't be much longer."

Finally, Cassie called some birds. Two of them flew screeching into the chapel and the diversion allowed us to make our escape.

"Your friend will betray herself, miss," Hannah whispered in my ear.

I edged my way over to Cassie. "You've got to stop using your gift," I murmured. "Hannah says so."

"Who?"

"My ghost!" I hissed.

She rolled her eyes. "Fine."

Once the birds had been chased out, Pastor Carruthers tried to lead us back inside to finish his sermon, but Ms. Deering said a firm no.

"Some of the students' parents will be picking them up from school, and I can't keep them waiting," she told him. "Thank you for the interesting tour and your hospitality. Mr. Rose, could you please show us the way back to our bus?"

Mr. Rose led us back to the bus without speaking while Pastor Carruthers asked Ms. Deering about the pastoral care at Etherall Valley Academy. She bent the truth, saying Mr. Boxe managed all that stuff. Then the pastor wanted to know about Mr. Boxe's faith, and she murmured vaguely that she believed he attended a church, but wasn't sure what denomination it was.

"Adam Rose has been worried about his daughter." Pastor Carruthers was one of those people who couldn't ever speak in a truly quiet voice. Maybe it came of a career of hollering about sin. "Mr. Boxe assured Adam that Patience would receive the necessary guidance and discipline she required, but we haven't seen much improvement. Adam is considering removing her from your school. She's a wayward girl, easily led." He glanced at the rest of us as if we were a bunch of hardened criminals.

"Patience? Wayward?" Ms. Deering kept her composure as best she could. "I must assure you, Pastor Carruthers, that Patience receives just the special attention she needs for the behavioral qualities she exhibits, and we've developed a management plan we wholeheartedly facilitate. She's in excellent hands. I think removing her from school might put her in danger of regression." I had to hand it to Ms. Deering. I knew exactly what she meant, but the pastor could take it totally another way.

"Well," he replied, "I wouldn't presume to make the decision for Adam, although of course he trusts my judgment as his pastor. I'd like to speak to Mr. Boxe himself and find out exactly what measures are being taken."

"We have a policy of dealing with the parent or guardian directly, rather than any third parties." Ms. Deering was bordering on icy. "I'll get Mr. Boxe to give Mr. Rose a call—or write him a letter," she corrected herself. "Then the Roses can confer with you as they see fit."

There wasn't much Pastor Carruthers could say to that. We reached the Rose house and Patience ran inside to get changed. A minute later she came back out in her jeans and t-shirt. She kissed her mother's cheek, gently untangled herself from Faith's hug and joined us on the bus. We all returned Faith's wave as Ms. Deering drove away, but there was a tense silence after we turned onto the highway.

Mona spoke first, trying and failing to keep the indignation out of her voice. "So, what was with that blessing? Was that pastor checking if we'd burst into flames as soon as we set foot in the chapel?"

Patience's face crumpled and she dropped her face into her hands. "I'm sorry, I'm so sorry!" Drew put an arm around her.

"It's okay, Patience." Ed shot Mona a look. "Not your fault."

"You knew what was going to happen once we got into the chapel, didn't you?" Gabe asked.

She nodded, sniffling. "Pastor Carruthers told Father I'm born of Satan." They were dramatic words, but Patience was deadly serious. She sucked in a deep breath. "I think he's wrong," she blurted. "I know he's my pastor, but I can't believe his word on this. I'm not a bad person and I don't hear the voice of Satan. I am one of God's children, a faithful servant. I don't see how the pastor and Father can be right."

Drew squeezed her shoulders as she dissolved in tears again.

Mona was contrite. "You're too smart to believe these gifts are from some big, scary devil. Sometimes parents are wrong. Mine are, a lot. It's not your fault, but I know it feels weird when the people you're supposed to believe in are just totally *wrong*."

Patience wept with total abandon. I wished I could say something to comfort her. Somehow she'd survived years of religious indoctrination and self-loathing, and here she was, emerging on the other side of that with enough clarity to see her community's prejudices.

"I suppose it makes sense now why Mimi's ghosts didn't want her there," Mona mused. "The whole time, I felt like that pastor knew something. Like he somehow knew we've all got powers."

"How could he know?" Drew asked.

Patience wiped her eyes. "Mona's right. Pastor prayed for us as though we've been turned by Satan. And Father was taken aback by Cassie's tricks with the animals."

Cassie flushed pink. "I had to do something to get us out of that church!"

"Your mother doesn't have the same feelings as your dad," Gabe told Patience.

Faint hope dawned on her swollen face. "Really?"

He nodded. "Your father is scared. But your mom, she's like Drew. A loud feeler. Avalanches of emotion spilling off her—surges of love and protectiveness for you. Anger at your dad and that pastor, plus deep, deep guilt. There wasn't one flicker of fear toward you, or any of us. I think she sees your gift for what it is, and hates that she can't protect you from your dad and the pastor."

Patience wept again, this time with relief.

"I can't believe you got through this without therapy," Cassie told her.

Mona snorted. "Why does everyone always think therapy is the answer? When I tried to tell my parents I could understand all the dialogue on the Scandi-noir network without subtitles, they humored me for a while. But when I started competing with online translators and doing a better job, they thought I was making up some elaborate story to impress them. Mom got all worried about my self-esteem and sent me to a psych!"

"No problem with Mona's self esteem." Gabe grinned.

"My parents did it too," Ed put in. "After the divorce, they caught me just once too often trying to heal animals that were already dead. They thought I was a future psychopath, murdering pets and forest creatures."

"What did you tell your psychiatrist?" Mona asked.

"I told him I was just healing them. He said, 'Your urge to heal these animals is a result of your need to mediate in the conflict between your mother and father.' I believed him for a while. Then one day he needed to finish our session early because he had a migraine. I joked that I could probably heal it. Maybe he thought it would be a good way to show me I was living in a fantasy world, so he got me to try. He freaked out—so I guess it worked. I didn't have to see him much longer, though, because it was pretty soon after that I got the scholarship offer from Etherall Valley Academy. Thanks to weekday boarding, I couldn't make the appointments anymore."

Mona thought this story was hilarious. "You showed him! When I told Dr. Mayer about my translating, he said it represented my struggle to be understood and—"

I gasped, and Drew sat up straight. "Dr. Mayer was the name of my psychiatrist, too," he said.

"Dr. Mayer! He was *my* psych." Ed's eyes had grown round.

"And mine," Cassie cried.

"Mine too!" I said.

Ms. Deering glanced over her shoulder, her face taut with shock. "Gabe?"

"I'm the odd one out who never saw a psychiatrist," Gabe said.

"Patience?" Mona asked, lunging for her notebook.

Patience shook her head. "When my father caught me conjuring, he asked Pastor Carruthers for help."

The hairs on the back of my neck had risen. In the rearview, we could see Ms. Deering frowning.

"Holy crap," Cassie breathed. "Do you know Dr. Mayer, Ms. Deering?"

"No. I've never even heard his name. He's not listed in any of your school records."

"Sus. Pish. Us," Mona mumbled, scribbling hard.

"Sometimes psychiatrists specialize in certain types of mental illness," Ed said uncertainly, like he wanted to convince himself. "Maybe Mayer specializes in teenagers with, I don't know, delusions of superpowers?"

"Are you serious?" Mona stopped writing, her eyes almost bugging out of her skull. "There are *seven* gifted kids in the county of Menoa, and Mayer's seen *five* of them! You think that's a coincidence?"

"Wait, Ed could be right," Drew said. "If Mayer's a known specialist and our parents all took referrals from our doctors, then it *could* be a coincidence that five of us saw him at one time or another. Also, Mimi and I already worked out that we both saw a Dr. Mayer, but it was a different guy. One works in Etherall Valley and the other works in Perry Ridge."

"Oh, mine was in Pinetree Glades," Cassie said, looking relieved. "They must be different people. Massive coincidence, though. Mayer's not exactly a common name."

"Bullshit," Mona declared. "There's something creepy going on. Mayer's got ginger hair and glasses, right?"

The five of us nodded, and Gabe grimaced. "So the guy has clones all over the county."

"Do you think he pushed us together, somehow?" I ventured. "He's the one who recommended Etherall Valley Academy to my parents."

"Mayer could know Boxe," Drew said.

"That makes sense." Ed ticked off the process on his fingers. "Mayer gets to know us through therapy, diagnoses our *delusions*, tells Boxe, and then Boxe grants us places at the school."

Mona looked skeptical. "Except *my* Mayer didn't suggest EVA. He just told Mom she should consider a private school with a smaller student body."

"Are there any other schools in Etherall Valley that fit that description?" Gabe asked her.

She twisted her lips. "One other. But when Mom brought me down to EVA to do the admission application, they said I could study multiple languages, so it was a no-brainer."

"I got a math scholarship when I applied," Ed said.

"And I got a literature one based on winning a county-wide poetry contest," Drew added. "The offer came out of the blue—I hadn't even applied to EVA."

Cassie raised her eyebrows. "And I got contacted with an offer of a place in the dance program after my dance school closed down."

"Dr. Mayer gave my parents two options for me," I said. "A clinic or this school."

"And Patience was hand-picked by Mr. Boxe," Mona said. "Only Gabe didn't start at EVA through any of the above, did you, Gabe?"

He shook his head. "My moms heard about the academy from somewhere. They go in for alternative stuff, so they put me into the feeder school when I was in junior high. But when I got to the ninth grade, they found it too expensive, so Ma told EVA I'd be leaving. Next minute, I got offered an athletics scholarship, which halved the fees."

"Patient zero." Mona had no doubt in her voice. "Gabe was the first one at EVA, then the rest of us were manipulated into coming here, too. And if that was nothing to do with you, Ms. Deering, I'm guessing it was down to Mr. Boxe."

Hairs on hairs rose on my neck this time.

"But what does Boxe know about us?" Drew was looking at Ms. Deering. "Does he think we're delusional or gifted? Does he think he's helping us get over a psychological condition? Or is he just letting you run a program for kids with arcane powers?"

Cassie rolled her eyes. "Always with the fancy words."

"I'll need to investigate," Ms. Deering said.

"How did you originally spot Gabe's gift?" Mona asked, staring at our teacher as if she'd never really seen her before. "What exactly is your process for identifying a gifted kid, Ms. D?"

Ms. Deering didn't answer for a moment, then she pulled off into a rest area on the side of the highway.

"Come on," she said, beckoning, and we all climbed out after her.

Outside, she sat down on a bench that faced a pine railing. The rest of us leaned against the railing, facing her in the soft afternoon breeze. We waited for her to speak, the occasional car whipping past behind us.

"When I was fifteen, my family came to the attention of the media."

I comprehended what this was in a rush: Ms. Deering was going to tell us her story. We'd all had the chance to tell ours, but we'd never asked for hers. We'd never even suspected she *had* a story. She was just there, our sentry, to protect us. But of course there was more to it than that.

I studied her petite frame, the honey-colored hair, the faint lines around her mouth and eyes, the sky blue of her irises. She looked tired—and not just post-camping-weekend-with-teens tired.

"We had a disturbance in our house. A poltergeist, people called it. Keys and pens flying around the room, plates throwing themselves across the kitchen. Rumors started among our neighbors, and before we knew it, we had reporters knocking at the door. They filmed and photographed us. I was what they call 'the focus' of the haunting; all the activity seemed to center around me. It's a common occurrence: a moody adolescent being the eye of a poltergeist storm."

Shock made my head buzz. *She's like me?* I flicked a glance at Hannah and Marvin, but they were simply hovering nearby without any apparent interest in the revelation. In fact, Marvin was kicking aimlessly at fallen pine cones, his feet going straight through them. Gabe must have felt my turmoil, because he took my hand and squeezed it. Drew saw it happen and quickly looked away.

"My parents consulted psychic mediums," Ms. Deering was saying. "One told us the house was built on a ley line, another an ancient burial ground. Someone else thought it was the spirit of a man who'd died alone in an upstairs bedroom. They carried out sage smokings and said incantations. Then priests were summoned. They came in groups and blessed the house, saying prayers to cast out the devil." Ms. Deering's eyes rested on Patience for a moment, a touch of irony in her expression. "Nothing made any difference. The disturbances continued and my confusion worsened, because all I could hear inside my head the entire time was one word, over and over again. *Fight. Fight. Fight.*

"I thought it must be the poltergeist—the angry spirit— trying to rile me up, as if it had unfinished business it was using me to get done. The urge to lash out was physically painful. It felt like my body was tied up, restrained with invisible chains, somehow. I was wound up like a spring with nowhere to release the tension. My parents couldn't speak to me without me screaming back at them, and it took every bit of my willpower not to become violent. They were at their wits' end when they sent me to stay with my grandparents—but the poltergeist activity followed me there. On my first night, my grandmother's teapot flew across the room and smashed into a wall.

"My grandfather was a gentle person, a military veteran who had rejected everything to do with war. He never even raised his voice after he left the forces. He might not have known what was going on for me, but he recognized what I needed. He had an old punching bag. He hitched it up in the barn and sent me out there to smack the hell out of it." She smiled. "It was like a miracle. The voice screaming *fight* inside my head abated. The more I kicked and punched that old bag, the better I felt. When I went back in the house, everything was still. I couldn't understand it, but I welcomed the relief.

"In the morning, the urge to fight was back and the spoons were flying around the kitchen. I went back out to the punching bag. Again, everything settled as soon as I obeyed the voice.

"Grandpa sent me down to a local boxing club. I trained. I got the crap beaten out of me in my first few fights, then I started to win. I got sent home and quit my usual hobbies. Instead, I learned every style of fighting and martial art I could find a teacher for. As I got older, I started target practice with firearms and crossbows; I learned fencing and broadsword fighting. The only time I got any peace was when I was fighting." She locked eyes with me. "I wasn't the focus of a poltergeist. It was me—all of that telekinetic activity. It was my excess energy sending objects flying and breaking things because I needed to fight. Fighting, defending—they're my purpose.

"I have these instincts—intuitions—that tell me when something's wrong or right. They're powerful. When I saw Gabe, I knew I had to protect him. Same with Patience. I was drawn to them magnetically—not even like a magnet, actually, it was more like a moth to light. Then to the rest of you. You all glow to me. And when Mimi arrived, I knew that was it, that you were all here now, and I had to protect the seven of you—with my life, if necessary. Any time you're under threat, the voice starts up again: *fight*."

There was a long silence.

"Hell, Ms. D," Ed breathed. "Why'd you never tell us this before?"

"It wasn't relevant. All that matters is protecting you."

"Wasn't *relevant*?" Mona said weakly.

Ms. Deering shrugged.

Drew shifted on the railing. "Your intuitions, what are they like? Like the voice, or something else?"

She considered the question. "Like a game of hot and cold. I don't know what the circle of seven is all about, but every now and then I get a strong feeling pulling me one way or pushing me another. You know—warmer, warmer—hot. Boiling hot. Then I know it's right. Or cooler, cooler, ice cold. Then I know it's wrong."

"You must have an amygdala the size of a truck," Mona said. "What sort of things make you cold?"

"Whenever anyone asks questions about you kids, I go ice cold. And when other kids try to join the gifted program? Ice cold. The instinct to keep your gifts under wraps is boiling hot, which is why I've always insisted on complete secrecy. The other thing that gives me the chills is when there's a secret being kept from me—or relationship lines crossed." There was no mistaking the looks she gave me and Drew. My heart stuttered and Drew looked at the ground.

"What is the intuition saying now?" Patience asked. "About Mr. Boxe and Dr. Mayer?"

"My intuition's always remained neutral around Mr. Boxe." She looked as puzzled as we were. "I don't get danger chills, but I don't get warm fuzzies, either. Dr. Mayer—well, I think I ought to make an appointment with him and see what I can find out."

Mona had two deep creases between her eyebrows and was clearly thinking harder than a Greek philosopher. "I always wondered if it was a higher power or a kind of deep connection that brought us together at EVA. But it's not that at all." She looked up. "Someone's pulling the strings. It's either Dr. Mayer or Mr. Boxe—or both—and I want to know what's in it for them."

25

Top Tips for Rumbling Your Friends' Secrets

Back at the school, Cassie went straight to her room. She had a plan to convince Sir Percival that her closet was a better place to live than her hair. In light of our newest discoveries, Mona said she was going to review her notebooks. Patience wanted to practice her conjuring. I was impressed by her ability to move on, considering she'd only just decided once and for all that she wasn't a vessel of Satan.

Olivia wanted details about the camp, but I'd promised to call my mom when I got back. I borrowed the phone in Ms. Samvedi's office and gave Mom the rundown on where we'd slept and what we'd eaten all weekend, strategically omitting the bits where I was escaping sinister men shrouded in darkness, or experiencing my first kiss. And then arguing with the kisser over whether his vision of me drowning was going to come true.

"Hey, Mom, I wanted to ask you something," I said when I'd run out of half-truths to tell her. "Back when Dr. Mayer suggested I come to EVA, what exactly did he say about the school?"

"Oh, heck, Mim, I'm not sure I can remember now. Pastoral care—that was the buzzword he kept using. He said you'd get twenty-four seven support and somewhere to be safe while you grew into your abilities."

A shadow formed on the ceiling. "Grew into my *abilities*?"

"Yes, your artistic talents and academic capability, I suppose he meant."

"Why did he think I was unsafe?"

"I don't know—your mood, I suppose. He seemed to think you were at real risk."

My skin prickled. "Of what?"

"A depressive decline? Isolation?"

"And there were absolutely no other schools closer to Perry Ridge that he could suggest?"

"Well, it's funny you should say that. Your dad and I have been doing some research and we've come across a school in Maidenvale that might be a suitable alternative to Etherall Valley Academy. It's got a similar ethos, but it's a quite a bit cheaper, and best of all, it's only forty-five minutes from home. You could commute by train and be home every night! Dad and I are going to attend a tour on Tuesday night."

This conversation had taken an unpleasant turn. "But Mom, I told you I love it here."

"I know, honey, but those incidents, the kinds of kids going to EVA..." She trailed off, then resumed brightly. "Maidenvale Prep hasn't had a reportable violent incident all year, and they don't accept kids with any kind of criminal history."

"Mom—these are my friends you're talking about!" I took a breath and attempted to change the subject. "Anyway, how's the planning for your Paris trip going?" She was silent. "Mom?"

"We've postponed the trip."

I was so shocked I didn't reply for a few moments. "What? But you've been planning it forever!"

"It's not the right time. Anyway, about the school tour—"

"Mom, *what*? I don't get it! You've been talking about this Paris trip for as long as I can remember. What went wrong? Did the accommodation fall through? Or couldn't you get leave from your new job?"

"No, I wouldn't have taken the job if there had been a problem." She paused and I got the feeling she was back-pedaling, trying to hide something. "Your dad and I just decided it was bad timing. We'll go another time. In a... a year or two."

My brain finally caught up. "Is it money?" Her hesitation was enough to confirm it. "It is, isn't it? Is that why you want me to change schools?"

"No! Well, it's not *just* that. There are several reasons. Anyway, Dad and I will do the Maidenvale Prep tour and we'll let you know how it goes. I know you love EVA, but imagine if we found you a school you liked even better!" Her voice was tight with faked enthusiasm.

"I don't think it's likely." I sounded like a brat, but I needed her to understand how important this was.

"We'll see." Now Mom just sounded tired.

I fretted alone in my room after the phone call. The thought of Mom giving up her lifelong dream of going to Paris made me ache. She'd been practicing her French using an app for over a year, not to mention the hours spent cross-referencing tours against her precious photo book of Paris's most beautiful sights. My eyes stung with tears of guilt—then despair. I *couldn't* leave EVA.

I made a frantic plan: we could dip into my college fund to pay the tuition fees. Then, surely, they could still go to Paris. I emailed Mom with the suggestion.

There was a message in my inbox from Aunt Aurora, thanking me for the birthday wishes. In her signature at the foot of the email was a blessing for Samhain, which made me think of Gabe calling Cassie a witch. I replied to my aunt, starting with some inane chitchat about my camp at Blackmere Pool, then asking her about her Wiccan practices and whether she'd ever had a familiar. I made out like it was pure curiosity, sparked by a book I'd been reading.

Mona came to visit me after dinner. "I have a theory," she announced, shutting the door behind her. "Where are they?"

I pointed at the floor where Marvin was slouched against the wall, and the end of my bed where Hannah was sitting. I leaned back, fully prepared for a long monologue on how Mr. Boxe and Dr. Mayer had conspired to get us all to the school and why. Possibly also something to do with codes.

That's why it was such a shock when Mona sat on my chair, opened her notebook and dropped it on my lap at a page from over a year earlier. "Drew's vision of a drowned girl," she said, tapping the page. "That was you, wasn't it?"

The astonishment on my face was all the answer she needed. "H-he told you?" I stammered.

"No, I worked it out myself. He freaks out every time we're near the water, and it's always focused on you." Mona's expression was a battle between pride in her discovery and deep concern. "Why didn't you tell us? Why didn't *Drew* tell us?"

"He did tell you about the vision—back when it happened."

"But he didn't tell us he'd realized it was you. That's not cool. And you—you knew, too. He told you, which explains a lot about your behavior toward each other. But you didn't tell us. Why the secrets?"

"Because he's wrong!" I said hotly. "Completely wrong. He's misremembered the girl in his vision. It wasn't me. Or he's misunderstood it."

"He said it was someone important." She stared at the words on the page for a few moments, then shook her head. "No, I don't think he's misremembered or misunderstood, Mimi. I think it's more that you don't like the truth."

Damn her, with her sharp intellect that could always cut straight to the truth. "Not all of his visions go the way he thinks they will."

"Most do."

"Maybe the ones we know about. He has plenty of visions where we have no idea how they turned out."

She observed me so closely that I started to fidget. "I can understand why you're upset," she said. "But how does denying it help? If we'd known about the vision, we could have all been looking out for you over the camp weekend. Ms. Deering's going to go nuts when she finds out."

"Firstly, I don't want you all looking after me."

"But that's what friends do."

Her words silenced me for a few moments. "Not that way, though. Friends don't hover around waiting for each other to fall into a lake. Anyway, secondly, Ms. Deering isn't going to go nuts because you're not going to tell her. I've asked Drew not to tell anyone about it. I don't want people thinking I'm in danger or getting worried. I'm perfectly fine. I can look after myself." I was sounding like an audio loop.

"Mimi, we can't lose you. We can't lose you because you're the seventh and we need you." Mona's eyes were big and earnest. "And I've never clicked with anyone the way I click with you. You listen when I blather on about stuff, and sometimes you even seem to think I'm interesting. You're my best friend."

I didn't know what to say. Her words almost didn't penetrate the old, long-hardened shell of my isolation—almost. But they did, and I sat there, suddenly close to tears. "Thanks, Mona. And you *are* interesting."

"So, I'll be telling Ms. Deering all about it," she finished.

"No—"

She held up a hand. "Save it. This is big, and you'll just have to put your self-worth problems aside. We need to work out how to save you."

When I got to gifted class the next day, it was obvious to me that Mona had already spilled the beans. Ms. Deering looked thunderously angry, standing at the front of the room, staring me and Drew down.

"Would you care to share?" she asked Drew, as if he'd been caught passing a note.

"Huh?"

"About your vision of Mimi?"

His green eyes widened and he swung around to look at me. I locked my gaze on the desk, sure my face was scarlet.

Hannah's voice came softly in my ear. "They're merely concerned for you, miss." It wasn't much comfort.

After a thick silence, Drew told everyone how he'd recognized me from his vision on the day I started at EVA. His voice was low and stumbled on the word "drowned." There was a stunned hush, broken only by the crows that cawed noisily from the garden shed roof.

Gabe swore and turned away so we couldn't see his face. Ed shuffled closer and put an arm around my shoulders. Patience stifled a sob.

Cassie scowled. "Great, she finally turns up and then we lose her."

Despite the awfulness of the moment, a candle flicker of warmth rose in my chest. They really seemed to mind that I might be fated to die.

"Mimi, I need you to focus," Ms. Deering told me, resting a hand on my desk, her eyes burning into my face. "This is a warning. We can prevent it, if we're smart. Drew's visions are warnings, not done deals. Look at what happened with Cassie's aunt. And the cyclist who was almost hit by a bus. If we're watchful, we can prevent this."

"I hate being treated differently," I protested weakly. "I don't want everyone watching over me. It's my nemesis."

"No. *Drowning* is your nemesis." It was so blunt, I practically jolted upright. "You need to manage your aversion to being cared for and accept our help. I know this, Mimi—in my intuition system, it's as hot as burning coals."

I said nothing. I was having a strange moment of realization that there were people in this world other than my family who really cared whether I lived or died. And if I wanted to hold on to their friendship, I'd have to allow them to look after me. It felt good, but also so horrible that I wanted to claw my own skin off.

Mona was writing a list. "Okay, Mimi. You need to stay away from lakes, ponds, rainwater tanks, wells, the ocean, bathtubs and swimming pools. That shouldn't be too hard."

An idea dive-bombed into my head, fully formed. "Wait—the well! Last week, I nearly fell into the old well! The grille broke, I was helping Axel rescue his library book, and I slipped. Axel grabbed me, stopped me from falling." I gazed around at them all in triumph. "*That* must have been the drowning in Drew's vision. And it got prevented!"

To my shock, nobody looked convinced except Patience. She was nodding eagerly, but Mona was chewing her pen, her expression doubtful. Drew looked close to losing the plot.

"Mimi." Ms. Deering held my gaze. "Accept our help."

I found myself crying in class. I *hated* crying in class and hadn't done it since middle school. Mona and Patience cried too, which made me cry more. The boys stopped looking at us, but I think they had manly tears happening. Cassie scowled, which was the equivalent of crying for her. Ms. Deering waited for us to get our shit together.

At last Mona blew her nose loudly. "Did you contact Dr. Mayer yet, Ms. D?"

Ms. Deering nodded. "He has offices all over the county, although I've learned that some have recently closed down. The Perry Ridge one and the Pinetree Glades one."

"I guess it's expensive, running all those offices simultaneously," Mona said.

"Expensive and inconvenient. But useful if you're hunting for a bunch of gifted young people who are scattered across the county. And it would make sense to shut the extra offices down as soon as you have them assembled in one location: Etherall Valley Academy."

As conspiracy theories went, Ms. Deering was hitting a standard Mona could only aspire to.

"So you're going to see him?" Cassie asked.

"Yes. On Wednesday, during my non-teaching time, I'm meeting him at his Etherall Valley office. I'll claim to need advice about a student's behavior."

Mona wriggled forward on her chair. "And have you confronted Mr. Boxe?"

"No. I'm still deciding what to do about him. I want to see what's what with Dr. Mayer first, then I'll tackle Mr. Boxe. This is a delicate situation, and if there's a secret to untangle, I need to do it carefully. My first objective is to work out whether the two men know each other—and how."

The seven of us sat together at lunchtimes now. This new arrangement felt permanent, as if we were now locked together as a group for the foreseeable future.

Except, on Tuesday, Axel joined our table uninvited. "How was your weekend away?" he asked. "What did you get up to?"

I rattled off some of our teamwork activities and he listened in silence. His envy was palpable.

"I've asked Ms. Deering if I can re-sit the aptitude test," he said.

"Nice," I replied weakly. God, this poor, lonely kid who thought he belonged in our phony genius program. "You know, I've heard that aptitude and IQ tests are often skewed. I wouldn't overthink it if you don't do especially well. There are so many ways to be smart."

He shrugged. "Yes, but I'm normally good at IQ tests." He was quiet for a moment, then seemed to make a decision. "Can I tell you something?"

"Of course."

He glanced around, but Mona and Gabe were consumed by a highly scientific argument about whether the body understood that non-sugar sweeteners were not sugar. Patience was listening, Ed was saying that artificial sweeteners tasted disgusting anyway, Cassie had gone to get some fruit and Drew was pretending not to listen to my conversation.

Axel leaned in. "I spoke to my parents about the gifted program. They're going to make a formal complaint to the board of the school. They believe Ms. Deering is singling out students for extra opportunities unfairly."

"Whoa," I said in alarm. "Don't do that!"

"Why not?" Axel looked quietly rebellious. "Olivia agrees with me. She's wanted to be in it for over a year. Diesel and Jackson want to join, too." I was aware of Diesel and Jackson—they wore anime shirts and geeked out over RPGs. Jackson was the only person I'd ever met who also listened to Hoodwynk.

"It's not all that great," I said in desperation. "It's pretty boring, actually. Like, if I have to do one more teamwork activity, I'm going to lose my sense of self. It's not for geniuses at *all*."

Axel's hazel eyes were puzzled behind his glasses. "I don't get it. Everyone I know wants to get into this gifted program, but whenever I talk to any of the members about it, they say it's boring and I wouldn't want to join. What's the deal?"

"There's no deal." The others had fallen quiet now, catching on to what Axel was saying. "It's just an offbeat way of running a program, I guess. This school is always doing offbeat things."

"But this is a whole new level of offbeat. I mean, you're all in the program together, even though every one of you has *different* talents. Ed's a math specialist, and Drew, you're doing extension literature, correct? And you with your art, Mimi. And Mona studying three different languages, like she's training to be in the UN or something. Gabe's in the specialist media class, and Patience is doing literature too."

Cassie arrived back with a tub of fruit salad.

"And Cassie's in the dance program," Axel went on. "So why are they teaching you all in the gifted program together like that?"

"What are we talking about?" Cassie asked, suddenly alert.

Axel was staring around at us all. "I mean, math, art, dance—they can't be teaching extension work on all those things in one class. And it's not about your grades, either. It's not like all of you are A averages, are you?" He sounded aggrieved. "So what is it? Why do you get to be in the program and I don't?"

We sat in wordless consternation, trying to think of a good reason. A *really* good reason, because Axel had obviously seen through all the other ones he'd been fed. Mona opened her mouth, but unexpectedly, Patience got in first.

"We all saw a psychiatrist," she said in her soft voice. "The gifted program is a ruse."

"A what?" Cassie sounded genuinely baffled.

"A façade." Patience had her eyes on Axel. "The psychiatrist recommended we attend this school. The gifted program is a space where we can work on getting better."

Mona rolled with it. "It's a support group, if you must know. Ms. Deering is a trained social worker, and we support each other to manage our various disorders."

"And now you know the truth," Drew put in, "we'd appreciate it if you could keep your mouth shut. It's not like we *want* to have these conditions. The gifted program helps us feel less isolated. Like we matter."

That wasn't far from the truth. We all sat watching Axel.

"It's a mental health support group?" he said slowly. "That's all?"

"It might not seem like much to you," Cassie sneered. "But it matters to us."

Axel raised a hand and waved it vaguely. "No, I didn't mean that. I'm just surprised."

"Are you still going to get your parents to complain to Mr. Boxe?" I asked.

He shook his head. "No. Of course not."

I went weak with relief. "Thanks, Axel. I know you just wanted to join, but now you know the truth, do you think you could stop drawing attention to us and getting other kids riled up about the program?"

"Yes. I'll stop. And I won't tell anyone." Axel got up. "Sorry, everyone. I had it all wrong."

He left us alone.

Cassie glared at Patience. "You *told* him about Dr. Mayer?"

Patience went instantly pink. "I didn't say his name. I just knew Axel wouldn't stop asking until we gave him some part of the truth."

"She did her best," Drew told Cassie.

"I didn't think it was a bad story," Mona said. "Specific enough to make him believe us, vague enough to protect the truth. I just hope he doesn't spread it around, or we'll all be branded with a whole new sort of reputation."

I honestly didn't care. I was used to having that sort of reputation, and was there really anything wrong with being a little disordered? I was just glad Axel would finally stop beating himself up about not being in the gifted program.

"I saw Ms. Deering getting into her car as I was coming to class," Mona told me in math on Wednesday.

"Going to visit Dr. Mayer?"

"I'd say so."

A frisson of excitement buzzed through me. "I can't wait to get some answers."

"Me too." She opened her file, but at that moment a bell started ringing.

"Attention, all students. This is an evacuation drill. Please follow the directions of your teachers."

The class groaned as one, and Ms. Huang told us to leave our gear where it was and head out to the quad in an orderly fashion.

We were halfway across the room when Mona stopped, causing a minor traffic pileup. "Wait—my notebook!"

"I said leave your things, Mona."

"Not my notebook," Mona said quickly. "I take it everywhere."

"Leave it," Ms. Huang ordered her in a tone that was not to be trifled with.

"But I can carry it in my hand—"

"Mona Thomas, in a life-or-death situation, there will be no going back for a notebook! Out!"

Poor Mona was forced to leave her precious notebook behind. She grumbled all the way out to the playing field. There, we split off into our homeroom groups and the teachers carried out a roll call. Drew sat beside me, but we didn't speak. We hadn't spoken since the weekend's disagreement. I knew I had to apologize; I just hadn't worked out how. Nor could I work out how to *not* feel like I did about him.

"This is the worst," Cassie grumbled. "It's hot in the sun, and I can't even put my hair in a ponytail, because Sir Percival insisted on staying with me today."

"Your bat's developing separation anxiety," Gabe told her. "You're going to have to put him in pet daycare while you're in class."

"You could try enrichment toys," Drew offered. "Something to distract him when you're leaving the room."

She gave them both a death stare. "You're so amusing, boys."

We were all finally sent back to class. I got into my seat, wondering if it was worth opening my math file for the final few minutes of the period.

"Oh, crap!" Mona was rummaging through her bag. "Where'd it go?" She rifled through her file and papers, then looked at me, her face draining of color. "It's gone. My notebook's gone."

To Ms. Huang's credit, she made everyone show her what was in their bags, but the notebook was nowhere to be found. Mona asked if she could go check the lost property box, but Ms. Huang made her stay until the bell rang for lunch. I went to the admin block with Mona, trying to reassure her.

"You don't understand," she said. "It's got everything in it! Everything from the past few weeks—all the discoveries we've made, all the changes since you got to EVA. God, why didn't I encode it all? I thought about doing it so many times, but I decided I would just never let it out of my sight instead."

"I'm sure it's just a case of someone mistaking it for their own. Maybe it even got bumped to the floor during the fire drill and one of the teachers picked it up. Has it got your name in it?"

"Of course not. Do you think I'm unhinged? But it's not like anyone could mistake it for theirs. I order those notebooks specially off this obscure website that makes one-of-a-kind stationery."

"There's no such thing as one of a kind, Mona. I guarantee you there's some massive online shopping site selling fakes."

We reached the great doors of the admin block and pushed our way through. The receptionist sent us down the corridor to the dim room where the lost property collection was kept, and we dug rather hopelessly through the plastic tub of books, pens, sunglasses, jackets and water bottles. At last Mona straightened up and gazed at me, tears welling in her eyes.

"What if Boxe has it?" she whispered. "Mimi, I've really screwed up."

I gave her a quick hug. "Let's go and see if someone's handed it to Mr. Boxe. Chances are, he hasn't even had time to look at it yet."

She trailed after me down the corridor. Around the corner, at the front desk, a student was asking the receptionist for a new password to the school intranet. It sounded like Axel. When we reached Mr. Boxe's office, the door was wide open and he was nowhere to be seen. A breeze wafted in through his open window and riffled the papers on his desk.

"Let's wait for him to get back," I suggested, but Mona gave a gasp and a moment later was striding straight into the office. She snatched her beloved notebook off the desk.

"He did have it! Thank God. Do you think he looked at it?" She flipped through as if to check that our principal hadn't left any graffiti on the pages.

"Come on, Mona, let's get out of here," I whispered. "We shouldn't be in Mr. Boxe's office!" I checked the corridor.

But when I looked back at her, a deep frown had creased her forehead. She wasn't looking at her notebook anymore, but at the desk. She reached down and shifted a couple of items, uncovering a yellowing piece of lined paper. On it was a black, hand-drawn circle of spidery writing with symbols all the way around. A vague memory nagged at me.

"Oh my God," Mona breathed, shaking it free from the other papers. "This is the drawing from Drew's vision."

A jolt of uncanny fear went through me. There was the feather, the skull, the star, the hand, the eye. There was also a heart and a paw print. Lines, dots and squiggles ran down the page like the lettering had bled at certain points. This was what Drew had attempted to sketch for us.

My eyes paused on the skull and something seemed to click deep inside me, a key turning in a lock.

"Mimi," Mona said softly. "This writing—it's the same code from the Lydenburg papers. Exactly the same."

"What does it say?" I asked.

"I need time to translate," she murmured.

"We can't *take* it!"

Mona looked at me rebelliously for a moment—then I had a brainwave. I pointed at a small printer/photocopier on the L-shaped part of Mr. Boxe's desk.

Mona didn't hesitate. She whipped open the lid and placed the paper facedown, then hit copy. It seemed to take forever to scan, then began aggressively spitting out the printout, one section at a time. It was so noisy I thought I was going to have a heart attack.

If that wasn't bad enough, just as the copier was finishing its hellish racket, a door opened further down the hall and Mr. Boxe's hearty voice rang out. "Well, I think that's a good as solution as we can manage, under the circumstances…"

Mona seized the printed page. She scrambled across the room to the open window, swung her legs over the sill and dropped to the grass below.

"Come on!" she whispered at me, ducking out of sight.

I fumbled open the copier lid and grasped the yellowed page by a corner, whipping it out and dropping it back on Mr. Boxe's desk. His voice was getting louder. Was it better to be caught in his office, or trying to climb out of his window? I could give a better explanation for being found *inside* the office. My shadows gibbered and heaved in every corner, and I gestured frantically at Mona to run, my nervous giggle threatening.

Mona didn't have to be told twice. She took off at a scamper. I turned and faced the door just as a head poked around the corner.

But it wasn't Mr. Boxe—he was still mid-conversation down the corridor. It was Axel. I sagged with relief.

"Mimi! What are you doing?" He came in to join me.

"Nothing! I just…" I couldn't find an end to the sentence. "We should get out of here."

At that moment, Axel noticed the drawing sitting on the desk. He froze and stared at it, then reached out and picked it up, holding it close to his face.

"I know this," he said slowly.

"What?"

"It's from the Lydenburg papers."

"How do you know about that?"

"I'm from Lydenburg," he said. "Everyone in town knows about the papers. But this drawing, not many people know about *that*."

Mr. Boxe's voice grew louder again—he was finalizing his conversation. I glanced at the window and then back at Axel.

"I think we need to talk." He paused, studying me. "Mimi, are you supposed to be in here?"

"No!" I said. "Come on!"

We didn't waste another second. I dashed for the window and climbed out, Axel scrambling after me. I ran in a blind panic until he grabbed my arm and pulled me toward a copse of trees near the fence, both of us giggling with the adrenaline rush.

I peered back at Mr. Boxe's office window, chest heaving. He was in there, standing in front of his desk, but not looking our way. "I don't think he saw us." I sank down onto the grass. "Thanks, Axel."

He joined me, took off his glasses and polished them on his shirt. He put them back on and pulled a yellow page out of his pocket.

I nearly choked. "Whoa—you took it?"

He cast a scowl back toward the admin palace. "I don't understand why Mr. Boxe has it. It doesn't belong to him." He glanced at me. "Or did *you* get it from somewhere? Did Mr. Boxe confiscate it?"

"No, it was on his desk when I went in there."

"Oh, right." He gazed down at the page as if it were a dangerous snake in his hand. "Have you heard of the Asterions?"

I scrounged in my memory for something to hang the slightly familiar word on. *Dad's email.* "Are they the cult that thinks there's an invisible city in the Lydenburg mountains?"

"Mind your words, miss," Hannah's voice came in my ear.

"Shut y'mouth, kid," Marvin added.

"Not a cult," Axel said. "An ancient order of spiritual leaders descended from druids."

I only knew of druids from my brother's D&D books. "Are you a member of the—the order?"

"My parents are members. This is an extremely important set of symbols." There was caution in his voice, and he seemed to be trying to gauge how much I knew. "Why are you interested in it?"

"Not sure," I said, which was mostly the truth. "I don't know what it means."

"I do."

"Will you tell me?" I was about to add "and Mona," but that would implicate her, and Ms. Deering wanted everything kept a secret.

Axel was rubbing his neck uneasily. "I don't know if I'm supposed to."

"I won't blab it around. Even if you can tell me what the icons around the circle mean, that'd be good."

He checked around us, but the schoolyard was deserted; people were still eating in the cafeteria.

"I don't want to talk about it here. I feel like the school has ears and eyes everywhere." Axel didn't know how right he was. "Do you know of somewhere private we can talk? Maybe after school, in the art room? Oh—no, actually. I'm not too happy about Mrs. Shaw always being around. She's been acting strangely."

I pictured our wise, colorful art teacher. "I think that's normal for her."

He shook his head. "No, she's been watching me. You and me both."

That made me feel a little ill. All those hours I'd spent after school and on weekends in the art room, with Mrs. Shaw hovering around. Oh, hell—my painting of Albert! What if she suspected something?

Axel got to his feet, pocketing the paper again. "Actually, on second thought, forget I ever said anything. I'll get this back to the people who are supposed to have it in their protection. Forget I mentioned the—you know. The order."

Mona would never forgive me if I didn't get this information from him. "Wait," I said. "I know the perfect place where we can talk—away from school. Follow me."

26
When the Stars Align

I led Axel along the school's fence line into the shrubbery and out through the split in the fence. A crow observed us from its position on the gate.

"Is this allowed?" Axel asked, glancing around. "I thought it was against the rules to leave the school grounds."

"We won't be long," I said. "We'll get back before next period so we're not missed, promise." I crossed the road and led him into the woods. "Okay, let's talk."

"The Lydenburg papers were found on an old farm," he began.

"Under the floorboards, right? And they thought it was a wartime code?"

"It's not, though. It's secret information about the flood prophecy."

"Yes. And an invisible city."

Marvin harrumphed in my ear—a warning noise.

"And about the Order of Aster." Axel said the words reverently.

I slowed my pace to a wander, the trees trembling around us in the chilly breeze. "What is it, exactly?"

"My parents are high up in the order. They're knowledge keepers. They've brought together prophecies from all over the world, saying there's going to be a great flood—a bit like the biblical one. A new set of world leaders will emerge and guide those who have faith to a refuge. They're called the Transcendents."

"Who are they?" I asked, heart racing.

"They have gifts. Powers. There are supposed to be seven of them, about our age. They were all born seventeen years ago, on nights when certain stellar bodies crossed paths in the sky. In fact, for a while, my parents thought I might be one of them."

"You!" I stopped and stared at Axel. "Did you show signs of powers?"

"No, but I was born at the right time. I'm not one of the seven, but I'm connected. I'm a trained sentry."

"*You* are?"

He put a finger to his lips. "Did you hear something?" he whispered.

I stood perfectly still and listened. The wind sighed through the treetops, and I thought I caught a cracking sound somewhere. I peered around us, but nothing moved except for the leaves and my shadows, which rolled and slithered all around us. Even the crows were quiet, for once.

I shivered. "Let's keep moving. We're visible from the school standing here." We walked on. "I thought sentries were born, not made."

"Why would you think that?"

"Because of the story Ms. D—"

"Hush, miss!" Hannah hissed.

"Watch your mouth!" Marvin snapped.

I stumbled over my words in an effort to stop myself.

"What did you say?" Axel looked bewildered.

"I said, I assumed being a sentry was something people were born to do."

"It's a role," he told me. "They're all just roles that anyone can take on."

"But you just said the seven were all born under some sort of stellar event."

"Yes, but so were thousands more, right? It's not like the seven were the *only* kids born on those nights. So why did *they* get the Transcendent roles and others didn't? Luck. Pure luck. I've been trained all my life to be a sentry, sworn to protect the Transcendents with my life. But if I died, there'd be someone else who could take the role. Just like if any of the Transcendents died, there'd be someone else to take their roles."

"Damn." We reached the water hole and stood on the shore, gazing at one another. "Just roles. Anyone could take them." I repeated the words in a numb haze. Hopefully I could remember all this for Mona—but if not, we could probably get Axel to repeat it if I could make him trust me. "So there are seven Transcendents…"

He nodded and pulled out the paper again. "The Transcendents are represented by this drawing." He pointed to the symbols around the circle in turn. "The eye—that's the prophet. The heart is the empath. The paw print is the beastmaster. The hand is the healer; the star is the conjurer; the quill is the scribe—"

"Scribe?" I echoed. I was still limp with shock, but somewhere, something stirred in response to this unfamiliar word. Another click. "I thought it was polyglot."

Axel frowned. "Polyglot? No. Are *you* the scribe? No, that's probably Mona, right?"

I pointed to the skull. "I'm the necromancer."

"No, don't speak it, girl!"

I whirled around when Marvin shouted the words. In my excitement, I'd completely forgotten my ghosts' instructions. *Oh, hell*—big mistake. I'd inadvertently disobeyed Marvin *and* Hannah. Would they both invade me at once? Could I even survive that?

But Marvin was standing straighter than I'd ever seen him, his bent old body alert. Not moving. Hannah watched from a few steps away, silent with sorrow.

Axel was whipping his head back and forth, peering fearfully around the woodland. "Who's there?"

Had he heard Marvin speak? Marvin faded into the daylight air, giving me my answer.

"Marvin!" I cried. "Wait, Marvin, I'm sorry!"

"That was a spirit?" Axel's eyes were wide with fear.

"He's gone." I choked on the words. Once more, one of my ghosts had revealed—sacrificed—himself, simply to give me a message.

"Who's gone?" Axel asked.

I sank onto my knees on the bank, tears spilling.

"Mimi?" Axel crouched beside me, putting a tentative hand on my back. "What happened?"

My heart drained of all the excitement I'd been feeling. Marvin was gone. I ached for the comfort of my friends. *Drew.* I wanted his arms around me. "We should go back. Lunch is nearly over."

Before I could get to my feet, I was shoved and went flying. I found myself on my back, my ears, eyes, nostrils filling with cold water. I struggled, lashing out, but something was pinning me down. The air in my lungs bubbled out until they were empty, then it hurt like my chest was being squeezed in a fist. *No air.* The pain was too much, and I gasped, sucking in liquid. This time it burned, as if the water had come from a boiled kettle. I choked and coughed but it was all water, nothing to breathe in or choke out except water. I thrashed and kicked, but my arms were being held tight. Silt and sunlight blinded me.

I'm going to die.

Screw that, I was *not* going to die. I fought with every grain of energy that remained in my body. But the hold on my arms was like an iron vise, and my kicks met empty air. I couldn't even see my assailant, let alone fight my way free.

Drew's vision of the drowned girl. A black-inked skull. Marvin's shout. Albert thudding his cane on the deck. Accept our help, Mimi. It all ran through my mind like a time-lapse video. My fury morphed into injustice. Then despair.

I can't save myself.

Something or someone was taking my life, and there was nothing I could do to make it stop. My vision was fading, turning gray. The cold water didn't feel cold anymore. The urge to fight faded into weariness, then stillness, then silence. My limbs slackened; my gulping and bubbling subsided; shadows descended.

The world grew dark.

Quiet. Still.

Hannah, leaning over me. "Miss, you must come with me."

I wept softly, hopelessly. "I didn't want to die, Hannah."

"You had to." She spoke calmly. "Take my hand."

"No."

"Take it."

"No!" But my will was waning.

"Miss." Hannah stood beside my killer, who was still hunched over, holding me under the water. It was Axel, his eyes fierce, glasses lost in the struggle, water dripping off his skin. For the first time I noticed his white and green sweatshirt. *The number thirty-four in dark green paint.*

"Miss, take my hand. Please."

I took Hannah's hand. It was rough-skinned and surprisingly strong. My own hand felt small and weak grasped in those fingers.

A girl's hand clasped by another girl's hand.

She pulled me up out of the water, which fell away like sand. I stood above my dead body while Axel released me and sat back, breathing heavily. He raised his wet arms and closed his eyes.

"Power of the necromancer, enter me," he called.

Hannah was touching me—why didn't it hurt? Why hadn't I been sucked into her memories of death yet? The whole Mimi was here, intact. *Oh. Because I'm a spirit, too.* I wasn't sharing body space with another spirit this time; my spirit had left my body.

I was dead.

Hannah's eyes had always been concealed by shadow, but now I saw them: soft, drooping at the edges, with compassionate velvet-brown irises.

"Why did Axel kill me?"

"He thought your gift could be his." We moved, gliding across the surface of the ground. "The lad thought he would become just as you were, miss. He only needed the name."

"The name of my gift?"

"Yes, yours or anyone of your friends' gifts."

"It wasn't enough for him to be a sentry?"

"He's not a real sentry, miss. A mere foot soldier, is all. And all he's ever wanted is to be important. To be a grand leader like his pa and his ma, and save his people from the flood. A hero."

"Is that why he tried to join the gifted program?"

"He's been endeavoring to become close to you all, one by one, for months. Doing his best to get one of you to name your gift, so he could do away with that one and take the power for himself."

"Will he become the necromancer?" I asked.

"No, miss. It's a fool's dream. He'll be sore ashamed when he realizes your murder was for naught."

I gazed at Axel, his arms still raised. "Power of the necromancer," he said again, more urgently this time. "Enter me!"

"Come away." Hannah sounded more urgent now. "We must hurry." Then, dreamlike, we were running through a place that barely resembled the woods anymore. The trees were dark lines in a colorless fog, gray on gray.

"Where are we going?" I asked.

"We must let them know what's happened."

"What's the point? They'll find my body soon enough."

"Your gift, miss. The gift of the crossing."

Voices were becoming audible through the fog now, in the same way sound travels underwater. Hannah slowed until we were hovering in place, gray mist all around us. The muffled voices grew nearer.

"I'll draw your young man to you," she said, her beautiful doe eyes on mine. "I shall place his hand in yours. You must lead him to the water, help him find your body."

Running footsteps were coming closer and a dark shape appeared, heading straight for us. Hannah reached upward, grasping the hazy shadow branch of a tree, then wrenched it firmly downward. It snapped with a great crack and fell in front of a human-shaped shadow, which stopped short.

Hannah tugged on my hand and placed it into another's, then quietly vanished. A rush of color and emotion swamped me, making me want to simultaneously laugh, cry and scream.

"Mimi?" Drew was staring at me in bewilderment. "What's happened to you?"

He could see me? He *could* see me! He could see everything I felt and knew and sensed. And I felt and knew and sensed everything of him, too. Hannah hadn't just joined our hands; she'd connected our souls. We saw each other's love and desire, like for like, a wild river through a burst dam.

"Axel hurt me," I said, but he already knew—my memories had seeped into his soul.

He ran for the water hole, my hand still clasped in his. Then the water came into view, my lifeless body submerged in the shallows. Drew howled in grief and fury, an animal sound. Axel was still kneeling there, arms raised like a religious fanatic.

Drew released my hand to shove Axel aside and drag my body from the water. He screamed and wept over the limp, sodden form with half-open eyes and blue lips.

I stood on the bank, unsure of the way forward. For a moment, with my hand in his, it had felt like there was a way back. But my body was dead and Drew had severed the connection of our souls when he dropped my hand, leaving me isolated in the gray place.

Mona and Gabe burst into my field of vision, blurred but recognizable. Then another shape appeared: Ed. He never stopped running, just threw himself at my body, sliding to a stop in the mud and thrusting his hands straight onto my heart and lungs. Drew held me, saying my name over and over, his arms supporting my shoulders while my head lolled lifelessly, eyes cloudy.

Mona strode toward Axel, vengeance in every tendon. "What did you do?" she screamed, slapping his face hard.

"I'll become the necromancer now," he tried, cradling his cheek. "You haven't lost one of your seven—just replaced her."

"We don't want *you*! We want Mimi!"

"Help her!" Drew implored Ed.

"No, don't!" Axel crawled toward my body.

But Gabe dragged him away. Then Patience was there, hands cupped to conjure, and something long and snakelike appeared. A rope. Gabe yanked Axel's arms behind his back, making him cry out in pain. He wrestled against Gabe for his freedom while Patience tied his wrists together. Then Cassie appeared, stalking him, baring her teeth and growling as deep and slow as a jaguar. Axel went still with uncanny fear.

I stood unanchored and invisible in a gray world, watching the blurred forms of my friends trying to save me. Ed trying to heal my dead body; Drew and Patience pleading with him; Mona shouting about thin boundaries. Cassie untangling the tiny bat from her hair and sending it for help.

A prod came at my consciousness, and I pushed back reflexively.

"She's still here!" Gabe cried. He had his eyes locked on the spot where I stood. "I can feel her. Mimi, we won't let you go. Stay with us."

"Mimi." Drew sobbed the word, cradling my head in his hands. "Come back."

And suddenly I understood how.

I went closer and touched Drew's hand. He felt it—the zing—and his hand opened to mine as if it were under my control. I grasped it, momentarily basking in the sensation of our souls meeting again—but there was no time for that, because a light tunnel formed and I was dragged through. Then I was in that cold, cold body, lying in Drew's arms.

My soul and body had reunited, and for a moment it felt so bad, so horribly, awfully bad, I was tempted to leave again. My lungs were full of water; every cell was icy and leaden, screaming with lack of oxygen. But something seemed to dislodge inside my chest in response to the warmth Ed was pouring through his hands, and my heart gave a twitch, then a glorious, painful thump. I heaved, rolling over so I could cough.

The coughing went on and on. Water gushed from me, more water than I'd ever imagined could fit in a set of human lungs. I coughed, vomited and choked water up onto the ground as Drew supported me across his knees. I was vaguely aware of sounds around me: relieved sobbing and a broken cheer. Slowly, the world became visible in full color again, sharp and firm.

They moved me onto dry ground, but Ed stayed at my side, his hand between my shoulder blades as I expelled a seemingly endless flow of water. The energy he passed me was as warm and smooth as molten honey, regulating my heartbeat, softening and regenerating my internal organs back into full function. Bit by bit, the water gave way to the air trying to enter my lungs. Patience covered me with a blanket so impossibly soft, warm and light, it could only have been conjured. Cassie called birds and butterflies to zip through the air above me as if trying to amuse a crying infant in a crib. I lay still, surrounded by magic, and the sun shone down onto us as if nothing at all was wrong.

It wasn't long before Ed's surplus of life force had done its work. My lungs were clear of water and working again, my heartbeat steady as a metronome, my hungry cells chowing down on oxygen. I was healed, but exhausted, and couldn't keep my eyes open. Mona fretted that I might be in a coma.

"It's okay," Gabe told her. "She's not unconscious, just tired."

Drew held me tight.

27

How to Stage an Average School Day

I was fine, honestly fine, by the time Ms. Deering and Mr. Boxe found us. I mean, I was utterly wrung out and exhausted, but physically fine. All I wanted was sleep.

Ms. Deering drove me to the hospital to get checked out, leaving Mr. Boxe and the other six to deal with Axel. The doctors listened to my chest and scanned my lungs, but they couldn't find a thing wrong with me other than the bruises on my arms. I claimed those had happened when my friends pulled me out of the water. Ms. Deering took me back to school, trying to ask me about Axel, but I fell asleep before I could tell her much. I woke up to her coaxing me out of the passenger seat.

I did a supported stagger back to the dorm, the cries from the crows in the oak tree following me all the way there. Ms. Deering told Ms. Samvedi a convincing story involving severe menstrual cramps, and said I'd need to spend the day resting. I sat on the floor of the shower and let the hot water run over me, thawing some of my emotional shock.

When I got out and dried off, it became clear that something was different. The shadows. I'd grown so used to them slithering around in my peripheral vision, I'd all but stopped worrying about them. But now I was alone, I couldn't miss the fact that they'd changed. They were bigger, and there were more of them. And they weren't wiggling around in the corners anymore—they were full-sized and hovering around the EVA campus. One was in the bathroom. There were two in the dorm corridor. Out of my bedroom window, the playing field swarmed with them.

Right. This was new and not particularly welcome. At least they weren't in my bedroom. In fact, for the first time since I could remember, I was completely alone.

When Ms. Deering came to visit me a couple of hours later, her face was haggard with worry.

She hugged me. "How are you now?"

"I'm okay. Sleepy. I'm surprised Ms. Samvedi let you in."

"I said you needed iron tablets." She presented me with a bottle of supplements. "Hey, maybe they'll help."

I laughed weakly. "Thanks." I slumped back against my pillow and looked up at her. "Where's Axel?"

"He's under lock and key." She pulled my chair up to the side of the bed and sat down. "Mona showed me her copy of the drawing you found in Mr. Boxe's office, but she doesn't know what happened next. How did you end up in the woods with Axel?"

"He found me in Mr. Boxe's office, and when he saw the drawing, said he knew what it meant. We sneaked out of the office because we weren't meant to be in there."

"No, you weren't." A grim smile.

"I wanted to hear what he knew, but he was worried about being overheard, so I took him over the road to the woods. He knows all about the Lydenburg papers and a flood prophecy. Oh—and he said he's a sentry, too. He says there are seven *types* of gifted people, not just seven gifted people." I stopped. It was all a little jumbled up in my head.

Ms. Deering's mouth tightened. "Mona says he was trying to take your gift. He thought if he killed you, your gift would be released and he could claim it for himself." I shook my head, still struggling to believe that Axel—a school friend—had wanted me dead. "He was following what it says in the Lydenburg papers."

I sucked in a breath. "It's written down?"

"I believe so. I'm trying to get hold of the full set of papers for Mona. They were written by members of the secret Lydenburg cult—the Asterions, they call themselves."

"Axel's a member."

"Yes, and so is Mr. Boxe."

As if it hadn't been through enough today, my poor heart practically smashed its way out of my chest cavity. "Mr. Boxe?" I choked out. "Oh my God! They're all in danger! Mr. Boxe will—"

"Mimi, calm yourself." She put her hand on my leg, which was kicking at the bedclothes. "They're fine. Mr. Boxe isn't a risk."

"How do you know?" My voice was an anxious yelp.

"Because I've spent the past couple of hours with him, hearing his story. He *was* instrumental in bringing you all here to the school. He did so to place you under my protection. He's aware you're in danger because of the beliefs of some of the Asterions—the ones who think they can assimilate your powers by sacrificing you. He and Dr. Mayer, who is also an Asterion, were both involved in bringing you all here. They're elders of some sort."

I chewed my lip. "So, some Asterions are dangerous and others aren't?"

"Yes. Mr. Boxe says there are rogue elements in his community. He's been doing everything he can to watch over you seven and ensure your safety. They even brought in two boys from their cult to help monitor you, but neither of them worked out."

"Axel?" I guessed.

She nodded. "And Tyler." My lip curled. "Yes," she agreed. "Tyler's story is that he was trying to drive Cassie to safety that night, because they were being followed. Mr. Boxe doesn't believe him. He suspects Tyler is rogue."

"And what's Axel's deal?"

"I understand he's a distant relative of Mr. Boxe's. It came as a huge shock that Axel also had his own agenda. Mr. Boxe genuinely trusted him, not realizing Axel had become warped by his need to be part of the circle of seven. I should have picked up on it myself—I heard the warning bells when Axel applied to the gifted program. I dismissed my intuition, thinking it was just the usual caution I feel when the secrecy of the circle is under threat."

"Why didn't Mr. Boxe just come out and tell you the truth from the start?"

She raised her eyes to the ceiling, and it seemed for an instant as if her exasperation was short-circuiting her brain, but when she spoke, she sounded calm. "I've been demanding to know the same thing. They're a secretive group. Theo Boxe says they believed it was better to keep us ignorant of their machinations—that they could better keep the rogue elements away from you all if you didn't understand your own significance. But he didn't count on

Mona's research skills. She's been conducting web searches that threw up beacons for the rogue Asterions. They tracked you seven down, sent in spies—even got to the ones who were supposed to be watching over you."

It sounded like the plot of a movie. I peered at Ms. Deering. "Do you believe all this?"

She relaxed into a chuckle. "Mr. Boxe is telling the truth. I didn't get any danger signals when he came clean."

"And what did Dr. Mayer tell you?"

"Nothing. He claims he can't discuss his clients with me, that his recommendations never include specific schools or clinics—that's up to the parents, et cetera. He pled ignorance, essentially. It was only when I spoke to Mr. Boxe that I got confirmation Mayer is involved."

"Who *are* these rogues?" Whether from tiredness or stress, tears were threatening. "Why don't Boxe and Mayer deal with *them*, instead of trying to protect *us*?"

"Because they don't know who they are," she said.

It pissed me off. My friends—my amazing new life—were under threat. I picked savagely at my blanket.

"Mimi, you need to rest now. We'll talk more soon, as a group."

I nodded. "Axel can't get to me?"

A cloud seemed to cross Ms. Deering's face, but she looked normal again before I could work out what it meant. "I believe Axel's been taken into custody of some kind."

"There were no police called or anything?"

Her face betrayed some internal pain—almost anguish. "If I could make this all *unhappen*, I would. I'm as worried and confused as you are. But you're all safe, and I've been assured that Axel is incarcerated. We stopped Drew's vision from coming true."

That wasn't quite accurate. Drew's vision *had* come true; it was just that we'd found a work-around.

"At least everyone can stop worrying about me now," I said.

"Oh, I don't know about that. I think we should all be looking out for one another more than ever. And following my rules. And listening to my intuitions and not keeping secrets from me."

"I won't keep secrets anymore." I slung my arms around my bent knees and rested my chin on the blanket, feeling suddenly very young. "Ms. D, I have shadow things around me, as well as ghosts. They're like—like swirls of black smoke I see in the corner of my eye. I thought they were something to do with bad vibes—my fear or worries, stuff like that. But I don't know anymore. They've gotten bigger—clearer—since this morning. They look more human now, and they're all over the academy grounds."

She took this in, utterly still. "I see."

"I don't expect you to fix it. I just wanted to tell you the truth."

"Thank you." Ms. Deering appeared to be having Big Thoughts, but she didn't share them.

I took a breath. "Do I still have to stay just friends with… everyone?"

"Yes. My instincts are screaming at me about that, at least for now." She saw the look on my face. "You remember I told you about the hot-cold thing? Well, when I think about you and Drew seeing each other…" She raised her hands helplessly.

"Cold?" I guessed.

"Very, very cold. Arctic."

Funny. It felt the complete opposite when *I* thought about me and Drew. "You didn't make this much of a big deal when Gabe wanted to take me to the dance," I reminded her, trying to keep the resentment out of my tone.

"Yes, but it's not Gabe for you. Is it, Mimi?"

I said nothing.

"I can't force you to follow my advice," she said at last. "I'm not going to forcibly separate you. But it would help immensely if you'd cooperate with me, just for a few months. Things might change—they do sometimes. But I have to follow these intuitions, Mimi. They're all I've got."

I still didn't answer. It felt like too much to ask of me. Just hours earlier, Drew and I could have lost each other for good. And that wave of love that crashed over me while my soul was connected to his—that wasn't something I could simply forget about. What if the rogue Asterions were still out to get us? What if they succeeded? Drew and I might only have "a few months" to be together, and she wanted me to forgo them.

"I'll think about it," I said.

"*Mimiiii,*" was the gentle sound I woke up to. "Mimi, we have cookies."

I smiled and opened my eyes. Mona, Patience and Cassie were all there, my bedroom door shut, the clock showing ten past three in the afternoon.

"It's study hour," I reminded them, and Cassie snorted.

Patience reached tentatively for my hand, as if she thought I'd push her away. "Are you all right now?"

"I'm good," I said.

Mona helped me hitch myself up, plumping my pillows like a nurse from the mid-twentieth century. Cassie perched on the end of my bed, detangling her curls with her finger rake.

"Did Ms. D tell you about Mr. Boxe?" she asked while Mona put a cookie in each of my hands. "We've got, like, an occult principal!"

"Principal of Darkness?" Mona suggested. "Beelze-Boxe?"

"Don't joke about it." Patience's cheeks grew pink.

"Ms. Deering says she's getting him to come and speak to us tomorrow," Mona told me. "He owes us an explanation."

"We thought it was *him* who had you," Cassie went on. "Mona came running into the cafeteria with the drawing from Drew's vision, and said she'd left you in Mr. Boxe's office. We waited for you for a while, then we figured you must've gotten caught. So we all went together to the admin block to talk Mr. Boxe out of expelling you, but when we got to his office, he was missing and you were missing, and we were like, *What the hell?*"

"Then Gabe said there was an emotion commotion coming from somewhere beyond the school gates," Mona put in.

"And all the crows were going *nuts*, croaking and screeching." Cassie's eyes were bright. "I tried to get them to shut up, but they kept saying, '*Come, come!*' and flying toward the gate. I think they like you," she added.

"And Drew went white as a sheet and said, 'The water hole!' and he just started running." Patience's eyes were huge. "Then Ed resuscitated you!"

My eyes flooded with tears. "I need to thank him."

"He's on top of the world," Mona informed me, grinning. "I mean, he's exhausted, but I've never seen him this high. Drew's still a bit freaked out. Gabe told him to chill, you're fine, and he has first dibs on a day pass with you now the vision of your drowning's no longer a factor. I thought Drew's head was going to implode."

"Guess what Sir Percival did!" Cassie looked as proud as a parent whose toddler had hit a new milestone. "He flew back to the school and beat his wings against Ms. Deering's office window! She'd just gotten back from her meeting with Mayer and knew something was up. *Then* he led her and Mr. Boxe back to us! She," Cassie corrected herself. "I keep forgetting. I found out Sir Percival's a she." She launched into an explanation of the coloring and lack of sex glands on the female bat.

"And Patience conjured this completely unbreakable rope," Mona interrupted. "And she helped Gabe tie up that…" She used several descriptive words for Axel.

"I know," I said. "I saw most of it."

"No, I mean during the part where you were dead."

"I was still there, watching."

They were all silent. Patience shuddered.

"Well, anyway, we're glad you made it back," Cassie declared, looking away.

"Glad!" Mona lunged for a hug, squeezing me hard. "That was the worst moment of my life, when we found your body!"

Patience was nodding. She fixed a stare on Cassie, who eventually shrugged in vague agreement. "It was pretty bad."

"Hey," I said to Mona. "Axel said you were a scribe. Not a polyglot."

Her eyes grew round, and I almost heard the click in her head. "That's one of the words I couldn't translate from the Lydenburg papers!" She opened her notebook. "I thought it was *archivist* or something."

"A scribe is a writer," Patience said. "A recorder of knowledge."

Mona scribbled in her notebook.

"Sounds better than polyglot, too," Cassie remarked.

"What's it like—on the other side?" Patience had her pale eyes on me and sounded a little breathless.

I was quick to reassure her. "No hellfire, demons or eternal torture. I don't know where I was exactly—somewhere in between this life and oblivion, I guess. Hannah called it the gray place." My eyes prickled again.

"They're gone, aren't they?" Mona said, her voice low.

I nodded, dropping my gaze to the blanket. "Both of them. No more ghosts."

"There'll be more."

She was probably right.

"That must be why they pick you," Mona said, opening her notebook. "You can move between the here and the hereafter."

"So she can't die?" This impressed even Cassie.

Mona thought about it. "No, she can die. If Ed hadn't been there, I think she'd still be dead now. But maybe a necromancer can come back, if the conditions are right. She can cross between life and death."

The gift of the crossing.

Then Ms. Samvedi came and kicked the girls out of my room, saying they should be studying and threatening them with official warnings. Mona seized my laptop off my desk and slid it onto my lap with a grin.

"I think you've got some messages."

The C8 icon was blinking from the toolbar, but my email inbox was open and there was a new message from Aunt Aurora.

From: Dawn Morgan
To: Mimi Alston
Subject: Re: Checking in
Ghostling!

So good to hear from you. Do you realize what a can of worms you've opened, asking me about my Wiccan practice? Now I have permission to bore you for extended periods of time!

How's school? You went camping at Blackmere Pool, did you? Interesting place. I'll tell you why in a minute.

So, familiars—most witches don't have them these days, except as family pets. But they were quite a thing in history. Cats, obviously, but also hares, toads, badgers, dogs— anything goes. Even imps, whatever they are. Some say familiars were gifts from the devil, or even lesser demons themselves, but that's your standard misogynistic anti-witch lore talking. Often familiars were gifts from other witches— basically companions to help with spells and protect the witch. I consider Toffee my familiar, although the only thing he helps with is yowling at 5am to wake me up if his kibble is low.

Now, Blackmere Pool. That place has a serious Wiccan and druidic history! It's supposed to be a spiritual place of gathering, where people go to recharge their mystical powers, or receive messages from the otherworld. Did you find the stone circle near the cabins? That's an ancient henge, very powerful. AND you would have been there while the Leonid shower was taking place—ooooh! Did anyone act unusual while you were camping? LOL!
Now, I've got to get to work, but are you going home for Thanksgiving? Let's have a long chat about this stuff then!
All my love, Aunt Aurora

Mona was going to love this.

The boys had sent a bunch of Collabor8 requests, including six from Drew. I hesitated for a moment, worrying about the security of the app—but I needed to speak to them. One quick chat couldn't hurt. I opened a group chat and requested everyone.

Drew Ellery accepted.
Gabriel Cavendish accepted.
Mona Thomas accepted.
Patience Rose accepted.
Edwin Farrow accepted.
Cassandra O'Meara accepted.

Miette: *Before anyone says anything, Ed, you are the best. Thanks for bringing me back.*
Edwin: *Anytime! All the bits doing what they should?*
Miette: *Two lungs sucking, one heart thumping, two eyes seeing, nine fingers tapping. All thanks to you.*

Edwin: *Stop it. I'm getting embarrassed.*

Gabriel: *Where's my thanks?*

Miette: *Excuse me, who are you again?*

Gabriel: *The guy who can feel you getting scared at 200 yards.*

Miette: *Oh, yeah. That must have been some loud fear. Thanks, Gabe.*

Gabriel: *See? Sometimes knowing how people feel without asking IS required.*

Miette: *And thanks, Drew, for finding me. And Cassie for sending Sir Percival for help. And Patience, for conjuring a rope and a blanket. And Mona, for slapping Axel's face as my proxy. But most of all Ed for being so generous with his life force.*

Edwin: *What can I say? I ooze energy.*

Cassandra: *Ew.*

The chat continued, silly and heady with relief and affection. Then a knock at the door and the sound of Ms. Samvedi's voice reminded me that we shouldn't be discussing this stuff online. She opened my door, and I slammed the laptop shut.

"Mimi, your mom's on the phone."

I blinked at her. "Did you tell her about me feeling unwell?"

Ms Samvedi gave me a stern look. "As the dorm head, I reserve the right to inform parents and guardians of anything I deem relevant."

I groaned and got to my feet, dragging myself down the hall to her office.

"Hi, Mom."

"Mimi, are you okay, honey? Isha says you had a menstrual episode!"

"What the hell is a *menstrual episode*, Mom? Seriously, it's a few cramps. I'm fine."

There was a long pause. Then a sob.

"Mom? What's wrong?"

"I don't think I can take it. The worry! I hate having you so far away. And Isha said that awful boy who tried to abduct your friend turned up at your camp! Why didn't you tell me?"

"Because it wasn't a big deal—it was just a coincidence. He happened to come to Blackmere Pool, not realizing we were camping there. He tried to talk to Cassie, which was stupid, but he left almost immediately."

"You still should have told me. This isn't okay, Mimi. Listen, your dad and I attended that school tour today, and Maidenvale Prep looks like a much better option. It's closer, you can live at home, and it has a strong code of conduct. Zero tolerance of violence—"

"Mom, I'm not leaving EVA."

There was a long silence. "Honey, we can't afford it. My new job hasn't been working out and the manager has suggested I resign. I don't know how long it'll take for me to find a new position. This school is costing us the earth. I'm sorry. I know you love it there. But we just can't do it." The tears were back in her voice. "We've already spent the Paris money, and the bank won't let us remortgage the house."

I swore, and she didn't even reprimand me. "Mom, I'm sorry. Why didn't you tell me you *used* the Paris money on EVA? Or about your job problems?"

"We were so relieved you were enjoying school that your dad and I wanted to make it work, whatever it took."

Tears were running down my face. Guilt—and also despair. "Please, please can we use my college fund to cover the EVA fees? It's important I stay here. Really important."

"Honey, even if I wanted to do that, we can't access that money. Your college fund is an investment plan. It's tied up until you graduate school."

It was too much. I was bone tired, and this was freaking me out. "I can't talk about this right now. I've gotta go."

"Wait, Mimi—"

"Bye, Mom. I love you. I'll call you on the weekend."

28

I'll Leave You with This

Despite Mom's bad news, despite Ms. Deering's request that I somehow not be madly in love with Drew, I still got excited when I saw him in homeroom in the morning. I still tingled in all the right places and went into a heightened physical state. I still devoured him with my eyes: the sweep of his cheek and the agate green of his eyes. The curve of his jawline and softness of his mouth. The way he looked up; the way his lips quirked into a smile when I walked toward him.

I'd seen into his soul, and it was lit up with love for me in there.

Drew had one of the shadows near him. It wasn't doing anything—just hovering. I eyed it, but it didn't move. Were they a type of ghost? The school had been a quarantine station once, after all—it made sense that the academy would be haunted by large numbers of the dead.

Maybe this was my gift developing. Not ideal.

I sat beside Drew, facing Cassie and Gabe on the opposite side of the table. We talked in low voices about Axel.

"Do you think he's in prison?" Gabe asked.

"Not a chance," Cassie drawled. "I bet they look after their own, these Asteroids or whatever they're called. That's why Tyler's still roaming free, turning up at our camp and

384

stuff. I bet they're like the Freemasons, with secret handshakes and special rules and friends in high places."

"Axel had better be in custody." Drew's expression had grown cyclonic. "Attempted murder… It's not like he did it by accident or anything."

"Do you think we can really be killed for our gifts?" Gabe's face was unusually grim. "Imagine how many people will be coming for us if it's true."

There was a general silence.

"Axel didn't gain my powers when he drowned me, did he?" I said at last. "Hannah said his beliefs were a fool's dream. He couldn't see spirits, as far as I know. He couldn't see *me*."

Gabe toyed with a pencil stub on the table. "That's true. He thought you were gone."

"*You* knew I was still around," I said.

"Yeah. Felt you there." His expression was guarded, and Drew's eyes flicked back and forth between us.

"It was lucky you tuned in. I was starting to think there was no coming back."

"I was worried you were right for a minute," Gabe said.

I grimaced. "We all have our black moments." He gave me a small smile.

Cassie shook her hair down her back. "Anyway, it's over now, and what happened gives us a damn good reason to keep our mouths shut about what we can do."

Drew leaned in. "If they come for us, we'll stick together. We'll be okay."

Gabe checked the clock. "The bell's about to go. I'm looking forward to hearing what Boxe has got to say for himself."

We got through our first couple of periods and assembled in the cottage for gifted class. Drew's shadow was still with him. They mostly seemed to hover in places rather than around specific people, but his was ever-present. *Should I tell him?* Maybe it would freak him out. There was another one in the cottage, skulking in the corner near a poster illustrating medicinal herbs.

Ms. Deering was late, so we sat down to wait in a huddle, united by our hostility toward Mr. Boxe and his cult. When it came to activating our team spirit, all those games on camp were nothing compared to one instance of mortal peril.

At last Ms. Deering arrived, Mr. Boxe by her side. He walked heavily and didn't look great. If someone had asked, I'd have guessed he hadn't slept. His fluffy hair stood on end, as if he'd been dragging his hands through it. He had coffee-colored shadows under his eyes and even his mustache seemed to be drooping. He pulled a chair across the carpet so it was right in front of us, and dropped into it.

"Morning, all." His voice was low and steady—not the bluff, blustery sea captain we knew and tolerated. "Thanks for giving me your time today. Are you all right, Mimi?" I nodded. "Good. Good." He sighed. "I'm sorry you had to go through what you did."

"Had to?" Mona couldn't hold it in. "*Had* to?"

He spread his hands, and, for the first time, I noticed his ring bore a gold triskelion, just like the one on EVA's logo. "The Asterions are a peaceful community," he said. Cassie scoffed audibly. "We live our lives lightly, and we work with people in business and government to reduce human impact on the planet. We live sustainably and eat no meat. We fund causes and try to do good in the world."

"And drown innocent people." Drew said it with steely composure.

It shut Mr. Boxe up completely for a few moments. He lowered his gaze to the floor, and, to our embarrassment, a tear ran down his cheek. "Axel has longed for a key role for years. I thought training as a sentry would be enough; I didn't realize his yearning had eaten away at him and made him rotten." He wiped his eyes. "I'd hoped the rogue section of the Order of Aster had lost impetus as a movement, but it seems they still pursue spiritual transcendence as doggedly as ever. The irony is, chasing after transcendence is the last way to achieve it, especially when it involves harming people."

"What do they want from us?" Ed asked.

Another helpless gesture. "They think the gifts you seven possess will allow them to reach a safe haven in the mountains in the time of flood."

"How?"

"The city is invisible to regular people. Without extra-sensory perception, it's hidden from view. The rogue Asterions need your powers to find the city."

"If it's invisible, how can they be so certain it's there?" Mona asked.

"There are prophecies…"

Cassie snorted again, and Mr. Boxe gave her an unexpected smile.

"I agree with you, Cassandra. I don't believe in the flood or the city. Not many members of my community do—but the rogue members are an exception. They're convinced it exists and that the flood is imminent, which is what makes them so dangerous."

"How do they plan to use us?" Gabe wanted to know.

Mr. Boxe hesitated and glanced at Ms. Deering. "Tell them, Theo," she said.

"Of course I can't know for sure," he said, "but if they were to take you into their keeping, one assumes they would induct you into the Asterion ways so you could lead them to the city."

"And if we didn't cooperate?" Mona asked.

Mr. Boxe coughed. "They're ruthless. They'd try to access your gifts for themselves."

Drew narrowed his eyes at Boxe. "You mean they'd try to cut them out of us? They'd sacrifice us to get at the powers." The shadow behind him seemed to darken and simmer.

Mr. Boxe gave a reluctant nod.

I discovered I was chewing my lip, making it bleed. "And you have no idea who they are?"

"They operate underground, so to speak. They're among us, living and moving through the Asterion community, but we don't know who they are."

"Except for Axel and Tyler."

He gave another of those great sighs, and the tears trembled on his lower eyelids. If he was acting, it was an award-winning performance. "Yes. But I assure you, neither of those boys will bother you again."

"What does that mean?" Patience asked, her eyes wide.

"Tyler's been removed from the school and the elders are monitoring him. They've also taken Axel in hand. He's to face the consequences. I can't say more than that."

I wanted details, but Mona broke in. "Is Olivia Candlish one of the Asterions? She's been almost as fixated as Axel on getting into the gifted program."

Mr. Boxe frowned but shook his head. "Olivia's simply ambitious."

Mona didn't seem satisfied, but she let it go—for now. "So how are we supposed to protect ourselves from your rogue members?"

"All I can do is warn you to be on your guard. Ms. Deering will of course provide protection, and you can trust in me to do everything possible to keep you safe, but the best strategy is vigilance—and complete secrecy."

He excused himself, saying he had an important meeting to attend, but before he left, he turned back and locked eyes with me. "Mimi, on behalf of the Order of Aster, I apologize for the attempt on your life. If there's anything I can do to make reparations, please don't hesitate to speak to me." He hurried away.

"You should ask him to change your marks to straight As," Gabe told me. "It's the least he can do."

"Do we trust him?" Cassie asked, her eyebrows hitched.

Ed laughed. "Like a kayaker trusts a great white."

"How much does he know about our gifts, Ms. D?" Mona asked.

"He knows you have them, obviously, and the Order of Aster know the titles of the seven powers, but Mr. Boxe doesn't know who has which gift or what the gifts involve. He only understands them in the most general terms."

"That's something." Ed glanced out the window at a skyful of darkening rain clouds. "Let's keep it that way."

"Going forward," Mona said, "I propose we only communicate verbally about our gifts—no email, no Collabor8. Check for eavesdroppers. No risks."

"Good idea," Ms. Deering told her. "We'll lock everything down."

A sinkhole seemed to open in my chest as I heard them make plans and remembered Mom's news about our family finances and the school.

"Mimi." It was Gabe, watching me with a puzzled air. "What's wrong?"

I didn't bother to rebuke him. He couldn't help it. "My parents are taking me out of EVA. They can't afford the fees."

Their faces reflected my own crushing devastation. For an instant, I felt a teensy bit better.

"Oh, perfect," Cassie spat. "We save her life then she gets taken away from us anyway."

Drew appealed to Ms. Deering. "You can't let it happen."

"No," she said. "We can't let it happen."

"It's not just the money," I said. "They don't like the stuff they've seen going on. I've only been here a couple of months, and my friend practically got abducted, then someone else had to be removed from a family violence situation. And both times, I was involved. I've been home safe with them for years, remember, so it's freaking them out."

"I'll call your parents," Ms. Deering promised me. "I'll talk them through those matters."

"Mimi." Mona's eyes were gleaming, and she was sitting up straighter than a preschooler looking for a gold star. "I've just had an idea about what *reparations* we can request from Mr. Boxe."

On Friday afternoon, I was alone in the art room—if you didn't count the presence of several looming shades. I'd told the others about them and Mona had come up with the term "shade," explaining that it had a double meaning of darkness and ghost. In the absence of more information about them, I went with it.

My artwork was practically painting itself. I'd added Hannah and Marvin standing at Albert's shoulders, so it resembled a peculiar family portrait. All three had their eyes in shadow, which added to the sense that they were related. It felt extraordinarily easy to paint the dead, after all that time struggling to paint a living human. It made sense: ghosts were what I knew best.

Mrs. Shaw came to stand by my side and gazed at my painting. "This is deeply eerie, Mimi."

"Thanks."

She took the paintbrush out of my hand. "Sit down. I need to talk to you."

I sat, and Axel's words about her flitted across my mind. But he'd been lying about everything. Mrs. Shaw settled across the table from me, twiddling one of her chunky rings.

She smiled. "Well, you've impressed people, haven't you, Mimi?"

"Pardon?"

"Mr. Boxe has asked me to give you some news. EVA just received a large private donation. The school board has approved a one-off scholarship covering the full tuition and boarding fees for an art student. Mr. Boxe recommended it go to you, I agreed, and the board has carried the motion."

I had to feign shock, but of course I knew it was coming. Mona had come up with the idea and even been the one to take it to Mr. Boxe. What was more, he'd promised to refund my parents the fees already paid for the year. When he called to tell them about my scholarship, he made assurances about the recent "anomaly" in an EVA student's behavior. Then Ms. Deering phoned them to say how proud the school was of my compassion when it came to Juliet's situation.

No parent in their right mind could ignore that level of kudos for their kid. Mom cried again when she called to tell me they'd changed their minds—but this time it was from happiness. I knew it was all going to be okay when she told me they were re-booking the Paris trip.

I was happy too—except for one thing: the conversation that had to take place with Drew. I kept putting it off. If it happened, then it would become real. For now, I could go on imagining things were fine. We could exchange secret smiles and sit beside each other at lunch and occasionally touch by accident and get flustered. And we weren't doing anything wrong, right? Because we weren't *seeing* each other, or *kissing*, or *dating*.

Never mind that I was painfully, wildly in love with him.

It took Drew to make the conversation happen. The bell rang after one of our gifted program classes and the other five left the cottage in a noisy throng. I was dithering so I could walk with Drew when he abruptly stopped and asked

Ms. Deering if he and I could use the room to talk privately. She eyed us for a moment, then clearly decided she could trust us. And if she couldn't, we were going to find somewhere else anyway. She left us alone, pausing to give Drew a meaningful look before she stepped through the door.

A crow landed on the windowsill, cocked its head at me, then flapped away. Drew joined me, dropping into the chair beside mine, albeit at a safe, non-touching distance. Suddenly my heart was raw and stinging.

"She gave you the hot-cold talk too, didn't she?" I asked.

"Yeah, she did." He seemed to be deciding where to begin. "I wanted to tell you this alone. I had another vision of you."

A sucker punch. "Oh, *great*."

A smile tugged at his mouth. "Not the bad kind. I saw you in an orchard, and there were a couple of people with you. A little boy in an old-fashioned brown cap, and a woman in a skirt and heels, carrying a handbag. Do you know who they could be?"

Hope stirred inside me. "Not yet."

Drew's expression was somewhere between resolve and misery. "I need you to know something. I'm going to do what Deering wants. But it's not what I want."

"I know."

"She wants me to not feel like I do. I don't even know where to begin with that."

"Yeah."

"So I've got to somehow be your friend—at least for a while. But these feelings—they aren't small." His cheeks were red, his eyes fixed on the desk.

I reached out and touched his fingertips. "I saw your soul."

Drew's head snapped up. His pupils expanded against those green irises like a drop of ink in water. "What?"

"Remember, after the branch came down in front of you?"

Comprehension dawned. "Is that what that was? In the woods, when you were suddenly there, holding my hand? I didn't know if it was a vision or something… else. It wasn't you, though—not the physical you." He frowned as if he couldn't make sense of it.

It didn't need to make sense. "Our souls touched. We knew everything about each other for a moment, inside and out."

"Everything?" A cloud crossed his face.

A smile spilled out of me. "I liked all of it."

Surprise lit him up and he held my gaze, his voice coming soft with wonder. "It… it felt like you were saying my name across the universe."

It was just our fingertips that were touching, but somehow that alone was heating me up. "I don't know how, or why, but when you touch me, there's a…" I stopped, suddenly embarrassed.

"A zing?" he said eagerly.

"Yes! And you felt it when I was caught in the gray place and you let me come back—through you."

His warm hand clasped mine fully. Joy bounced around my heart like a kid at a trampoline park. Then I remembered Ms. Deering's request and the joy backflipped into a ball pit of desolation.

"Ms. D says we need to stay apart for a *few months*," I said. "What does 'a few' mean? Like, two?"

He grimaced. "Two's a couple. A few is more like three or four. At least three."

"Three, then. Twelve weeks. I can live with that. I don't love it, but I can live with it."

He nodded. "Me too." He brushed my fingers with his thumb, featherlight. Who knew fingers were an erogenous zone?

I shifted a little nearer and summoned some bravado. "Can you at least kiss me? If we have to wait three months, I need something to keep me going."

Drew's gaze landed on my lips as if a magnet had drawn it there. I caught my breath, sure he was about to move closer, then he shook his head and pulled away, disentangling our fingers. "That's only going to make me want to do it again. Then we might get in a loop and never break out."

"Doesn't sound so bad to me," I joked, but I was secretly crushed. Yes, it would be more difficult to drag ourselves back to the friend zone if we kissed again, but at least I'd have something to replay in my most yearning-filled moments.

Drew straightened up. "I'd better go. I have work to do."

I was a little insulted. "Schoolwork?"

"Psychological work. Trying to get over you."

Oh. "Please don't try to get over me. Not fully."

His gaze softened. "Like I could."

That made me smile. He stood, gave me one last scorching sweep with those green eyes, then turned and left the cottage. I listened to his footsteps going down the wooden steps and sighed a sigh that came from the lowest echelon of my being. I stood up, feeling hollow. Lovesick.

Footsteps sounded on the steps again and Drew reappeared in the doorway, his eyes glittering and wild.

"Fuck it," he muttered, then his hands were holding my face, his lips crushing mine, our hearts smashing up against each other through our ribs. I found myself twisting his t-shirt with one hand, the other twining through his hair, every movement an attempt to bring him closer. He made a noise so low and taut with desire, it sent an ache through every nerve ending in my body. We kissed, and kissed, and kissed, and I drowned all over again in the best possible way.

There was no way it was going to keep us going for three months.

The Intruder

The C8 icon was blinking blue. *How?* It was eight p.m.—well after the time the app got locked.

Whitefox has opened a Collabor8 under GIFTED PROGRAM PROJECT.
Accept session?

In this session: You, Mona Thomas, Gabriel Cavendish, Edwin Farrow, Patience Rose, Drew Ellery, Cassandra O'Meara and Whitefox.

Mona: *"Whitefox"? Seriously? Who are you?*
Whitefox: *It doesn't matter. I need to talk to you about the Asterions.*
Mona: *Tell us who you are if you want us to listen.*
Whitefox: *Listen to me. All of you being in one place—it's not safe. You court disaster when you're together. You need to separate. Scatter. The further apart the better.*
Gabriel: *Why?*
Whitefox: *It makes it harder for them to monitor you, control you. None of you should be anywhere near one another. You shouldn't even be in the same county, let alone the same school.*
Cassandra: *That's bullshit.*

Whitefox: *It's common sense. While you're together, the convergence draws attention. You're practically inviting them to come and get you.*
Mona: *WHO ARE YOU?*
Whitefox: *A well-wisher. You need to disperse. The sooner the better.*

Whitefox has left the session.

THE END

From the author:
Psst ... I have something for you.
Subscribe to my newsletter for an exclusive *Ghostling* post-credits scene and other bonus content.

SIGN ME UP!

About *Darkling*

Circle of Seven Book 2 (May 2025)

Darkness is building.

She's survived a terrible fate and discovered why she's perpetually followed by ghosts. The worst is behind her now. Right?

Mimi simply wants to enjoy her newfound circle of friends—and being in love—but even that is fraught with drama. She's banned from being with him and they're struggling to resist their urges. Surely stealing a moment with Drew couldn't be that bad.

But there's something dark at the academy, and it's targeting Mimi. Day by day, an army of shades grows in strength and numbers. When the abilities of her friends falter, Mimi must ask herself if she's the cause. Will this darkness destroy the people she loves?

When two of their number are taken from them, the group descends into desperation. The mysterious enemies who want their powers are closing in, ready to take advantage of any weaknesses in the circle, and the Academy's gifted ones don't know who to trust. In the face of devastating betrayals and fractures, how can their circle ever be whole again?

And can Mimi fight the rising darkness before it gains total control?

Acknowledgements & Author Note

Many years ago, some friends who also live in my hometown stumbled across a story about the lost city of Astroeth in our local area.

In the 1930s, a Dr. Smith and his psychically gifted wife built a cottage in the hilly area of Glen Forrest, Western Australia, overlooking a valley and abandoned granite quarry. One day, while standing looking at this quarry, Mrs. Smith "found herself engulfed and surrounded by a strange ancient city" She used her extra-sensory perception to trace the outline of the city and buildings. She also discovered the large Sun Temple Healing School which sits partway down the valley where there is a sheer wall of granite. Apparently, the quarry workers had to stop working as their instruments went haywire. The quarry wall was presumed to be part of the vast eight-sided granite wall of the ancient school and Initiate Temple.

According to the *Digital Seance* blog, the builders of the city "were very highly developed in spiritual powers, close to non-physical Astral beings and workers and could 'leave their bodies at will' to transfer by teleportation. They used levitation and sound wave methods of life and beam ray." Unfortunately, those tyrants from Atlantis (damn them!) invaded and the residents had to sacrifice Astroeth in an explosion.

My friends and I decided to search for the temple. Using Google Earth and donning our tinfoil hats, we went hunting through the bush until we found the quarry, then sat and tested our instruments (phones) to see if they would go haywire. It was indeed quite a spooky and spiritual place. One of my friends, Megan, put together a beautiful illustrated booklet about the experience and I fondly remember this experience as one of the most exciting explorations I've ever been on. This experience was loosely the inspiration for the Circle of Seven series. I loved the idea of initiates learning to develop their psychic gifts and reimagined the whole scenario with young, (fairly) normal people as the protagonists. Huge thanks to the friends who shared that adventure with me.

This book was originally published by the excellent independent Canada-based press, Evernight Teen, in 2015. I owe them a huge, heartfelt thank you for believing in my book and offering me my very first publishing deal. I've since gone on to publish 18 books and become a fulltime author, and it was this first contract that started me on the incredible journey to achieve a lifelong dream.

Thank you to Camille Booker, my editor, who did brilliant work helping me tease out problems and fill in gaps in the story. And thank you to Arran McNicol who did a fantastic job with the Americanization and proofreading. Thanks also to the people who helped with the cover design process (I know it was torture by a thousand changes): Thomas Woodward and Fionna Cosgrove. And thanks to Nattie and Kristy for your honest feedback when I needed it! Lastly, thank you to H.M. Waugh for her sage advice on cold-water swimming.

This book was soft-launched through Kickstarter in 2024. Massive thanks to kidlit author Kristy Nita Brown for the idea of doing a Kickstarter! I wish to thank the 101 backers who pledged their support for the book. I am also deeply grateful to Trevor, Georgie and Reef, my talented family, who created artworks for the project including the art page in the book, the Circle of Seven mandala and the tarot art card designs, as well as assisting with merch and stretch goal goodies such as the charm bracelet and bookmark. Shoutout again to Fionna for her excellent support with social content during the campaign!

More by Ash Harrier

The Arcane Scholars

The graduate students at Oxford University's Cornix College can choose between a masters in Divination, Necromancy, Hecatology or Countermancy. With a degree from the elite Faculty of Arcane Sciences, the world will be at their feet – even if their lives are in mortal peril.

Totally Starcross'd

A modern retelling of the classic Shakespeare play, *Romeo and Juliet*.

Romilly Montague and Julian Capulet are two love-struck teens whose parents are about to slug it out for the job of Governor of Verona. For Romilly and Julian it's never been truer that you can choose your friends but not your family.

Will this story end in woe—or can there be a happily ever after for this modern-day Juliet and Romeo?

The Alice England Mysteries

Three quirky middle reader mysteries about Alice England, the girl who works in her family's funeral parlor and receives messages from the dead.

www.ashharrier.com

www.ingramcontent.com/pod-product-compliance
Lightning Source LLC
Chambersburg PA
CBHW050856210726

48290CB00004B/1252

9781763583825